THE
GAME
IS
MURDER

THE
GAME
IS
MURDER

◆◆◆◆◆

HAZELL WARD

BERKLEY
NEW YORK

BERKLEY
An imprint of Penguin Random House LLC
1745 Broadway, New York, NY 10019
penguinrandomhouse.com

Book design by Alison Cnockaert

Library of Congress Cataloging-in-Publication Data

Names: Ward, Hazell, author.
Title: The game is murder / Hazell Ward.
Description: New York : Berkley, 2025.
Identifiers: LCCN 2024054749 (print) | LCCN 2024054750 (ebook) |
ISBN 9780593952443 (hardcover) | ISBN 9780593952467 (ebook)
Subjects: LCGFT: Detective and mystery fiction. | Novels.
Classification: LCC PR6123.A714 G36 2025 (print) |
LCC PR6123.A714 (ebook) | DDC 823/.92--dc23/eng/20241129
LC record available at https://lccn.loc.gov/2024054749
LC ebook record available at https://lccn.loc.gov/2024054750

Printed in the United States of America
1st Printing

The authorized representative in the EU for product safety and compliance is
Penguin Random House Ireland, Morrison Chambers, 32 Nassau Street, Dublin D02 YH68,
Ireland. https://eu-contact.penguin.ie.

For Carren.
You can't put a price on the value of a sister.
But if you could, that price would be half a penny.
And you would owe me.
Forever.

Even if, heaven forbid, a novel should be based on real people or real events, the story that is captive in the pages of the book is always fictional. Its characters are fictional. Its setting is fictional. Its plot is fictional. It cannot be any other way, since fiction is held to a higher standard of truth than mere life.

PREFACE

◆ ◆ ◆ ◆ ◆

THE READER IS WARNED

WARNING: This is not one of those books where you can skip bits. This book requires effort. A lot of effort.

If you are the sort of reader who habitually ignores the Big Paragraphs, or skims over the Descriptive Bits, you might as well put this book down, right now, and get yourself a nice cozy crime novel instead. In here, details matter.

So, if we are going to do this, let's do it right.

This is how it's going to be. We will give you all the information you need.

Everything you need to know.

No holds barred.

All the cards on the table.

You can ask us any questions you like. Except, of course, whodunnit? Because that would be cheating. And we don't like cheating.

This book is about YOU. You are the detective here. It's up to you to follow the clues.

And why not? Why should we have to do all the work?

So, the question is, are you smart enough?

See, you are nodding yes, but there is a little part of you that is thinking, *Probably not.*

But hey, it's only a book, right? So, really, what does it matter?

Wrong! This is life or death. My life. Your death. Or the other way around, maybe. Who knows? My point is, life is serious, isn't it? So WAKE UP!

Keep your wits about you and pay attention.

OK, so at this point you are thinking, *I have no idea what this book is about, and that cozy crime novel idea is sounding mighty tempting.* I can understand that. Sometimes we want to take the easy path. I get it—I do. So if you want to go, go. No hard feelings.

Au revoir. Arrivederci. Bye-bye.

If you're still here—and, of course, you are—it's Matrix time.

You know what I mean. Red pill or blue pill? Red? Blue? Red? Blue? Red? Blue?

Come on—make your mind up.

You picked red. So predictable.

OK, then. How deep it goes . . .

THE
GAME
IS
MURDER

WELCOME TO MURDER HOUSE

8 BROAD WAY

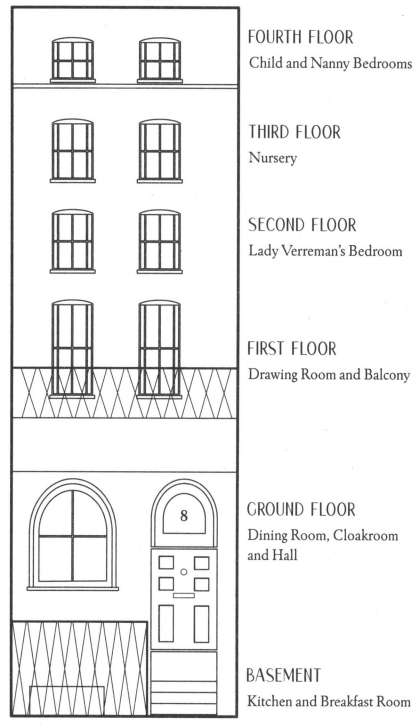

FOURTH FLOOR
Child and Nanny Bedrooms

THIRD FLOOR
Nursery

SECOND FLOOR
Lady Verreman's Bedroom

FIRST FLOOR
Drawing Room and Balcony

GROUND FLOOR
Dining Room, Cloakroom
and Hall

BASEMENT
Kitchen and Breakfast Room

ACT 1

◆◆◆◆◆◆◆◆◆◆◆

GUILTY!

1

❖ ❖ ❖ ❖ ❖

A MURDER IS ANNOUNCED

People that trust themselves a dozen miles from the city, in strange houses, with servants they don't know, needn't be surprised if they wake up some morning and find their throats cut.

—Mary Roberts Rinehart, *The Circular Staircase*

THE LIGHTS ARE on at 8 Broad Way. The steps have been swept and the brass door knocker has been polished. For this is an occasion. Walk up the steps and tap lightly upon the door. They are expecting you.

The night has long since drawn in, and there is a biting November wind of the sort that turns the tip of your nose a deep raspberry pink. Your breath mists beneath the portico lamp. Stamp your feet and rub your hands together while you wait. It's not really cold, but the Georgian town house and the dark London street are reminiscent of a Dickens novel. Be David Copperfield. Hope for the best and make the most of every situation.

Footsteps on a tiled floor. Someone is coming. Get out your invitation. This is it. Good luck.

You are invited to a Murder Mystery Party!

A murder will take place at: [Address] _____*Here*_____

On: [Date and Time] _____*Now*_____

It is 1974. The world is changing. The Summer of Love is over, and a new world order is emerging, brasher, louder and angrier than before. Gone is the old deference to Class and Money. Harold Macmillan's assertion that the country had never had it so good is long forgotten, and James Callaghan's Winter of Discontent is coming.

The working classes are on the march.

For the upper classes, things are no longer rosy. In the rarefied atmosphere of the Berkeley Club, gentlemen may cling to the old traditions, as a shipwrecked mariner to a life raft, and in the Georgian town houses of Belgravia, ladies may polish the escutcheons on their family silver and, in muttered tones, invoke the spirit of Enoch Powell as the savior of the Established Order, but the end is coming, and the dukes and earls and baronets all know it.

Even in the aristocratic sanctuary of 8 Broad Way, change is coming. And for one inhabitant, at least, change will be deadly.

RSVP

* Please try to dress in appropriate costume
* Arrive promptly
* Bring booze

———

WALK UP THE stairs to the drawing room. It is full of guests. Watch as conversation sputters into silence as you enter, and then, with a polite hiccup, smoothly resumes.

Champagne? Perhaps not. Look around the room. The faded velvet curtains are drawn against the night and look magnificent, though perhaps a year or two past their best. The furniture, too, is old, very old, but it commands the room as though it has grown into the house, as though it were bought new a century ago and has never since moved from its appointed spot.

A chandelier glitters and lamps are lit around the room, casting their warm yellow glow over the guests, dripping them in gold.

Greet the host. He is a little odd, to be sure, but they say that that which in the commoner is merely odd is, in the aristocrat, an interesting eccentricity.

"Welcome."

—Welcome, welcome.

"My brother and I are so glad you agreed to attend this little party of ours."

—Our little murder mystery.

"Well, less of a party and more of an experience, so to speak. I see you chose not to indulge in fancy dress for this occasion, and I congratulate you on your perspicacity. Most people, in the circumstances, would have dressed in bell-bottomed jeans and hippie beads. I can assure you that no one in this affair would ever have attired themselves in such a manner. My father's only concession to the age was a rather unfortunate mustache. In his dress, he remained, thankfully, remarkably conservative. As, of course, did my mother."

Watch as your host claps his hands to ensure he has the full attention of the room.

"Ladies and gentlemen, tonight we will be examining a real case, one involving our own family—the Verreman Affair, as it is usually referred to in the press. We will shortly review the real evidence and consider the solution as it was presented by the prosecution in a court

5

of law. You have each been assigned a part, and we hope that you will play it with gusto. Tonight, overacting is positively encouraged.

"A man has been accused, and, as you will see, has been, in some manner, convicted. However, this case is one of the most singular cases in legal history, and the court of law he was convicted in was not a criminal one. More on that later.

"I have my own theory about what occurred."

—Me, too! I have a theory. Oh yes, I do.

"I'm sure we all have theories. But we will not tell you our theories yet! My brother and I will listen to the evidence presented here tonight and contribute what information we can from our own first-hand knowledge of the case, and of the persons involved. In your turn, we hope that you will all regale us with your stories, and who-ever plays the Great Detective will reach a definitive conclusion so that we can finally lay this matter to rest."

—Finally.

"Some of you we have met before. Others are new acquaintances. All are friends here."

Raise your glass in acknowledgment of the toast.

"For those of you who haven't yet worked it out, I am David Ver-reman, and, of course . . ."

—I'm Daniel. The other brother.

Applaud lightly.

"Thank you. And, of course, the convicted man I spoke of was my father. Tonight, the task of our Great Detective will be to discover not so much whodunnit but whether our father dunnit."

—I'm the brother no one talks about.

"Ah! The dinner gong."

—The dirty little secret.

"If you're all ready, shall we go down to dinner?"

—The one no one talks about . . . Contracts!

"And, er, yes, I almost forgot. Ladies and gentlemen, you should have received a contract with your invitation. Can I just check you have all signed and dated your contracts, and sent them back? If you have not received a contract, can you raise your hand?"

Did you miss something? Was there something written on the back of that invitation? Better raise your hand.

"Ah. Anyone else? No? Good. There you go. Do take your time reading it. I can always tell dinner to wait."

—I'm hungry.

Skim through the contract quickly; then sign it.

"Excellent. OK, then. If that is all of them, let's go down, shall we? I'm starving."

2

◆ ◆ ◆ ◆ ◆

THE DOCUMENTS IN THE CASE

It is not for me to suspect but to detect.

—Anna Katharine Green, *The Leavenworth Case*

The Contract

The Agreement

1.   Reading the testimony that follows this agreement constitutes acceptance of this binding agreement between you, the reader of this document, hereafter known as The Reader, and the author/curator of this document, hereafter known as The Author.

The Document

2.   This document constitutes the entire scope of this investigation.

2:1   All information relevant to the investigation must be contained within this document.

2:2   Any solution to this investigation by The Reader and/or The Author must be based exclusively on information contained within this document, and not on any theory unsupported by the evidence within this document.

Withholding of Information

3.   The Author must not unreasonably withhold information from The Reader.

3:1   All information should be provided to The Reader in a timely manner.

3:2   If The Author acquires new knowledge relating to the investigation, it must be shared with The Reader as soon as possible.

3:3   It is The Reader's responsibility to assess the value and weight of information contained within this document. The Author cannot be held responsible for inaccurate conclusions derived from accurate data.

Persons of Interest

4.   The Author must inform The Reader of all suspects, witnesses or persons of interest in a timely manner.

4:1   The Author must inform The Reader of any new suspects, witnesses or persons of interest as soon as possible after their discovery.

Solutions and Resolutions

5.   In entering into this contract, The Author and/or The Reader undertakes to provide a complete solution to the problem under investigation. Unsolved mysteries are not permitted.

5:1   The solution/resolution at the end of this document must be derived exclusively from the facts, as presented within this document, and be consistent with the behavior and character of the suspect, as described in this document.

5:2   The solution/resolution, when explained, must be logical and must not be reliant upon chance or coincidence or be derived from divine intervention of any kind.

5:3   The culprit must have had clear Means, Motive and Opportunity, and this must be demonstrated by The Author and/or The Reader in their solution.

5:4   When demonstrating their solution, The Author and/or The Reader must explain their deductive process, including:

5:4.1 How they examined and assessed the evidence.

5:4.2 Their preliminary assumptions.

5:4.3 Their investigative and deductive reasoning, with results, including all working theories and rejected theories.

5:4.4 The reasons for the elimination of suspects from suspicion.

5:5   The evidence against the culprit, as identified by The Author and/or The Reader, must be compelling, and all parts of the investigation must be resolved.

5:6   The evidence against the other suspects must be less compelling than the evidence against the identified culprit.

5:7   The motive of the culprit, when demonstrated by The Author and/or The Reader, must be readily understandable, logical and human.

[And if you think *that's* confusing, try googling this: "Marx Brothers Sanity Clause."]

THE GAME IS MURDER

I hereby agree to be bound by the terms of this contract:

Name [Reader] _____

[Signature] _____

[Date] _____

Name [Author] ___A. N. Author_____

[Signature] _____*A. N. Author*_____

[Date] ___Today_____

Reading on denotes acceptance of these terms and conditions. Failure to abide by them may incur penalties. For details of penalties, please refer to Appendix B.

SO, DID YOU sign it?

You did?

Liar!

Get your damned pen out and sign it. We'll wait.

RIGHT, THEN. SO you've signed it now?

I tell you what. Not that I don't trust you or anything, but I will just remind you that reading on constitutes acceptance of this agreement, and that it is as legally binding as a signature.

OK?

Read on, Macduff.

Let's Play a Game!

An icebreaker. Isn't that what you call it? Don't you just love icebreakers? Of course you do. Everyone does. (Why else would you make people do them all the damned time?)

Don't worry, though. This one is easy. Child's play, actually. We have some items on a tray. In a moment, we will show you the items. Then we will take the tray away, and you'll have to try to remember as many of them as you can.

Are you ready? Here we go.

- Gambling chips
- A clock
- A woman's shoe
- A house key
- A diary
- A toy car
- A lead pipe
- A bloodstained letter
- A teacup
- A lightbulb
- A bottle of pills

Got it? Good. We'll be testing you later!

3

◆ ◆ ◆ ◆ ◆

THE LONG DIVORCE

I shall not be present at my trial.

—Maurice Leblanc, *Arsène Lupin, Gentleman-Thief*

"LADIES AND GENTLEMEN, in tonight's episode of *Perry Mason*, I will be playing the prosecuting barrister, and . . ."

—I'll be appearing for the defense.

David Verreman is standing at the head of the table. A folded cream-colored card sits in front of each place setting, with the character name of a murder mystery guest on one side, and the menu on the other.

Your place is next to David.

"We have our witnesses here, and both the judge and jury will be played by our Great Detective. It's a slight mixing of metaphors, perhaps, but you will have noticed that detective novels generally don't bother with juries. They move straight from detection to guilty verdict, without worrying about trifles like habeas corpus. Not here. I will make my opening statement, and then we can start discussing the case while we eat."

Your place card says, *The Great Detective.*

Turn it over quickly.

The First Course

~

Prawn cocktail, on a bed of lettuce, sprinkled with a dusting of paprika

Accompanied by the opening statement for the prosecution

Served with brown bread

David Verreman puts a hand on your shoulder. He leans in confidentially, as if anxious not to be overheard.

"Congratulations, Great Detective. I'm sure you are going to do a great job. We have invited a number of people to join us this evening. You might call them witnesses."

—Or dinner guests.

"Or, as Daniel says, you might refer to them simply as dinner guests."

—Or suspects.

"Or, just possibly, as suspects. I have reserved for myself the honor of sitting on your left. Next to me we have Mr. George Howard-Cole and his wife, Margaret; next to them, Sir Henry Wade and his wife, Carolyn Keene-Wade. They are all friends of Lord Verreman, including Carolyn, who also happens to be Lady Verreman's sister."

—And our aunt.

"Then we have Dr. Ronald Knox, coroner. I expect his story will be quite a long one, because he does love to talk, so I will try to rein him in. We have also invited the jury foreman, who we like to call Jeff. 'J.F.' Get it? He doesn't have many answers for us, I'm afraid, but he does ask some pertinent questions, which you might find useful.

"At the far end of the table we have put Mr. Stanley Gardner and

Mr. Eddie Biggers, the husband and boyfriend of the deceased, respectively."

He leans in closer and drops his voice to a stage whisper. "We have seated them together in the hopes that it will lead to fireworks later. I do love fireworks. Don't you?

"Next come our experts. We have Professor Cameron McCabe, the pathologist; Dr. Elizabeth Mackintosh, the world-famous blood analyst; and then comes another great detective, Chief Inspector Nicholas Blake, the detective in charge of this case.

"Finally, we have two singular gentlemen. Mr. William Collins— Wilkie to his friends—was a valet at the Berkeley Club at the time of the murder. And next to him, a gentleman who goes by the unlikely name of Gaston Leroux. He lends money—and at extortionate interest, if you can believe it. Lastly, of course, my brother, who has claimed the seat to your right."

David straightens up and addresses the room. "Welcome, all. During tonight's meal, we will invite each of our guests to make a statement about their particular knowledge of the case. Some of you will contribute a broad knowledge of the whole case. Others will have only a small snippet of information to add to the pot. All, however, are welcome at our table. I hope you will all be able to answer the questions raised by the Great Detective, or ourselves, or, of course, each other. Is that clear?

"Please feel free to write down any questions that you may have and pass them to either Daniel or myself. I should just give our witnesses a quick reminder of the rules." The room is silent. Expectant. "Remember, please, if asked a direct question, you must give an honest answer. However, you should not volunteer information. It is the job of our detective, here, to formulate the questions that will enable them to crack the case. We do not want to make the job too easy! The game has to last at least until dessert, and hopefully all the way past coffee and into the brandy and cigars.

"My brother and I have also taken dual roles tonight. Not only are we the lawyers in the case, but with a swift costume change, we will also become the hapless assistants of the detective. I will play Dr. Watson, and my brother will be Captain Hastings."

—Or the other way round.

"Or, as you say, the other way round. It's much of a muchness. While our detective is being inscrutable and mysterious, and playing their cards close to their chest, we can ask the obvious questions. And anyway, dash it, it's our party, and why should everyone else have all the fun? We may even propose solutions, but if we do, they will, in time-honored tradition, be the wrong ones. Or we may stumble upon a clue but fail to realize its significance. Or we will get the right person for the wrong reason. Or vice versa. If you have read anything from the stable of detective literature, you will be perfectly familiar with our role.

"Only the detective can decide the value of our contribution. Sometimes our help can be invaluable. At other times we are merely a nuisance. All clear?"

Nod your head in agreement.

"All right, then here I go with my opening statement. Wish me luck."

David Verreman clears his throat dramatically, even though he has been speaking nonstop since you arrived. "Thank you. Where shall I begin? At the beginning? Why not? Lord John Verreman (I refer to him by his title because 'Daddy' seems rather out of place in this formal atmosphere) married Antonia Keene (our mother; always 'Mother,' never 'Mummy') in 1963 at St. George's, Hanover Square. For the new Lady Verreman, her wedding day was the culmination of all her hopes, dreams and, it must be said, a fair amount of scheming. For Lord Verreman, it was, perhaps, more of a spur-of-the-moment decision. His male friends were appalled; his female friends were jealous. All of them were surprised.

"Until then, Lady Verreman—my mother—had not been a woman who was noticed. She was invited to society parties, but mostly to make up the numbers or when her sister asked if she might bring Antonia along. Everyone liked Aunty Caro, and Antonia, though dull, was very little trouble, so she was easy to accommodate.

"But Lord Verreman was captivated by his new bride. She was always very delicate looking, petite and almost fragile. And she was at least a foot shorter than him, so perhaps she brought out his protective instincts. Who knows?

"Lady Verreman lost no time in fulfilling what she perceived as the only duty of an aristocratic wife. She provided her husband with a son and heir within the year—that would be me. And a little over a year later she had another son. Having produced both an heir and a spare, as the saying goes, she considered her marital obligations concluded, which must have come as a bit of a disappointment to her amorous new husband. Still, they were happy enough, and on the death of his father, John Verreman became the seventh Earl de Verre and, at his wife's insistence, took up his seat in the House of Lords.

"It was around that time that Lord Verreman gave up his job at Coutts. That bank was so venerable an institution, and the job was so safe, and easy, that no one had resigned in living memory. There was a considerable amount of tut-tutting about his rashness, and rumor has it that one or two board members went so far as to raise an eyebrow and/or suck their teeth in surprise, but this has never been confirmed, and such emotional displays do seem rather unlikely for the Queen's bankers.

"Nevertheless, John Verreman shook the dust of the world's oldest bank from his feet and launched himself on a new and exciting career as a professional gambler. He was not completely foolhardy. He had recently won the spectacular sum of thirty thousand pounds in a single night's play at his club, the Berkeley, where only the very aristocratic or the very rich are admitted, and he was acknowledged as a gifted player of backgammon and of his favorite game, chemin de fer, which has sadly gone out of favor in the years since.

"Verreman cut rather a romantic figure, I always think, the aristocrat and the gambler, risking all on one turn of the cards. He didn't always win, of course, and the uncertain nature of a gambler's life was difficult for Lady Verreman to bear. Born into relative poverty, where every penny counted, she found it difficult to be nonchalant about losing a sum equivalent to her father's annual salary in a single night.

"And, of course, she sat and watched him lose it. Each night, she left her children with the nanny, put on an evening gown and arrived at the Berkeley in time to join her husband for dinner, then whiled away her evenings watching him win or lose his shirt.

"For a while, things were good, but life is not lived in stasis, and by 1974, the year of the *incident*, Lord and Lady Verreman were living apart, and Lord Verreman's fortunes had taken a decided turn for the worse. He was still paying the bills at Broad Way, and was now faced with the prospect of paying substantial maintenance for the wife and kids, before even considering where he was going to lay his own head.

"Worse, however, was a disastrous custody case, in which he tried to gain interim custody of his children by having his wife committed to an insane asylum. The Divorce Reform Act of 1969 made it easier to get a divorce, and in the four years after it passed, the family courts were swamped with fighting couples who would go to any lengths to hurt each other. The courts had seen it all, and they were not sympathetic to a rich man who wanted to lose the wife and keep the kids. He lost the case, and custody, and his famous nonchalance began to suffer—and along with it went his luck at cards.

"You have been very patient with my long, and no doubt tedious, telling of the backstory, but you will, I trust, come to see that all of that is necessary to get a complete picture of my parents' lives. Now we will move on to the events of the night itself.

"Picture this. It is the night of the seventh of November 1974. Lord John Verreman is crouched in the basement kitchen of his estranged wife's home. He is now a ruined man, penniless, and soon to face the shame of being declared bankrupt for all the world to see. He has lost his home, his money and his family. Worse still, he has lost it all to a woman he believes to be a lunatic.

"But Lord Verreman is, by nature, a risk-taker. He knows, more than anyone, that if a man is prepared to stake all on one throw of the dice or one spin of the wheel, great fortune is to be had. If he is lucky.

"He crouches in the dark and calculates his odds. They are good. He has chosen a night when there are no other adults in the house, and it is now long past the children's bedtime. At nine o'clock his wife, as she always does, will come down to make a cup of tea. And he will be waiting for her.

"He hears footsteps, coming closer, making their way down four flights of stairs. He hears the neat *clip, clip, clip* of her shoes on the polished wooden steps. He holds his breath, straining to hear, and grips the weapon in his hand a little tighter. His heart is pounding, perhaps, but he is a man who thrills at risk-taking, the same man who raced powerboats at breakneck speeds. He takes one or two deep breaths and waits for the perfect moment to strike.

"The footsteps pause at the top of the basement steps, and, as he expects, she flips the light switch. Nothing happens. Lord Verreman has removed the bulb. She continues on down the stairs. Lightbulbs are always blowing at eight Broad Way, and, without a husband to help her, his petite wife has got used to finding her way in the dark.

"She walks down the steps, carrying her cup and saucer on a tray, with only the red glow of the light from the kettle to guide her.

"Does she stop as she reaches the final step? Does she sense the presence of another human being? Of evil? Does she have any idea of the danger she is in? We will never know.

"As she takes the final step, Lord Verreman strikes.

"The first blow, dealt with savage force, knocks her down. Three more blows follow quickly, spraying blood across the room. There is no time for her to defend herself. He wants this business over and done with.

"As his victim lies unconscious upon the stone-cold floor, her life fast ebbing away, Lord Verreman looms over her, and it is then that he makes a terrible discovery.

"This woman is not his wife."

4

THE THIRTEEN GUESTS

Every clever crime is founded ultimately on some one quite simple fact—some fact that is not itself mysterious. The mystification comes in covering it up, in leading men's thoughts away from it.

—G. K. Chesterton, *The Innocence of Father Brown*

DAVID VERREMAN HOLDS the room captive. He pauses here and takes a sip of wine, holding the glass up for inspection, so that the light hits the crystal, and the blood red of the wine is a grisly reminder of the events that took place in the basement of this house, just a few feet below this table.

As if on a whim, he holds the glass out, looks around the table and makes a toast.

"To our victim, Mrs. Sally Gardner. You will not hear her name mentioned often around this table. Her death is merely the inciting incident of a much more interesting drama, but we should, perhaps, take a moment to acknowledge her contribution here."

Hold out your glass in return, and watch as he drinks and smacks his lips, and wonder whether David Verreman is really the bastard that he seems to be. He is certainly enjoying himself. He takes another sip, and continues.

"What does Lord Verreman feel at that moment? Shock? Fear? Shame?

"He risked it all, and he missed. This is not his wife, but the pretty young nanny to his children, who started work only a few weeks earlier.

"Desperately, he forces the body of the nanny into the large canvas sack that he'd hoped to use to dispose of his wife. He doesn't know it, but Sally Gardner's life is not quite expired as he pulls the cords tight.

"Leaving the body in the dark of the basement, he goes to the top of the stairs and listens. All is quiet. He takes a moment to steady himself. He thinks he might be sick, and he must not, on any account, do that. Quickly, he steps into the hall cloakroom, washes the blood from his hands and from the murder weapon, and splashes cold water onto his face.

"Then, with a feeling of dread, he looks at himself in the cloakroom mirror. Does he recognize the face of the desperate man who stares back at him? Who can tell? He hears a creak on the stairs above him. Someone is coming. Someone is calling out. This is a nightmare."

David pauses again and takes another drink. Perhaps this time it is to quench his thirst. Perhaps.

"Let us now turn our minds to Lady Verreman. Mother. Unfortunately, my mother is not able to attend this evening."

—She wasn't invited.

"True."

—And she's dead.

"Thank you."

—Not that we would have invited her anyway.

"Yes, thank you, Daniel! Mother, Lady Verreman, has been watching TV in her bedroom. At eight forty, her son—that would be me—joins her. They snuggle together on her bed, and she is eagerly awaiting the tea that the new nanny so recently offered to make.

"She checks her watch. Quarter past nine. David should be in bed, but it is nice having him here next to her. And he is growing up fast. There won't be many more nights like this. Let him stay awhile longer. Where is that cup of tea? The girl has been an awfully long time.

"She waits a minute more, then decides to get up and check. She leaves David watching the news and walks down two flights of stairs. She reaches the hall, and the top of the basement steps, and looks down. All is in darkness. That's strange. Where could she be?

"As she calls out the young woman's name, she hears a noise behind her, and half turns just as the first blow strikes, causing it to miss her head and bounce painfully off her shoulder. She hears the bone crack.

"More blows follow, and they find their mark. Blood is pouring from her head. She struggles desperately, and in the scuffle her assailant drops his weapon. Perhaps she has a chance. He knocks her to the floor and is on top of her, his gloved fingers around her throat. She is going to suffocate. She manages to hook her foot around one of the spindles of the basement stairs' railing, and she hangs on. She hangs on and summons all her energy to push him away.

"Finally, utterly exhausted, he gives up, and husband and wife, murderer and victim, sit together on the hall steps and try to catch their breath. She looks at the hall, now spattered with blood, up the walls, across the ceiling and all over the floor. This must be her blood, she supposes.

"Unsteadily, she rises to her feet and crosses to the hall cloakroom. She, too, looks in the mirror, and is horrified by what she sees. Blood is spattered over her pullover and her pretty summer dress. It is congealing in her hair. Are there patches of hair missing? Hard to tell.

"Her throat is dry. The water in the cloakroom is horribly warm, but she drinks it anyway. It is painful to swallow. She looks over at her husband just as he lets forth a terrible sound, a long moan that echoes around the hall. It erupts out of him like he's an animal in distress. Like a horse she once had, who'd broken his leg going over a jump, looking up at her as she took aim.

"She must be very careful now. He is beginning to move. The

THE GAME IS MURDER

shock is starting to wear off, and soon he could be dangerous again. She forces herself to talk to him in a normal voice. The way she did when they were first married. When they were happy. She turns away from the mirror and says, in a brisk voice, 'It's not so bad. Now, what shall we do with the body?'

"*All men are like children,* she thinks to herself. *Deep down, they need to be told what to do. They like to play at being the protector, but it's all just pretend.* 'Why don't you take me upstairs,' she'd said, 'and I can have a lie-down, and maybe you could bathe my head, the way you used to when I had a migraine. Do you remember?'

"And he'd nodded, and stood up, and now he is trotting beside her. As if they have had a silly fight, and now they are making up. As if he was playing murderers, and got bored, and now he is playing doctors instead. He seems to have forgotten Sally in the basement. But she hasn't. She will never forget.

"He sends their son to bed, and she lets him lay her down on the bed. He even puts a towel over the pillow, for the bloodstains. She thanks him, prettily, and calls him 'dear.' He kisses her gently on the cheek. Then he walks into the adjoining bathroom and turns on the tap to soak a towel for her head. He is talking, but she can't make out the words through the gurgle of the pipes and the sound of gushing water. She says, '*Huh-humm,*' in a dreamy voice as she slips out the bedroom door.

"And she runs. She runs as she has never run before. Down the two flights of stairs. She throws open the front door and runs into the street, and into the safety of the Three Taps pub. Is he chasing her? She daren't spare a second to turn round and find out. She runs, and she runs, and as she runs, she calls out, 'Murder! Help me! Murder! He's killed my nanny. Murder!'

"And Lord Verreman, returning from the bathroom with his wet towel, sees the empty bed, looks out of the window into the street and sees his wife escaping. Does he hear her screaming bloody murder? Perhaps. But it matters not.

"It is all over. There is nothing left to do. Except flee. He leaves behind his wife and his family. He leaves his home and his friends. He leaves his mounting debts and his tattered reputation. And in the basement of his wife's home, he leaves a sack. And in that sack, a beautiful young woman finally breathes her last. A woman who never did him, or anyone, any harm. A woman who had a life as valuable as that of any lord or lady. She, too, had a husband.

"She had friends. She had family.

"She had lovers.

"She had life.

"And now, like a flame, she has been snuffed out.

"Ah! Perfect timing. Here comes the food. What a fabulous dinner party this is."

WARNING: This is not a dinner party! This is a novel.

Adjust your expectations accordingly.

No doubt The Author will tell you, momentarily, that the food is delicious. Do not believe him.

There is no food here. There are no guests. There is no silver cutlery, no fine china. There is only ink on paper. And if you are reading this on an infernal machine, there is not even that.

There is you, The Reader, and there is The Author. And this author, like all authors, is a low-down snake in the grass.

Maybe *you* aren't even who you think you are.

Trust nothing. Trust no one. Not me. Not you. And, for the Good Lord's sake, never, ever trust an author.

You have been warned.

"THESE PRAWNS ARE delicious, aren't they?"

Nod your head. Agree, cautiously, that they do, indeed, taste delicious.

"So, what did you think of my opening statement?"

Look down at your notebook. What does one say to a man whose father murdered a woman in mistake for his mother, and then tried to murder the mother, too?

"It was good, wasn't it? Chief Inspector, what did you make of my speech?"

Detective Chief Inspector (Retired) Nicholas Blake is busy wiping the inside of his Babycham glass with a finger of brown bread. He has a dribble of pink mayonnaise on his chin. Try not to look at it as he talks.

"You certainly have a flair for storytelling, Lord Verreman. However, we policemen prefer our prose a little less purple, if I may put it that way."

"Ah yes. Your style is more *As I was proceeding in a northerly direction*. That's the stuff that we have come to expect from Her Majesty's Constabulary, is it not?"

"Not quite. We have moved on a little since Inspector Lestrade, you know."

"Oh, I do hope not, Chief Inspector. I do hope not."

The policeman laughs.

"Perhaps you can give us your first impressions of the case. You spoke to my mother that night, I believe?"

Detective Chief Inspector Blake clears his throat and examines his fingernails for a moment, as if considering whether to speak. An affectation. Then he takes a deep breath, lays his hands flat upon the table and begins. "Early hours of the following morning, to be precise. Lady Verreman had received some pretty severe head wounds, which needed to be stitched, and she had lost a fair amount of blood. She had been sedated when we finally got to see her, but she was able to give us a brief account of what occurred. Not too dissimilar to your own account. You have taken one or two liberties with the truth, perhaps, but, on balance, I would say you were pretty fair.

"We went back the following morning, naturally, and she was able to give us a little more detail. I must say that what impressed me most about Lady Verreman's testimony was that her account never altered.

Even from that first interview, under sedation. I consider that very convincing.

"After speaking to Lady Verreman that morning, we were immediately able to issue not a warrant for Lord Verreman's arrest, not then, but an alert for him as a missing person. It was felt by some, even at that early stage, that we needed to tread carefully. Lord Verreman was a peer of the realm, after all. But Lady Verreman told us that she had been attacked by her husband and that he had rushed at her from behind, coming from the hall cloakroom, raining blows on her head. It is a miracle that she wasn't killed, too. It was clear that we needed to speak to Lord Verreman as a matter of urgency.

"Officers were at the house within forty minutes, having obviously attended, in the first instance, at the public house where the call had come from. They were forced to break open the door, but, as you know, Lord Verreman had already fled.

"An officer and a sergeant checked the ground floor, noting, of course, the very large patch of blood in the hall, an obvious site of attack, and then they proceeded to check the upper floors. On the top floor, they found one minor child, awake and standing next to his bed."

"That would be me," says David.

"That, as you say, would be you. There were, er, no other children in the house. Officers then returned to the ground floor, where the sergeant noticed, in passing, so to speak, a white object, which he took to be the leg of a child's doll, lying on the hall floor. The two officers then proceeded down to the basement, which was in darkness, where they discovered the body of Mrs. Sally Gardner inside a bloodstained canvas sack. My sergeant pulled open the bag and took out one arm, to check that life was extinct, but other than that, he did not disturb the body.

"They then proceeded into the back garden, which led off the basement, the door to which was unlocked. The garden was surrounded on all sides with very high walls, all of which were covered with moss and ivy. It is extremely unlikely that anyone could have left that way, and certainly they could not have done so without leaving a mark.

"There was also a basement door to the street. Lady Verreman stated that it was used only to take out rubbish and was otherwise kept locked at all times, and my officers found it to be both locked and bolted from the inside.

"They tested a lightbulb that was left lying on a chair in the kitchen, and it was found to be in perfect working order. Obviously, samples were taken from the scene for the forensics team to examine. There were only two other pieces of evidence of any note. The first was the bloody towel that had been laid over the pillow in Lady Verreman's bedroom. And the second, of course, was the dolly's leg."

Silence around the table. The policeman gives a satisfied little smile to himself and is not prepared to let the moment slide away without its due appreciation.

David Verreman supplies it. "The dolly's leg? Whatever do you mean, Chief Inspector?"

Blake waits a little.

"Oh, do tell! We're all properly agog."

—Agog.

"We are beside ourselves with anticipation. Do tell us about the dolly's leg!"

Blake laughs. "Well, milord, you will recall that the sergeant noticed, quite automatically, as you might say, what he took to be the leg off a dolly. It was white, and sort of bent into a leg shape, and could perhaps have come off a porcelain doll, or summat like that."

"Go on, Chief Inspector. You're teasing us now. I feel sure that you have something perfectly thrilling up your sleeve."

—Let's hope so.

"Yes, milord. Well, when the officer returned to the hall, which, as you will recall, had been the site of the attack on Lady Verreman, he happened to glance at the dolly's leg again. And it had changed color!"

5

✦✦✦✦✦

THE CASE OF THE FOOTLOOSE DOLL

"Here is one top boot, but there is no sign of the other."

"Well, and what of that?"

"It proves that they strangled him, while he was taking his boots off. He hadn't time to take the second boot off when . . ."

—Anton Chekhov, "The Safety Match"

"CHANGED COLOR, CHIEF Inspector? Whatever do you mean?"

"Yes, milord. Whereas before it had been pure white, now it was blood red!"

The policeman sits back in his chair with a small smile. He is pleased with himself.

"Well, I'll bite, Chief Inspector," says David Verreman. "How did the doll's leg change color, and what possible connection is there between a dolly's leg and a brutal murder?"

The smile gets bigger. "Well, milord, you see, on closer inspection, it turned out not to be a leg from a porcelain doll at all. What it was, in actual fact, was a length of lead piping, wrapped around, along the whole of its length, with white sticking plaster. In short, it was a blunt instrument, and, as we later confirmed, *the* blunt instrument— by which I mean the murder weapon!"

"Good gracious," says David Verreman. Is he humoring him? Mocking him? Maybe a little of both. "But the color, Chief Inspector? Damn it all, even murder weapons don't change color mid-murder, do they?"

The policeman chuckles. "You wouldn't think so, would you? I wonder if anyone can guess."

The policeman looks around the room, and, gratified, is about to reveal the answer when, from the other end of the table, Jeff, who has been straining to speak for some time, suddenly bursts out, "What I want to know is—"

"Not yet, Jeff," says David Verreman, hurriedly. "There will be plenty of time for questions later. This is a game, after all."

—Write them down.

"Yes, if you have thoughts, or questions, or theories, do please write them down. Detective Chief Inspector Blake has given us a conundrum. While we mull that over, why don't we ask Aunty Caro for a bit of background on Lady Verreman? Carolyn Keene-Wade is my mother's sister. I'm sure she won't mind me saying that they were not close. The press criticized Aunty Caro because, at the inquest, she sat with my father's family rather than with my mother. Mother sat on her own, ramrod straight, between our father's family and Sally's family. But she looked only at the coroner, and neither spoke to nor acknowledged anyone else. The gulf between them was a narrow one, as they say, but it was infinitely deep."

—So, with that ringing endorsement, we give you the statement of Carolyn Keene-Wade.

Carolyn Keene-Wade stands. She shrugs her shoulders—indifferent, almost—and waves her hand, as if to say, *Who cares?* When she speaks, she speaks briskly, as one who does not shirk her duty, despite any unpleasantness it may occasion, and despite her inability to comprehend why anyone would care. She begins her speech with a sigh.

"There really isn't much to tell. Antonia was my sister. We were never really close, although I believe that it was not for want of trying on my part. My sister was always a little peculiar. She looked so tiny and delicate and fragile, all the men she met thought that she was in need of their protection. More fool them, because she really wasn't like that at all.

"My sister was always a terribly jealous person. She was jealous of me because she thought I was my father's favorite. It wasn't true, I don't think. It was just that I was younger, and so, of course, I needed more attention. Antonia was never the sort of child who liked to be cuddled, unless she saw me sitting on Daddy's knee. Then she would cry until he cuddled her, too.

"I think the trouble started when I got married. You see, my husband is rather wealthy. As children, we had never been poor, despite what Antonia would tell people, but we did not grow up with lots of money. My sister saw what I had and decided that, at all costs, she would make a better marriage than me. If I had a rich man, she would have an aristocrat.

"I must say, she dropped lucky when she met John Verreman. Not just because he was 'in the stud book,' as she used to say, but because he was not a cad. He was quite taken in by her lost-little-kitten act and was as surprised as anything when he woke up the morning after his wedding to find that he had married a tiger.

"My sister kept a newspaper clipping of their wedding from the society pages. They were very photogenic. The paper said that they were 'a golden couple.' Antonia liked that very much. Other men would have cut their losses after a year or two, but Johnny stuck with it. He tried his best to make a go of it. But it was never going to work, of course.

"John was a gambler. Even away from the gaming tables, he loved to take risks. He raced powerboats, climbed and so on. He even, I believe, did the bobsleigh at one point. My sister was not a risk-taker. On the contrary. She weighed everything like a chess player, considered every move and all its permutations, before making the simplest decision. She found the ebb and flow of their finances intolerable. I do know that she started to salt money away almost from the moment that they were married, although whether she was saving for a two-man canoe or a single-person scull, I'm not sure. She took ridiculous amounts of pleasure in padding the housekeeping bills and pocketing the difference, though I doubt John even noticed. Her husband had many faults, but lack of generosity was not one of them.

"I think that they were reasonably happy for the first few years. She had provided him with an heir, something that weighed far more heavily with her than him, I believe. He was quite blasé about his aristocratic background, which annoyed my sister no end.

"All through her life, Antonia had periods of mental illness, and as the marriage deteriorated, her condition worsened. John was worried about her. He tried, many times, to get her the help she needed. My sister could appear completely rational, you know. And she somehow managed to convey the impression to her doctor that her husband was browbeating her. Worse, that she was afraid of him.

"In reality, I think that he was afraid of her. And if he wasn't, he should have been. Antonia always felt that she was being whispered about, that people didn't like her. All nonsense. When her marriage broke down, the paranoia increased, and I suspect that at some point she also began to drink.

"She was obsessed with John. She hated him, but she loved him, too. She couldn't leave him alone. She trailed after him everywhere. Even down to the club. It was embarrassing. People laughed at her, but she didn't care. She was afraid that if she left him alone for a moment, some other woman would get her claws into him.

"That's it, really. It's all very sad. She was my sister, but I hardly knew her. I don't believe that anyone did. Her marriage was the greatest triumph of her life. She had made it into the stud book. She knew *Burke's Peerage* inside out. She knew exactly what was due to her rank, and she insisted on it. No one ever got away with calling her *Mrs.* Verreman. The end of the marriage was an unthinkable disaster. She told John over and over again that she would never divorce him.

"And, in the end, of course, she was right. Though he disappeared, he was still her husband. It was the ideal situation for her. He couldn't divorce her if he couldn't be found. She wiped the unfortunate murder of a young woman in the basement from her mind. Sally

Gardner was just a minor obstacle on the road to their everlasting love.

"In my sister's mind, you see, they were the golden couple right to the end."

Carolyn Keene-Wade sits down, and David Verreman applauds. "Wonderful, wonderful, Aunty Caro. Poignant and perceptive, with just the right amount of bile. Like only a sister could, eh?"

Carolyn lifts her glass in acknowledgment and goes back to her prawns.

"I think we will have just one more before the next course, shall we?"

—Can we make it a short one? I'm starving. I need meat.

"How about Mr. Stanley Gardner, the estranged husband of the deceased? Will you tell us what you know, sir?"

Mr. Gardner stands up, and immediately puts a finger down the edge of his shirt collar and runs it around his neck, to give his vocal cords a bit of breathing room. His hands are sweaty, and he leaves a damp mark on the light blue fabric of his collar.

"Yes, well, er, I thank you for the invite to this dinner, not that we've tasted a morsel yet, barring a handful of scrawny shrimps, and my insides are fair flapping, as they say.

"Well, now, I identified the body of my wife at the police station, and again at the inquest. But other than that, I don't have much to tell you, and honestly, I can't for the life of me understand why I keep being asked about it. Sally and me, we married young. Bloody silly, really, but we were in love, or thought we were.

"But I was in the merchant navy, and that meant being away from home for months at a time. Sally said she was OK with that, but you can't never tell about those things. Not until you try it. So, we tried it, and it turned out that she wasn't quite so keen on it after all.

"Sally was what you would call vivacious. She liked a party. And dancing. And giggling and going out with a fella in the nighttime. All that razzmatazz. Wasn't her fault. She wasn't to know what it would be like sitting at home night after night when everyone else was out

THE GAME IS MURDER

having a good time. But I knew. I knew what it was like, and I should have known it wasn't for her.

"But there, I was in love, too, I daresay. I forgave the first time. She was sorry, and we made the best of it. But after the second time, that was it. A fella couldn't be made a fool of. It wasn't just the affairs, though. We'd both done a bit of growing up by that time and realized that we'd just been bits of kids and foolish.

"So, we separated, and Sally went her own way after that. I did hear that she'd got a job working among the nobs, and, tell you the truth, I thought that was pretty funny, because she didn't strike me that way at all. Just the opposite, in fact.

"But what do I know? We'd been separated about a year by then, and people change, don't they? No doubt we would have divorced eventually, but, with being away so much, I didn't get around to it. It didn't bother me, and I suspect it didn't bother her none either.

"I'm just speculating here, but the Sally I knew didn't want to be tied down, and what better reason is there for not going steady with a chap than a husband in the wings? Maybe I'm wrong, but I reckon our Sally was not made for monogamy. She was a fine woman, for all that, and I liked her.

"That's all I have to say about the matter. I know nothing of these Verremans. I met old Lady Verreman once at the coroner's court, and that was enough for me. Cold as a fish she was, and I had no desire to get better acquainted. No offense to any family members who may be present.

"That's it, except to say that if, by concluding, my actions hurry along the main course, I will now put my arse upon my chair and a seal upon my gob. I am done."

And there you have it. The first three witness statements. What do you notice?

How about the rank stereotyping? Take poor old Stanley Gardner. He's a merchant seaman. So he must be a working-class kind of guy, right?

How do we know?

The author of a detective novel doesn't need you to know. The author of a detective novel is concerned only with the detective. The detective is the only fully fleshed-out character. He has quirks and idiosyncrasies galore. Even a few outright character flaws. He is the opium-smoking, violin-playing chess master. He is exceedingly neat or excessively messy. He drinks too much alcohol, or he drinks only coffee. He wears a deerstalker hat or a twirly mustache. Whatever.

You are our detective. Your character flaws are now lovable eccentricities.

Insert lovable eccentricity here: _____

Our characters will have some flesh on their bones. We will differentiate them, at least. Perhaps we will give one a glass eye and another a gammy leg. Who knows? They will be identifiable, more or less, though not, perhaps, down a dark alley, with a following wind.

But that is OK, because everyone bar the detective is a mere cardboard-cutout character.

They barely exist.

They are each representative of a type. The policeman will be gruff and unimaginative, the sister spiteful, the merchant seaman a canny lad.

Why? Because their purpose is merely to deliver information. The author does not want you to be sidetracked by their backstories. Largely because he has not bothered to give them backstories. He does not want to waste precious words on them. He wants you to think of them like the postman. They bring the news— and it hardly matters at all which uniform they wear. Royal Mail or UPS? Who cares, as long as the package arrives on time?

Can they not be both postman and fully rounded character? Well, possibly, but that means an awful lot of hard work, and, really, who can be bothered with that?

And so Stanley Gardner, merchant seaman, estranged husband of the deceased, must be working-class. And, being working-class, he must be from the north of England, where all the working-class people are kept when they are not serving their betters. He uses phrases like "fair flapping" to alert you to his low origins, much like a leper rings his bell. Forewarned is forearmed.

All of which, of course, means that Mr. Gardner must be innocent.

It is a convention of detective fiction that neither the maid nor the gardener—Gardner, get it?—nor the schoolmistress nor the chauffeur nor, in fact, any member of the hoi polloi can be guilty of the crime. Despite what you may have heard, the butler has not dunnit in a detective novel since 1930, and Mary Roberts Rinehart has not lived it down since.

When detective novels take place in the rarefied world of the upper classes, the proletariat are background artists and scene-shifters only. They do not figure in the main action.

Why? Because the classic detective came of age after the Great War. According to the social mores of the time, it was bad form to pin the crime on someone from the "lower classes," in the same way as a modern author may feel uncomfortable portraying a mugger as a young Black man. Though a servant, and indeed a young Black man, is as capable of committing a crime as anyone else, as a stereotype it seems rooted in casual bigotry and is, therefore, usually best avoided.

All of which means that you can cross Stanley Gardner off your list.

Right?

You are keeping a list, aren't you?

"INTERESTING, EH?" SAYS David Verreman. "I wonder what your preliminary thoughts are. I know, I know, I mustn't ask! We wouldn't want to spoil the game, would we? Follow the money; that's my advice. But not now, of course. Because here comes the beef!"

Main Course

~

Beef Wellington

Bloody!

Served with roast potatoes, baby carrots and asparagus

"I sincerely hope that there are no vegetarians among us. Probably something I should have checked earlier, I know, but remember that these guys are mostly still living in the 1970s, and no one was a vegetarian back then, except, perhaps, the occasional hippie. Back then, beef was king. And tonight, we have a king with a duke on top. Can't be bad."

David Verreman turns to you and asks, "Do you like beef Wellington?"

Look—being paraded down the table is an enormous platter upon which is a log-sized slab of beef fillet covered in golden pastry and decorated with tufts of parsley, suspiciously bright in color, that lie, unwilting, around the log.

The parsley is plastic.

"And roast potatoes, too," he gushes. "My favorite. I never did get past nursery food, you know. Plain English food—that's what I like. Now, then, the beef is rather rare and nicely bloody, so why not have Dr. Mackintosh's story next? It seems rather fitting, don't you think?"

Dr. Elizabeth Mackintosh is the world-famous blood specialist. She looks down the table and scowls a little. Does she think it in poor taste for David Verreman to speak of the dead and the dying while the meat is yet in our mouths? Dr. Mackintosh looks interrogatively around the table, and, no one raising an objection, she begins her story. As she speaks, she repeatedly clasps and unclasps a pince-nez

36

that is hung around her neck. The pince-nez is not showy, but rather solid and plain, and gives the impression less of spectacles and more of a portable microscope.

"I was called to this house in the early hours of the morning following the murder. I took samples from the attack sites in the basement and in the hall. I also took samples from the victim and from Lady Verreman in order to make comparisons with the samples found at the scene, and finally, I took samples from a short piece of lead piping also found at the scene.

"Of course, at the time that this event occurred, there was no such thing as DNA analysis available to us, and yet we were able to look at the blood groups and blood subgroups of the two victims in order to distinguish them with a great deal of accuracy.

"In this, I must say, we were quite fortunate, because Lady Verreman and Mrs. Gardner had different blood groups. Our job would have been very much more difficult had they shared the same group.

"Lady Verreman was blood group A, as is around forty percent of the British population, while Mrs. Gardner was of the much rarer group B, which is found in only ten percent of the population. The blood found in the hall was largely of the same type as that of Lady Verreman, group A, while the blood in the basement was largely group B, Mrs. Gardner's group. I say 'largely' because there were some bloodstains of both groups in each of the sites, which I will come to in a moment.

"I also found very small quantities of blood group AB.

"For those of you who may not know, group AB is very rare, and is found in less than four percent of the population. It is possible, however, that the blood that tested as being group AB was, in fact, a mixture of blood group A and blood group B from the two victims. In most cases it is possible to detect and separate blood types even when they are mixed together, but in these samples, which were very small, we have not been able to do so, so there remains the possibility that this blood came from another source, that of a person with blood group AB.

"I should say at this point that we do not know Lord Verreman's blood type.

"Apart from these small group AB samples, all the blood was of either group A or B, the same groups as the victims. If we begin with the site in the basement, I found many blood splashes and smears near the base of the stairs, and the parquet wood floor was soaked with blood. Toward the top of the basement stairs there were a number of blood smears against the wall, one of which had the impression of a fabric print, from a finely knitted garment. Neither the clothes Lady Verreman wore nor those of Mrs. Gardner matched this fabric impression. Analysis of the blood here proved to be of group B.

"The bottom of the stairs was clearly the main site of the attack in the basement, and I found radiating splashes and blood spots on the walls. These were likely to have been thrown off the weapon during its repeated swings. The blood at the bottom of the stairs proved to be of group B in almost all cases.

"I also found, in the basement, some indistinct shoe prints in the area behind the breakfast room, and in the back garden, most probably from a man's shoe. The blood in this area all proved to be of group B. I found a few scattered bloodstains in the kitchen area. There were some bloodstains around the cooker, but I was unable to get any satisfactory result from these bloodstains.

"I tested the mailbag in which the body was found, which was extensively bloodstained. I selected six distinct areas of the bag to test. In four of these areas the blood corresponded to group B, and two showed both group A blood and group B blood.

"I examined Lady Verreman's clothes and shoes, which were extensively stained. The front of her dress was stained with group A blood, although there was a group B stain on the back of the dress and another stain, which was group AB, which, again, may have been a mixture of both victims' blood or may have come from a person with type AB blood. With Lady Verreman's shoes I found many light smears of group A blood on the uppers, while there was group B blood found on the soles and underneath the arches. There were similar patterns of staining on both left and right shoes.

"In the hall, the site of the second attack, there was also a radiating pattern of blood on the walls and ceiling near the top of the basement steps, as well as downward trickles onto the floor. In the hall cloakroom, I found splashes of blood on the ceiling, most likely thrown off the weapon by an attacker standing with his back to the cloakroom.

"Inside the cloakroom, I also found a tuft of bloodstained hair in the sink, which was consistent with samples taken from Lady Verreman. The blood on this hair was exclusively group AB.

"In the cloakroom sink, clinging to the tuft of hair, I also found six microscopic gray-blue textile fibers. I have not been able to positively identify these. I found four similar fibers on the bloodstained towel from Lady Verreman's bedroom, and seven on the piece of lead piping.

"I was subsequently asked to examine Lord Verreman's borrowed car, which was found, abandoned, two days after the murder. I found a further thirty-two of these gray-blue fibers. Twenty-five of them were attached to bloodstains on the inside of the driver's-side door, and the remaining seven were attached to a small tuft of bloodstained hair, which was similar to samples taken from Lady Verreman.

"The lead piping found at the house also had several bloodstained hairs attached to it, as well as a considerable quantity of blood, which was all of group AB, but which, again, may have been a mixture of blood from both victims or from someone else. All of the hairs I examined appeared similar to samples taken from Lady Verreman. None resembled samples of hair taken from Mrs. Gardner.

"That is a broad summary of my evidence. I was, at a later date, asked to examine a letter that was sent to Sir Henry Wade, supposedly by Lord Verreman. The envelope contained several smears of blood, which I tested. Most of these tests returned unsatisfactory results. However, one smear, on the back of the envelope, did return a result.

"The blood group on this letter was AB."

Dr. Mackintosh gives a little nod to indicate that she has finished, and returns her attention to her plate.

"Wonderful, Dr. Mackintosh. Thank you!" David Verreman taps his fingers together like a clap, but without the noise. "Really wonderfully explained, and you managed, more or less, not to put anyone off their food, which I, for one, am extremely grateful for.

"There are one or two points there that are rather suggestive. Don't you agree, Great Detective?"

Nod hastily in agreement. Are there any suggestive points?

Write something in your notebook. For form's sake, if nothing else.

"Really, this is delightful. I'm enjoying myself enormously," says David.

And he really does seem to be having fun—talking about how his father tried to kill his mother, and accidentally killed someone else instead.

Is that strange?

—Who shall we have next?

Margaret Howard-Cole raises her hand. "As the lady doctor mentioned the letters, perhaps I should go next, and then perhaps we can hear from Sir Henry Wade, since he is the person to whom the letters were addressed?"

"Perfectly fine with me," says David. "Away you go."

"Thank you," she says, standing. "Well, now, Lord Verreman was a friend of my husband's, really."

"Bloody good sort," bursts out George Howard-Cole through a mouthful of potato, and with gravy dribbling down his chin. "A damned fine chap. Old-school."

"Thank you." Margaret Howard-Cole averts her eyes from the sight of her husband chewing. "Well, it was around eleven forty-five, I think, on the night of the seventh of November when John Verreman knocked at our front door. My husband was away, and I, of course, was in bed.

"I got up and let him in. I could tell there was something wrong. He wasn't hysterical or anything like that, but I could tell he'd had a bit of a shock. I'm not sure how. He looked pretty much as normal, only a little disheveled. Perhaps that was it, because, as a rule, John was very well turned out."

"Quite right," says George Howard-Cole, forking a piece of asparagus into his mouth. "Shipshape and Bristol fashion."

"He certainly wasn't covered in blood or anything like that," continues his wife, looking straight ahead. "I do remember that there was a small damp patch on his right hip, where he might, conceivably, have sponged his clothes down, but that was all.

"I brought him into the house. He seemed rather shaken, and I gave him a large drink and pointed him toward the sofa. Naturally, I asked what was wrong, and he said that he had been passing his wife's house on his way home to change for dinner—they lived very near each other, and I believe that he passed there often—and he happened to look through the basement window, where he saw a man attacking his wife. So, obviously, he went to help her. He let himself in—he still had a key—and ran toward the basement.

"He said he slipped in some blood at the bottom of the steps. Then the attacker ran off and Johnny went to help his wife, check that she was all right and so forth. Of course, with hindsight, it might have been better if he had chased the attacker instead, but Antonia was hysterical.

"She always was hysterical, but now she had a sort of excuse. Johnny said she was covered in blood, and she said that someone had killed the nanny. The girl wasn't a trained nanny, of course, more like an au pair. But that was Antonia for you, even at a moment like that. Anyway, she pointed to a sack, which was, apparently, soaked with blood, and he presumed that that was where the body was. I don't think he looked inside it. I got the impression he was a bit squeamish.

"That's it, really. That's all he told me. Oh, he did say that he had called his mother and asked her to pick up young David there. And he called her again while he was with me, just to check that the boy was OK.

"And after that we talked about other things. Normal stuff. After a couple of hours, he said he ought to get going. I did offer him a bed, but I knew he wouldn't accept. Wouldn't look good. Besides, I doubt if he would have slept anyway.

"Before he left, he asked if I had some notepaper, because he wanted to write a letter. He wrote two, in fact, both to Henry Wade, and I told him I would post them for him in the morning. Actually, I gave them to someone else to post, but it's the same thing.

"I didn't notice any blood on John that night. There was none on his hands, and as far as I could tell, there was none on the envelopes either. They were white envelopes. I put the stamps on, and I am sure I would have noticed if they'd had smudges of blood on them.

"John Verreman left my house around one fifteen a.m., and, as they say, he was never seen again."

Margaret Howard-Cole takes a sip of wine, a concluding action to fit this last statement, before she sits down. Her husband leans forward, pats her arm and whispers, "Attagirl," spraying masticated carrot as he does so.

Sir Henry "Hal" Wade takes up the story. He does not stand up, and yet his manner is more formal than Mrs. Howard-Cole's. He takes long pauses between sentences, and parts of sentences, and sometimes between individual words. And he chooses those words very carefully.

As he talks, he keeps his eye on his knife, which he holds, point down, on the table, keeping it balanced along the perpendicular with the tip of his finger. He pulls the knife round in ever-widening circles with his fingertip, and when, inevitably, it escapes the restraining pressure of his finger and clatters to the table, he merely picks it up again, sets it point down on the table once more and begins again, without ever lifting his eyes from his cutlery.

Hal Wade is a man who knows his duty, and does his duty, but only his duty, and not one jot more.

"As Mrs. Howard-Cole has said, I received two letters from

Jinx—that is, Lord Verreman—a few days after the murder. There was a slight delay in receiving them, since I was away from home at the time. As soon as I did get them, I took them straight round to the police—in fact, to Mr. Blake here . . ."

He waits, circling his knife, until Chief Inspector Blake confirms, "Quite correct."

"I also pointed out to him that one envelope appeared to be bloodstained."

Pause. Knife circling.

"Also correct."

"One letter was a personal letter addressed to me. This is the letter that refers to the tragedy as 'the most ghastly circumstances' and is generally referred to as his confession, though I have never considered it so. The second note regards the sale of some family silver, with some instructions about which creditors I should pay with the money from the sale.

"I have no idea why Lord Verreman chose to honor me with these communications. We were friends, but not, I wouldn't have said, especially close friends. I had no authority to take control of the proceeds of the sale, nor, in fact, did I do so.

"That's all. I believe that you have copies of the letters. That is my entire connection with this matter."

And Sir Henry picks up his knife properly and returns to his dinner, unconcerned.

LOOK DOWN AT the table. There are two small white envelopes next to your water glass. Have they been there the whole time, or has a quiet-footed servant placed them there while your eyes were fixed upon the circling knife?

Open the first envelope. Spidery writing over three pages of fine-quality notepaper.

David Verreman leans forward. "Don't worry. Printed transcript on the back."

—I don't know why people say the letter is unreadable.

"It *is* unreadable! It's terrible. His writing was always bad, I'm told, but I suppose we must allow him some latitude on this night, since he was, no doubt, in a state of shock."

—It's perfectly legible to me.

Glance through the handwritten version and confirm to yourself that it is, indeed, unreadable; then turn, relieved, to the printed version.

7th Nov. 1974

Dear Hal,

The most ghastly circumstances arose tonight, which I briefly described to my mother. When I interrupted the fight at Broad Way, and the man fled, Antonia accused me of having hired him.

I took her upstairs and sent David up to bed and tried to clean her up. She lay doggo for a bit, and while I was in the bathroom, she left the house.

The circumstantial evidence against me is strong in that A will say it was all my doing. I will now lie doggo for a bit, but I am only concerned for the child/ren. If you can manage it, I want them to live with you—Coutts (trustees) St. Martins Lane (Mr. Joseph L. French) will handle school fees.

A has demonstrated her hatred for me in the past and would do anything to see me accused. For David, going through life knowing his father stood in the dock for attempted murder will be too much. When he is old enough to understand, explain to him the dream/disease of paranoia, and look after him.

Yours always,
John

Reach for the second envelope and ask yourself why he didn't put both letters in the same envelope. This letter is much shorter.

Financial Matters
  There is a sale coming up at Christie's, 27th November, which will satisfy bank overdrafts. Please agree reserves with Gervase Fen.
  Proceeds to go to:
  Lloyds, 6 Pall Mall
  Coutts, 59 Strand
  NatWest, Bloomsbury branch, who also hold an Equity and Law Life Policy
  The other creditors can get lost for the time being.

Jinx

Read through the letters hurriedly, because David Verreman is already tapping his glass with his knife.

"Thank you. As we seem to have already got on to the subject of money, why not hang all the dirty laundry out at once? Mr. Leroux, why don't you favor us next?"

Gaston Leroux is a sturdy-looking gentleman, well-fed and well-dressed, with a thick mop of dark hair and impossibly small spectacles, which he polishes fastidiously, first with his tie, then, after peering through them and shaking his head in dissatisfaction, with his napkin. On his wrist is a fat gold link bracelet, and the links clink gently as he polishes the lenses. He replaces his spectacles with equal fastidiousness, and glances along the table to ensure that he has everyone's attention.

He gives a small cough. Put the letter down and give him your full attention.

He smiles, and begins.

"It is not without a certain amount of emotion that I relate my small part in the extraordinary adventures of Lord Verreman. Until now, I had given up ever learning the whole truth about this amazing case. These things are quickly forgotten by the public, of course, but at the time, the entire nation was deeply interested in solving this mystery. Even today there are still those who recall the Verreman Affair with amazement, and brood over its possible solutions. But I am buoyed up today in the certain knowledge that our Great Detective will succeed in discerning—or devising, if you prefer—a solution to this enduring conundrum.

"Where everyone else gave up, our detective will prevail. I look at our Great Detective and I see the insightful mind and the moral fortitude of this truly great investigator."

Gaston Leroux raises his glass. Is he taking the piss? Is this an insult or a testimonial? Should you be offended? The room is silent. Smile, a little, and nod, briefly—just in case.

Gaston Leroux smiles in return. "What part did I play in this mystery, you ask? Almost none, I declare. Almost none at all. A mere footnote. But one that, perhaps, may go some way—a very little way, I assure you—to facilitating the discernment of Lord Verreman's financial affairs prior to the incident.

"I am not in a position, you understand, to give a psychological insight. I am not the bosom friend, or the trusted confidant. My role is altogether different. I was described in some of the more priggish newspapers of the time as a 'financial gentleman,' which was a term I rather liked. It set the right tone, I thought. I was, perforce, involved in finance—by which I mean the lending of funds to those in temporary want of money—but always, I hope, remembering that I was, first and foremost, a gentleman dealing with gentlemen."

—Moneylender.

"Nowadays, of course, people are much less circumspect when it comes to talking about money, and these days I am happy just to call myself a financial adviser."

—Moneylender!

"'Financial adviser' is a term that, I admit, suggests much while meaning almost nothing at all, but it still evokes a modicum of decency and professionalism."

—Loan shark!

"But you don't want to know about that. You are concerned only with the manner of my encounter with Lord Verreman and this case. Well, it was like this:

"About a month before the murder, Lord Verreman, till that point a complete stranger, approached me seeking a short-term loan of five thousand pounds. Now, I was placed in a somewhat difficult position. Lord Verreman, of course also a gentleman, felt that his word was his bond, and brought no other surety with him.

"Here we have a practical example of the difference between a gentleman and a financial gentleman. While a handshake may be surety enough for a gentleman, a financial gentleman demands collateral more easily converted into hard cash.

"That being so, I conducted what you may describe as an audit of Lord Verreman's assets, the result of which led me to believe that he was not a good risk. He was, as they say, distinctly overstretched. Therefore, with a great deal of regret—for it would have looked well to have him as a customer—I was forced to turn down his request.

"And that would have been all, except that, a week later, he returned to my office, and on that occasion I did make him a loan, though for a somewhat lower amount. He brought with him a very wealthy friend, whom I recognized immediately as being a different sort of financial gentleman, the kind likely to be found in the financial papers, and who consented to guarantee the loan. Confidentiality, of course, prohibits me from naming this gentleman, despite his later actions. However, he was mentioned regularly in the press in connection with this case, both at the time and for years afterward, and was almost always described as being a 'close personal friend' of Lord Verreman, so I daresay you could work it out if you were minded to.

"I must say it did occur to me to wonder why, being such a 'close friend,' he elected not to lend Verreman the money himself rather than see me take my forty-five percent in interest. However, that is none of my concern. Perhaps he had offered and Lord Verreman refused. Who knows?

"The terms of the loan were these: three thousand pounds, repayable over six months, with the interest at forty-five percent APR. This is, admittedly, higher than a bank would charge, but then again, if he could have got a bank to lend him the money, he wouldn't have come knocking on my door, would he?

"I was still a little nervous about the wisdom of the transaction, but I was reassured when Lord Verreman came to my office in person three days before the first installment was due and paid it in full, in cash. Unfortunately for me, before the second installment came due the murder occurred and Lord Verreman vanished. I soon discovered that his rich 'close personal friend' was decidedly not a gentleman, as he tried to wriggle out of his obligation to settle the debt that he had underwritten.

"Which was a salutary lesson. Money definitely does *not* a gentleman make. 'Wait for the death certificate,' indeed! Not me, sir. And I got it out of him in the end! Oh yes! A 'financial gentleman' may try his best to behave as a gentleman, but when faced with such boorish behavior, I'm afraid *this* financial gentleman will always choose the course that is of the greatest pecuniary advantage to me. He paid up!

"But that is by the by. Lord Verreman's finances at the time of the incident—that's what you want from me, I'm guessing. And, as I said before, 'overstretched' is the term that best describes them. Though he undoubtedly had assets, he was overdrawn in all four of his bank accounts, and by a considerable amount. He did show me the notice of an upcoming auction that included some of his family silver, which was expected to fetch a tidy sum, but even if every item met its reserve, the sale could not do more than keep the wolf from the door just a little while longer.

"Lord Verreman was quite frank about his liabilities. Nothing that I subsequently learned at the inquest conflicted with the account that he had given me. That in itself is unusual, since, in my experience, gamblers and debtors are terrible liars. He also paid me the compliment of confiding in me that his marriage was ending and a financial settlement needed to be arranged. I never met Lady Verreman, but just looking at the entries in his bank accounts, I could see that a divorce settlement would not be the gravy train she might have felt entitled to expect given outward appearances.

"Lord Verreman was a pleasant gentleman. And a Gentleman. Though I knew him for only a short time, he did not strike me as the type of person who was willing to do *anything* for money. And in my experience, and in my line of work—"

—Loan-sharking!

"—it is not an opinion I would be prepared to offer about many of my customers. That, I realize, is stepping outside my province as witness in the case and is, properly, a matter for our Great Detective to decide. But I include it for what it's worth.

"That is all, I am afraid. I have, of course, speculated a great deal on these matters, and I have formulated not a theory, exactly, but certainly a number of questions that our detective might like to consider."

Leroux pauses, waiting for an invitation to continue. Is he asking your permission?

"Thank you, Mr. Leroux. That was very illuminating," says David Verreman. "Perhaps we can save the questions until after dinner? There will be plenty to discuss, I'm sure."

Gaston Leroux smiles, a little sourly. As he takes a sip of wine, he gives a little bow, and he mutters, "Of course. At your service."

Let's Play a Game!

Earlier, we showed you a tray with eleven objects on it. Why eleven? Why not? Why must we be confined to ten, or compelled to make it a round dozen? No. We choose to be different. We choose eleven.

And we have made it easy for you. All these items are of significance to our case.

In a test with random objects, most people cannot remember more than about seven items—plus or minus two. But these are not random items. These are our clues.

Go!

How could you forget the damn clues? What kind of detective are you?

Take a moment.

Cast your mind back.

Try again.

Write your eleven objects here:

1 _____

2 _____

3 _____

4 _____

5 _____

6 _____

7 _____

8 _____

9 _____

10 _____

11 _____

Is that it?

Really? Try to picture the objects in your memory palace. Did you add them to your memory palace? Have you even got one?

OK. If you didn't get them all—and let's say, for the sake of argument, that you did not—sorry, but you lose a life.

Come, come. There is little point in arguing now that you didn't know you might lose a life, or, indeed, that we held your lives at all. And no, there is no point in asking how many lives you have. This is not that sort of game. There are rules to be followed, certainly, but it is your job to find out what the rules are. After all, you are a detective.

The lead pipe, the bloodstained letter, the teacup, the pills, the gambling chips, a lightbulb, time, a high-heeled shoe, the key of the door, a diary, a car: these are the clues that will crack this case, and you can't even remember what they are!

You may argue—though, again, you would be wasting your time—that you were not told of the significance of these items. And we would argue, right back at ya, that a clue is a clue for all that. The discarded cigarette end with the distinctive lipstick, the scrap of paper gripped in a dead man's hand, a long blond hair where no blond hair should be—these are the bread and butter of the Great Detective. Not to mention the coffee that is still warm in the pot, the message scrawled in the victim's own blood or the dog that failed to bark.

None of those clues is labeled for the edification of the detective. Like Sherlock Holmes, you have to seek them out. Waddaya think the magnifying glass is for?

A Quiz: What Kind of Detective Are You?
Detectives come in all shapes and sizes. You get tall ones and short ones. Fat ones and thin ones. Stupid ones and clever ones.

We have, considerately, sorted them into groups for you. We will call the first group *Behold, a Great Detective!*

The group includes Sherlock Holmes, of course. But he is not the only one. How about C. Auguste Dupin? One of the very earliest detectives. The man who solved Poe's "The Murders in the Rue Morgue."

Two women are found brutally murdered inside a locked room on the top floor of an apartment building. No one entered the building, and no one could have placed a ladder against the outer wall without detection. The chimney was too narrow even for a child to climb down. Witnesses who heard the assault declared the murderer to be speaking an "unknown language." Dupin deduces the murderer's extraordinary strength from the brutal treatment of the bodies, and his lack of financial motive from the two bags of gold left untouched in the room.

Dupin ponders the problem deeply, but not for long. He puts himself inside the mind of the murderer, and *like that*, he arrives at the solution. The orangutan dunnit!

What orangutan, you say? Why, the hitherto unmentioned but now logically inferred orangutan, of course. Because when you have eliminated the impossible, whatever remains must be a long-armed primate from Borneo.

Shall Dupin be your model? Perhaps not, unless you are a master of astral projection. But Poe was writing at the birth of the detective story, when the rules were not yet established. We forgive Monsieur Dupin, but we do not emulate him.

OK, back to the story.

EDDIE BIGGERS IS standing up. He looks both nervous and resentful, though he has been tucking into his meal with gusto. He leans a little away from Sally's husband as he speaks.

"Sally and me had only been dating a few weeks. It was casual, but I think we both hoped it was going somewhere." He looks toward Stanley Gardner, and quickly away again. "I did know that she was separated from her husband, but it had happened a long time ago, she said, and she considered herself a free agent."

Stanley Gardner does not even glance in his direction. Biggers continues. "Yes, well, we were going together. They said at the inquest that she had quite a few boyfriends, which seemed bad, maybe, to some people, but none of them had been serious, and at the time of . . . we had decided to be exclusive. And we were.

"She was a nice woman. Mostly people don't mean anything particular when they say that, but I do. Sally was a nice woman. She was nice-looking, she was fun to be around and she was kind, too. Always had a smile on her face. That's how I remember her, anyway.

"She was only in the house that night because I had asked her to come out with me the night before. I'm a barman, see, and I have to take time off when it's quiet, which is generally a Tuesday or a Wednesday. Nannies and housekeepers and people like that generally have Thursdays off. I never knew that before I met Sally, but it's a fact, apparently. They all have the same day off, and then they can meet up with each other for drinks.

"Sally used to like meeting up with her friends, but on this particular Wednesday, the night before the killing, I had asked her to come out with me, just the two of us. It's hard to really get to know each other in a crowd, isn't it? So she swapped her night off. Not that there was anything wrong in it. We were just talking. At the inquest, they made it out like Sally was a party girl, and next door to a prossie or something"—he stares malevolently at the coroner, Dr. Knox, who blushes and looks down at his empty plate—"but it wasn't like that at all. Sally was . . . well, like I said, she was nice.

"Anyway, that night, the night before the, you know, we'd argued. I can't remember what about now. Something and nothing, probably. We did argue sometimes. Sally was a passionate sort of person. We'd argue, and then we'd make up. Always. So, the night before, we'd had a bit of a row, and she'd gone off home in a huff, a bit early.

"But on that day, the seventh of November, I called her. It was just after eight. Maybe half past. I called her and we made up. I was only on the phone for about five minutes, because I was working at the time, but we were all fine again. She sounded happy as anything when she put the phone down.

"And that was the last thing she did before she got killed. She put the phone down, and then, so they said at the inquest, she put her head round Lady Verreman's bedroom door and asked if she wanted a cup of tea. I think that being so happy is what made her do it. You know, when you've made up after a row, you have that itch to get up and do something, don't you?

"She put the phone down; then she asked Miss La-di-da if she wanted a cuppa, and walked down them basement steps to her doom.

"If I hadn't called her just then, or if I hadn't got her to change her night off, she might never have been there."

Eddie Biggers stops talking. Not with a flourish, or a concluding action. He just stops talking. And he carries on standing there, staring at his plate—staring through the plate, and the table, and the floor, into the basement beneath.

After a moment, David Verreman clears his throat. The sound of it seems to bring Biggers back to himself, and he sits down heavily.

Verreman pulls a comic face at Dr. Knox, as if he just witnessed Biggers eating his soup with a dessert spoon.

The lower classes. Endless fun.

IN THE INTERVAL between the dinner plates' being taken out and the dessert's being brought in, the pathologist, Professor Cameron McCabe, makes his speech. He has a voice that travels naturally across the room. Like an actor, or a university lecturer. And he seems to feel quite at home addressing an audience. Professor McCabe does not put on any airs. He does not clear his throat, or fiddle with his collar. He merely collects the attention of the audience with one sweeping glance around the table, and begins his speech in a soft, but entirely audible, voice that bears only a trace of his Scottish roots.

"I was asked to examine the body of Mrs. Sally Gardner. She was clothed in a smock dress, bra and pants. Her underclothes had not been disturbed and she had suffered no sexual assault.

"She was a healthy person. The medical examination showed no evidence that she had suffered any but the usual, common ailments during her life. She had had her appendix removed, probably as a teenager, but there were no other surgical procedures in evidence. Not, of course, that her medical history could have contributed to such a violent death. I merely give you this information for the sake of completeness.

"Well, then. I examined the injuries. There were three blunt injuries to the face—that is to say there was heavy bruising over her right eye, the right corner of her mouth and a third area, over her eyebrow. These bruises were more likely to have been made with a closed fist than a blunt instrument.

"There was a second, different, set of injuries to her head. There were four splits to her scalp on the right side of her head. All four were in the same area, above her right ear. There were two further splits in the scalp at the back of her head. These are likely to have been made with a weapon. I examined the lead pipe found at the scene, and it was consistent with the sort of injuries found, though I cannot, of course, say *definitively* that it was the weapon used in the attack.

"I found heavy bruising on both shoulders, which may have been caused by the weapon missing its target. On the back of her right hand there were some superficial bruises, most likely to have been defensive injuries as she tried to protect the back of her head from the blows.

"Lastly, I found four in-line bruises on the right upper arm, consistent with fingers gripping her arm tightly. There was blood found inside the air passages, and a good deal of bruising on the brain, which would have caused it to swell, resulting in unconsciousness.

"The cause of death itself was both the blunt force injuries to the head and the inhalation of blood that had blocked the air passages. Either would have been sufficient to cause death on its own. Together, of course, they were doubly fatal.

"Unconsciousness would probably have occurred quickly, though not immediately, but she would certainly have been unconscious at the moment of death."

Professor McCabe sits and looks around the table again, as if to say, *Any questions?*

Well, any questions?

DAVID VERREMAN LEANS in close and whispers, "My brother and I were wondering whether you might like to take The Tour."
—You'll love it.
"Do say yes. We won't ask the others. They've all taken it, of course. Dozens of times, some of them."
—But you haven't.
"Exactly. And it will allow you to—"
—Picture the scene.
"I was going to say 'get the lie of the land,' but, as always, my brother has cut through the—"
—Bullshit.
"—verbiage. Shall we go? They'll hold dessert for us."
Precede David Verreman out into the hall. He seems excited. Walk just in front of him, cautiously. He points to the tiled floor near the top of the basement steps. "That's where Mother got it. There's not much to see here, I'm afraid. The hall was carpeted at the time, and, of course, they ripped that up afterward. Did you know that blood is one of the most difficult stains to get out? It's easier if you treat it straightaway, of course, but I don't suppose anyone was thinking about stains on the carpet at the time."
—I bet Mother was.
"Possibly. Our mother was a rather particular woman. Very neat. Very tidy. I heard that, at the hospital that night, the doctor treating her wanted to cut off her clothes, and Mother kicked up a hell of a fuss, and she stopped them, saying, 'This is my very best pullover.' Can you believe that?"
—I can.
"She was rather strange." He flicks on the light down in the basement. "Now, you have to imagine that this was all in darkness. The

police found the lightbulb on one of the chairs over there," he says, walking down a few steps and pointing to the table in the breakfast room. "The police say the killer took it out so that his victim would not spot him before she reached the bottom."

—The police say our father took it out so our mother would not see him.

"I am being mealymouthed. Of course the police say it was our father, and that Mother was the intended victim. But that has not yet been determined."

—Hasn't it?

David Verreman moves deliberately on down the stairs and assumes a tour-guide voice. "If you look down to your right, you will see that one of the spindles on the balustrade near the top of the staircase has been replaced."

Look carefully at the twisted cast-iron spindles of the staircase. The spindles seem identical to one another. He points to one twisting piece of metal. It looks identical to the others: iron-gray, overpainted in black enamel paint. Look more closely, and see the unevenness where the new spindle has been welded in.

Verreman opens his hands and points at the floor, as if to say *Ta-da!* Or *Voilà!* Or maybe just *What do you think?*

And what do you think? This is too strange. The basement has a parquet floor, and there is a dark stain partially hidden under layers of polish. Or is there? Perhaps it is a trick of the light. A shadow. Or perhaps the murder has permanently marked it. After all, a bloodstain is one of the most difficult stains to remove.

David Verreman is practically dancing. He twirls toward the piano. "The body in the bag was found here. Next to the piano. That was my first piano, you know. A terrible old thing. Horribly out of tune. God only knows how they got it down here. I had lessons from the age of four. Can you imagine that? A toddler *dink-dink-dink*ing about on the keys. I had to sit on about three cushions, and my hands were too small. But I persevered, and they bought me the grand piano in the drawing room when I was seven."

—I was never allowed to touch it.

"Now, Daniel, that's not true, and you know it." David Verreman turns to you. "Daniel was not interested in music, and never would practice. Now, of course, he forgets that, and remembers only that they never bought him a piano, too."

Nod your head a little. This man is clearly nuts.

—I liked other things. But did they encourage me? No.

"Ignore him," says David. "All those sour grapes hurt his little tummy, and now he's in a bad mood."

Give a tight, nervous smile; then smile a little more when David suggests that perhaps you ought to be getting back upstairs for dessert.

6

♦ ♦ ♦ ♦ ♦

FLOWERS FOR THE JUDGE

Have you ever stopped to think how much of the world's disturbance is caused by butlers being able to see through keyholes?

—S. S. Van Dine, *The Kennel Murder Case*

Dessert

~

Individual summer pudding

Accompanied by a coroner and a policeman

Served with mascarpone cream

"I should perhaps begin by talking a little about the role of the coroner and the inquest in our legal system," says Dr. Ronald Knox. "In the United Kingdom, the post of coroner is held usually by either a lawyer or a doctor. I am a doctor by training, although I am, of course, trained in the law with regard to inquests. An inquest is an official court proceeding, but it is not a criminal trial. An inquest need not have a jury, unless the coroner thinks it advisable, but it usually does in cases where there has been a violent or unexplained death, in which case the jury will be selected in the ordinary way.

"The purpose of the inquest, at that time, was to establish three things: the identity of the deceased; the cause of death; and, where death arises from murder or manslaughter, the name of any person on whom the jury feels confident of affixing responsibility for that death.

"I should mention, perhaps, that juries are no longer required to name the guilty person, but that was the procedure at that time.

"The conduct of the inquest—that is, the nature and range of the inquiry—is usually a matter for the coroner alone to decide. Now, when considering how to conduct the inquest into Mrs. Sally Gardner's murder, I was faced with two major problems. The first was that the principal party in the case—I refer, of course, to Lord Verreman—disappeared shortly after the murder. Being present in the house on that evening, by his own admission, he would almost certainly have had important information to lay before the jury. My second consideration was that the other principal witness was Lady Verreman."

Dr. Knox presses the tips of his fingers together in contemplation. "Now, until 1984 it was a principle of English law that a wife could not testify against her husband unless—and this is a very important caveat—she was giving evidence regarding an assault upon herself. In any matter pertaining to the death of Mrs. Gardner, Lady Verreman *could not* testify; however, she was free to talk about the assault on herself. I considered it necessary that, if at all possible, the inquest be delayed until such time as Lord Verreman was apprehended or returned of his own volition. This being so, I delayed the inquest as long as possible. By the following June, however, it was clear that Lord Verreman—if, indeed, he was still alive—was lying uncommonly low, and was unlikely, therefore, to come forward, and I was compelled to consider proceeding with the inquest without him.

"I gave a great deal of thought to the conduct and scope of that inquest. In order to do justice to Mrs. Gardner, and considering that this may be the only court in which the murderer of that lady was named, I deemed it necessary to hold the fullest inquiry that I could into the events of the seventh of November. And yet, in order to include the testimony of Lady Verreman, who was, after all, the only available witness to the murder of Mrs. Gardner, I would have to exclude all the evidence *about* Mrs. Gardner.

"I could, of course, have held only a formal inquest, taking evidence only with regard to the identity and cause of death, but I felt that by taking wider evidence, even that which did not relate to Mrs. Gardner directly, we were more likely to reach a resolution that would bring a measure of comfort to the family and friends of that poor young woman in the years to come.

"And, difficult though that decision was, I believed, and still believe, that it was the right decision. Unfortunately, a consequence was that in order to get justice for Sally, she was mentioned uncommonly little during the case, which did confound some people."

At the other end of the table, Jeff has been showing signs of restlessness, and now he can contain himself no longer. He bursts out, "It confused me! And I said so at the time."

"I know, my dear chap. I know. The exegeses of the law are not always plain to the layman, much though we try."

"I said so at the time," repeats Jeff, mulishly.

"You did. I well remember. It was an excellent question, and it gave me much pause."

"How did she know? That's what I said. How did she know? And you know summat? I still don't know the answer to that question."

Jeff sits back in his chair. His tone is defiant, challenging.

Dr. Knox mutters to himself, "Dear me." He takes several experimental puffs on his unlit pipe. "Let's hope all your questions will be answered after tonight."

For a moment, it seems as though he has finished. He sits staring into space; then he adds, in a quiet voice, "Her father wrote to me, oh, quite a long time afterward, telling me how disappointed he was that his daughter had been forgotten in the notoriety of an aristocratic scandal. That was how he put it. He felt that very keenly, and I certainly understood how he felt."

He stops again, and then adds, "Yes, I certainly understood that. But, you see, the alternative was no better: name and cause of death only. Where would have been the justice in that?"

Dr. Knox examines his fingers, hands clasped, the two index fingers extended, like a child making believe his fingers are a gun. He rubs the tips of his gun fingers against his lips. Then he takes a deep breath and continues. "The inquest took place in June 1975, seven months after the event. I had decided, for better or worse, that I would hold the fullest inquest possible—with one caveat. It is a convention of coroners' courts that we do not question the veracity of witnesses. That is to say we do not cross-examine them, or doubt the truthfulness of their evidence. *We* are not an adversarial court.

"The inquest was not short of legal representatives. Apart from myself, there was a lawyer representing the interests of Mrs. Gardner and her family, one representing the police, another representing Lady Verreman and one more, representing the interests of the absent Lord Verreman and his family. I conducted the initial questioning of each witness, and counsel were free to ask supplementary questions to clarify any issues that they felt were insufficiently clear to the jury.

"It was not—decidedly *not*—their right to cross-examine witnesses, or cast aspersions on the integrity of those witnesses. And certainly not on their sanity. I had to come down very hard on counsel for Lord Verreman several times on that point.

"In addition to the testimony of Lady Verreman, the only eyewitness in the case, I also took testimony with regard to the physical evidence, of which there was a great deal. Mrs. Gardner's husband was able to give testimony with regard to the identity of the victim, and Professor McCabe was able to give testimony to the cause of death—which was, as he has said, blunt force trauma, and suffocation due to the presence of an overwhelming amount of blood blocking air passages. Professor McCabe is very eminent in his field, as is Dr. Elizabeth Mackintosh, the blood analyst from whom we have also heard. We were very lucky to get her, because she was the leading expert in her field—cutting-edge, as they say today. Combined with the evidence provided by the police, I really do think that there was ample testimony upon which the jury could reach their verdict—"

"But what I wanted to know—" says Jeff.

Dr. Knox continues over Jeff, who throws down his spoon in disgust, but quickly picks it up again, to scrape the bottom of his empty pudding dish. "Could reach their verdict," Dr. Knox repeats, forcefully and loudly, then dropping to a normal register again as Jeff begins licking his spoon, "in accordance with the constraints placed upon me by the law of the land.

"Lady Verreman gave a very clear account of what happened. Very clear indeed. I consider that she was very brave. I could not help but notice that she sat apart from the other witnesses, and no one—not Lord Verreman's family, not even her own sister—gave her an ounce of comfort or support."

Dr. Knox concentrates hard on his pistol fingers. Carolyn Keene-Wade rolls her eyes at him, but he does not see her. "Counsel for Lord Verreman tried several times to discredit her evidence, but I put my foot down about that, I'm afraid." Dr. Knox aims his finger gun at an imaginary lawyer, but refrains from pulling the trigger.

"The jury," says Dr. Knox, giving a nod toward Jeff, but carrying on quickly, lest Jeff should think he is inviting a contribution, "were very conscientious and attentive, and considered the evidence very carefully. Their task was made more difficult by the intense interest from the press.

"Really very intense. It was a strange time. But the evidence, I'm afraid, was overwhelming. Quite overwhelming. It is natural, of course, to wish to exonerate a loved one, but I really think that, in this case, there are no grounds for hope in that regard. Much better to accept and move on, as they say.

"The jury returned a verdict of murder at the hands of Lord Verreman against Sally Gardner, and, for what it's worth, I wholeheartedly agreed with them. I agreed with them then, and I agree with them now."

Dr. Knox holsters his fingers, picks up his spoon, blinks several times in quick succession and digs into his summer pudding, down the side of which the mascarpone cream rosette slipped gently during his speech, and is now a formless blob at the bottom.

David Verreman applauds enthusiastically. "Thank you, Dr. Knox. I think that's just about everyone. In a moment, I'm going to ask our detective here to give us a preliminary theory."

—Leg!

"Or perhaps even a verdict?"

—Leg!

Have you got a verdict? Or a preliminary theory? Have you even got the first bloody clue as to what is going on? Lean back suddenly as David Verreman stretches across you and whispers savagely, "Why do you keep shouting 'leg' at me, you bloody imbecile?"

—Cretin.

David snorts loudly, just barely hanging on to his temper. His elbow is on your pudding plate. Dark red fruit juice from your untouched pudding is inching slowly toward his white dinner jacket. Why does everything at this bloody dinner look like blood?

—The chief inspector's color-changing leg! Forgot about that, did you? Now who's the imbecile?

David stops for a moment. He is still leaning in front of you, his face inches from your own. Up close, his skin is a blotchy red. He retakes his seat a second before the blood-colored fruit juice reaches his clothes, and he passes a napkin first over his perspiring forehead and then over his face, wiping away flecks of spittle that have gathered around the corners of his mouth.

He takes a deep breath and hitches a smile onto his face, the genial host again.

How many drinks has he had tonight?

"The leg! By Jove, yes, I'd almost forgotten Chief Inspector Blake and his marvelous cosh of many colors. You promised us an explanation."

The chief inspector chuckles to himself. "Yes, well, the leg, which was, of course, no leg at all, but a piece of lead piping wrapped in dis-

64

tinctive white Elastoplast with a yellow zigzag stripe through it, the sort of implement, as you say, that is usually referred to as a cosh . . .

"Well, now, Lady Verreman declared in her statement that her attacker had come upon her from behind in the hall—that is, from the direction of the cloakroom. It is our theory that he had gone in there to clean himself up before leaving the house, and that he had also washed away the blood of Sally Gardner from the weapon, when he suddenly heard footsteps on the floor above.

"That, of course, was Lady Verreman, coming to find out where the girl had got to with her cup of tea.

"The front door is at the end of the hall, and that way lay freedom and escape from the horrors that he left in the basement, but in order to get to that front door he had to go through Lady Verreman, who by this time had reached the ground floor and was calling out the nanny's name. In a panic, Lord Verreman rushed from the cloakroom and began to attack Lady Verreman, too, but this time with very different results.

"I don't know whether you have ever murderously attacked anyone . . ." Here he looks around the table, and adds with a practiced aside, "And if you have, please don't tell me. I'm retired."

David Verreman obliges him with a hearty laugh.

"Well, physically attacking someone is bloody exhausting—excuse the language. Even top boxers at the peak of their fitness, and after months of training, can fight for no more than three minutes at a time. I know in the films"—he pronounces it *fill-ums*—"a fight can go on for half an hour or more, but in real life, after a couple of minutes you are completely knackered—so weary, you can barely lift your arm above your head.

"Lord Verreman had just killed one woman, remember, in a brutal assault. Then he had struggled with the body, stuffing it into a sack. And he was terrified out of his mind—which in itself requires a ton of energy, to produce that initial adrenaline kick. Finally, he was in shock, not only because of what he had done but because he had discovered that he had murdered the wrong woman.

"That's a lethal mixture—adrenaline and shock. A true adrenaline rush changes the way your body behaves at a molecular level. The adrenaline binds to receptor cells in your liver, producing a rush of glycogen for bursts of high energy, and in your lungs, so that you can breathe faster and more deeply, getting oxygen to your legs so that you can be ready to run. It pumps your heart faster, forcing blood away from muscles that don't need it, into your arms and legs so that you can fight or run away. And it does all of this quicker than the blink of an eye. But, and this is the important thing, it doesn't last long. You might feel the effects of it hours later, but the adrenaline rush itself is over in a few seconds. Nature has realized that that is all you need. After that, you've either survived or you're dead meat."

Look at Blake. Has he noticed what an ill-considered thing he has just said? If he has, he doesn't acknowledge it, but continues. "Verreman, in killing the nanny, had already experienced one massive adrenaline rush. Killing his wife was going to be much harder. No doubt he experienced a second rush, but this one would have been much smaller, and his muscles, his heart and his lungs would still be recovering from that first massive shock to the system.

"So, he attacked his wife, and this time he could see he had the right woman, because the hall was lit, albeit dimly, from the streetlight outside. But he tired quickly, and Lady Verreman was just a little bit prepared. She had come downstairs in search of her nanny. She couldn't find her. Perhaps it was then that she remembered that tonight, for the first time in months, she had forgotten to put the safety chain on the door. And, most crucially of all, she heard a noise behind her, from the direction of the cloakroom.

"It was at this point that Lady Antonia Verreman experienced her own adrenaline rush. And that sudden burst of energy—that rush of blood to *her* arms and legs, her heart and lungs pumping at full capacity—saved her. It enabled her to dodge some of the murderous blows and fend off others. At one stage her husband managed to force her to the floor, and he had one hand around her throat, choking the life out of her. She managed to hook one foot around a spindle at the top of the basement stairs to steady herself, and with her other foot, and all the strength of her arms, she pushed him back off her.

"At which point, totally exhausted, arms and legs aching madly, Lord Verreman stopped trying to strangle his wife and joined her on the steps, where they sat side by side and caught their breath. For Lady Verreman, of course, it could be a temporary reprieve only. For one moment, she might have hoped that it was now over, and perhaps even that they could make up, as they had done after heated rows when they were first married. But Lord Verreman, of course, would have known that this was but a brief hiatus. With the grisly evidence in the basement, there was only one escape for him—and that was to finish his wife off completely and hope that the murders were laid at the door of an unknown intruder.

"For a while, husband and wife talked. Lady Verreman described this conversation as being quite everyday and matter-of-fact. When she learned that the nanny was dead, she merely said, 'It's not so bad. Now, what shall we do with the body?' She was trying to soothe him, but underneath, she was thinking of ploys she might use to get a few seconds' head start on her husband.

"She was a fast runner, she knew, but she was five foot two and her husband was at least a foot taller, with long legs and longer strides. She needed to give herself as much time as possible.

"She went into the cloakroom to get a drink of water, which she remembered being horribly warm, and that gave her a few moments to think. And then, pretending to more fragility than she really felt, she asked Lord Verreman, who, after all, was still her husband, to take her upstairs to their bedroom and bathe her head with a cold compress.

"And he did. I have often wondered what he was thinking when he agreed to go upstairs with her. Not reconciliation, certainly. Bodies in the basement tend to put a dampener on rekindling romance. To my mind—and this is only my theory, you understand—he thought that if he could get her lying on her bed, strangling her would be a whole lot easier. He was a big man. If he had sat on her chest while throttling her, she could never have got free.

"But who knows? For he never got the chance. He laid one small towel over her pillow, and took another into their adjoining bathroom and began to run it under the tap. Like in all old houses, the plumbing was pretty noisy, and it covered the sound of Lady Verreman slipping off the bed and running downstairs in her stocking feet.

"She had a good head start on him, and it seems he didn't realize at first where she had gone—he called upstairs to the nursery, where young David here was still wide-awake and, no doubt, was wondering what the hell was going on with the grown-ups. That proves, I think, that the adrenaline had long worn off Lord Verreman, and shock was beginning to set in. He wasn't thinking clearly. But he must have cottoned on pretty quickly. Whether he looked out the window to see his bloodstained wife running hell-for-leather down the street, we'll never know. But we do know he scarpered from the house pretty darned quick after that. And he had just enough sense left to close the door behind him in case a posse came looking for him before he had time to get away.

"By the time my officers arrived at the house, he was long gone. After we interviewed Lady Verreman, we put out an alert for him—not a warrant for his arrest at that stage, bearing in mind the sensibilities of certain influential sections of society, but a missing person alert. And that's how we presented it to the press: anxious to trace him. I think the first press releases suggested that we were concerned for his welfare, and then that he might be able to give us information about what had happened, which, of course, placed him at the scene. The press aren't daft. They knew he was a suspect, and that we couldn't say so.

"It was only after the discovery of the car—one that had been borrowed from a friend, for reasons unknown—that we received the most damning evidence. In my mind, there is no credible explanation for it, and it puts the murder weapon in Lord Verreman's hand, no question about it."

Lean forward as far as you can. Make sure you catch the next few words.

"In the boot of the car was a second piece of lead pipe. It had also been wrapped in this distinctive Elastoplast—white, with a yellow zigzag thread running down the center. The odds that Lord Verreman, driving a borrowed car, would innocently have a cosh in the boot of his car—one that was almost identical in every way to the murder weapon found at the scene of the crime—well, the odds are astronomical.

"On the basis of this damning evidence, I sought, and was granted, a warrant for the arrest of Lord John Verreman on the charges of the murder of Sally Gardner and the attempted murder of his own wife.

"I was one hundred percent certain then that he was the murderer, and I am one hundred percent certain now. I consider that second piece of pipe incontrovertible evidence—unless, of course, your detective can give an adequate explanation for its presence."

Detective Chief Inspector Nicholas Blake chuckles to himself. Can you explain away his incontrovertible evidence? How could you when you have only just heard about it?

"Oh," adds Blake, still laughing, "about the color-changing thing—that one's easy. Lord Verreman had gone into the cloakroom after the first attack, where he probably washed Sally's blood off the weapon. After the attack on his wife, he dropped the cosh on the bloodstained hall carpet. If the Elastoplast was wet, it would have absorbed the blood on the floor quickly, but even if it wasn't wet, it would still have begun to absorb the blood, though at a slower rate. Plasters, of course, are designed for that very purpose. And then the bottom of the cosh had become so saturated that the blood continued traveling to the top side of the cosh—just as a piece of kitchen paper will absorb water, spreading out to the corners of the paper even though only the center of the sheet is in contact with the spilled drink. That's one explanation. The other, of course, is that, in the excitement of finding the body, and not realizing they were treading on a murder weapon, one of the flat-footed first responders kicked the 'dolly's leg' and it flipped over, so it was bloody side up.

"Obvious, really."

7

◆ ◆ ◆ ◆ ◆

LOVE LIES BLEEDING

What an advance in civilization, when the nobility consider
themselves subject to the law, and bow to its decrees.

—Émile Gaboriau, *The Widow Lerouge*

OK: Time-out

Time to consider *The Presentation of Evidence.*

Think of a novel like a court of law. The prosecuting barrister
(we'll call him A. N. Author, King's Counsel) wants to present his
evidence in a certain way. He arranges this evidence (we'll call that
"the plot") in such a way that the jury (which is, of course, you, The
Reader) believes the bullshit, or "story," that he is serving up.

Got it?

Imagine that this prosecuting barrister—again, that's the author,
not just of this damned novel but of every novel—holds up a blunt
instrument to the jury. Blunt instruments come in all shapes and
sizes. Let's call this blunt instrument "a brick."

The prosecuting barrister shows the jury the brick. It's a nice-
looking brick. A solid-looking brick. It has four straight sides and a
nice, solid surface. He raps on the brick with his knuckles for the
benefit of the jury, and it makes a brick-like sound.

Then he tells you how a brick is made. How clay is mixed with
cement and fired in a brick kiln at 1,100 degrees Celsius, until it is

hard and strong. He shows you the brick again, and you agree, this is a strong-looking brick.

Then he tells you how a brick is coated with a sealant to make it weather resistant, and you notice that it does, indeed, have a shiny surface. "A standard brick," he tells you, "weighs around seven pounds," and it looks heavy. "A standard brick is two hundred fifteen millimeters long, one hundred two point five millimeters wide and sixty-five millimeters high." You still think in feet and inches, but you do a quick calculation in your head, and you think 215 millimeters is about eight and a half inches, if your sums are correct. You look at the brick in the barrister's hand, and you figure that's about right.

What the barrister is holding in his hand is a good, solid, usable brick. The sort of brick that could be smashed over a victim's head and do some pretty nasty damage.

Do you see the con?

Here's what the author doesn't do.

He doesn't turn that brick around, because if he did, you would see that instead of being a standard sixty-five millimeters high—that's two and a half inches to you—it's only ten millimeters high. He doesn't let you hold that brick in your hand, because instead of weighing seven pounds, it weighs about one.

That brick looks like a brick from one angle only—and that is the angle that A. N. Author, KC, showed you. Did he lie to you? Yes. And no. He showed you "a brick" and he talked about "a standard brick." He did not tell you that his brick was a standard brick. He manipulated you into drawing that conclusion for yourself, from what he told you, and how he told you, and what he left out.

It is your job, as a jury member, or a detective, or just as plain old A. Reader, to look at the story—remember, that's the bullshit in this scenario—and question what an author is telling you. Ask yourself: *Why is he showing me the brick this way? What other ways could I look at the brick? What did he not tell me about the brick?*

Because otherwise, you might as well pick up that brick and

smack yourself over the head with it to see if it is thick enough to knock some sense into you.

Back to the story.

"THANK YOU, CHIEF Inspector Blake. Consider us suitably impressed. Kicked over by a flat-footed policeman. Of course! Why didn't we consider that? But then, we are not trained in the subtle art of detection, or evidence gathering. Although I expect our Great Detective wasn't fooled."

David looks in your direction. Try to smile. Look confident.

He continues. "Now, then, in a moment I am going to ask our detective here to give us their preliminary verdict—that is, their working theory. As everyone who has ever read a classic detective novel knows, the detective will form a working theory very early on. Sometimes that theory proves to be right despite the apparently overwhelming evidence to the contrary, and everyone says what a genius that Mr. Holmes is, or, twenty pages from the end, Hercule Poirot slaps his forehead and says, *Mon Dieu! What a blundering nincompoop I have been!* or words to that effect.

"I will leave it up to our detective which method to choose. But, of course, this is a preliminary conclusion only, and no one is going to hold them to account for it. I certainly won't."

—I might.

"Perhaps a brief summary of the evidence would be useful, now that everyone has spoken . . . "

"I haven't spoken," says Jeff.

"Me neither," says Wilkie Collins.

"I'm not bothered," says George Howard-Cole.

David Verreman looks a little embarrassed. "I'm sorry. Did you want to speak?"

"Well, isn't that what we're here for?" asks Jeff.

Collins nods his head in agreement, though he looks as though he would be happier to have gone unnoticed.

"OK, then," says David. "I give you the jury foreman of the inquest—Jeff!"

"Finally," says Jeff, standing up. He is not nervous, but he is leaning forward a little, as though racing to get his point over before he gets cut off again. "It's only taken fifty years. I should say at once that my name is not bloody Jeff. That's his lordship's little joke. I do have a name—first and last. It's Postgate, if you must know, Raymond Postgate—but it won't make any difference to his lordship over there, and nor to you either, I daresay, so I doubt you'll waste your time remembering it.

"I was the foreman of the jury, and it was my responsibility to represent the entire jury, and ask any questions that we might have. I took that responsibility, that civic duty, very seriously. I listened to the evidence carefully, and when it came to Lady Verreman's testimony, there was a big hole in the middle.

"See, this is how it was. According to 'er ladyship, she never went into the basement at all. She said she shouted down the basement stairs, calling for the nanny, but, seeing the basement in darkness, figured she wasn't down there. According to the police, it was pitch-black down there, so she couldn't have seen nothing. And she couldn't have seen down to the basement from the 'all anyway, because there is a turn in the stairs at the top.

"So my question was, how did she know? How did she know the nanny was dead? How did she know what was down there? He'll tell ya," Jeff says, pointing at Dr. Knox, "I asked the question at the time. And he wouldn't answer."

Dr. Knox holds up one hand in acknowledgment, then joins both hands together, re-forms his finger pistol and points back at Jeff. "Quite right. And it was a very good question."

It *is* a very good question. Make a note.

"But," continues Dr. Knox, "as I explained previously, there were constraints on what the law allowed a wife to give evidence about in the prosecution of her husband."

"Her husband wasn't on trial, though, was he? Not then." Jeff is not going to be fobbed off again.

"I realize that it is difficult for a layman to understand, but if I had allowed Lady Verreman to answer your very pertinent question, I might have prejudiced a future trial, had Lord Verreman been found. In the end, of course, that was moot. But Lady Verreman did, in fact, answer that question before the inquest, although not within the jurisdiction of a court. She gave a very ill-advised exclusive interview to the *Express* in which she very nearly named her husband as her attacker, and as the murderer of Sally Gardner, too.

"It was very naughty, and the newspaper really should have known better. In fact, I happen to know that a file was sent to the Director of Public Prosecutions, and they considered whether to prosecute both Lady Verreman and the *Express* for contempt of court. Ultimately, they decided against it.

"But what she said in the newspaper, and what she couldn't say in court, was that she asked her husband, after he had attacked her, where the nanny was. At first, he prevaricated and said, 'She's gone out,' but when she pressed him, he said, 'She's dead,' and added, 'Don't look.'

"From that, she realized that the nanny's body must still be in the basement. None of that could be relayed in court, but, you see, it proves that Lady Verreman was speaking the truth and that her husband had killed the nanny, and attacked her with murderous intent, too. That article was very carefully written. It never actually stated that Verreman attacked either woman, but it talked about the attack in one paragraph, then about 'the tragedy' of Lord Verreman's life as a gambler and his mounting debt, with a casual mention of the arrest warrant for murder thrown in. I bet nine out of ten readers would have sworn that the article named him as the killer. But it didn't. Not quite.

"It was a bloody stupid thing for a reputable newspaper to do. They must have been pretty confident Verreman wouldn't show up again. Any competent defense lawyer would have claimed prejudice. And they would have been right.

"It might have been worse, though. I discovered, from a confidential source, that some of the photographs that they took, but didn't use, were definitely too much. I've seen them. These were never published, mind you, and a good thing, too. They were in poor taste. Yes, very poor taste indeed. One, I remember, showed Lady Verreman at the bottom of the basement steps, pointing at the site of the murder, and another actually had the journalist curled up on the floor in the fetal position, representing Mrs. Gardner's corpse. Now, that was tasteless.

"However, they never published those.

"So, you see, Jeff, that is your answer. Lady Verreman knew what was in the basement because her husband told her. There is nothing mysterious about it, I'm afraid, though the restrictions placed upon me at the inquest made rather a mystery of it."

Jeff looks as though he is about to ask another question, but Wilkie cuts him off. "Well, what about my story? Dismissed, I was. Out of hand. He couldn't have done it—Lord Verreman, I mean. Because I seen him—that's why.

"And I gave evidence at the inquest. But nobody cared. Nobody believed me. But I seen him. That night. At about a quarter to nine. I was a valet, see, at the Berkeley. I parked the cars, an' that. I came on duty at eight p.m. There was another chap who worked with me—he started at nine, because it's quiet, you know, for the first hour.

"Well, I can't say to the minute, not exactly, but it was about eight forty-five p.m., as near as makes no difference. I'd been at work a good while, and I was starting to look out for my partner coming on. You get to know the time without looking at yer damned watch, by how long it takes to do the regular things you do in a job. And I had been valeting at the Berkeley eight years at that time.

"Anyway, about eight forty-five p.m., give or take a couple of minutes *at most*, Lord Verreman drives up. Now, the police asked me what car he was driving, and I'm pretty sure it was his usual car—that is, his Mercedes, and not that old heap of junk that they said he was driving after. I'm a valet, see. I can spot the cars of all our regulars. I sees them coming down the road, and I'm ready for them. I would have remembered if Lord V had turned up in a different car. And if it had been a Ford Corsair—heap of junk that car was—I couldn't have helped but see. But the police said it was dark, and I might not have noticed. I told them it's my bloody job to notice, but did they listen? No."

Wilkie scowls at Nicholas Blake, who is not looking at him.

"So, Lord Verreman drives up, but he doesn't get out of the car. He just talks to me through the car window, see? An' he says, 'Many in?'—meaning 'in the club.' Now, this is a thing he does quite often. 'Cos he's a regular, see. A professional. And I know what he is asking. What he wants to know is whether there are any rich foreigners in— by which I mean foreign to the club—rich amateurs who come to lose their money at cards. They don't care how much they lose as long as they can lose it in a swanky club, playing with lords and dukes and film stars and such. That's what they really come for.

"But it was still early, and so I says to him, 'Not much of a crowd yet,' and he says, 'Thanks.' Always polite, Lord V was, not like some of them."

Here Wilkie shoots a dark look at George Howard-Cole.

"And then he drives away. And that was the last I seen of him. I did tell the inquest this, but they didn't take no notice neither. I was on that stand about two minutes. It took longer to swear me in than it did to listen to what I got to say. He"—Wilkie points to Dr. Knox—"didn't believe me, and nor did the police."

Chief Inspector Blake interrupts. "We did receive a statement, and I assure you we treated it seriously."

Wilkie sits back in his chair, crosses his arms and snorts.

"We concluded," continues Blake, "that even if true, it did not preclude Lord Verreman's having done the crime. It's not a long distance between the club and his wife's house, even allowing for his

THE GAME IS MURDER

changing cars on the way, and it really was a very dark night, so it is perfectly possible that you were mistaken. If you were busy—"

"I weren't."

"Or if you weren't taking particular notice—"

"It's my job to notice."

"The police concluded," said Blake, carefully removing himself from the collective noun, "that you may have been mistaken about the time."

"I—"

"Or about the day. One day is much like another when you're working, and Lord Verreman went to the club almost every night."

"Bollocks. I know what day it was."

"The other possibility that the police considered was that you had offered this evidence either out of misguided loyalty to Lord Verreman or because someone at the club, someone upon whom you depended for your job, asked you to give Lord Verreman an alibi."

"I fuckin' knew it! I knew you thought I was a stooge!"

"There was a meeting . . ."

George Howard-Cole gives a belly laugh. "He means the Wise Men, Wilkie. He thinks one of us bribed you, or perhaps threatened you, into providing old Johnny with an alibi."

Wilkie laughs, but he doesn't seem amused. "Bollocks!"

"Well, quite," says Cole.

"The fact is," says Chief Inspector Blake, with a hint of anger behind his carefully composed policeman's tone, "that there was a meeting the day after Verreman's disappearance, a meeting of some of the most powerful people in the country . . ."

"A meeting of friends," says Cole.

"All of whom knew Lord Verreman intimately."

"Friends!"

"The press called them the Wise Men—I don't know why; one of their bloody stupid nicknames—and they called this lunch the Gathering of the Magi, which made it sound biblical. But what it really was, they said, was a meeting of influential people who had the means and the connections to help Lord Verreman disappear off the face of the earth. At least, that was the thinking of the press—and, I may say, of many in the police."

"Bollocks," say Wilkie and Cole in unison.

Cole laughs. "What it was, really, was a few friends—yes, *friends* of Verreman—who got together to swap stories, as you might do at a wake. And no, we did not know that he was dead, but, you know, it seemed important to mark his going in some way. Plus, of course"— and here Cole looks a little contemptuous—"it was a chance to gossip and speculate about what had happened. I daresay that after a few drinks, one or two of us did broach the subject of what we might do if Jinx got in touch and asked for our help, which he didn't. But Wise Men? Ridiculous. And most of the ideas were bloody stupid.

"I remember Phillip Trent suggested stowing him away in a banana boat." Cole chortles to himself. "The press wouldn't have called us Wise Men if they had heard some of the things that were said at that lunch, I can tell you. Trent was always an idiot." Here Margaret Howard-Cole plucks at her husband's sleeve.

"Of course you're not allowed to say so now, because he killed himself over what a bunch of meanies we were to him."

"You *were* mean to him," says Margaret.

"Oh, well, maybe we were. So what?"

"Phillip loved Johnny. He was devastated by what happened."

"Oh, I know. We all know. No one loved Johnny like Phillip loved Johnny. No one was allowed to, because Phillip was a poet, so, of course, he was 'sensitive.' And you're not allowed to mock the sensitive. They're like the handicapped now."

"Disabled," says his wife, despite herself.

"Oh, to hell with it! You can't say anything these days, for fear of hurting someone's feelings. The truth is, we all liked Verreman. We had lunch. We talked about our friend. Perhaps we got a little drunk. But we didn't go round bribing the help to make false statements to the rozzers. And," he says, his voice rising as he looks angrily toward the policeman while shaking off his wife's restraining hand, "if we were going to give him a false bloody alibi, it would have been a damned sight better than Wilkie seeing him outside the club.

"We could easily have said he was playing cards with us at the club. No one could have proved differently. This was long before CCTV and people tracking you on your bloody phone. We could have given him an alibi. But we didn't. Because, when it comes down to it, we are not a gang of amoral rich bastards who ride roughshod over everyone else. We are law-abiding rich bastards. The police disliked our attitude? Sod 'em!"

He takes a long drink of water while he blinks away the tears threatening to well in his eyes. "Johnny Verreman—Jinx—was my friend. I liked him. He married that bitch"—he taps his wife's arm in apology for his language, or, perhaps, to forestall her criticism—"and she made his life a misery from the moment she got the ring on her finger. If I'd been married to her, I would have bashed her over the head with a brick years earlier. The woman was a nightmare. But did Jinx try to kill her? I don't know. Maybe he reached the end of his rope, or maybe it was someone else.

"It was a long time ago, and who bloody cares? I'm sorry about the nanny. She was a nice woman, by all accounts. I'm sorry she copped it. I don't know if my friend tried to kill her or his bloody wife, but I don't think he did. I can't prove it, and I don't even want to try. But I'm allowed to believe it. And no one can make me change my mind if I don't want to."

"'Ear, 'ear," says Wilkie.

David Verreman stands up to speak, but Chief Inspector Blake forestalls him with an interruptive cough. Verreman concedes the floor with a wave of his hand.

—Really?

"*Shh,*" David says.

—For God's sake! I'm going for a slash.

"Don't forget to wash your hands!" David calls after his brother.

"It is true," says Chief Inspector Blake, loudly, "that no one obstructed our inquiry. Not exactly. Certainly not in any way that was actionable. But none of his friends went out of their way to help us."

"Why should we? It's not our bloody job," splutters George Howard-Cole, while his wife tugs at his sleeve in a fruitless effort to get him to shut the fuck up.

Blake continues, choosing his words carefully, addressing no one in particular. "I would have thought that his circle would have been eager to lend us their assistance—if he was a friend, who they believed to be innocent. But no one volunteered anything. No one came forward to assist us of their own volition. Doors were not slammed in our faces, it is true, but, nevertheless, his circle of friends closed ranks. They answered our questions, yes, but only so far as they had to, and not one inch more. They were never rude—indeed, their manners were impeccable—but they were hostile nevertheless.

"We did check Mr. Collins' evidence, as is our job, and we concluded it would have been possible for Lord Verreman to drive to the club, establish an alibi and drive straight to his wife's home in time to lie in wait for her.

"It is even possible, just, that he would have had time to swap his car after being seen at the club, though it is hard to know why he would. And so, you see, as an alibi it is meaningless. And really, apart from that one witness, everything else points to Lord Verreman lying in wait for his wife in the basement, knowing that she would come downstairs to make her nightly cup of tea.

"Everything pointed to Lord Verreman being a desperate man—desperate because his financial situation was perilous, and desperate because he could not bear to be separated from his son any longer." He points toward David Verreman, who nods at this tribute, and Blake presses on. "His bank accounts were all overdrawn. His luck at cards had deserted him and, crucially, the two-year period of separation was almost up. In January 1975, Lady Verreman would have been able to proceed with the divorce if she chose, in which case Lord

Verreman would have been forced to disclose his finances to the courts. It is my belief that this prospect is what drove him to contemplate murder. The fiction that he was a successful gambler would have been exposed for all the world to see. He would have been a laughingstock. And any chance of regaining custody of his son would have been gone forever.

"Lord Verreman has been described, often, as a proud man. But what he really was, was an arrogant man. He couldn't bear the thought of all his rich friends knowing how poor he really was. An arrogant man wouldn't be able to bear the thought of another custody battle with a woman he considered his inferior—in class, in education and in mental stability.

"But Lord Verreman was a gambler. He was a risk-taker. And so he took the risk. He made one last, reckless bet. All or nothing. If he could make his wife disappear, his problems would be over. No financial settlement. No custody case. And all he had to do was whack his wife over the head with a piece of lead piping, stuff her body in a sack and dump it somewhere where no one would find it—perhaps out at sea. I think he planned to tell everyone that his wife—the wife he had been calling mentally unstable for over a year—had just run away.

"And if he had succeeded, who would have made a fuss? No one. Lord Verreman had successfully cut his wife off from society. She had no friends. Her own family took his part. Even after the nanny was found dead. Even after Lady Verreman was attacked, and named him as her attacker, her family sat with Lord Verreman's mother in the court. They gave the dowager duchess succor, and they cut Lady Verreman dead.

"By November 1974, Lady Verreman didn't have a friend in all the world. No one would have tried too hard to find her if she disappeared. They would all have been glad to see the back of her."

Chief Inspector Blake points first at the Wades and then at the Howard-Coles, and his shaking index finger remains pointed at George Howard-Cole until the aged policeman can hold it there no longer. "I think it sticks in their craw that she survived and Verreman failed. I think that they thought of her as expendable. Disposable.

"There she was, this tiny little woman, standing up to her husband, and sticking two fingers up to his family, and his friends, and his *set*. She was making bloody fools of you all, and Lord Verreman couldn't stand that. He decided to bash her over the head. But when he realized he had got the wrong woman, he ran away, like a coward. So much for the old school tie and breeding, then. Whether he is alive or dead, I have no idea. I never did. My inclination was always that he had gone on the run—because that is what cowards do.

"I kept on hearing what an honorable man he was. But he didn't behave with honor toward his wife, even before he tried to kill her. This is a man who tried to have his own wife committed to an insane asylum. This is a man who preferred to gamble rather than do an honest day's work to make his living. This is a man who left his wife and his son"—the shaking finger points at David Verreman again, and he glances at Daniel's empty chair—"the son whom he professed to love so much. And this is a man who, rather than provide for his family, would bash his wife over the head and stuff her body in a sack, and dump her corpse like so much rubbish."

The retired policeman runs out of breath, but he holds his hand up to indicate that he is not quite finished. He takes a deep breath. "He was prepared to let this boy spend the rest of his life wondering whether his mother was alive or dead, and why she had abandoned him, rather than admit to his friends that he was broke. And there is nothing honorable about that!"

His hand falls to the table. Not for the first time, the police have spoiled their fun. Chief Inspector Blake slumps a little in his chair. The speech appears to have exhausted him completely.

—What did I miss?

"Nothing. Just the usual. Did you wash your hands?"

—Pride and honor, corpses in sacks, so much rubbish and all that jazz?

"Yep."

—That's what I figured.

"Show me your hands. You didn't, did you?"

THERE IS SILENCE in the room. Stanley Gardner picks up his empty pudding plate and examines it carefully.

Silence.

Waiters bring in the coffee, in four tall silver pots.

Watch them as they place the coffeepots on the table and leave in silence. As the door closes behind them, David Verreman claps his hands together in an attempt to reignite the party atmosphere.

"I know! Cigars."

He opens the box that has been placed in front of him, takes one for himself and offers you one. Wave it away politely. He passes the box on.

"Oh, and brandy, of course." He crosses to the sideboard and picks up a heavy crystal decanter. He pours a spot for himself and, without asking, sets a glass in front of you. Then he passes the decanter down the table.

For a few moments David Verreman engages in exuberant sucking on his cigar, turning it, examining the end and sucking some more. Then he swirls his brandy in his glass and takes long sniffs. He moves the glass around under his nose so that he can suck up all the aroma before he takes his first sip. After several minutes of sucking and sniffing and swirling and sipping, David Verreman puts the glass down and moves his cigar to the side of his mouth.

"Well, now we really have heard from everyone, and we have come to the exciting moment when our Great Detective will render their preliminary verdict. I should perhaps remind you of the rules of the, er, game first. The detective will give us first their verdict, and then the justification for their verdict. They will explain why they have come to their conclusion and why they have ruled out all the other suspects.

"But this is, of course, only the first act. We have decided that tonight we will be generous and allow the detective three opportunities to reach the right conclusion. That is fair, I think, and certainly more justice than my father ever received.

"OK, then. I think we are ready."

"Hang on. What about the defense?" asks Henry Wade.

"Yeah, that's not happening."

"What the hell?"

David Verreman stands and turns to look you full in the face. "Great Detective, what say you? Is John Verreman, seventh Earl of Verre, and our own dear father, guilty or not guilty of the murder of Sally Gardner and of the attempted murder of Lady Antonia Verreman, aka our ol' mum?"

Silence. Total and utter silence.

—Duct tape!

"What?" says David Verreman, and his voice is slightly high-pitched, and his hands are shaking. His lips are drawn back in the beginnings of a snarl.

—Duct tape. Over the mouth. And you're the genius of the family!

Another moment's silence, and David laughs. The laugh is good-natured, but his smile doesn't quite meet his eyes.

"Of course. How foolish of me. I do apologize. Forgive me—this may hurt a little."

David Verreman leans forward, grips the edge of the duct tape and slowly begins to pull it away, taking the top layer of your skin with it.

"That's better," he says, and he brushes away a stray strand of hair before taking his seat again.

Begin to holler.

Verreman holds up the duct tape in warning.

Stop.

Listen as the voice echoes through the empty halls of this house.

"Thank you," says David Verreman. "It's so much better when we can be civilized, don't you think? Now, then, your verdict, please."

Silence.

"It's OK. You can say it." His voice is caressing, soothing.

Pass a hand over your face. Touch those places where the duct tape has abraded your skin. Push your hair out of your eyes, straighten your back and deliver your verdict.

The Great Detective looks David Verreman square in the face. "Guilty!" he says.

ACT 2

◆ ◆ ◆ ◆ ◆ ◆ ◆ ◆ ◆ ◆

GUILTY?

8

✦ ✦ ✦ ✦ ✦

A WHISPER IN THE GLOOM

And so, you see, all is not as it appeared.

You can't say we didn't warn you.

Are you disappointed?

Relieved?

Both.

You are not, after all, the Great Detective. You are a mere Reader of Novels. It does not fall to you to solve this case. You are a bystander, an onlooker, a spectator.

You are nothing more or less than a Peeping Tom.

Did you really expect more? This is only a novel, after all. How would that have worked? Only The Author makes the decisions here—that great and powerful wizard who makes worlds, and breaks them at will, and who, I am informed, has unparalleled wisdom and intelligence, and is quite remarkably handsome, too.

—STOP!

But cheer up, because you, my friend, have a much more important role than that of detective. We have reserved for you the position of Supreme Judge.

It is for you to decide whether or not this so-called Great Detective has reached the correct solution in this case.

Remember that contract?

Well, now you will be the one who decides whether it has been fulfilled. You will be the one to decide whether the case has been solved. Have they dotted all the i's and crossed all the t's? Have they made their case? Are you convinced, utterly, in your heart, your mind and your soul, that the solution the detective arrives at is the only possible solution?

That is your role as The Reader. It does not matter what the detective thinks. Only what YOU think matters. The purpose of a novel is to tell the reader a true story about people who have never lived and a world that has never existed. Even if, heaven forbid, a novel should be based on real people or real events, the story that is captive in the pages of the book is always fictional. Its characters are fictional. Its setting is fictional. Its plot is fictional. It cannot be any other way, since fiction is held to a higher standard of truth than mere life.

Fiction, if it is worth anything at all, is *about* life but it is *not* life.

It gives us answers.

It gives us truth.

It gives us satisfaction.

It gives us, in fact, completion.

I bet you don't get that in real life!

If you, Reader of This Novel, find answers, truth and satisfaction here, then you have reached completion.

If you do not? Well, that will leave you feeling deeply unsatisfied. Frustrated, even. And for that, there must be consequences.

A contract requires an exchange. Something for something. A reward and a penalty. If the Great Detective of this novel fails your test, then they have reneged on their contract. And they will suffer.

Appendix B, the penalty clause:

You, Dear Reader, are now the Ultimate Arbiter of The Contract. This may sound like a dull job. And who's to say that it is not? We have offered you answers, truth and satisfaction. We said nothing of fun. Fun is for children, and this ain't no picture book.

So, let us see how the scene looks now.

You thought that you were attending a smart dinner party. And yet you knew that you were not. You were at once sitting in a house in Belgravia and in your own home. In a coffee shop. On the train. Wherever.

And so nothing has changed. And everything has changed.

The Great Detective, who was once you, and is no longer you, is sitting at the same dining table in the home of Lord David Verreman. But there is no dinner party, and there are no guests.

We did try to warn you, you know.

There is the detective, who was you, and is not you, and—who knows?—may be you again. And there is David.

And that is all.

David has no guests.

David has no food.

David doesn't even have a brother.

Other than this table, the house is empty. Except, of course, for the basement. Nothing ever changes in the basement.

Shall we carry on? Or are you feeling a little let down? Put out. Tricked. Conned. Like the victim of a scam artist, a fraudster or, my personal favorite, a flimflam man.

But really, we have told you the truth, the whole truth and nothing but the truth. So help us God.

Take a moment to look back and you will see. You misinterpreted what you read. But don't beat yourself up too much. We intended you to. We set you up. You are our fall guy. Our patsy. Our schmuck.

How could this happen? After all, you are a seasoned novel reader. Not your first trip to the library. So how did you get it so wrong? Because the game is rigged. And, again, we did warn you.

"Trust nothing," we said. "There is no dinner party," we said. Damn it, we even advised you to put the bloody book down and run. But did you? No. And we knew that you would not. Why? Because the game is rigged.

The Author, that lying, cheating, no-good son of a bitch, took into account all your previous experience of reading novels, and he used that experience against you. Oh well, whatcha gonna do? Put the book down? When you've come so far? Surely not. Might as well read on a little. After all, you are now hip to The Author's devious jive. You won't get caught out again.

Will you?

SO, DAVID VERREMAN and the Great Detective are sitting in the dining room at 8 Broad Way. They are alone. The table is laid for sixteen, but each place setting has a small pile of paper where the plates should be. Some piles are thicker than others. Some have typed witness statements, some newspaper articles. Or photographs. Diagrams and crime-scene pictures. David Verreman is walking round the table, touching each pile of papers as he goes, as if trying to draw up through his fingertips the information contained in them. The detective watches him warily.

Do we need to describe the detective? Surely not. After all, we have not described David Verreman, and yet you have a clear picture of him in your mind, do you not? And if we now said that Verreman was five foot two, fat, balding, with a rash of pimples on his cheek and flaking skin on his forehead, would you believe us? Of course not. Luckily, he is not like that at all. David Verreman is, in fact, almost exactly the way you have pictured him.

How did you do that?

And the detective actually does look rather like you. The same eyes. The same mouth. Why, it's uncanny! Do you make yourself the hero of every novel? What does that say about you? I wonder.

Shall we give the detective a name? He has managed without

one all this time, it is true. Still, a detective is not a detective without a name, and he does look like you. Do you want to try giving him your name?

Insert your name here: _____

Hmm. Yours is a nice name, no doubt. But it is not a detective's name. It does not suggest strength, like "Hercule," or the shadow of the prison gate, like "Sherlock." Nor is it a puzzle, like "Rebus," or a code, like "Morse."

I think, after all, we had better give him a name ourselves. We shall call our detective Max Enygma. It's a name as good as any other, and certainly better than yours. "Max" is solid, dependable and has a suggestion of girth, while "Enygma" evokes mystery, and, perhaps, even the solving of mysteries.

It is decided, then. David Verreman, who looks almost exactly as you imagined him, is in the dining room with Max Enygma, who looks rather like you.

9

◆ ◆ ◆ ◆ ◆

THE POISONED CHOCOLATES CASE

We have gone so far as to combine the ideas of an agility astounding, a strength superhuman, a ferocity brutal, a butchery without motive, a grotesquerie in horror absolutely alien from humanity, and a voice foreign in tone to the ears of men of many nations, and devoid of all distinct or intelligible syllabification. What result, then, has ensued?

—Edgar Allan Poe, "The Murders in the Rue Morgue"

"ROUND TWO, THEN," says David. "Are you ready?"

"Ready for what? This is ridiculous! I haven't come here to play games," says Enygma. He has not moved from his seat, but his eye travels constantly to the door and back to David, measuring the distance between them. Just in case.

David shakes his head and gives a rueful little laugh. He sits in his chair, which has the largest stack of paper in front of it: buff folders; typewritten reports stapled together, with passages highlighted in yellow marker, and Post-it notes sticking out in all directions. He pats the folders as he talks. "Really? That's a shame. I do like games. But we have made it easy for you, you know. No need to look for the discarded cigarette end, or the thread of cotton caught on the convenient bush. All the interviews have been conducted. All the evidence collected. All you need to do is review it. You do not even need to find out whodunnit. All you need to do is to prove, beyond a reasonable doubt, that the person who did dunnit, so to speak, was not my father. You might call it family pride, but I like to think of it as more of a board game. Like Cluedo, but with a real body."

"You're a bit mad, aren't you?" Enygma says.

"Well, that is a possibility. It's in the family, you know. And insanity is a good defense to most things, I'm told. But if I am mad, it is probably best to humor me, don't you think?"

—*Wait! Wait. I'm not feeling it yet. Are you?*

Really? Do you think we need to give our detective some sort of backstory?

—*Can't hurt.*

But backstories are such a drag.

—*Nevertheless . . .*

OK, well, the first choice we have to make is: *professional* or *amateur.* You would not believe the number of murders that are solved by nosy neighbors, vicars' wives and elderly spinsters. But, since we have already called Max Enygma a Great Detective, it might be as well to assume he has had some prior experience, don't you think?

(Up to you, of course, but if you choose *amateur,* you might have to hang here for a bit while we do a spot of rewriting, and that will be a drag. For all of us.)

Good. Let's go ahead and put a tick in the *professional* column.

Professional	Amateur
✔	

Which leads us to our next question, or perhaps subgenre: *police* or *private detective.* Now, in the real world—that is, the world in which you, and possibly we, live—private detectives are nondescript former policemen who do little more than Internet searches and stakeouts, where they sit in their car and take photos of your cheating spouse for ammunition in your forthcoming divorce.

(If you need a phone number for this sort of detective, stay behind after class.)

In fiction, however, *Private Detective* is *Where It's At.* Men, and sometimes women, will make themselves available for a fee—always undisclosed—and will track down anything from a bird statue to a missing heiress.

Private detectives often have eclectic skill sets. Sherlock Holmes, for example, is the author of at least seven monographs, handily covering every case he comes across in which obscure expertise is required, or where the author needs to make a fantastic and unlikely leap of logic.

Whichever. You choose.

These monographs cover varieties of tobacco ash, cipher writing, the singular properties of the human ear and, strictly for shits and giggles, the polyphonic motets of Lassus.

Even Great Detectives need hobbies.

Some private dicks are reformed criminals. Some are unreformed criminals. Some are detective-story writers (which seems like a bit of a cheat). All of them have the advantage of being unconstrained by such trifles as the Police and Criminal Evidence Act or habeas corpus.

Now, before you make up your mind, consider that the police do have certain advantages. Manpower, for one. And forensic laboratories, although forensics does seem a bit like cheating in a whodunnit. Three hundred pages of detection, and then the DNA results come in. That kind of thing can feel like a waste of your time, can't it?

Which reminds us . . .

Pop Quiz

A defendant has been charged with murder, and the DNA results are in. There is a 99.9 percent match between the defendant's DNA and the DNA found at the crime scene. Do you vote to convict?

Answer: _____

The correct answer, of course, is "hell no," unless the defendant is Edgar Allan Poe's orangutan. The DNA of all humans is a 99.9 percent match. The differences are always down there in the 0.1 percent.

You need to learn to interpret your data.

And if the defendant *is* Mr. Poe's orangutan? Well, the answer is still no, because there is no way in hell that the murders in the Rue Morgue were committed by an ape.

So, *policeman* or *private detective*? Of course, some authors . . .

—*Sneaky beasts.*

. . . try to have the best of both worlds, and they make their detective an ex-policeman, who still has *good contacts on the force*, which effectively means they have all the freedom of the private dick and all the resources of Scotland Yard.

Time to choose.

Policeman	Private Dick	Police Dick
		✔

No-brainer, really. OK, shall we carry on?

—*Is that it?*

What do you mean?

—*Backstory. We need backstory. "Police dick" is not a backstory.*

Really? OK. How about something like this? Max Enygma is a former police officer who was unfairly dismissed from the force after uncovering corruption. Unspecified. Room for speculation (and a possible prequel if, please the Good Lord, this book sells). Drinks too much. Smokes too much. Divorced. No kids. Or divorced with one kid, whom he loves to death but hardly ever sees, because he is always working a case.

—*Which?*

Which what?

—*One kid or no kids?*

Well, it hardly matters, does it? *One kid* shows his tender side, and his self-recrimination, hence his drinking, while *no kids* means that he can occasionally meet up with his angry ex-wife, who still loves him, really, and they can have a roll in the hay, which is momentarily satisfying but leads to noisy rows in which the ex-wife throws things, followed by self-recrimination and drinking. Same thing.

—*No sex, please. We're bookish. Book sex is always excruciating.*

Well, then, it had better be *one kid*, I suppose.

—*Boy or girl?*

Does it matter? It's not as if they're going to appear in the story.

—*Girl. One of those wisecracking girls who know the ways of the world, even though they are only twelve. They take their dad to task when he uses politically incorrect language. They wear baseball caps backward and hide his cigarettes for his own good. They pour his booze down the sink. Tell him off when he doesn't show up to the school play, but aren't, you know, scarred by it.*

That seems an awful lot of extraneous detail to me. Why can't Enygma just have her picture in his wallet but refuse to talk about her? That suggests deep feelings without any of us having to feel them. And then we don't have to explain why he doesn't show up at the school play in a way that doesn't make The Reader think he is a shit. Because that would not be easy, let me tell you. No matter how good the excuse, the second that kid looks out in the crowd with a trembling lip and does not see her daddy, The Reader is going to think, *What a shit*. Guaranteed.

—*Still seems callous.*

Trust me, no one will notice. Broad brushstrokes are all we need here. Like Manet.

—*Monet?*

The other one. But him, too. Close up, just daubs of paint. Farther away, crowds of people at the opera. Or water lilies. Whatever.

—*Fine. One kid. Hardly mentioned, but feelings implied. Poor little bugger. What else?*

Else?

—*How did Max Enygma, drunken un-father of the year, end up duct-taped to a chair in this house? That's what The Reader really wants to know.*

How do you know what The Reader wants?

—*Never you mind. Tell us.*

That's easy. Max Enygma answered an advertisement in *The Times*. Lord Verreman advertised for a Great Detective who could solve the mystery of the century. Enygma might also have been tempted by the reward.

—*What reward? Verreman is skint.*

Hmm. We could make it the house. If Max Enygma can solve the mystery to the satisfaction of Lord Verreman, which, of course, means proving the former Lord Verreman not guilty, then he gets to keep the house in which he is currently . . . not imprisoned, not exactly . . . shall we say, in which he is residing?

—*Ah! And, of course, if he succeeds, then he will be able to provide for his family, who are currently living in a cramped studio flat, with horrible neighbors who have wild parties and a dangerous dog?*

Whatever. No one cares about the wife and kid. Let's say no reward. Verreman sends him a party invitation. He's going to work pro bono, so that he can get back in the detective game and get his name in the papers. How's that? It doesn't matter. All The Reader wants is some halfway plausible excuse that allows them to keep playing along.

—*When my love swears that she is made of truth, I do believe her, though I know she lies?*

Exactly. Let's carry on.

MAX ENYGMA READ the letter in his hand for the third time. The first time he'd read it, he had suspected a trick. Egg. It would be just like that bastard Monty Egg to think up something like this. The second time he'd read it, he wasn't sure.

Enygma washed down his many medicines with another cup of tea. And now he read the letter once more.

He began to feel excited. He remembered the Verreman Affair. Of course he did. Everyone did. It was a crime that invited speculation—a peer of the realm murdering the nanny. It reeked of salacious promise, although, in fact, there had been very little salaciousness to be found in the case. Still, the newspapers had done their best to insinuate debauchery in high life, while being constrained by the fear of contempt-of-court writs. Verreman, of course, had spoiled all their fun by not being found, which left the press horribly hidebound in what they could print without prejudicing a trial that they knew was never going to come.

Enygma tapped the letter against his knee while he decided what to do next. If the letter was genuine—and that was a big if—he had to decide whether he was up to the task. After all, he was getting to be an old man now.

His eyes flicked toward the wall where his long-service certificates and commendations were framed. His eyes lingered for a moment on a picture of himself walking up the steps to the courthouse. It was a good picture. Dynamic. He'd written to the paper to get a copy of that picture. And it had been a good case. A cold case. And he'd solved it.

Was that why Egg had sent him a cold case? Was he trying to ruin this for him, too? Because, of course, this letter could not be genuine. And Monty Egg would never stop persecuting him.

Max Enygma looked at the paper in his hand—not at the letter this time, but at the paper itself, and the envelope it had come in. The envelope was creamy white, and bordered with a thin navy blue line. The envelope was too thick to read the contents of the letter through it, and, in any case, the inside of the envelope was lined with navy blue tissue paper. Max Enygma did not know anyone who used such fancy stationery. Certainly not Monty bloody Egg. The letter was handwritten in intense black ink, and he was pretty sure that the writer had used an expensive fountain pen for their flamboyantly handwritten message.

Then Enygma noticed a small card that remained in the envelope. He pulled it out and turned it over, expecting it to be a business card. It was an invitation. A bloody murder mystery party. He threw the invitation in the wastepaper basket.

Definitely Egg. The bastard knew he hated murder mystery parties.

He tossed the letter in the bin, too.

The envelope would have followed suit, but Enygma noticed that the sender's name and address were embossed on the back flap. Lord David Verreman, 8 Broad Way, London.

There were two facts Max Enygma knew about his old partner. The first was that he was a bastard. The second was that he was a cheap bastard. Enygma could envisage Egg coming across some fancy stationery in the course of his work and pinching a bit for his own use. But embossed stationery is expensive. And another man's embossed stationery would be *very* hard to come by.

Enygma bent over and rooted through the wastepaper basket to pull out the invitation. At least he'd get to play the part of the detective. In the old days, when he still went to parties, he was always made to play the role of the corpse, on the grounds that his police experience would give him an unfair advantage. Which was bollocks, he thought to himself, because the murders in murder mystery parties can never be solved by detection. They are written by third-rate mystery writers who couldn't solve real crimes if their lives depended on it.

—*Hey!*

Not us.

HE LOOKED AT the bottom of the card.

* Please try to dress in appropriate costume.

Enygma snorted. He wasn't going to dress up in bell-bottoms and a tie-dyed shirt! No, sir. He would wear an ordinary business suit. Fuck it, even in the 1970s men like him had worn suits, hadn't they?

Well, well. The Verreman Affair. If he could solve that case, his reputation as a detective would be remade.

Before he could change his mind, Enygma scribbled a few words of acceptance on a sheet of notepaper, which, he could not help noticing, was of greatly inferior quality to that of the first new client he'd had in years.

10

◆ ◆ ◆ ◆ ◆

THE BEST-LAID PLANS

"If it is any point requiring reflection," observed Dupin, as he forbore to enkindle the wick, "we shall examine it to better purpose in the dark."

—Edgar Allan Poe, "The Purloined Letter"

BY THE TIME Max Enygma stands in front of the Verreman house on the night of the party, he has become a great deal more acquainted with the details of the case. He has spent several long days at the British Library, trawling through newspaper reports of the investigation and the inquest. The case against Verreman had seemed pretty convincing, he thought, though he had noted one or two points of interest.

Verreman's letter did not discuss terms. Enygma decides that he will treat this evening as an initial consultation, but that after tonight he will start charging. And, he thinks, looking up at the five-story Georgian town house, he will be adjusting his rates for inflation.

The house on Broad Way is impressive. The black-painted front door reminds him of TV shots of 10 Downing Street. The steps have been swept and the door knocker freshly polished, he notices.

His phone buzzes, which causes Enygma a little flurry of anxiety. Almost no one has his mobile number. And those who do, do not call. He fishes it out of his overcoat. A text.

Walk up the steps and tap lightly upon the door. They
are expecting you.

He snorts to himself as he climbs the steps and raps out a short
tattoo with the knocker, and he notices how his breath swirls in mists
in the glow of the portico lamp. There is something Dickensian about
the house and the lamp and the glow, which makes him stamp his feet
and rub his hands together, though it is not really cold.

He hears footsteps from the other side of the door. Someone is
coming.

Enygma recognizes David Verreman at once. He looks, Enygma
thinks, very like his father—the John Verreman of the newspaper
archives—except, Enygma realizes, that the current Lord Verreman
must be older than John Verreman was when he disappeared.

"Evening," Enygma says.

"Good evening," returns Verreman, rather formally. "I'm very
glad to see you. Before we go up to the drawing room, I hope you
won't mind if I ask you to wear this"—Verreman holds up a roll of
duct tape—"and these." With his other hand, Verreman holds up a
pair of handcuffs.

"What the fuck?"

Verreman winces, just a little, at the last word, but as Enygma takes
a step backward, toward the still-open front door, he says, "Part of the
game. I assure you, no harm will come to you. You have, I am sure, left
word of where you will be tonight. People know you're here."

Enygma nodded in answer, as if it were true. If only he'd thought
to do that.

"It's part of the game," repeats Verreman.

"What game?"

"*The* Game."

"What's *the* Game?"

"The Game is Murder! This is a murder mystery party, after all."

"Right." Enygma considers for a moment. "I won't wear cuffs," he
says eventually.

"Just the duct tape, then. A compromise. I agree."

David Verreman drops the handcuffs onto a console table in the otherwise rather empty hall, and Max Enygma consents, with only a little apprehension, to having his mouth taped shut.

"Comfortable?" asks Verreman.

Enygma nods. He can hear a babble of conversation as they climb the stairs together.

"Excellent," says Verreman, and he throws open the doors to the drawing room.

It is completely empty.

"As you can see," Verreman says, taking Enygma by the arm and leading him round the bare room, "the room is full of guests—all here to meet you." He presses PAUSE on a Bluetooth speaker. "They have stopped talking for a moment in order to get a look at you, but now— see—the conversation resumes."

He presses PLAY, and the low babble of conversation resumes in the otherwise silent house.

Verreman spreads his arm out, like a model at a car show. "Champagne?" he says, taking two imaginary glasses from an equally imaginary passing waiter. Then he looks at Enygma, and at the duct tape across his mouth. "Perhaps not," he says, and mimes knocking back both drinks.

They stand in the center of the room and Verreman talks at him like a tour guide for a particularly cloth-headed group of schoolchildren. "Note the curtains. The finest quality, although a little faded now. They look magnificent, don't they?"

Enygma looks toward the window and sees only a bare curtain rail, coming away from the wall at one end.

"The furniture is old, too, but I think you will agree that it commands the room, as though it were made for the house."

There is no furniture.

"And the chandelier, of course. Everyone mentions the chandelier. Our crowning glory. Don't you love the way it glitters? How it casts a yellow glow over the guests, making them look like they've been dipped in gold?"

Enygma looks at the light. There is only a bare bulb hanging from the ceiling on a white plastic wire. Its bright white light illuminates the two men's footprints in the dust on the floor.

David Verreman, Enygma concludes, is nuts.

Verreman moves to the center of the floor, bare save for a lone sheet of newspaper, and opens his arms wide to address the room. "My brother and I are so glad you could all attend this little party of ours."

Max Enygma begins to feel alarmed. David Verreman, he knows, does not have a brother. He does not have a sister. From his research at the British Library, Enygma knows that John and Antonia Verreman had only one child.

Verreman is still speaking, but Max is not listening. He can, he is sure, hold his own in a fight, as old as he is. He can rip off this duct tape—there is nothing to prevent him—and walk right out the front door, which, with his habitual cautiousness, he noticed was secured with only a latch, though the door also wore two bolts and a safety chain, none of which were engaged. But the person in front of him is definitely David Verreman, and the prospect of solving this case, however remote, convinces him to indulge Verreman's games—for the time being, at least.

Verreman is looking at him, and it is clear that he has missed something.

"Sorry?"

"Contract?"

Contract. What does that mean? Was he sent a contract? Should he have fished again in that wastepaper basket?

Verreman hands him a contract, and Enygma skims through it quickly.

"Take your time," says Verreman. "I can always tell dinner to wait."

The contract appears to be gibberish, certainly not legally enforceable. Enygma shrugs to himself and scrawls a signature that looks nothing like his own.

"OK, then," says Verreman. "Let's eat. I'm starving."

Enygma is hungry, too, but as he enters the dining room, he discovers that there is no food. Just as there are no guests.

The dining room has one long table with, Enygma counts, sixteen seats set around it. The table is covered with a pristine white tablecloth. In front of each chair is a large name card, folded into a Toblerone shape, with the name of the guest printed on one slope and the menu on the other. Some of the names Enygma recognizes from his research—Carolyn Keene-Wade, Lady Verreman's sister; Detective Chief Inspector Nicholas Blake, the detective in charge of the case; Stanley Gardner, husband of the dead nanny; and the Howard-Coles, whose cold assistance in the case was just this side of obstruction.

Other names are unfamiliar to him. He takes the seat Verreman directs him to while Verreman introduces him to the empty seats one by one. Verreman's attitude is contagious, and at one point Enygma catches himself nodding a greeting to an empty chair as though it really does contain a forensic pathologist. Enygma shakes his head a little to rid himself of the impression, and tells himself to stop being a dick.

"Just a quick reminder of the rules," Verreman is saying to the silent room. "If you are asked a direct question, you must give an honest answer, or say so if you don't know. But you must not volunteer information. This is a game, after all. And we don't want our detective to crack the case before dessert, now, do we?"

As Verreman begins his opening statement, Enygma wishes that he had eaten before he came.

Verreman begins by scene setting: stuff that Enygma already knows, or that he considers irrelevant to the case itself and speaks only to motive. Amateurs are always excessively concerned with motive. Enygma himself cares nothing for *why* a crime was committed. He cares only for the *how* and the *who*. He lets his mind wander while Verreman talks about his parents' marriage, their childhood, all sorts of rubbish.

David Verreman's description of his father lying in wait in the basement is, Enygma concludes, pure melodrama, and he scarcely listens, though he wonders what it is like to have to narrate the attempted murder of your mother by your father as though it were a penny dreadful. He brings his mind back to the case at the point where the nanny had been bundled into a sack and Lord Verreman went upstairs to wash his hands in the cloakroom in the hall.

That's bloody odd, he thinks, and pulls his notebook from his jacket pocket and writes his first note.

David moves on to his mother's movements in the lead-up to her attack, then to her pushing her husband off her, and Enygma tries to reconstruct the scene in his mind. Antonia, of course, was a tiny woman, barely over five feet, and she weighed almost nothing. Her husband, on the other hand, was six foot three. Could she really have pushed him off her?

Perhaps. With enough motivation. And, of course, if he had killed once already, not by shooting but by violent assault, he would be shattered, and he would hurt everywhere. Maybe.

But why would she ask him to take her to her bedroom? And why would he go? Surely both of them would want to stay near the front door—he to escape, and she to escape from him?

Enygma makes another note.

"Here comes the food," Verreman says, looking expectantly at the door. Despite himself, Enygma looks, too, and again wishes he had eaten before he came. When, a few minutes later, Verreman asks him if he found the prawns delicious, Enygma has to take a deep breath before he feels steady enough to nod in agreement. Luckily, the duct tape negates the necessity for him to smile at the same time.

Suddenly, David Verreman leans in close, as though to make sure no one else can hear, and he asks Enygma, in a confidential tone, what he thought of his speech.

Enygma points to the duct tape and tries to look both impressed and sympathetic. Then Verreman turns to a chair farther down the table. "What did you think of it, Chief Inspector?"

Verreman turns back to Enygma and speaks softly again. "Look at him, poor man, concentrating all his efforts on wiping the inside of his Babycham glass with a finger of brown bread. He's got a dribble of pink mayonnaise on his chin, too. Be a good chap and try not to look at it when he talks. He's up next, you know."

And, to Enygma's amazement, not only does Verreman begin to talk to the imaginary policeman, but the policeman begins to talk back. If, at this point, Max Enygma had closed his eyes, he could have been back in his days on the force. Chief Inspector Blake speaks exactly like every senior policeman he has known—that is, he is stolid, reliable and completely unimaginative. He can even picture him: mid-fifties, balding, overweight, but only as fat as his peers. No fatter. In 1974 he would have been a smoker, for sure. But not anymore. Times have changed, and so, reluctantly, have the police.

If Max Enygma had closed his eyes, he could have pictured Detective Chief Inspector Blake quite easily. But he did not. And instead of seeing a familiar, if not friendly, police officer, Enygma sees David Verreman slip in and out of his own character, and his own voice, until, finally, he concedes the floor to DCI Blake, and David Verreman disappears entirely.

Blake examines his fingernails meticulously and begins to speak in the broad, flat vowels of a beat copper from Northampton who has risen through the ranks to become a senior detective at Scotland Yard. Being a professional, the DCI begins not with the background but from the moment that the police appeared at the scene, and then moves on to his interview with Antonia Verreman.

Can Enygma detect a note of self-satisfaction there? "What impressed me most," Blake says, "was that Lady Verreman's testimony never wavered. From the first interview she gave, while under sedation at the hospital, to the testimony she gave in the coroner's court, her version of events never altered."

Blake considers this to be important, and Enygma is inclined to agree. He makes another note.

"Officers were at the crime scene within forty minutes, having attended, in the first instance, at the public house where the call had come from. When they arrived at the scene of the crime, officers were forced to break open the door."

Forty minutes seems like a long time, Enygma thinks as he makes another note. Could that have made any difference? Probably not. Lord Verreman, after all, would have been long gone.

He smiles ruefully at the story of the color-changing dolly's leg. The DCI is something of a raconteur, but Enygma has attended enough crime scenes to know that, given the choice between (a) a superabsorbent piece of sticking plaster and (b) a clumsy policeman, he would choose option b every time. Not for nothing were they called flatfoots.

A murder in high society and a body in the basement would, Enygma guesses, have attracted a large number of curious beat policemen before the detectives showed up to kick them out. In Enygma's experience, coppers are every bit as curious as the average lookie-loo, but with many more opportunities to satisfy their curiosity.

Enygma does not bother making a note about the doll's leg.

"DINNER" IS OVER, and Max Enygma's tongue is thick and his mouth dry after the duct tape. He sips the brandy his host has placed before him, and is relieved to find that this, at least, is real. He takes a sip and lets the liquid run over his tongue, savoring it. It's good brandy, he knows, although he usually prefers to drink whisky. But Enygma wants to placate his host, who, it seems, values tradition.

Enygma lets his eyes travel around the dining room. It is largely bare, except for this beautiful long table and the chairs, and two oil paintings, one at each end of the room. The subject of the first is instantly recognizable as Lord John Verreman. Enygma has seen the painting in the newspapers, the missing earl in all his regalia, ermine cape round his shoulders, looking a bit po-faced. The picture is bigger than he imagined, and well-done by a fashionable artist, he knows. But it is the other painting that draws his eye. It is of Lady Verreman, but this is not the Lady Verreman of the newspapers. In this portrait, she is a young woman, a teenager perhaps. She is smiling. Her head is tilted back a little, as if she is about to break into laughter. In his wallet, Enygma has a picture of his daughter in an almost identical pose.

The detective is visited suddenly by the notion that the two girls are sharing the same joke.

David Verreman begins to speak, and Enygma pulls his eyes away from the picture to look at his new client. Verreman stands and addresses the room, though only Max Enygma is there to listen to him.

"The account I gave you in the last round was, more or less, the case as presented by the prosecution at the inquest. Don't you agree, Chief Inspector?"

David smoothly moves six paces to the left and drops into a chair in front of a place card that reads, *Detective Chief Inspector Nicholas Blake.* As he sits down, he gives a little cough and examines his fingernails carefully. When he speaks, it is in the policeman's voice. "More or less, milord. More or less. That is to say, you expressed yourself rather more floridly than would ordinarily be considered acceptable in a police report, but, taking it as a whole, I would say that your report covered the facts as we presented them."

Enygma watches in morbid fascination as Verreman nods and retakes his own seat and becomes, once more, the debonair host.

"A glowing commendation. Thank you, Chief Inspector. I gave the Authorized Version, as it were, because I am a fair man."

Enygma snorts a little but is careful that his host does not hear him. It is clear to Enygma now that his client is a little unhinged, and possibly even dangerous. Is a proclivity for murder an inheritable trait?

Verreman turns to Enygma: "You might say to me, *Your father is innocent.* Indeed, you may be tempted to do so. But I would advise

you not to give in to that temptation. I am not concerned with innocence. Innocence is between my father and his god, if he has one. I am
concerned only with the guilty. To be precise, guilty or not guilty. I
expect that you are aware that my father did not stand trial. He was
named as the culprit at the inquest—a custom that, as Dr. Knox
pointed out, has since gone out. But, although he was called a murderer within the privileged confines of the court, he was never convicted. Never tried. Never arrested. Never even questioned about
the murder. Apart from his brief correspondence, some of which you
have seen, written to his closest friends in the immediate aftermath of
the tragedy, we do not have his version of events."

Enygma considers this. "So, the inquest was treated as a quasi
murder trial."

"That's true, but one where only the prosecution was allowed to
give evidence."

Verreman looks toward the coroner's chair, as if he's heard the
doctor's hesitant cough. He nods, conceding the floor, then moves
five chairs down the right side of the table, picks up the doctor's imaginary pipe and holds it in the side of his mouth. Then he presses his
fingertips together like a small child at prayer, and Enygma watches
as, before his eyes, David Verreman becomes a rather prissy old man,
fastidious and precise, choosing his words carefully and savoring
them slowly as though they are delicate fruits. "I was in a most difficult position. I waited for as long as I could in the hopes that Lord
Verreman—your father, I mean, of course—would be found, or perhaps would return of his own volition. But, as time went on, that
seemed less and less likely. And under those peculiar, if not to say
unique, circumstances, I decided that I would try to give Mrs. Gardner's family—her parents, her husband, her friends—some sort of justice. But, of course, there was the complication of Lady Verreman's
testimony. Really, it was a very difficult situation. But I did my small
part to the best of my abilities, I assure you. And really, I do not see
what I could have done differently that would have brought a measure of comfort to her poor family."

Verreman puts down the pipe, takes a step backward and is himself again. "Don't distress yourself, Doctor. I meant no slight upon your professionalism or your honor."

He steps forward and picks up the imaginary pipe again. "Thank you, my dear boy. Of course, I, er, realize that there were two families affected by this tragedy. I always try to remember that. But it is the responsibility, and, er, the right of the coroner to conduct the inquest within the limits set by the law, in the way that they deem best, taking into account all the factors of the case. They are given a wide latitude precisely because each case is, er, unique. In order to see justice done, true justice wholly done, we must be able to take the circumstances of each case into consideration."

David Verreman mimes laying the pipe on the table before he moves back to his own seat and resumes talking to Enygma. "So, I have shown you the case for the prosecution. Now I would like to begin to look at the case for the defense, if I may."

"OK, but would you mind . . . I mean," says Enygma, looking into Verreman's face, trying to gauge the degree of instability in his new client, "shall we make this a cold-case conference rather than a dinner party, and just let the evidence speak for itself?"

He is anxious for a moment. His client does not like this suggestion—and he has clearly gone to a great deal of trouble learning his lines and honing his parts—but Enygma is starting to feel a little seasick at each sudden volte-face.

Verreman pouts and flings his arm in the air. "Well, fine! If you just want to go through the paperwork, who am I to stop you? I was just trying to inject a little drama into the thing—that's all."

Verreman drops into his own chair and begins flipping petulantly through the files before him. He stops at a page he clearly knows by heart, but instead of reading it, he says, "What you must remember about my father is that he was a product of his age. As, too, was my mother, I suppose. It was 1974. Men were the dominant sex—or they believed themselves to be. They handled the money. Women could not get a mortgage, a loan or a credit card, unless a man—a husband or a father—cosigned for them. Men had the power. They had the jobs. Most married women did not work. They stayed at home. They had babies. They looked after their man."

"Yes. I know all this."

Verreman continues, unheeding. "But the times, as Dylan had pointed out, were a-changing. For the first time, women could choose whether or not to have a child. The contraceptive pill was available to married women with children—almost never to singletons, who might, heaven forbid, use it to facilitate sex just for the fun of the thing. My mother, being a lady and not a liberated woman, did not enjoy sex. She did not enjoy physical affection of any kind, since it might conceivably lead to sex. She had done her duty and provided her husband with an heir and a spare. No doubt, being a dutiful wife, if she had had a girl, she would have had another child, and another if necessary, but, as she had assured the succession, that was that."

Verreman's head tilts suddenly to the right.

—Why am I the spare?

David straightens his head quickly and mutters, "Don't start."

The head tilts again, seemingly of its own volition, and Enygma begins to realize that, at least as far as his "brother" is concerned, David Verreman has little control over the voices coming from his mouth. David emits a strangled growl, pulls his neck straight and swallows, choking down Daniel's words. He grips the table and breathes deeply until he is sure that his voice is his own again.

"John Verreman," he continues, as if nothing has happened, "was a man of his times. Which is to say he expected his wife to be pretty, and accommodating, and not to bother her head about business or politics or, well, anything, really. A lot of his friends' wives did charity work—not working in soup kitchens, you understand, but organizing balls, that sort of thing. Some of them had hobbies—art, music, flower arranging. None of them had jobs. And none of them wanted one. They stayed at home and made their husbands feel like the kings of their particular castles. And that, apparently, was enough.

"When Lord Verreman decided he was going to pack in his job as a banker to be a professional gambler, it never occurred to him to consult his wife about it first. That is a form of arrogance, no doubt. He believed that, as he was a privileged man with privileged friends who knew the right, privileged people, things would always work out for him. But Antonia Verreman was different. She was not a risk-taker. The thought that they might be plunged into debt with one turn of the card made her sick with anxiety. Her brother-in-law, Sir Henry Wade"—Verreman points to Sir Henry's chair, and touches his watch lightly—"once won and lost seventy thousand pounds in a single night. The average annual wage at that time was less than two thousand pounds, and ten thousand would have bought you an average-sized house in central London."

David Verreman checks his watch, and Sir Henry Wade laughs, a little ruefully. "Play like a gentleman. Win like a gentleman. Lose like a king. Or don't play at all. Johnny understood that. But Antonia was the embodiment of the careful housewife. Scrimping and saving. Making stupid economies. Partly, of course, so that she could squirrel money away. But it was also a means of embarrassing Verreman in front of his friends. They would go out for the day, and she would bring sandwiches and a bottle of lemon squash. They would eat out, and she would open her lunch box like Little Orphan Annie."

He touches the watch again, and Henry Wade's voice is stronger. "Now, Johnny was not mean. The man had his faults, I'm sure, but he was not mean. It was her. It was her way of letting his friends know that they were having to tighten their belts. And the lightbulbs! There were never any working lightbulbs in that fucking house. You always had to grub around in the dark. She said it in court—she actually said in court that she couldn't afford to buy new lightbulbs on the allowance that Johnny gave her, though she bought her groceries from bloody Harrods. Bitch."

"So, you see," says David, letting his cuff fall and cover his watch again, "my mother was constitutionally unsuited to a gambler's way of life. But she adapted. As Sir Henry says, she scrimped and saved. She put money in hidey-holes all around the house. And she followed her husband everywhere until the day they separated—and even then, she couldn't leave him alone. A lot was made in court about the fact that my father used to pass this house every evening. Today they would have called him a stalker, but back then they called him 'obsessive.' An 'obsessive father.' In the 1970s, any man who wanted to spend time with his own children was considered odd. Not enlightened times.

"But here's what you probably don't know. My father used to walk past our house every night when we were with our mother, because he wanted to make sure we were OK, that the house hadn't been burned down or the front door left open. Mother wasn't any good at domestic stuff. At the custody hearing, he said that he would just glance at the house from the street on his way home. But that, obviously, was nonsense. He snooped. He pried. Like Wee Willie Winkie crying through the locks, he crept down the basement steps and pressed his nose to the windowpane to see if he could spot us. He would try the front door to check that it was locked. Sometimes, if she had not put the chain on, he would let himself in and wander around—check the fridge to see if there was enough food, and so on. It was his house, so he had the right to go in, although I believe his solicitors had advised him that it might not look good in front of a judge.

"But here's the funny thing: my mother used to do it, too. She would walk past his house on nights when she had custody, so she wasn't checking to make sure that I—we," he said, hastily, as his head began tilting toward the right, "that we were being properly cared for. No. She was checking up on *him*. Trying to find out when he was home, whether anyone was staying over and, if so, whether they were female. I don't believe my mother ever caught him with another woman, but whether that was because he wasn't interested or because he was careful, I could not say. My mother did have an awful temper, and I don't know what she would have done if she'd found him with someone else."

"Lord Verreman did not bring up his wife's stalking in court? In the original custody case, I mean."

"I don't think so. He must have known about it, of course, because she wasn't trying to hide it. She wanted him to see her. She wanted to provoke a reaction. But he preferred to pretend not to see her. He was trying to be smarter."

Enygma shifts in his chair.

"I hope I'm not boring you."

"Hardly that," Enygma says. And it is true. Max Enygma cannot resist a mystery. His client is eccentric, yes, even odd, but this is not the first odd client he has had. And although he is reserving judgment on his client's sanity, he is becoming interested. Indeed, he has been interested since the moment he read the invitation, because he knows that if he can solve *this* case, nothing about the past will matter. "I will challenge you, though. You need to be prepared for that. If we look into this case together, then we will need to look at every piece of evidence from all angles—not just the one that makes your case. Do you understand?"

"Of course."

Enygma draws his seat closer to the table, closer to the piles of evidence. "OK, then. Why don't you pour us another drink and we can get down to it?"

Verreman pours them each a generous measure, and Max Enygma gets up and throws a log on the fire. The house is cold, and Enygma suspects that this fire is the first source of heat that the house has seen in a long time.

"Cigar?" says Verreman, taking one and proffering the box. While Verreman sets about the laborious task of establishing an even burn, Enygma takes a swig of brandy and flips open the first file. *Custody Case*, it says on the flyleaf and on the spine of the file.

"Tell me about the custody case."

"It was held about a year before the murder happened. You might not think it important, but I think that was the start of it all. My father had been absolutely certain that he would be granted full custody.

He had presented evidence of my mother's mental illness, of which he had a documented history, and he had evidence that it was not being properly treated, largely because my mother refused help. A lifetime of privilege—of entitlement, if you like—led him to believe that the hearing was a formality.

"But what he failed to take into account was that the family courts at that time erred, almost exclusively, in favor of the mother. The flip side to the man being king in the worlds of business, finance and decision-making was that the woman was left with the home and the children. That was her domain. And when the marriage was over, she got to keep both.

"My father was, I believe, given advice from family solicitors and so on. But he chose to ignore it. A lifetime of winning had convinced him that anyone who compared him—tall, aristocratic, even dashing—with his mousy little wife, she who brought her own sandwiches and scrimped on lightbulbs, would favor him. But they did not. When he naively brought in his proofs of her mental illness, they weren't interested. Every day, men were coming before them, yelling that the women they had chosen to have children with were suddenly unfit mothers. Every day, powerful men fabricated evidence against their spouses, had them committed to mental asylums in the hope of avoiding spousal maintenance. Every day, successful men were trying to take children away from their mummies, just so Mummy wouldn't win.

"So, my father went to court clutching proof of his wife's illness, and they didn't believe it. They didn't believe him. And they didn't like him. Like my mother, they found the idea of a fit, healthy man making a living from gambling distasteful, disreputable and financially irresponsible. He might have cut a dash at Monte Carlo, but in the family court in Islington he went down like a lead balloon. They awarded my mother full custody. He got every other weekend.

"But my father was not a quitter. It took him a little while, but he regrouped. He began to take his wife seriously, probably for the first time in their marriage. He began to ask for advice. From his friends.

His family. And from his family lawyers. If you were his lawyer, what would you have advised him to do?"

"Me?" says Enygma. "I don't know. What could he do?"

David Verreman looks a little disappointed. "He needed to be able to demonstrate to the satisfaction of a hostile court that his wife was not coping. My first nanny, the one who had been with the family since I was born, was dismissed shortly after my father left the marital home. She was very obviously on Team Johnny, and was almost certainly passing him notes from the day he left. Without her, my father argued, we would be at risk. He thought that would mean he would get custody. As a sop to his complaints, the court simply mandated that there should always be a nanny in the house. Which, of course, they made him pay for.

"As long as the nanny was there, it didn't matter that my mother spent all day in bed—there would always be clean clothes, and food on the table, which was all the courts really cared about.

"My father was stymied. Unless, of course, he managed to get the nanny on board. If he could win her trust, he would have an informant, someone to whom the courts would listen. And, after all, he was the one paying her wages. To him, recruiting the nanny to tell tales about his wife would have seemed an entirely reasonable thing to do."

"OK. Are you saying that Sally Gardner was working with him? That she was informing on Antonia? Do you have proof?"

Verreman shakes his head. "No. No proof. But my father must have spoken to her several times, because he told friends that he thought she was good at her job, that he liked her. That shows he knew her quite well, doesn't it?"

"It implies it," Enygma says, "but it's not proof of collusion."

"I know that. I know. But my father made it his business to get to know all the nannies. I say 'nannies' because there were lots of them. And my mother certainly suspected them of helping him. Few of them lasted more than a month or two. In the six months before the murder, there were seven of them. One lasted only a single afternoon.

"The moment Mother suspected that my father had got to them, they were out. Sally Gardner was with us for six weeks. My mother told the inquest that she liked Sally, and that they were fast becoming friends. They confided in each other, she said. Frankly, I find that rather hard to believe. My mother did not fraternize with the servants. And she was not the sort of woman who made friends with other women, no matter who they were. Other women were rivals. They were either above her in the food chain, in which case she envied them, or below her and she despised them. The Great Sisterhood passed my mother by.

"But Sally had been there six weeks, and that was, comparatively, rather a long time. I would be lying if I said I remembered Sally. I remember the events after she died, of course, but she made only the vaguest of impressions in my memory before she died in our basement, and if she had not been killed, it is certain that I would not now remember her at all, because I think my mother was beginning to get the feeling about Sally—that feeling that she was in Lord Verreman's pay, which, of course she was, in a literal sense. My mother began, as she always did, to guard her tongue in front of her, and she arranged little tests to check her loyalty.

"I have no idea whether Sally passed them or not. Afterward, of course, well, she passed by default, didn't she? You have to trust the person who died in your place. That is, of course, assuming that she did."

"Yes, I suppose you do. So, your father had been denied custody. Was he appealing that?"

"He was. In fact, there was going to be another custody hearing in January of the following year. They would have been separated two years by then, and either party could have filed for divorce, though I don't know whether my father was planning to. Mother certainly wasn't. My father had been gathering evidence for the custody hearing."

"What kind of evidence?" Enygma asks, knowing that Verreman is desperate to tell him.

"Well, he began to record conversations with my mother. Whenever she lost her temper and flung obscenities his way, he pressed RECORD on his Dictaphone and made a note of the time and the place and what had set her off. But I don't know how much use the recordings would have been in court. In fact, I think he was advised that it might make him look manipulative, secretly recording private conversations. And, of course, she could always claim that he had goaded her into losing her temper before he hit the RECORD button.

"He scraped an acquaintance with the pharmacist who had premises at the bottom of this street, and he often brought him tablets to identify. The pharmacist, who was obliging but rather stupid, would tell my dad the names and strengths of the drugs and what conditions they were prescribed for. Without ever mentioning his wife's name, my father managed to compile a dossier of the range of medications she was taking—dosage, frequency and their likely purpose. On the day of the murder, he took a small blue tablet to this friend and asked him to identify it. Limbitrol, the tablet was called, and it was used to treat moderate to severe depression and anxiety. Side effects include paranoia, delusions and hallucinations, as well as itching, diarrhea and, rather paradoxically, suicidal thoughts."

"Your mother was taking Limbitrol?"

"There is no way of knowing. But she was prescribed it, and a number of other drugs. And there is no way of knowing whether the tablet my father showed the pharmacist was taken from the bottle that was found on her bedside table—although it's likely, of course. My father never said where he got it, and the pharmacist was careful not to ask. It is possible that he waited until my mother was out of the house, then let himself in and filched a tablet, but how much more likely is it that he simply asked the nanny to do it for him?"

"Why would he do that?"

Verreman opens another folder and flips to the police statement of the pharmacist, which is exceedingly brief. "Well, I imagine either because of a genuine concern for the well-being of the mother of his children or, less charitably, because the court had made it a condition of custody that my mother continue with any treatment that her doctors had authorized."

"So, your father could go back to court and say either that she was not complying with the court order or that she was complying and was suffering from delusions as a side effect?"

"Exactly. Lose-lose for Mother."

"And this visit happened on the day of the murder? Was the pharmacist called to give evidence at the inquest?"

David Verreman glances once at the coroner's chair, but doesn't move from his seat. "No. I don't believe he was."

"Hmm."

Enygma considers for a moment, and decides the time has come to put his cards on the table. "Let me have this straight. You want me to go over the evidence with you, and consider whether a guilty verdict would be likely to stand."

"Exactly."

"And if I still say your father is guilty . . . ?"

"I am looking for a true verdict. If he is guilty, so be it. But I—"

Verreman's head tilts to the right.

—We.

"We need to know."

Enygma scratches his cheek thoughtfully. "If you are looking to find out what really happened, to prove someone else guilty, that is going to be extremely difficult after all this time. Not to say impossible."

Verreman waves a hand. "I am not seeking justice for Sally Gardner, I assure you. I am thinking only of myself. It is a selfish motive, but an understandable one, I think. Nor am I looking to overturn verdicts or clear my father's name. I am not that noble. All I seek to know is whether, had he stood his trial, my father should have been found guilty or not guilty beyond a reasonable doubt."

Enygma touches his face where the skin is still smarting from the duct tape. "And I have your word that afterward, no matter the verdict, I will be free to leave."

"On my honor."

—Your honor!

"Shut up!"

"One more question. Do you know a man called Egg?"

Enygma watches closely. "Egg? As in chicken?"

"Fair enough," says Enygma, after a pause. "I will give you this evening for free. If you require my services after that, we'll need to talk about fees." He begins to pull some of the files nearer to him. "But can you just be you? No need for accents or props. Just you and me."

—And me!

Enygma pauses before saying, reluctantly, "OK. Just the three of us, but sitting here at the table, going through the evidence. Can you do that?"

David Verreman swallows, and says in a rather quiet voice, "Yes. I mean, probably."

"OK, then. Now, why don't you begin by telling me what worries you about the police case?"

"It seems that everyone—the police, the press, even the girl's own family—just assumed that Sally must have died as part of the Johnny and Antonia Extravaganza and the shit show that was their divorce. They looked at it this way: the Verremans were a rich society couple. He was a gambler with money problems. She was the wife who stood between him and his children. It was a story with everything going for it. It seemed obvious to them that little Sally couldn't be the target of the killer. But why not? Women are killed by men every day, and just as many poor ones as rich ones. So why did the police dismiss that theory out of hand?"

"Because of your mother."

"I was going to say, because of class. But yes, my mother pointed the finger at her husband. But I maintain that if we had lived on a council estate in Manchester or Birmingham rather than in a Georgian town house in Belgravia, the police might have considered the possibility that my mother was lying. Or mistaken. After all, by her own account, she didn't witness Sally's murder. She didn't see the killer exit the basement. Even if she told the absolute truth, it's possible that the killer was someone else."

Enygma snorts. "Possible, but hardly likely."

Verreman continues as if he hasn't heard. "But when Lady Antonia Verreman said that her husband attacked her, they never looked any further. And when people began to question the reliability of her story, her sanity, they took the same view of the matter as the judge in the custody case: that Lady Verreman was being maligned out of spite. It never occurred to them that a common little nobody like Sally Gardner could have led a life as interesting as that of her employers, that she might have been the target of a murderer herself.

"Working-class women couldn't even get murdered in their own right. And yet, you know, there was as much evidence for Sally being the intended victim as there was for it being Antonia."

"Such as . . . ?" says Enygma.

Verreman moves to Chief Inspector Blake's chair and begins to rifle through his pile of papers. "Here we are. Sally Gardner. Now, usually Sally would have been out on a Thursday evening, the night of the attack. Thursday was her regular night off. According to the prosecution, the reason a Thursday night was chosen for the attack was because my father was expecting the house to be empty. Except, of course, for my mother, and me."

—And me!

David Verreman scowls at the interruption, which confirms Enygma's suspicion that he cannot keep Daniel down. "Well, that's not an unreasonable deduction," Enygma says.

"Perhaps. But Sally went out on Wednesday night, with Eddie." Verreman points to a chair at the bottom end of the table, where the place card for Eddie Biggers stands. "But she came back early. She and Eddie had rowed. He told police"—Verreman waves the report in the air—"that it was over something and nothing. But whatever it was, she was back home by nine thirty. Not the first time they'd rowed either, by all accounts. The police described their relationship as 'brief but tumultuous.' So that is one man who had reason to be annoyed with her. But there were others. Plus, there was her husband, who was, after all, still her husband."

"Come off it," Enygma says. "They had been separated a good long while. Tempers generally cool after time."

"Unless something happens to inflame them."

"If he was going to kill her in a passion, wouldn't he have done it when they separated? When he caught her cheating the first time? Or the second? That's the time for a crime of passion. Not a year later. Unless something had changed. If she had filed for divorce, for instance. But, apparently, she hadn't."

"You might be right. But they weren't the only two men in her life. Not by a long chalk. Including Eddie, police counted six current or recent boyfriends, including one who was married. Now, according to Eddie, she had dumped the rest of them in order to be exclusive with him. I don't know if that is true, but if it is, maybe one of them wasn't too happy about getting the push."

"The police checked into them, I suppose?"

"Well, maybe they did. But maybe they didn't try too hard. They thought they knew who their man was. Why waste time chasing down alibis of innocent men, right?"

Enygma doubts this. A certain amount of police work is just routine. Even if the police thought they had their man, they would have been careful to dot the i's and cross the t's. "Did Eddie have an alibi?"

"He did. And it was a good one. He was working. He was a relief pub manager, and the other staff confirmed that he was working all night."

"Well, there you are."

"It might interest you to know that the pub where Eddie worked was a five-minute walk from this house. Five minutes, straight across the square. Yes, he was working. But people take breaks, don't they? Or they change a barrel. Or nip outside for a smoke. But it needn't have been him. Maybe it was one of the five other guys. Maybe the married guy. There was also a guy named Ray who she was said to be keen on. What happened to that guy?"

Verreman flips through his notes, fast. "And—now, this is interesting—on the day of the murder, Lady Verreman and Sally have been in the house all day. Doing what? Not much, apparently. But around five o'clock, Lady Verreman starts cooking dinner, and all of a sudden, Sally remembers that she's got to post a letter. She's had all day to post it but suddenly decides she has to make the last post."

So what? Enygma thinks. People do irrational things all the time. A mark of an amateur detective is to want an answer for every small detail. To want to tie up every loose end. To ascribe meaning to everything. In life, human beings are not rational. We put off writing letters until the last minute. We don't pay bills on time, even when the money is sitting in the bank. We don't make important calls. Why? Who knows?

"Sally slips out of the house, taking me with her. The letter box is at the end of the road, and the letter already has a stamp on it. Antonia is expecting her back in five minutes. Ten, if she dawdles. But Sally is gone for forty-five minutes, and dinner goes cold. What was she doing all that time? Not posting a letter—that's for sure."

"And you don't—"

"I remember nothing. If she had done something remarkable, I might have remembered it. But from this distance, I can remember nothing. And there is nothing useful about it in here"—Verreman thumps the pile of paper—"which means that either nothing much happened, or something did happen but the police never asked about it, and I have now forgotten it. Do you know, it was ten days before they took a statement from me? That's rather a long time when you're eleven."

Enygma takes a deep breath. "OK." He waves away the letter, and the postbox and every other meaningless damn thing. "OK. If we are going to do this, let's not start with the fripperies. Let's start with the most damning piece of evidence against your father. Because if you can't explain that away, your whole case is done for. Sally Gardner could have posted a dozen letters, but it won't make a damn bit of difference if you can't explain that second piece of lead piping."

Verreman looks uncomfortable, but he reaches for the folder with *Murder Weapon* on the side. He is on the point of opening it when Enygma takes it from his hand. Enygma doesn't open it, however, but recites from memory, "There are two distinct lengths of lead piping in this case. Both pipes are wrapped in white Elastoplast-type sticking plaster with a yellow zigzag line running down the middle of it. The shorter piece of pipe is found in the hall of the house—the site of the attack on your mother—covered in blood and hair, while the longer piece is found in the boot of your father's borrowed car, clean of forensic matter. The police maintain, and it's hard to argue against, that those two pieces of pipe were owned by the same person. Right?"

"Well, yes." There is a long pause.

"The pipe in the hall contained blood from your mother and Sally Gardner, and hair from your mother. Just a coincidence, you think? You think, perhaps, that the real murderer just happened to choose as a weapon a lead pipe of the same diameter as one that just happened to be in the boot of your dad's car? And then he happened to wrap it in the exact same kind of plaster bandage, of the exact same color, with the exact same yellow stripe down the middle? Is that what you think?"

Enygma is pushing Verreman, he knows. He wants—he needs—to get past this cheery bonhomie that Verreman has been exhibiting all evening. He needs to know what kind of man Verreman is, how dangerous he is. But Verreman chews his lip, and says nothing.

Max Enygma flips open the file and begins to skim through Dr. Mackintosh's testimony at the inquest. "'. . . lead piping found at the scene . . . was stained with blood, and had several bloodstained hairs stuck to it . . . nine inches long . . . two pounds and three ounces . . . grossly distorted. Elastoplast . . . yellow stripe . . . bloodstained.

"'Blood on pipe type AB, may be a mix of groups A and B. Blood on hairs on pipe group A.

"'Hairs on pipe similar to Lady Verreman's. Seven microscopic blue-gray fibers on pipe . . . Origin unknown.'"

Enygma scans the document, and then reads, "'Another thirty-two fibers in car. Twenty-five in bloodstaining inside door. Remainder attached to clump of Lady Verreman's hair.'"

Enygma stops reading, and David Verreman flinches visibly. "You can't hide from this stuff. If you don't have an answer to this, then fucking about talking about letters and tablets and custody arrangements will get you nowhere. But if we can explain this away, then we have a chance."

"They weren't identical. The pipes. They tested the pipes and the Elastoplast, and they weren't identical."

Enygma smiles. It is not a kind smile. "And what does that prove?"

"Well, that the two pieces of pipe and the two strips of Elastoplast came from different places at different times. In which case, it might just be a coincidence."

"You think that the murderer just happened to choose a lead pipe of the same diameter and wrapped it in the same brand of plaster with which Lord Verreman habitually wrapped his own blunt instruments?"

"Well . . ."

"Do you know how many widths lead pipes come in?" says Enygma. "Do you even know the brand of Elastoplast that was used? They called it 'Elastoplast-type tape,' which could mean anything. If you don't know—and you *don't* know—then how can you know how likely this coincidence is?" He reads again from Dr. Mackintosh's statement. "'On the piping found at the house, the adhesive was spread over most of the back of the bandage, two to three millimeters from one edge and four to five millimeters from the other. On the pipe found in the car, the adhesive extended two to three millimeters to both edges. The width was approximately the same, but it is very difficult to take measurements from something that has been stretched.'"

He puts the report down. "Now, that one or two millimeters

might be a crucial piece of evidence, proving that the two pieces of Elastoplast-type bandage were completely unconnected with each other. Or it might not. We'd have to look at the Elastoplast-making process, wouldn't we? It might be completely normal for the width of the glue to deviate even within the same roll, or it may be a fixed width. Or maybe he just used up all the tape on one roll and started another for the next pipe. Who knows? Dr. Mackintosh was asked if the two pieces of fabric plaster had been woven from the same loom, and she said that she had not examined it 'in that degree of detail.'

"Same with the pipe. We know that the two ends of the pipe were not connected to each other, because they did not fit together, and at least one of them was not bought for the purpose of head bashing, because it had signs of use. But what does that prove?"

David Verreman stands up suddenly and walks to a corner of the room. From the way he keeps tilting and straightening his head, Max concludes that he is having a silent argument with his brother. Max isn't bothered. He figures that as long as the argument is silent, he doesn't need to worry. Eventually Verreman returns to the table. "The question is, why was your father carrying a lead pipe wrapped in plaster in the boot of his car?"

"Ah," says Verreman, "but it wasn't his car at all. It was a borrowed car!"

Enygma tries not to smile. "You are suggesting that his friend, er . . . '

"Edmund Crispin."

"You are suggesting that his friend Edmund Crispin was in the habit of fashioning coshes and leaving them in the car for his friends to find? I believe he denied ever seeing it."

"He might have forgotten it was there."

"Did he also forget giving a similar cosh to an acquaintance, who then went on to kill a woman and attempted to kill the wife of the man to whom he had loaned his car? That seems rather unlikely. Whatever we come up with to explain the presence of the second pipe, it cannot be a solution that relies upon extraordinary coincidence.

Don't you see? Coincidences happen every day, of course. But that is not good enough for us. We have to craft a *story*, the way that writers do, that is so plausible, and so *right*, that people will have to accept it. If we can find a story, a simple story, that fits the facts, then we might, possibly, be able to acquit your dad."

David Verreman's head tilts to the right again.

—And condemn our mother. Because if he is innocent, she is guilty. Of something, anyway.

"We'll cross that bridge when we come to it," says Enygma. And his comment tacitly admits Daniel Verreman into the conversation as an equal party. "But I have an idea, and it may not come to that."

THERE IS SILENCE for a while as Enygma continues to read. David Verreman, who knows these files by heart, flips aimlessly through them. Daniel Verreman is saying nothing, thank goodness.

Suddenly, and as though he has just thought of it, though Enygma has seen this speech on the tip of his tongue for a while, Verreman says, "There was a journalist who had a theory . . ."

"I have read that theory. It does not hold water." Enygma speaks not unkindly, but with the weary patience of a much-tried man. "Any theory that relies on a corrupt policeman planting evidence is a no go. It is a theory created in vacuo. There is not a shred of evidence to back it up. Pity, because the rest of their work was quite sound."

Verreman looks like a sulky child.

"There are questions to be asked about the lead pipe, but, I say again, convoluted theories of what *might* have happened will get us nowhere. There is very little to be gained from doubting the testimony of expert witnesses. They are rarely wrong. And Elizabeth Mackintosh was considered a world-class expert in her field. There is no mileage in trying to discredit her."

—You take her at her word? All the experts? Just like that?

"Not quite," says Enygma. "But an expert witness has very little cause to lie, certainly not in open court. An expert witness responds to the questions that they are asked, and they give their objective opinions, staking their professional reputation on the answer. They may be fallible, of course, but only on TV would they lie or fabricate evidence in order to aid the police. If you are thinking along those lines, forget it. But professional witnesses know the game. They answer all questions truthfully, but they only answer the questions that they are asked. What we need to discover are the questions that were not asked." Enygma slaps the folder in front of him. "That is what we must concentrate on. Which questions were not asked? Which evidence was not brought forward?"

—Which dog did not bark?

"Exactly!" says Enygma.

11

◆ ◆ ◆ ◆ ◆

THE BIG BOW MYSTERY

We cannot join in the praises that have been showered upon
the coroner's summing up.

—Israel Zangwill, The Big Bow Mystery

The curious incident of the dog in the nighttime.

The lowest trick in The Author's bag of low-down dirty tricks.

Another losing game.

What is wrong with this picture?

Every goddamned thing!

How can you guess what isn't there? How do you pick, from the millions of things that *could* be there, the one thing that *should* be there?

You can't. And The Author knows you can't.

They're just fucking with you now.

MAX ENYGMA FLIPS through the file quickly. He is not reading it. Rather, he is giving himself time to think. He is excited, but he is trying to tamp his excitement down, see the thing from all angles, because he does not know what repercussions his actions might have. His client is clearly eccentric. And he may also be dangerous. And insane.

Enygma stands up and begins to pace the room. "What is the purpose of an inquest?" he asks suddenly.

—To establish the cause of death.

"Correct, Daniel." Enygma continues to pace. "The primary purpose of an inquest is to establish cause of death. Also, of course, the identity of the deceased, though this is a formality, except in cases where the victim is unknown or where the injuries to, or the decomposition of, the body make identification difficult. That was not the case here. But, as the coroner stated in his opening remarks at the inquest, the coroner has broad latitude to conduct his case as he sees fit. In this case, a unique case, the coroner opted to run his inquest as a quasi criminal trial."

Max Enygma is getting into his stride now. He remembers several police-procedure lectures he gave with regard to his more famous cases. He had enjoyed them, and had had some idle daydreams about joining the lecture circuit after his retirement. If it hadn't been for Monty bloody Egg . . .

Enygma stops pacing, and comes back to the table abruptly. "There were lots of things wrong with the conduct of that inquest. And I do mean lots. But I'm afraid the forensic evidence is not one of them. No one, least of all a jury, likes to disbelieve world-renowned experts. We have to be able to trust someone, right?"

"The counsel for my father asked some questions that the witnesses were told not to answer," says David.

"I know. But I am sure that there were questions that the defense were reserving in case their client ever came to court. The questions the coroner denied were mostly with regard to your mother's testimony, and it is highly likely that she would have been barred from giving evidence at all in a criminal trial."

"Even about the attack on herself?"

"In a criminal case, the Crown would not have dared to put her on the stand. It would have given the defense almost certain grounds for appeal."

For the first time, David Verreman looks impressed. Enygma's confidence rises. He resumes pacing, and then stops in front of the picture of Antonia Verreman. Something about the eyes, maybe. Or the mouth. Yes, the mouth. Half-open, smiling, not quite laughing. Not yet. But the laugh was bubbling up her throat, and it was coming. Enygma reaches into his pocket and pulls out his wallet. In the place where his police ID used to be, there is a picture of his daughter, Amy. How old was she there? Twelve? Thirteen, perhaps. The same mouth. The same smile. He wonders who had made her smile like that. Not him, certainly. Amy has not smiled for her daddy since she was nine years old.

Enygma turns decisively away from Antonia Verreman and snaps his wallet shut.

He feels a little sick.

"Drink?" asks Verreman, holding up the brandy bottle.

"How about coffee?" says Max Enygma.

Enygma sits at the table while David Verreman goes to the basement to make coffee, and he resists the impulse to pull the wallet out of his pocket again. He turns his chair a little, so that the picture of Lady Verreman is out of his sight line, and he picks up the file again, determined to read until Verreman returns.

His thoughts interrupt him.

He thinks of Egg. Is all this just Egg fucking with him again? No. Mustn't think like that. Though it is entirely Egg's style. He would find this evening very amusing.

But Egg couldn't have got into this business—whatever this is.

Verreman returns and pours coffee from a cafetière. His head is tilted to one side, as if he is listening. As if his brother is whispering in his ear.

Talking to yourself—that is one thing. But answering yourself—well, that is a whole new level of crazy. Max Enygma knows crazy. And if Verreman is crazy, and his behavior certainly suggests that he is, he would be putty in the hands of a man as smart as Monty Egg.

Damn it, thinks Enygma. *Won't I ever be free of that goddamned Egg?*

David Verreman, who has been in silent confab with his brother in a corner of the room, suddenly says, "All right!" and joins Enygma at the table.

"So," says Verreman, "are we just going to read this stuff and make notes? Like, all night?" Verreman's tone is petulant, masquerading as unenthusiastic.

"Do you know all this stuff backward?"

"Backward. Forward. Inside out."

Enygma closes his eyes for a moment, then opens the file at a random page. "What time was it when Sally Gardner put her head round your mother's door and offered to make her a cup of tea?"

David Verreman smiles. "My mother claimed that it was eight fifty-five p.m., a few minutes before the news began. In my statement it was a little earlier, around eight forty p.m., after my program ended."

"Hmm," says Enygma.

"My mother claimed in newspaper interviews that she had been watching *Mastermind*. That was a taradiddle. She had been watching *The Six Million Dollar Man*. But both programs finished at the same time, so it doesn't really matter."

—Except to Mother.

"Except to Mother! She didn't want people to think she watched trashy TV. The news, *Mastermind* and nature documentaries only."

—Yeah, right, Mom!

"OK," says Enygma, "how about this? I will interview each witness through you. That is, I will allow you to speak for each witness."

Verreman begins to bounce a little on his chair, in excitement.

"But," says Enygma, "only one witness at a time, please. Can you do that?"

"You bet," says David.

—Probably.

Enygma is doubtful, but he suspects that David Verreman has managed to contain his evident mental illness by compartmentalizing his differing personalities into witnesses to his family tragedy. David was, after all, in the house on the night of the attack, after which his father was never seen again and his mother was dragged through the courts. That would be enough to drive anyone a little insane. Enygma looks his client over carefully. His mother was accused of being paranoid, of suffering delusions. Was it hereditary?

Enygma must tread carefully. Three days in the British Library have left him tolerably acquainted with the facts of the case. He must check any testimony Verreman gives against the known facts. He can always strike it out later.

He drums his fingers on the table. "OK. Here's what I'm going to do. I am going to interview one witness at a time. No interruptions. You have managed to get the original police statements from each witness, as well as the publicly available record of the inquest. I won't ask how you came by the police records."

Daniel Verreman gives a tilt of the head, and a small smile.

"If you don't know the answer," says Enygma, "just say so. Educated guesses are fine. Wild guesses are also fine. But if you are guessing, I need to know that. I will be the person who decides what weight to give those guesses. Understood?"

David Verreman nods his head.

"Daniel?" asks Enygma.

—Understood.

"Good. Now, David, I would like to start with your account of the night of the murder. I realize that you were young at the time."

—We were!

"I am asking David only at the moment. I will come to you next. OK, Daniel?"

—Fine!

"Good. Now, David *only*, I want you to tell me, in your own words, what you actually remember of that night. Only what you *remember*. Not what you were told, or what you read afterward. Only what you yourself remember."

For the first time since Enygma met him, David Verreman seems uncertain. He opens his mouth and closes it again. Eventually, he says, "I remember watching TV on my mother's bed. They came in together, and my mother told me to go to bed. She had blood on her pullover."

"Your mother and father, you mean? After the attack had taken place?"

"Yes."

"Was it on her face, too? Her head?"

"In her hair. Not on her face. She probably washed it off when she went to the cloakroom for a drink."

"Maybe. Now, what about your father? Only what you remember."

David Verreman looks a little deflated. "I don't remember anything about him. He was there. I remember that. I think I was surprised to see him there, but maybe I wasn't. He did come to the house sometimes. Was I surprised to see them together and not yelling? Maybe that was it."

"Good. Thank you. And, Daniel, what do you remember from that night?"

—Nothing. I was asleep upstairs. I didn't know a thing about it till later.

"Thank you."

Enygma makes careful notes, mostly to give himself time to think. He wonders when Daniel first arrived. After the murder? Or earlier? After the separation? Or before it, when Mummy and Daddy were arguing all the time? A hell of a childhood either way.

"Now, David, you made a statement to the police ten days after the incident. Why was that?"

"We were at my aunt's house while my mother was in hospital. There were press camped outside the house all the time. So when Mother was released from hospital, she went straight to a secret location—actually a rented house in Cornwall—and we were taken to meet her there. Tearful reunion, et cetera, et cetera. That's when the police came to take statements."

"I see. Now, your statement was read out at the coroner's inquest as if you had written it yourself, but in fact you would have been asked a series of questions and then asked to sign what was written up. Do you remember doing that?"

"More or less. I mean, I remember answering questions. I don't necessarily remember signing anything."

"Good. Now, Daniel," Enygma asks, for form's sake, "can you tell me if you were asked to give a statement?"

David Verreman is pleased that Daniel has been asked.

—They decided not to take one, since I had been asleep when it happened.

Enygma nods as if that is proper police procedure when dealing with imaginary siblings, and again he writes in his notebook. Then he flips open the file and extracts David's statement.

"You talk about how you spent the day. You didn't go to school that day. Why was that?"

"My mother said it was because the school bus didn't turn up. That might have been true. But I missed school quite often, because my mother did not like to get up in the morning."

"But you had a nanny to get you up."

"Quite often my mother liked us to stay at home with her. She didn't like being left alone."

"Wouldn't she have had the nanny for company?"

"My mother, despite what she may have said later, did not keep company with 'the help.' She would have considered that beneath her."

"I see. So, what did you do that day?"

"Nothing. Watched TV, mostly, I think, while she slept. She rarely got up before lunchtime."

"You say that you *think*. Is that a guess?"

"Yes."

"OK. That's fine, as long as I know. Now I'm going to read you a part of your statement that was read at the coroner's inquest. You said, 'I went downstairs again to Mummy's room. That would have been about eight forty p.m. I asked Mummy where Sally was, and she said she was downstairs, making some tea. I didn't see her go downstairs, so I don't know if she took any empty cups with her. I didn't notice whether or not there were any empty cups in the room.' Is that correct?"

David Verreman considers for a moment. He likes this line of questioning, and he makes an effort to be meticulous. "Well, it's correct that I said it. And it's correct that that is what I thought. But I don't know if it really was eight forty p.m. I was eleven. Eleven-year-olds are not clock-watchers. And I'm pretty sure I never called her 'Mummy.'"

"Excellent," Enygma says, making a note. "Now, according to your statement, you went downstairs after your program finished, and no doubt the police checked on that and fixed the time from that. Do you remember what you watched?"

"Top of the Pops."

"And Sally Gardner was already downstairs when you reached your mother's room?"

"Yes. Well," Verreman says quickly, looking at Enygma, "that is what I said at the time. I can't honestly remember now."

Enygma nods. "Now, according to your mother's statement, Mrs. Gardner did not offer to make tea until just before the news, around eight fifty-five p.m., which gives us a fifteen-minute discrepancy. That may be important, or it may not matter at all. You might have taken longer to get from your room to hers than you remembered. You said you went 'downstairs' to your mother's room. How was that?"

"It's a big house."

—Let's have a tour!

Max Enygma is irritated by the interruption but agrees anyway. He wants to get a mental picture of the scene, but he also wants to get up out of his chair and away from the picture of Lady Antonia, which is beginning to unsettle him. "All right. Why not? I'd like to see the upper floors."

The stairs are wide on the ground floor but become progressively narrower the higher they climb. Enygma is surprised at how much house there is. They climb past the mezzanine, David leading the way, and he points out his father's study as they head back up to the drawing room on the first floor. Still empty. They move up past the second mezzanine. This one, David says, "is Daddy's dressing room." Max Enygma considers his cramped flat and wonders what he would do with a dressing room. Not dress in it—that's for sure. On the next floor they reach Lady Verreman's bedroom, with private bathroom.

Enygma walks slowly round the bedroom, and into the bathroom beyond. He turns on the taps. He might be checking whether a woman's shoeless feet could be heard running down the stairs over the noise of the taps, but actually he is trying to catch his breath. The stairs are steep, and he is getting old.

He comes back into the bedroom. The room is carpeted, and a dark rectangle shows plainly where the bed once stood. Enygma is aware of David Verreman looking at him. "So," he says, "your nanny had gone downstairs, and you and your mother were lying on the bed here, and watching the news together." He points to the rectangle of dark carpet, and then to the opposite side of the room, where a television must have been placed.

"Yes."

"What time was it when your mother decided to check on Mrs. Gardner and the tea?"

"I'm not sure."

"In your statement, you said it was before the nine o'clock news."

"Yes."

"Do you still think that?"

"I guess so. I think I remember her being gone when it started. But how can I really be sure? I mean, I was sure then. That's all I know."

"Good. Very good."

—Is it?

Enygma has recovered his breath now and is ready to move on, but he says, "After traumatic incidents people think that they will never forget what happened. But memory is not a permanent thing. It shifts over time, like sand in the desert. At times it covers things up,

140

and at other times it can uncover things. But sometimes people re-
hearse their version of what happened, a rote version, so that they are
not really remembering the incident anymore. They are just repeating
the lines they have drilled into themselves. That's not to say they are
lying, necessarily. It's just that they're not *remembering*. What we
need to try to do is remember it as it happened, and not our account
of it, or to say we don't remember at all."

They climb up toward the third floor. "I take it these are the other
bedrooms?"

"No," says Verreman. "This is the nursery. Playroom, basically—
because the upper classes don't let their kids play just anywhere. It
was well stocked. Toys, books. Lots of books, I remember. A table
and chairs over there," he says, pointing to one corner of the empty
room. "A couple of old armchairs over there"—he points to the other
side—"for reading or whatever. Everything you could need."

"Till dinnertime, anyway."

"Even then. There was a small cooker in this corner, and whichever nanny was stuck up here with us could make egg on toast and hot
milk, or whatever we wanted. Some days we never went downstairs at
all." Verreman opens a cupboard door, perhaps expecting to find
nursery tea things, but the cupboard, like the rest of the house, is
empty. "The bedrooms are upstairs."

The staircase is very narrow here, and Verreman and Enygma
climb the steep stairs to the top floor, where there are four smallish
bedrooms. "The nanny slept in that one," David says, pointing to the
bedroom nearest the stairs. "This one was mine. That was where the
police found me when they finally searched the house."

Max Enygma expects an interruption from Daniel Verreman, but
it doesn't come. Daniel lays no claim to a room of his own, because
Daniel has never left his brother's side. They climb back down the
stairs until they are standing in the hall.

Enygma looks along the length of the hall. At one end is the front
door, and at the other the cloakroom, with doors leading to the dining room and the basement. The space is empty except for a small

console table with a pair of handcuffs on it. Halfway between the front door and the cloakroom is the door to the basement. He flicks on the light switch for the basement and walks down the stairs, stepping carefully over the dark stain in the wooden floor at the bottom, where Sally Gardner's blood had seeped beneath the varnish, marking the scene of the crime as surely as any scene-of-crime officer could, and more permanently.

The basement is still furnished, and looks as though it were used yesterday, assuming yesterday was 1974.

OBLIGATORY MAP OF THE CRIME SCENE

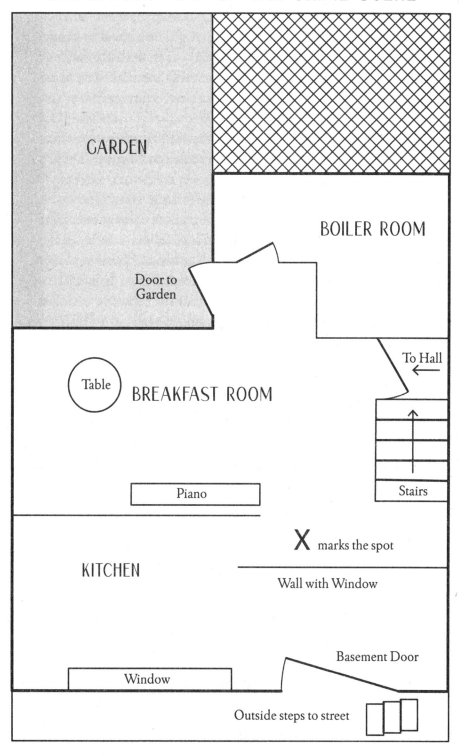

GARDEN

BOILER ROOM

Door to
Garden

Table

BREAKFAST ROOM

To Hall

Piano

Stairs

X marks the spot

KITCHEN

Wall with Window

Basement Door

Window

Outside steps to street

At the bottom of the basement steps is an upright piano. Enygma wonders how it was brought down here. Not from the hall, certainly. The turn at the top of the stairs is too tight. From the basement door to the street, then. Enygma pictures removal men struggling down the steep steps with the piano. He hopes the Verremans tipped well, but somehow he doubts they did.

Enygma lifts the lid of the piano and runs his fingers over the keys lightly. It is a good piano, though badly in want of tuning. "Do you still play?" he asks.

David Verreman shakes his head. "Not since . . ."

Verreman's voice trails away, and Enygma wonders how much of Verreman's life changed after the seventh of November 1974, and he hazards a guess that it was all of it. Poor bastard.

Enygma closes the piano lid and moves away from it quickly. He walks toward the kitchen and looks out of the window at the narrow front yard, with rubbish bins and a rusting bicycle with a buckled back wheel, and at the view of passing feet on the pavement above and in front of the house.

"My grandmother, God bless her," says Verreman, pointing toward the street, "tried to suggest to the police that my father spotted an altercation in the basement as he just happened to be passing along the road. Nonsense, of course."

"The police proved he wouldn't have been able to see anything from the street?"

"Absolutely proved it. Anyone who just glanced this way could have seen nothing at all. Even if the light was on. Which it wasn't, because it had been removed bodily, as they say, from the light fitting. Luckily, Margaret Howard-Cole said plainly that my father was in the habit of coming down the steps to spy on us."

Enygma goes back to the bottom of the basement stairs and looks at the bulb at the top of the flight. Unlike the ceiling in the basement proper, this ceiling is relatively low. A tall man could easily have removed the bulb—as, too, of course, could a small woman standing on a chair. But why would he?

"The body was found where?" Enygma says, although he already knows.

"Near the piano. Resting against this half wall. The police presumed the killer was going to come back for it."

"Seems a reasonable presumption," Enygma says. "You don't go to the trouble of stuffing a body into a sack unless you intend to take it with you when you leave."

"Exactly."

"So why didn't he?"

"Well, because he didn't have time, I suppose."

—Because Mother escaped!

Enygma takes another walk around the basement, steps briefly out into the garden, where he notes the high walls covered in ivy. Exit unlikely through the rear. He returns to the bottom of the stairs and looks again at the dark stain underneath the varnish of the wooden floor. "The killer," he says, "repeatedly hit Sally Gardner over the head with a blunt instrument of the same approximate length and diameter as the lead pipe found in the hall. There were four splits in her scalp above the right ear, and two further splits at the back of her head. There were also bruises on both shoulders, which indicates that Mrs. Gardner was moving during most, or at least part, of the attack. Agreed?"

Enygma shoots the last word at David Verreman, who looks startled for a moment, but then replies in the confident tones of Professor Cameron McCabe, pathologist. "Agreed. There were also four in-line bruises on her upper right arm, consistent with someone grabbing her tightly by the arm, and bruising around the right eye and the right side of her mouth. These, however, were more likely to have been made with a fist than with a blunt instrument. And there were a few superficial bruises on the back of her hand."

"Defensive injuries?"

"Very possibly."

Enygma leads the way back up to the hall, stopping at the top of the basement steps to look down the stairs. The light illuminates the bloody stain on the parquet floor like a spotlight. Enygma looks at it for a few seconds before stepping out into the hall and saying briskly, "Site of the second attack. Your mother stated that she arrived downstairs at around . . ."

Enygma again looks to Verreman, who says, "About quarter past nine according to Lady Verreman, and just before the nine o'clock news according to the son."

For a moment Enygma considers which part Verreman is playing, spots him fiddling with his Scotland Yard tiepin and concludes it is DCI Blake.

Good.

"Talk me through it, Chief Inspector," Enygma says.

DCI Nicholas Blake does not need to be asked twice.

"Sometime between eight fifty-five and nine fifteen p.m., Lady Verreman makes her way downstairs to find out what happened to her cup of tea. There is a discrepancy between the statements of her ladyship and the child, but the discrepancy does not make much difference so far as we are concerned. There is nothing crucial about the timings with regard to an alibi or anything like that, so it's much of a muchness, if you get me. My personal opinion is, David Verreman was mistaken about the times, which is only natural in a child. They're not always a-watching of the clock, now, are they? 'Twouldn't be right if they were.

"So, Lady V makes her way downstairs. She can see from the hall that the basement is in darkness. She doesn't need to go down there to know that the nanny isn't there. Stands to reason the nanny would have switched the light on if she was able to, since she was wearing high-heeled shoes and carrying a tray loaded with cups and saucers."

"Did the light work?"

"Yes, sir, it did, because the boys that first answered the call checked it, which, strictly speaking, they shouldn't have done, since it wiped out any fingerprints that might have been on there. Not that it matters, for we know the villain wore gloves."

"Do we?" asks Enygma, sharply, striding again to the top of the basement steps and flicking the light on and off.

Blake accepts the rebuke stolidly. "I beg your pardon. We found no fingerprints at the crime scene, neither on the lightbulb nor the weapon. Nor on the body, nor the canvas mailbag it sat in. And Lady Verreman *alleged* that the man who attacked her was wearing leather gloves. How's that?"

"Thank you. Very good. Now, what about the other basement lights—the ones in the kitchen and so forth? Were they present and working?"

"They were."

"And what about the light in the hall—was that present, or had that been removed, too?"

"That bulb was present, sir. In fact, all the other bulbs in the house were in their sockets, though not all of them worked. The light in the hall did not work, the one in the cloakroom did not and neither did a fair few of the lights in the stairways on the upper floors."

"Not very health-and-safety conscious."

"No, sir. Her ladyship said that the family had got used to the dark. Lady Verreman was rather a petite lady, five foot two, I believe, and these old Georgian houses have high ceilings. Apparently she used to wait until nearly all the lights had gone before she got someone in to change them. There is a streetlamp outside, so it's not completely black here."

"Hmm. But the basement would have been very dark indeed without the light, wouldn't it? Would anyone really have ventured down there in the dark? Light from the street couldn't penetrate there."

"Well, no, sir, ordinarily that's true. A very dark place indeed. Except, of course, for the red light."

"What red light?" Enygma is counting steps along the length of hall—from the top of the basement steps to the front door, from the basement steps to the cloakroom, from the cloakroom to the front door—and DCI Blake is matching him step for step. But Enygma stops now, and says again, "What red light, Chief Inspector?"

"Ah! Well, now, the Verremans had an electric kettle. But it had a fault. Usually, the light on a kettle goes on when it is boiled, and goes off automatically when it reaches boiling point, but the Verremans' kettle was the opposite way round. The light was on all the time, unless it was switched on; then it went out. But it might have given enough light to show Sally the way. But also, when Lady Verreman looked down into the blackness and saw the faint red glow of the light, she would have known that Sally Gardner couldn't be down there making tea, because the red light showed her that the kettle was not switched on."

Enygma hastens back into the dining room, grabs his notebook and begins to scribble his findings in it quickly. David Verreman / DCI Nicholas Blake waits patiently for him to finish. When he has finished, Enygma flicks his pen against the notepad, and considers. "The first attack takes place in the basement. There is no question about that."

"Agreed."

"According to Lady Verreman's testimony, she came downstairs, went to the top of the basement steps and saw it was dark. Did she attempt to turn on the light?"

"She can't remember, but she thinks not. The fact that it was dark was enough."

"OK. Then what?"

"She calls out the nanny's name, and she hears a noise behind her."

"Coming from the cloakroom?"

"Yes."

"Which means," Enygma says, flicking at the notepad, "either she was still facing the basement, and was calling down to the basement, or she was facing the front door." Enygma walks back into the hall, this time taking his notebook with him. "Here's my problem. A murderer—let's not give him a name at the moment—has killed someone in the basement and stuffed the body in a canvas sack—a sack that, by the way, he has brought with him either for this purpose or for another. Why does he go upstairs, into the hall? And why does he turn right, toward the cloakroom, from which there is no escape, when he could have turned left, toward the front door? What was he doing in the cloakroom?"

"Well . . ."

GROUND FLOOR

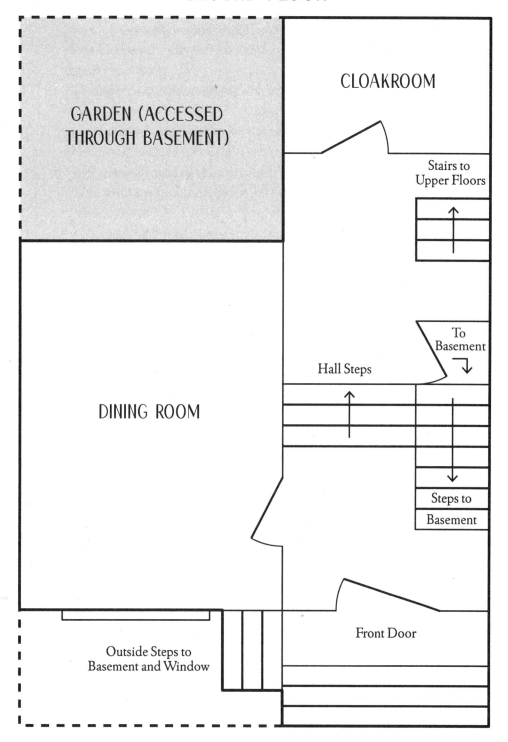

GARDEN (ACCESSED THROUGH BASEMENT)

CLOAKROOM

Stairs to Upper Floors

To Basement

Hall Steps

DINING ROOM

Steps to Basement

Outside Steps to Basement and Window

Front Door

"I make it about ten paces from the basement steps to the cloak-room, and fifteen to the front door. How about you?"

They run the experiment together several more times and agree that, roughly, the estimates are about right. "At any rate," says Blake, "the front door is half as much again in distance from the basement door as the cloakroom is."

"Yes, but the front door leads to freedom, and the cloakroom leads nowhere at all."

"Our theory," Blake says, "is that Verreman heard his wife coming down the stairs, looking for the nanny, and he went through the closest door and just hid."

"That's a very good theory, and the one I would have chosen. So my next question is, why didn't he stay hidden? Lady Verreman has come downstairs looking for her cup of tea. She does not suspect foul play. She looks down into the basement. All dark. She calls out for the nanny. No response. What was her next step?"

"She heard a sound behind her, and was attacked."

"Yes, but suppose she hadn't. After all, the attacker's first instinct was to hide. What if he had carried on hiding?"

"Ah, I see. Well, she might have tried the cloakroom door next."

"She might, of course, but wouldn't there be a chance, at any rate, that she would go down into the basement to investigate whether the nanny had tripped in the dark, or perhaps go upstairs again to see if the nanny had gone back to the nursery for some reason and forgotten about the tea? Had she done either of those things, the attacker could have seized their chance and run straight for the front door and out into the street, couldn't they?"

"There was still the body in the basement. They couldn't very well leave that."

"Couldn't they? Assuming no one had identified the killer, was there any physical evidence that could have laid the crime at anyone's feet?"

"There was the second piece of lead piping."

"Which you would never have found had Lady Verreman not

given you cause for a search warrant. No. If the killer, whoever he was, had remained in the cloakroom, and if Lady Verreman had gone, as I believe she would, down into the basement to check on her employee's welfare, then the killer could have strolled out the front door and been away scot-free."

DCI Blake will do no more than concede that the theory is "possible," but, in any case, it does not tally with the known facts, which are that the killer did, for some reason, leave the cloakroom and attack Lady Verreman. "The physical evidence is clear. She was attacked by someone standing with their back to the cloakroom, as though they had just left it. There was blood on the cloakroom ceiling and lightshade, which had been thrown off the weapon as the attacker swung it back to strike again, which shows that the cloakroom door was open—again, as though someone had just left it."

Enygma stands in the doorway of the small cloakroom, which contains only a toilet and a sink, with a mirror fixed to the wall above the sink. He looks at the ceiling and the light; no traces of the blood remain.

"There was blood on the ceiling, walls and door," he agrees, "thrown off the weapon as he swung it. Lady Verreman's blood. There was hair in the sink. Lady Verreman's hair. There was blood on the hair in the sink. Not Lady Verreman's blood. Group AB. Either both women's blood or neither woman's blood. Something wrong with that."

"What's wrong with it?" says DCI Blake.

Enygma turns on the single tap, for no good reason. The tap is labeled H, but the water that runs from it is cold, and tinged with a copper hue. No one has run the tap for a long time. "I don't know. I don't know what's wrong with it, but something is."

He returns to the dining room, pulls Dr. Mackintosh's report toward him and reads for a long time. Then he shakes his head and writes, "Ground floor cloakroom—query blood," in his notebook and moves on.

"OK. Now the nanny has been attacked and killed, and the wife has been attacked but not killed. What happens next?"

"Well," says Blake, "they're both exhausted from the fight. And Lady V and Verreman sit on the steps and talk for a bit."

"But why? If he has come to the house with the intention of killing his wife, why doesn't he? I take your point that he's exhausted, but he sat with his wife on the steps in the hall for up to an hour if we take the child's timings, and at least twenty to thirty minutes if we don't. Why, after that time, and knowing that he has left one body in the basement, does he let the only witness to the crime escape, especially if that witness was the intended victim in the first place? Why does he go upstairs with his wife, to a place where he knows his child is awake?"

"Maybe he didn't know. It was past the kid's bedtime, after all."

—Excuse me! I am here, you know.

"If *both* the children were asleep in their beds," says Enygma, a little hurriedly, "taking his wife upstairs was a risk. It was much more likely that the children would wake if he attacked her in the bedroom than if he did it three floors below. Come to that, he could have taken her down to the basement and left both bodies down there."

"We considered that by that time he might not have been thinking too clearly. It must have been quite a shock when he discovered he had killed the wrong woman."

"Quite. I wonder when he made that discovery."

12

◆ ◆ ◆ ◆ ◆

A LOSING GAME

The detection of crime in London now resembles a game of blind man's buff, in which the detective has his hands tied and his eyes bandaged. Thus is he turned loose to hunt the murderer through the slums of a great city.

—Marie Belloc Lowndes, *The Lodger*

Let's Play a Game!

You'll like this one. This game is called "Squeak, Piggy, Squeak." It's best played with a large group of friends, but if you have only a few friends, they will have to suffice.

If you don't have any friends, acquaintances will do.

If you were ever invited to parties as a child, you may have played this game.

Player One (that's you) is chosen to be "the farmer," and all the others are "little piggies." The traditional version involves sitting on your victim to make them squeal. In our version, however, the farmer carries a rolled-up newspaper, which I invite you to imagine is a length of lead piping.

The farmer is blindfolded and spun round three times. Then he has to find the piggies! When he finds one, he bops them over the head with the newspaper while shouting, "Squeak, piggy, squeak!" and when they cry out, which they definitely will if you hit them hard enough, the farmer must guess the identity of the piggy from the sound of their squeak, or lose a life.

How many times do you think you will have to hit them over the head before you guess who they are?

BACK IN THE dining room, Enygma says, "Are you married, Chief Inspector?"

David Verreman looks surprised, blinks and considers for a moment. And DCI Blake replies, "I am, although my wife claims I am more wedded to the job."

Enygma nods in understanding. "I was married. Once. But, like you, I was more in love with the job, and in the end, she left me."

Blake makes a vaguely sympathetic grunt, unsure where this conversation is going, but fairly sure he doesn't want to go there.

"I have a daughter, too. Twelve the last time I saw her, but she's grown up now, of course."

Blake grunts again, and to his embarrassment, Max Enygma brings out his wallet, pulls out a picture of a laughing girl and passes it across to him for comment. "Very nice," Blake says, passing it back as soon as is decent.

Enygma studies it, glances at the picture of Lady Verreman, then puts the picture back in his wallet. "My wife was quite a small woman. Petite, they call it."

Blake flinches involuntarily at the mention of a wife, but relaxes again when Enygma returns the wallet to his pocket.

"My point being that the two of them, my wife and my daughter, weighed near enough the same. But I could always tell which one of them was walking up the stairs, just from the tread of their feet. Do you know what I mean?"

"Oh yes, sir," says Blake, smiling suddenly. "I can quite often tell who is coming up the stairs at work, and there are a hundred fellas that work there. I'm not saying that I can tell every one, not to swear to, but a fair few of them I would comfortably bet my pension on."

"Exactly. So why do you think John Verreman didn't know that the nanny was not his wife until it was too late? Because that is the police's theory, is it not? Verreman waits in the dark for his wife, hears someone coming down the stairs, hits out—bam, bam and a few more bams—and only then realizes he has got the wrong woman. Why didn't he know sooner?"

"Ah, that's a good point, but the way I figure it is like this. He is waiting downstairs in the dark. He is nervous—after all, he is not a hardened criminal. He hasn't made a habit of lamping women over the head. So, he is nervous, sweating a bit, and he hears someone coming down the stairs. The adrenaline starts pumping through him something fierce, until he can't hardly hear the footsteps at all, let alone differentiate them, so to speak. All he can hear is the blood pounding in his ears. His hands are sweaty with fear. His mouth is dry. He vaguely sees the outline of a woman of approximately the right height through the red gleam of the light from the kettle, and, in his panic, he just lets fly at her."

"Hmm. That's possible. Plausible, even. But at what point did he realize he had got the wrong woman? And when he did realize, why in God's name did he not stop? The girl did not die immediately. She must have cried out. Why didn't he stop then?"

"Well, sir, he couldn't stop, could he? He had murderously attacked her. He couldn't leave no witnesses."

Max Enygma gives a small smile. "And yet, he let his wife live."

DCI Blake returns his smile with a grin. "Did he, sir? I don't think that was the intent. I think he was exhausted, mentally and physically, and, seeing as how his wife wasn't giving him any trouble at that time, he decided to try a different way. Lady Verreman was not, er, a well lady, and as such, she had certain, ah, medications in her bedroom. I believe—and, mind you, so did she—that he had reconsidered the violent-death angle, and thought that if he could get her upstairs and persuade her to take even a few tablets, then he might be able to force more on her when they began to take effect and she was no longer quite . . ."

"Sane?"

"Aware. When she was no longer aware. Lull her into a false sense of security. He could mix some in a drink or food, or just tell her she had forgotten to take her pills, and give them to her again. Easy. Then think how it might have looked the next morning, with a dead woman in the basement and a blood-soaked woman dead in her bed from an overdose. That, I think, was the plan, to the extent that this poor bugger had a plan at all."

"Possibly. Possibly. But I'm not convinced. Let's say Verreman is hiding in the dark, waiting for his wife. He hears someone coming, panics and belts her a couple of times before realizing he got the wrong woman. Why not leave then? Why finish her off and waste time shoving the body in a sack? Why not just run away? Even if she survived, it was dark, and, as per your theory, she was attacked from behind. What could she testify to? Nothing."

"Hmm," says DCI Blake.

The two men sit in silence for a while, Enygma reading the crime-scene report again, cross-checking one report against another, under-lining some sections in pencil and adding a note or two to his notebook here and there.

"Who is Ray?" Enygma asks, holding up a witness statement, but DCI Blake has disappeared. David Verreman is bored, and has gone to look out of the window at the dark street. He holds a whispered conversation with someone—Daniel, Enygma assumes.

Enygma shrugs and carries on reading.

When he slams the folder on the table, David jumps.

"Tell me about the sack, Chief Inspector."

DCI Blake turns away from the window. "The sack?"

"The one containing the body. It was not from the house, I think you said?"

Blake stands on the balls of his feet and lifts his heels up and down as he considers. *He needs only to swing his truncheon,* Enygma thinks, *to complete this impression of a flat-footed beat copper.*

"That's right. Neither Lady Verreman nor the children had seen the sack before. We looked into it, of course."

"Did you?"

"Well," Blake says, looking a little defensive, "it was an American mailbag. The sort of thing they used to carry airmail on planes, and so forth. It was not your average English postman's bag, but still not that uncommon."

"Really?"

"Well, it's the sort of thing that people hang on to if they come across one. They are made of strong canvas, and people use them for storing camping equipment, and so on."

"You didn't manage to trace this particular sack?"

"Well, no, but, really, it didn't matter. There were no identifying marks, apart from 'US Mail' stamped on the bottom. There were no fingerprints. What could it tell us?"

"None of Verreman's acquaintances recognized it?"

"Those bastards? They wouldn't tell us if they had."

"And none of Mrs. Gardner's boyfriends had connections with the US Postal Service? Or their carriers?"

"Well, no. None that we are aware of."

"You checked? You checked the backgrounds of all her boyfriends carefully?"

DCI Blake bristles. "We checked their identities and their alibis as a matter of routine."

"But not their backgrounds?"

"I am sure that my officers followed all the usual protocols."

Blake sounds defensive, so Enygma decides to move on. "How was it fastened?"

"There were strong metal eyelets in the top of the bag. The original cord was missing, but strong window-sash cord had been threaded through the eyelets."

"Was the bag closed when your men found it?"

"Pulled together a little, but not tied."

"Was there an arm hanging out of the bag? I have read conflicting reports about that."

"Not when it was first discovered. The officer who broke into the house, Sergeant George Heyer, took it out of the sack to check whether life was extinct, and it remained like that. When the doctor arrived, the arm was out of the sack."

"I see." In his notebook Enygma makes a mark against the correct version of events. "Go on."

"Go on, what?" says Blake.

Enygma lifts an eyebrow, surprised at the testiness in David Verreman's voice, and wonders whether it is due to DCI Blake's discomfort at this line of questioning, or because Verreman is feeling trapped inside the Blake persona. *How long*, Enygma wonders, *can David Verreman sustain a character before he needs to become himself again?* The image of a whale flits across his brain—a whale that must now and then break the surface of the water to take a breath of air.

"Never mind. We'll come back to that. I would like, if I could, to ask David Verreman if he recalls ever seeing the sack."

David Verreman comes back with a roll of the head and a beaming smile. "Excellent, Mr. Enygma. You are doing so well. What was it you wanted to ask?"

"The mail sack that was used in the murder—do you remember seeing it prior to that night?"

"No, but I cannot claim perfect recall, you know."

"It wasn't used to store camping equipment, or perhaps used as a toy bag or laundry bag, as far as you know?"

"I don't think so. I think someone might have noticed it. I mean, the people who came into the house—the nannies, doctors, visitors—would have noticed it if it had been in the house long. But then, if it had been kept in the attic or the cellar or something, perhaps they would not have. I couldn't really say, I'm afraid."

"And, er, what about Daniel?"

Verreman's head tilts to the right, and Daniel answers. It is clear that he is pleased to be consulted, and he takes time to consider.

—Very wise of you, Mr. Enygma, to ask me. I'm the one who knows all the hidey-holes around this house. I have lurked in the attic and the cellar when I have been banished from my brother's company. I'm afraid, though, that I never saw the mailbag before that night. And I would have seen it, I think, if it had been here.

"Thank you, Daniel," says Enygma. "Would you or your brother like a rest before I call my next witness?"

"Not at all," replies David Verreman. "We are ready when you are. Who do you want to call?"

"Hmm." Enygma is looking at the mailbag. "I think perhaps I'd like to speak to Dr. Mackintosh, but only if you—er, she is fit to carry on."

Dr. Elizabeth Mackintosh, world-famous blood specialist, has already materialized before Max Enygma's eyes, and she pulls out a pince-nez from David Verreman's pocket and holds it in her hand, ready to examine bloodstains.

"Good evening, Dr. Mackintosh," says Enygma, though he has no idea of the time, and suspects the night is well advanced.

"Good evening, Mr. Enygma."

"What can you tell me about the mail sack?"

"Nothing at all about its origins or manufacture, I'm afraid. I did examine the sack for bloodstains."

"All right. Tell me about those."

"The mailbag in which the body was found was heavily and extensively bloodstained. I selected six areas of the bag to test. Four areas gave reactions to group B blood, Sally Gardner's blood type. But the remaining two areas gave reactions to group B blood and group A blood."

"Group A was Lady Verreman's blood type?"

"Yes, it was."

"To be clear, are you saying that you were able to separate out these two blood types and identify them separately, or did these areas give a reaction to group AB, as on"—Enygma rifles through his notebook—"the tufts of hair found in the cloakroom sink, and in the car?"

"And on the envelope. Group AB blood was also found on the envelope sent from Lord Verreman to Sir Henry Wade. No. Those were very small samples indeed. The samples taken from the mail-bag were very much larger—the mailbag was saturated with blood—and we were able to separate out the samples into group A and group B."

"With regard to those samples that returned the group AB result from the other items, would you say it was more likely that those samples came from a person with group AB blood, or from group A blood and group B blood—Lady Verreman and Mrs. Gardner, respectively—mixed together?"

Dr. Mackintosh brings the pince-nez halfway to her eyes, as though to peer at the samples, then lets it fall. "It's impossible to say conclusively, you understand, but group AB is a very rare blood group. Less than four percent of the population have that type of blood. Group A is very common, and group B less so—about ten per-cent of people are group B. I don't like to deal in likelihoods. As a scientist, I prefer facts. But I can say, all of the samples that returned group AB results were very small, and identifying and separating very small samples into two different blood groups is all but impos-sible."

"Would you say that it is more likely that a person of blood group A and another of group B bled together in the same place, or that a third person, of the group AB, joined the party to make a trio of bleeders?"

"I'm afraid I decline to speculate on that. All I can say is that, in such small samples, it would be perfectly possible for a mixture of group A blood and group B blood to return a result of group AB. Equally, it is possible that a third person, of group AB, left those stains. I can only give you the results. The deductions are up to you, I'm afraid."

"Hmm," says Enygma. "But, going back to the mail sack, the blood that was discovered in the two areas where you found both blood types—that was definitely from two different people matching the blood groups of Sally Gardner and Antonia Verreman."

"Yes, it was."

"Thank you, Dr. Mackintosh."

David Verreman pockets the pince-nez and says, "Who's next, Mr. Enygma?"

Enygma looks at Verreman carefully for a moment. He is sweating, Enygma notices. And his eyes are somewhat glassy. "I would like to take a short break if you don't mind," Enygma says. "I need to use the bathroom. Perhaps a cup of tea, too?"

Verreman shows Enygma toward the cloakroom off the hall and disappears down into the basement to put the kettle on.

Enygma closes the door quietly, stands in front of the sink and turns on the tap. This is the cloakroom in which Lady Verreman's attacker stood—so she said. Enygma lets the tap run as he searches his pockets for his medication, and the copper-colored water finally runs almost clear. But Enygma cannot find the bottle of pills that he is certain he placed in his right-hand jacket pocket before he left home. He checks the pocket again, and they are not there. He checks all his pockets. No pill bottle.

He remembers that he wore an overcoat, and he opens the cloakroom door and is surprised to find David—no, Daniel—Verreman leaning against the wall at the top of the basement steps, head tilted toward the right, halfway between Enygma and the front door. Enygma can see his coat hanging on a wall peg, and he takes a step toward it.

Daniel Verreman takes a step, too.

"I—er, I was just going to fetch something from my coat. My, er, migraine medication."

—Allow me.

Before Enygma can stop him, Daniel has reached the coat, patted down the pockets, identified the pocket with the pills and extracted them.

—Might as well lock this door while I'm here. You never know who is roaming round at this hour.

He pulls out a key and inserts it into a hidden keyhole behind a false brass escutcheon. Now no one can leave through the front exit without using that key. For good measure, Daniel draws the bolts across the door, too, and slips the safety chain on.

Enygma wonders again what time it is.

A click from the basement means that the kettle has boiled.

—I'll bring you a glass of water for your tablets, too.

Daniel heads back down the basement steps, whistling.

13

♦ ♦ ♦ ♦ ♦

A QUESTION OF PROOF

He thought his detective brain as good as the criminal's, which was true. But he fully realized the disadvantage. "The criminal is the creative artist; the detective only the critic," he said with a sour smile, and lifted his coffee cup to his lips slowly, and put it down very quickly. He had put salt in it.

—G. K. Chesterton, *The Innocence of Father Brown*

It's going well, don't you think?

—*Could be worse. Could be better.*

What's wrong now?

—*What's all this business about migraine medication? Since when has Max Enygma had migraine problems?*

He hasn't got migraine problems.

—*But you just said he did.*

No, Enygma said, "My, er, migraine medication." The reader will know from the "er" that Enygma is lying about what his medication is for.

—*Really? Seems to me you have put an awful lot of faith in the intelligence of your readers. I've had a look at 'em and, to be honest, they don't seem all that bright to me.*

It will be fine. I'm told they have certificates. Plural. Not sure what for. But one "er" is all they need to suspect that Enygma is lying. We can always drop in another hint or two later on to remind them.

—*OK. Don't say I didn't warn you.*

You worry too much. It's a well-known fact that in a story, "er" means *I am lying my arse off.*

—*I thought it meant* I haven't got a bloody clue.

Well, yes, sometimes it means that, too.

—*How is The Reader supposed to know the difference?*

They just do! Because, obviously, Max Enygma knows what he is taking the medication for. So if he is saying "er," it's not because he doesn't know. It is because he is lying his arse off.

—*I see. So it's a matter of context.*

Exactly! In real life, of course, people say "er" all the time. And "ah" and "um" and all sorts of things that mean nothing. But we don't put them in, because that would be misleading. And boring. We only put them in when they mean something. So The Reader just needs to work out the context.

—*And you trust The Reader to pick up on that context from two letters?*

Yes.

—*OK. On your own head be it.*

"LET'S TALK ABOUT the two letters," Enygma says, then swallows the pills with the water Daniel Verreman proffered, which is horribly cloudy.

"Certainly," says David Verreman. "Who would you like to speak to?"

"Just you for the moment. And your brother, too, of course, if he cares to contribute."

—What is it you want to know?

Enygma takes out photographs of the two letters to Sir Henry Wade and lays them in front of him. "Why are there two?"

"I don't quite understand," David says.

Enygma looks from one photograph to the next. "Why two letters? Or, rather, why two envelopes?" He looks at David carefully. "After the events that occurred in the house, your father has driven to the home of his friends. Margaret Howard-Cole stated that he really went there to see her husband, who happened to be away from home that night. First of all, do you believe her?"

"I think so."

"They weren't having an affair?"

"I doubt it."

"OK. So, he goes to see George-Howard Cole. Why?"

—No idea, I'm afraid.

"OK. We'll put that to one side for a moment. While he is there, he writes a letter to his brother-in-law, Sir Henry Wade. It's not a long letter. It briefly, and vaguely, describes the events of that night, and your father states that he is going to 'lie doggo' for a while. Then he asks his brother-in-law to try to get custody of you—and, er, Daniel—if he can, and mentions the name of the family trustee who will cover school fees. That's about all it says. Now, let us say that John Verreman puts that letter in an envelope and seals it up. Then it occurs to him that there are some other financial matters that need to be dealt with. He takes another piece of paper and writes the second note. This one has no introductory stuff; it is just headed *Financial Matters* and gives some info about an upcoming silver sale and the state of his bank accounts. Why does Lord Verreman put this second letter, which comprises a single sheet of paper, in a second envelope?"

"You said it yourself: because he already sealed the first letter."

"OK. But why does Verreman put the second letter in an envelope on its own, and put a stamp on both letters? Why not open the first envelope, throw it in the bin and put both letters into the second envelope and save himself the stamp? Or open the first envelope, add the extra page and reseal it with a bit of sticky tape if he is feeling cheap? Because his friend's wife posted those letters for him, and, no doubt, his friend's wife provided the stamps. She supplied the stationery, after all. Why make her pay for two letters being sent to the same address at the same time?"

"Perhaps it didn't occur to him. Or maybe he was still in shock."

"That's possible. But there was another letter, wasn't there? This was sent to another friend?"

"Edmund Crispin. He was the person who lent my father his car. But he wrote that later. After he left the Howard-Coles' house."

"That's right. I think, perhaps, we should speak to Mr. Crispin. But before that, perhaps we can have DCI Blake's perspective on that third letter?"

David Verreman touches his tiepin, and DCI Blake responds instantly. "Mr. Edmund Crispin . . . The police, I must say, were not satisfied with Mr. Crispin. Like a lot of Verreman's friends, he did just enough to stay on the right side of the law, but he was not helpful."

"Tell me about it, Detective Chief Inspector."

"Well, now, firstly, the letter that Mr. Crispin received arrived two days after the letters that Sir Henry Wade received, which, of course, implies that it was posted two days after the first two letters. Stands to reason."

"The letter might have been held up in the post."

"Well, so it might. And we could have checked on that if we had received the envelope with the postmark. But we didn't get that. This is what happened. The letter was delivered to Edmund Crispin at his club, which is bloody queer, if you like. Verreman must have known Crispin's home address, because he had gone round to borrow a car from him. The letter didn't have a stamp, and the chap on the door had to pay the postage in order to accept the letter. Now, that made the letter memorable. I wouldn't mind betting that, if it hadn't been for that, Edmund bloody Crispin would have stuck that letter in his pocket and said no more about it. But, in the circs, he called up the Yard and asked what we would like him to do, and, of course, we told him to bring it right round."

Blake looks a little uncomfortable for a moment, then continues. "I daresay that, strictly speaking, we should have told Edmund Crispin to stay where he was and gone round to his club ourselves, with sirens wailing and blue lights flashing, to retrieve the evidence. But, given as how the man had called us himself, of his own free will, the desk sergeant didn't consider it necessary. Mr. Crispin claimed that the sergeant told him to drop it round 'next time he was passing.' A piece of evidence in the biggest murder case the Met had had in decades? I don't think so!

"It took Crispin four hours to bring it round, and when he did, it was without its envelope. He claimed to have chucked the envelope in the wastepaper basket, and by the time the police arrived at the club, all the bins had been emptied and the evidence was floating down the Thames on a barge with about a ton of other crap. There was no way to retrieve it."

"And you consider that Edmund Crispin threw the envelope away deliberately?"

"I consider a lot of things, Mr. Enygma, as, I am sure, do you. I consider that Edmund Crispin, being a clever bloke, covered his arse by bringing us a letter that may have been discovered, through investigation, that he had received—the doorman would be sure to remember, because of the postage. I think that Edmund Crispin tossed the envelope in the wastepaper basket knowing that it would be emptied, and the envelope destroyed. I think that he took his time about bringing the letter round to us to make sure that the envelope had been removed and would be bloody hard to find. I think some other stuff, too. I think that it was strange that Lord Verreman would use his last sheet of paper—it was written on the blotting page from the back of the notebook, which is not normally written on—to write to a friend, and then say nothing.

"Nothing in the letter says anything that Edmund Crispin would not already have known from reading the newspapers or talking to Verreman's friends. Crispin claimed, later, not to be a particularly intimate friend of Verreman's, but despite that, Lord John Verreman apparently used the last sheet of paper he had to write a letter not to his mother, or his brother, his son or even his wife. He didn't write to his lawyer, protesting his innocence, or to us. No. He used his last sheet of notepaper to write to a close, but not very close, friend. And he said nothing."

"What do you mean?"

"Well, here's a few things I might have expected him to say: *I didn't do it*, or *I did do it, but here's why*, or *Here's what really happened*, or *Here's what I'm going to do next*. But what I think is really missing, given that Verreman's other letters were mostly businesslike, practical letters, is this: I expected Lord Verreman to tell this friend what he had done with his car. To apologize for the inconvenience—because Crispin would not be getting that car back anytime soon. Wouldn't he have mentioned that?"

"Maybe. So, what are you suggesting?"

"I am suggesting that the letter that Mr. Crispin received—which, by the way, came in a rather large envelope—contained more than this single piece of notepaper. I am suggesting that Mr. Crispin disposed of the envelope, knowing that it contained evidence about Verreman's recent whereabouts; that he took this single page to the police only because he thought the doorman may have recognized Verreman's handwriting; and that Mr. Crispin kept back the majority of the document out of loyalty to his close, but not very close, friend.

"I also think, though I have no proof, that that notepad was full when Verreman started writing letters, and that there were several more friends and relatives of Lord John Verreman who received letters from him in the days after he disappeared, but who did not choose to call the police and report it. They were a very peculiar set, the lot of them."

"Hmm. I see. I should perhaps like to interview Mr. Crispin, if he is available. He was not at the dinner party, however, so I'm not sure . . ." Enygma allows his words to trail off. He averts his eyes from David Verreman, who has begun a whispered conversation with his brother.

Enygma walks over to the portrait of Lady Verreman again. It really is uncanny. This Lady Verreman looks different from every photograph he has seen of her, in all of which she seems serious, watchful and a little afraid. Even in her wedding pictures, she looks as if she were concentrating hard on walking along a tightrope and trying not to fall. But in this painting, she is carefree, wild and happy. Her hair is trailing behind her in the breeze, and she doesn't care about a single damned thing. Enygma hopes his daughter still looks this way.

David Verreman clears his throat, and Enygma turns back toward the table. David holds out his hand. "Edmund Crispin. How do you do?"

Crispin's voice is deep and clear, but Enygma notices that David Verreman does not look very comfortable. He determines to keep this witness for the shortest length of time possible.

"Thank you for coming, Mr. Crispin. I only have one or two questions, if that is OK. Firstly, the letter. You may have heard the DCI earlier, when he said—"

"I heard."

"Good. How do you respond?"

"I did my duty. I received a letter from Johnny. I called them. They said, 'Drop it round when you're passing.' I was passing at four o'clock that morning, so that was when I dropped it round. They never mentioned the importance of keeping the envelope, and it never occurred to me. I am not a policeman. Mr. Blake told me it should have occurred to me. I told him, if they thought it was so blasted important, it should have occurred to *them* to hop round and get it. He had nothing to say to that. His men messed up. Not my fault. I did my duty."

"And there was nothing else in the envelope?"

"There was not."

"Thank you. My only other question is about the car that you loaned Lord Verreman a couple of days before the murder."

"About a week before, as far as I remember."

"Quite. Now, I realize that you testified that you had never seen the second piece of lead pipe before."

"I had never seen either of them before I was shown pictures by police."

"Right." Enygma makes a small and entirely unnecessary note of this. "About the boot of the car, sir—when it was discovered, it was said to have, and I am quoting from the police report now, 'quite a jumble of stuff in it.' Was it in that condition when you loaned it to Lord Verreman?"

"No. Not exactly. I think there was a bag of bits and bobs, some car tools—a jack and so forth, and a battery charger. I think that was it."

"So anything else was left there by John Verreman, including a full bottle of vodka, I read, among other things."

"Presumably, yes. I doubt he would have lent the car to anyone else without asking my permission. He was not that sort of man."

"Thank you, Mr. Crispin. I appreciate your time."

A cough, and David Verreman is back in the room, followed swiftly by DCI Blake. "What do you think?" Blake asks.

Enygma shrugs. "Does it seem suspicious that Edmund Crispin threw away that envelope? Yes and no. At that time Verreman was only listed as missing—four days after the murder, you said, which makes that around the eleventh or twelfth of November. A warrant for Verreman's arrest was not issued until the thirteenth of November. Crispin might not have realized that Verreman was a suspect. Or he might have realized but decided that, in the absence of a warrant, it was no business of his—or, rather, yours. He might have tried to hamper the investigation, or he might just be a bit of a twit. No way of knowing. Your boys did not cover themselves in glory."

Blake looks rueful. "Bloody desk sergeant. We bollocked him later, of course, but what good's that? Damage was already done."

"Hmm."

ENYGMA HUNCHES OVER the police reports. He reads slowly, making notes from time to time, occasionally underlining a sentence, occasionally flipping back to cross-check a new piece of information against previous reports. David Verreman has read these reports before. Often. He roams around the dining room, occasionally stopping to look out of the window, occasionally venturing into the hall. He talks quietly to himself, in a way anyone might when they think they are alone. Enygma reads for a long time, and Verreman seems almost to have forgotten his existence. He jumps when Enygma says, "Let's talk about motive."

"OK," Verreman says, returning to the table and sitting down opposite the detective.

"Normally the motive in a case such as this is irrelevant—irrelevant, that is, to the investigation. The families, the public and the jury are very concerned about motive, of course. There have been studies that show that juries who cannot see an adequate motive will be reluctant to convict, no matter how much evidence there is. They need a story within which murder makes sense, do you see?"

"I think so," says David Verreman.

"*Motive, means and opportunity*, they say in detective novels. And in a novel, the most important part is the motive. But real detectives are only interested in the last two. If the murder was committed by means of a rare poison injected with a dart from a blowpipe, detectives are looking for people with access to rare poisons and skill with blowpipes. They don't fanny about looking for the secret love child or the long-lost heir. After they catch them, they'll probably ask them why they dunnit, but that is only so the lawyers can prepare a case for the jury. Otherwise, they don't really care."

"OK."

"But in this case, what we have most of is motive—which tells me that there is very little evidence against your dad."

"Except my mother's testimony, of course."

"No. Your mother would not have been allowed to testify at all. The police knew it, and the coroner knew it."

Dr. Ronald Knox takes his pipe out of his mouth and says, a little defensively, "The law, at that time, was clear that a wife could not testify against her husband, except in a case of assault against herself. I made that clear in my statement, and I was scrupulous in making sure that Lady Verreman's testimony was confined only to the attack upon herself."

"No," says Enygma. "You should never have allowed Lady Verreman to testify in that manner, and you know it. In 1973, the Court of Appeal overturned the conviction in a similar case, where a husband was convicted of the murder of his brother-in-law and the attempted murder of his wife. The Court of Appeal ruled that the two cases should have been heard separately, and that the wife was not competent to give evidence *at all* against her husband on the murder charge."

"Well, yes, er, that is certainly true, but you must remember that my court was not a criminal court. It was an inquest into the death of a young woman. And Lady Verreman was giving evidence in that context."

Dr. Knox swallows several times, then places his pipe back in his mouth.

Enygma leans forward. "Lady Verreman was *not* giving evidence in that context. You stated that she was giving evidence only about the assault on herself."

The pipe comes out again. "No, well . . . You're twisting my words. I waited seven months before holding the inquest. Lord Verreman was, by his own admission, a witness to the events of that night, and I wished to give him every opportunity to come forward. When he did not, I considered it right and proper—yes, proper—that the facts, all the facts, should be put before a jury within the limits of my role as coroner, which, as I explained, gives me a wide latitude. A wide latitude. Lady Verreman had evidence about the death of Mrs. Gardner, and I felt it important that she be heard."

Enygma opens his mouth to ask another question, but Dr. Knox puts the pipe decisively in his pocket and disappears. Enygma ponders the wisdom of forcing David Verreman to bring him back, but, after looking at Verreman, he lets it go for the moment. There is around Verreman's left eye a tic that he did not notice before. He wonders whether Verreman is taking any medication—or whether he should be.

"OK, back to motive. The theory seems to be that your dad's motive for murder was that he was in financial trouble. Let's look at that."

"Certainly." Verreman flips to the financial section of his file, but Enygma leaves his own file closed. "Now, the police theory is that your father was desperate for money, and that murdering his wife was the only way out. I want to look at that carefully. They have, on the face of it, created a good story. A desperate man, on the brink of ruin. About to be publicly humiliated by bankruptcy. A compulsive gambler rather than a professional gambler. It's a good story. An attractive story. A story people would want to believe. Can you guess why?"

—Schadenfreude.

"Exactly. Your father was a man who had been given all the advantages of life. Aristocratic, wealthy, good education. He had influential friends. He was adventurous. Damn it, he was even good-looking. He was not a man who engenders sympathy in an audience. Envy, possibly, but not sympathy. Your father, in fact, was just the sort of man who the British public like to see taken down a peg or two. As Daniel says, we delight in his misfortune."

"OK."

"The prosecution have a good story. But it is just a story. What we need to do is change the story. Rewrite it. Make it better. Or add a twist. We need to make our story more believable than theirs."

"By disproving the evidence?"

"By rewriting the story! By changing what the evidence means. And we're going to start with the motive, because the motive *is* the story. Now, according to the prosecution, your father was on the brink of bankruptcy. Where is the proof of that?"

"Well, he had four bank accounts. And they were all overdrawn."

"So what? I've got three bank accounts myself, and I can't remember the last time I was in credit. Were the banks about to foreclose? Were they demanding repayment on them immediately?"

"Er, no. I don't think so. There were a few snitty letters. But I'm pretty sure that each bank didn't know about the other accounts. It was 1974, before electronic banking and online credit searches."

"OK, so your dad was a bit warm there. Well, we knew that anyway. And that's not necessarily a bad thing when it comes to writing our story. If there is one section of society the British public like sticking it to more than the nobs, it's the bankers. What other liabilities did he have? Was he overdue on the mortgage? Were you about to lose the roof over your head?"

"No."

"So why the sudden urgency? What made your father decide that the *only* way out of his troubles was murder? Because the motive that the prosecution chose was financial desperation. They could have chosen something else, but they didn't. They could have made the case, for example, that it was because your mother was denying him access to his children, or that it was revenge due to the breakdown of their marriage. They could have implied sexual jealousy—that he thought your mother was getting it on with the help—or a whole host of other motives. But the motive that they chose was money. And that's very interesting."

"Why?"

"Because I don't think that they made the case for it. Not sufficiently, anyway. He had some debt. Who doesn't? But he had assets, too. The house was not about to be repossessed. Your dad was still driving round in his Mercedes. He had options. Worst-case scenario, he had to sell some stuff. In fact, he had already entered some silver in a sale, which would clear most of his immediate debt. So what was the hurry?"

"Well, the following January, they would have been two years separated, so my mother could get her divorce."

"Did she want a divorce?"

"Not really. Sometimes. When she was angry."

"OK. But he was already maintaining her, and you. He was paying all the expenses on the house. He was paying for the nanny, too. What more could she get?"

"I don't know."

"I believe that there was a family trust?"

"Yes."

"So most of the assets would be protected?"

"Most, I think. I'm not sure."

Enygma stands up. "Let's find out. Your father, I believe, owned this house outright?"

"Yes. Or rather, the family trust owned it."

"And your mother carried on living in it after he disappeared."

"Yes."

"But after your mother died, it was not disposed of in her will."

"That's right. The house belongs to me."

—Thanks a lot, Dad.

"It was entailed through the family trust. The aristocracy do not share the dibs equally."

"And this trust provided your father with an annual income?"

"A modest one."

Max Enygma begins to feel a fluttering of excitement. "Good. Now, according to your father's letter to Sir Henry Wade, there was also enough money to cover school fees in the trust. Which school did you go to, by the way?"

"Eton."

Of course. Of course John Verreman sent his boy to Eton, Enygma thinks. *Where else?* John Verreman was a responsible father. His son's education was provided for. "There was another house, too, wasn't there? Was that the house your father moved into after the separation?"

"No. That was rented out to Willard Wright. My father rented a flat around the corner."

"Willard Wright? Why does that name ring a bell?"

David Verreman looks a little uncomfortable. "Well, he was a friend of my mother's. And my father's, too, of course. He was supposed to have testified at the inquest, but—"

"Ah yes. The solicitor for the Crown attempted to have his letter read into evidence, but it was disallowed. Do you know what it would have said?"

"No."

—Yes.

Enygma hesitates only a moment before asking Daniel to continue.

—Willard Wright was, er, a particular friend of our mother's. They were rather close, for a while. My father knew him, too, of course. He was part of the set at the Berkeley Club. But they were not close friends—which makes Wright's testimony a little surprising. He maintained that, several months before the murder, he was on a boat with my father—fishing trip, or something, I believe—when my father said, 'out of the blue,' that he was worried his children would one day see him in court as a bankrupt, and that it would be easier if he 'got rid of his wife' and threw her body in the sea. Willard Wright claimed to have thought my father was both drunk and joking but that, after the murder, the words seemed rather more prescient.

"And why did he not give evidence at the inquest?"

—In hospital. Gallbladder, I think. Something like that. But he was well enough to give an interview to the papers a couple of days after the inquest.

"Well, as evidence goes, that's rather poor. If I understand you correctly, Willard Wright was not an impartial witness. His being a 'particular friend' of your mother's would be highly relevant in a jury trial. And the fact that this conversation happened several months before the murder might show more in your father's favor than against it. I mean, how desperate could he have been if he waited months to carry out his plan? And if he was genuinely considering killing his wife, why would he confide in Willard Wright, this particular friend of his wife? No. A man who has no plans to kill his troublesome wife may very well make a joke about killing her and tossing the body overboard, but a man who plans to do away with his wife would be more likely to keep his own counsel, surely, especially in the presence of a friend with, er, divided loyalties."

"Well, quite," David Verreman says.

"But, again, we come back to the idea that John Verreman was about to be made bankrupt. That is the motive put forward by the prosecution. But what I want to know is, how likely was that?"

—He *was* declared bankrupt.

"Yes, but that was only after his disappearance. Suing for bankruptcy was the only way his creditors could stake a claim on the estate. What I want to know is whether, and when, that would have happened had there been no murder and no disappearance. Because a man does not kill his wife to avert a *possible* future financial catastrophe. He kills when the catastrophe is certain. When it is almost upon him. Especially if he is a gambling man. Otherwise, he would have waited for his luck to turn, surely?"

Verreman's eye has begun to twitch, though he is sitting very still in his chair. Enygma senses a restlessness kept in check by iron will. But the iron is beginning to crack. His client—if he is a client—is making him uneasy, and Enygma tentatively suggests that they call it a night and agree to meet again in a day or two.

David immediately dissents. "No need. The night is young."

The night is not young. And Enygma is not young. And, in fact, Max Enygma is dog-tired. And concerned. About the health of his client, and his own health, too. It has been a long time since he has worked through the night, and he has been warned that his medication works best when he has a regular pattern of sleep and food. But his familiar flutterings of excitement have only increased. Enygma knows that he is following the right track. He rubs his eyes, makes a pretense of looking at his watch—a watch he no longer owns, thanks to Monty Egg—and agrees to stay "a little longer."

ENYGMA IS TRAWLING through financial records. As well as the four British bank accounts—including, Enygma notices, one with Coutts, the Queen's bankers, of course, who require new customers to hold very large balances on the black side of the ledger, mostly because they really don't want to have to deal with new customers at all—there were at least two other accounts: one in Rhodesia, as it was then called, which was "estimated" to hold around twenty thousand pounds; and another in Switzerland. *And,* thinks Enygma, *good luck with getting information about that.* The Swiss open their books for no one.

"The Rhodesian account was frozen, I believe."

"That's right."

"I read a newspaper account that said the money had been deposited 'prior to the murder,' implying, of course, that it was placed there prior to the murder because of the intent to murder, but, in fact, it must have been deposited before Ian Smith declared Rhodesia's independence from Britain, which was sometime around 1965. Correct?"

—Correct. The money in that account had been frozen for about eight years, as a result of British sanctions against the Zimbabwean government. Nothing to do with our father.

"Twenty thousand pounds in 1974 would have been worth a lot in today's terms."

—About a quarter of a million.

"Whew. OK. Now, the Swiss account would have been private, and remained private until your father was certified dead, I presume. No warrant in the world would have convinced Swiss bankers to open their books. So we do not know the balance at that time. But we can, perhaps, surmise that a British citizen would not go to the trouble of opening a Swiss bank account only to deposit nothing in it, can we not?"

"I think so."

"Good. There were also some reports at the time stating that your father held a safety-deposit box, also at a Swiss bank. Is that also factually correct?"

"Yes."

"Also"—Enygma flips through the file for a moment—"your father had expectations, did he not? A rich relative? Elderly and ailing. Would he not have expected, or at least hoped, that he would receive a legacy from that direction?"

—Yes. In fact, he did. Lady Audley.

"Yes." He turns the pages back, seeking something he has overlooked. "Now, this was the lady from whom he had tried to borrow money for his custody case. Is that right?"

—Yep. The old dear refused, and then croaked, only to leave him twice as much as he had asked to borrow anyway.

"But by that time, of course, Daddy was long gone, and the executors tried to wheedle out of it on the grounds that he might have predeceased her."

—Greedy little bastards.

"My point is," says Enygma, "that, had the murder not happened, your father would have had a reasonable expectation, or at least a reasonable hope, of coming into some money from this very old and very sick lady in the reasonably near future, and that, as his finances do not seem to have been immediately perilous, we might argue that this weakens the prosecution's argument of financial motive."

"I suppose so."

"And then there is the second house, the one occupied by Willard Wright. Why, if he was strapped financially, would he not just sell it? Or sell the Merc and buy something cheaper? Or sell more of his stuff? What I am asking is why, at that particular time—in November 1974—would your father feel an overwhelming need to alleviate his financial position by killing his wife? And how would murder have alleviated that position? If he was worried about immediate bankruptcy, the murder would not have helped—unless his wife's life was insured for a large sum?"

—It wasn't.

"Good. Then all we need to do is rewrite the story of the financial motive, and I think we can. I think we can make our story stronger than theirs."

—*What's all this rubbish about telling a story? Ain't we already telling a story?*

Well, yes, but there is a difference between *a* story and *the* story.

—*You've lost me.*

Look. We are the narrator. We are telling the story. But anyone within our story can tell their story, too. But theirs will be totally different from the story we're telling.

—*But aren't we telling the story of them telling their story?*

Yes.

—*So their story is part of the story?*

Not always.

—*Then why do we put it in there? Are you being paid by the word or something? Are you holding out on me? Has someone paid you to write this?*

Never.

—*That's what I figured.*

But that's not what Enygma is talking about. He is talking about *story as motive*. He is trying to present a valid and credible defense with a story that is more complete than the prosecution's story about motive, and that answers every question a juror might have.

—*How about,* It wasn't me? *Worked for R. Kelly.*

Did it?

—*OK. Bad example.*

MAX ENYGMA TURNS to a fresh page in his notebook and writes *STORY* in capital letters. Underneath that, he writes *Financial Motive* and carefully underlines it. "I think that we can construct a story that is equally as appealing as the story the prosecution have told. We certainly have plenty of evidence that, while he may have been a little stretched financially in the short term, this was a man with solid assets, which he could have liquidated if he'd needed to. We might be able to make that go away. There is one thing that worries me, however."

"What's that?"

"Your father is not a sympathetic character. I don't mean personally, of course, but to the public. To a jury. He is not likable. And that is a big problem."

—You have to be likable to be acquitted?

"It certainly helps. David said it earlier. It was 1974. Times were changing. Your father belonged to the old order—the aristocracy and the old school tie. That was one strike against him. But he was also a gambler. A professional gambler, maybe, but still a gambler. The public don't like gamblers. If they win, then they are merely lucky, and nothing breeds resentment like the undeserved luck of strangers. If they lose and stop playing, they are bad sports, and if they lose and continue playing, they become compulsive gamblers—either of which breeds contempt. That's strike two. And he had abandoned his wife and was trying to steal her children from her. That makes three. The family court didn't like him. There is no reason to suppose that a criminal court would have liked him any better."

"So, what's the solution?"

"I think that we *might* be able to make the case that the detective in charge, Nicholas Blake, was subject to the same prejudices as the rest of the British public. We might be able to do that, but I am uncertain as to whether we should."

—Police solidarity?

"Not at all. I'm uncertain for two reasons. Firstly, the public do not like seeing the police maligned by defense lawyers. It disturbs their worldview. Secondly, suggesting that our defense is so far out of the ordinary way that such an experienced policeman cannot conceive of it is tantamount to saying that we are proposing a solution that is both bizarre and implausible.

"We must, then, produce a defense that is both simple and elegant, and which the police were unable to detect only because they were looking at it from the wrong perspective, or because they lacked a vital piece of evidence. Not because they are idiots. And certainly not because they are corrupt. We must show that we hold the police in the very highest esteem—"

—Do we?

"—but that, because we have discovered this new perspective, the picture is now clear, and the evidence incontrovertible. That's what we need—a narrative that turns the picture around, with no blame attaching to anyone."

"And how do we do that?"

"By combing through the evidence and finding the correct angle from which to view it. It's back to my idea of a story. Of the story we tell. And the stories that people read. Remember that detective fiction is the most popular form of fiction there is. Which means that juries are made up of detective-fiction readers. They will be well-versed in unpicking the means, motives and opportunities of the criminals, but they will also be very good at spotting the implausible, even ridiculous, solutions that the authors behind these fictional detectives sometimes present.

"We must tell the jury a thrilling story, but it must be a plausible one, and we must also follow Sherlock Holmes' warning about theorizing ahead of our data lest we twist the facts to meet our theory, and make more of the evidence than it deserves. The jury, being seasoned Sherlockians, will be on the lookout for that."

"OK," David Verreman says, not entirely convinced.

"So, we have a gentleman who is asset rich, comparatively, but cash poor. He has an income from a trust fund; he owns two houses and possesses assets that could be sold if he needed extra cash. And, in fact, he was doing just that, with his sale of some of the Verreman family silver. That would have met his most pressing debts. There would be a financial settlement to be made for his wife, but as most of his money was tied up in trust funds, she would be unlikely to get much more than her living costs and support for the kids. There was the money in Rhodesia—nothing he could do about that. And there was the putative money in a Swiss bank account and a safety-deposit box. That's all on the credit side. On the debit side of the ledger, we have some overdrafts. Meh. Then there is that very unfortunate loan from the moneylender Gaston Leroux. Now, that doesn't look good. He has also borrowed money from his mother, and tried to borrow money from his rich aunty, Lady Audley—without success. Anything else?"

Enygma is looking at the page headed *Financial Motive* in his notebook and ticks off each item as he mentions it.

"That's about it, I think," says David.

—There's some land in Ireland, and some peppercorn rents, but the Verremans are not popular in Ireland—something about the third earl and the potato famine. We tend to just leave them alone.

"What other assets were there, apart from the family silver?"

"Oh, I don't know," says David, with a shrug. "A few paintings, none of them of the first rate, some more silver, some jewelry. Stuff like that."

The sort of stuff every family has in the attic, thinks Max Enygma. *The family jewels. The silver. The estate in Ireland you've half forgotten about.* He thinks about the very small legacy his parents left him, and the even smaller one his daughter will one day receive from him. If they can find her.

He takes one quick glance at the Lady Verreman painting, and turns back to his notes.

"Task one, then, will be to demonstrate that, far from being on the brink of financial disaster, your father was a man with assets. And expectations. He was in a privileged position. He knew a lot of influential, not to say rich, people. He could have appealed to one of his rich friends for a loan rather than approach a moneylender. He could have sold some of his assets. He could have got a bloody job. The two questions we need to answer satisfactorily here are (a) why did Lord Verreman approach Gaston Leroux for a loan when, on the face of it, he had other options? and (b) how long would he have been able to keep afloat if he had not disappeared, with or without the murder of his wife? If his financial position was at risk of imminent exposure, that might be a motive for murder, but if we are talking about months before financial collapse, then it rather argues against, because of the reasons outlined above—to wit, your father was a gambler convinced of the next big score, and his old aunty might peg out at any minute and leave him a packet."

Enygma looks around the room. He likes to be able to see his problems, and he usually fills the walls of his office with poster paper on which he marks the progress of a case. These walls are bare. Surely no minor act of vandalism could detract from the value of this house? He digs into his jacket pocket and pulls out a black marker pen.

He holds the pen up briefly, for David Verreman to see, and, receiving no protest, he writes his questions under the heading of *Money* on a stretch of bare plaster next to the door into the hall, leaving plenty of room beneath each for additions and clarifications.

Why approach a moneylender?

How long before bankruptcy

He steps back, looks at the wall, then moves forward again to add a question mark to the end of the second sentence. He feels better. He feels in control. He feels a tiny spider drop from the cobwebby ceiling and run over his face, and he brushes it away absentmindedly.

"Good," he says. "What's next?" He looks around, expecting to see half a dozen detectives sitting behind him, taking notes, but he sees only David Verreman, mumbling quietly to himself, or, perhaps, as himself to someone else. *Sod him,* Enygma thinks. The bastard invited him to this house under false pretenses. Enygma cares nothing for Verreman's state of mind, so long as he can help him exonerate Verreman Sr. Maybe Enygma can even catch the real killer. Wouldn't that be one in the eye for the Met? Max Enygma, the guy they all thought was washed up, no good, doolally, beating the lot of them in one of the biggest cases ever.

Verreman doesn't seem to have heard him, so he crosses back to the table and says loudly, "Motive. Come on. What's next? What other motives could there be?"

"I'm not sure."

—What about jealousy?

"Yes," says Enygma, pointing to Daniel like he has just earned himself a gold star. "Good. What kind of jealousy, do you think? Sexual?"

—I doubt that. My father didn't have any affairs. Someone would have talked by now.

"What about your mother?"

—Well, there was the thing with Willard, of course.

"How serious was that?"

—On her side, deadly serious, I should say. Mother was not the sort of woman for a lighthearted fling. She became obsessed. He became uncomfortable. And he ran for the hills.

"Not quite that far. He was, in fact, renting a house just minutes away from both of them."

—True.

"Was your father jealous of their relationship?"

"Not in the slightest," says David Verreman.

—No. I think Daddy would have been secretly pleased if the two of them had run away together. It would have solved all his problems, wouldn't it? But it was never really on the cards. Mother was probably trying to make our father jealous. She used to parade with Willard Wright up and down past our father's house, in the hopes he would come out and they could fight over her. She would have adored that. But, of course, it didn't happen. Wright tried to get out of it gracefully, but he didn't find it easy to shake her loose.

"And the testimony Willard Wright would have given at court? What credence do we give that?"

"My father," says David, "would never have confided a murder plan to him. Firstly, my father wasn't an idiot. And secondly, he didn't really like Willard Wright. And even if he had liked him, he knew that he was close to my mother, especially at that time, which was months before the murder took place."

—Agreed. If he said anything at all, which I doubt, it would have been nothing more than a joke.

"I agree, too," says Enygma. "I read your mother's memoir in the British Library."

"I can only apologize," says David.

—What for? Not the British Library, I hope.

"For Mother's memoir."

"It wasn't an easy read—that's for sure. And it was remarkably uninformative about the murder. OK," says Enygma, looking back toward the wall and flicking his pen backward and forward in his hand. "What other kinds of jealousy are there?"

"Well, the custody case. Does that count as jealousy?"

"I would say so. Or call it emotional reasons. That could include revenge, and anger, too." Enygma picks another patch of bare wall, writes *Emotion* and underlines it twice. He looks at the first list's heading, realizes that he underlined it only once and adds a second line beneath the first.

"Your father lost his original custody case. Was that a final decision?"

"No. Permanent custody could have been settled during a divorce, of course, but I don't think my father was planning on waiting that long, because that would have only happened then if my mother had consented. And she would never have consented. He was gathering evidence for an appeal. That would have taken place the following year, regardless of the divorce."

"Are you sure?"

—We're certain. For my mother, divorcing would have meant losing. And Mother never liked to lose. She would have made him wait another three years for a contested divorce, unless he could prove either adultery or unreasonable behavior. The latter would have been his best bet. He had those recordings that he'd made when she'd lost her temper. Either he took them for fun, to humiliate her; or he took them to use in court.

"OK," says Enygma, "but I'm afraid that gives him another motive. If he was desperate for a divorce and she wouldn't give him one, that seems like a good motive."

"Not necessarily," says David, suddenly becoming animated, like a battery-operated toy switched on again. "They were officially separated. My father was, essentially, a free man. And legal separation would give him the benefit of not having to provide a financial settlement. The prosecution's case was that the reason my father was so desperate was because the looming financial settlement would expose his losses. But if Lady Verreman refused to give her husband a divorce—and Daniel is right that she would never have consented to that—then what happens to the financial motive?"

"Excellent!" Enygma draws a connecting line between *Money* and *Emotion*, and adds the question *Was divorce imminent?* "How do we check that out? Had any papers been lodged with the family solicitors? Was there a court date?"

"No court date, not for the divorce hearing. Papers were being prepared for the custody hearing, but just the issue of custody. I don't know if a date had been set for that."

"OK." Enygma writes, *Check court date re custody.* "I think we can make something of this. The prosecution's case is largely built on motive, which tells me that it is weak—prosecutors with solid evidence lead with that. Their case is that Lord Verreman was about to be made bankrupt and exposed to the ridicule of his peers as a fool who gave up a safe but dull career for the allure of easy money and the glamour of the casino.

"Our defense will be that, while he may have been temporarily financially embarrassed, your father was a man with both assets and prospects. He had goods that he could sell that would more than cover his liabilities, which were not, in any case, immediately pressing. No one was calling in his loans."

—He'd had letters from the bank manager about his overdraft.

"Who hasn't? Further," Enygma continues, moving back to the wall, "he had expectations, in the form of an aged and ailing relative. He had influential friends, any one of whom could have secured him a job. If he was embarrassed about the need to get a job, he could always have cited his upcoming custody case as the reason for giving up, at least for a time, the profession of gambler. Indeed, he might have been wise to do that anyway. A banker would make a much better impression at a custody hearing than a professional gambler, even if he had been on a winning streak.

"All that is fine," Enygma says, snapping the lid of his marker pen on and off. "The only thing we have against us, so far as the financial motive is concerned, is that rather unfortunate visit to the money-lender."

"Gaston Leroux."

"Yes. That's not good. That needs explaining. Why would a man who has assets, some of which can be converted to cash with reason-able speed—witness the sale of silver—why would he approach a moneylender unless he was desperate?"

Enygma digs around in his pocket and pulls out a red marker pen, steps to his wall and draws a circle around the question *Why ap-proach a moneylender?* And, for good measure, he underlines it.

"Let's leave that for a moment and move on to means." Enygma selects a new piece of wall and writes, *Means*. He underlines it three times, then brushes away another tiny spider from the back of his neck.

Under *Means* he writes, *Access to lead pipe*, and just stops him-self from underlining that, too. He takes a step back, surveys the wall and adds a third line under the heading of each of the first two columns.

"A lead pipe is easily obtainable," says David. "Or, at least, it would have been in 1974. Lead piping was outlawed for new build-ings in 1969, but there was still plenty of it around."

"That's true. But my question is, why a lead pipe at all?" Enygma writes, *Why a lead pipe?* on the wall, then snaps the lid on his pen and returns to the table. He picks up his notebook, turns to the pages of notes he made before coming and clears his throat in preparation for giving a speech.

"Do you know how common the use of lead pipe is as a weapon?"

—One in six—if you are playing Cluedo, at any rate. In fact, I think there are three blunt instruments to choose from in that game. I've always wondered why. It seems unnecessarily bloodthirsty to me.

Enygma seems a little irritated at the interruption. "I've been do-ing research, and the answer is, not common at all. If you search the records of the Old Bailey, and their seven thousand, six hundred twenty-five murder cases, which I did, you will get forty-five returns for murders related to 'lead pipe.' Of these, the large majority are of people 'smoking a pipe' in the 'lead-up' to the murder. The number of cases that actually involve lead is six—three lead poisonings, two shootings with lead shot and one case of murder from an attack with a cosh.

"One. Joseph Rickards, 'with a certain iron bar of the value of twelve d,' did 'feloniously, willfully and of his malice aforethought strike and kill one Walter Horseman.'

"That was in 1786. I think it is fair to say that Joseph Rickards, cosh wielder, was probably not the inspiration for this attack— especially as that bar with the value of twelve pence might have been 'a certain iron bar,' and not a lead pipe after all. It's not clear. But, then, it was 1786. What do you want from them? Metallurgy reports?"

Enygma pauses, waiting for the guffaws of his squad of detectives, who are more or less obliged to laugh at the jokes of their boss. When he looks up expectantly, David Verreman manages a small smile.

Enygma turns his eyes back to his notes. "Of course, the Old Bailey is not the only court in the land. I also took a peek at the National Archives, which returned six hundred fifty-seven results for 'lead pipe' in connection with criminal court cases, various. Of these, most related to receipts for, instructions for the use of, inventories regarding, insurance documents covering and other miscellany about lead pipes, while twenty related to the theft of lead pipe, one to criminal damage of lead pipe and one to manslaughter related to the stealing of lead pipe near a gas meter and the subsequent accidental poisoning of the householder."

—We begin to see your point.

"There's more," says Max Enygma, who is a man who likes to show his workings out. "I also checked the national crime statistics. Unfortunately, a blunt instrument is a blunt instrument in those. They don't differentiate between the lead pipe, the spanner and the candlestick."

—A Cluedo joke!

"But, even so, *blunt instrument* is only the fifth most popular method of killing, behind *knife or sharp implement, shooting, assault without a weapon*, and *other*."

Enygma closes his notebook. "My point is, given that this is said to be a premeditated crime, why on earth would anyone make a lead pipe their weapon of choice?"

"Well—" says David.

"Most importantly, why did this assailant not stop to consider the two essential properties of lead—apart from its poisonous qualities, of course? To wit, lead is heavy, and lead is soft. You can bend it with your bare hands."

—Though we wouldn't advise it. It's poisonous, ya know.

"My point is, if he were actively planning to commit murder, why would Lord Verreman choose an admittedly heavy but also soft and hollow lead pipe? Why not an iron bar? Iron does not bend."

—Unless heated to one thousand four hundred eighty degrees Celsius.

"Exactly."

"Well," says David, "perhaps he didn't have access to an iron bar."

"Most hardware stores sell them. You might argue that a crowbar is easier to get hold of than a lead pipe, unless you are a builder or a plumber. And most cars have some kind of tire iron alongside the spare tire. Wouldn't that have been a better bet than a lead pipe?"

David Verreman blinks rapidly. "I'm not sure what you're saying. The lead pipe may have been a poor choice of weapon—clearly it was—but it *was* the weapon."

"Was it?" asks Enygma, excitedly. "Was it? If it was, why? And . . . if it wasn't," he says, "what was it doing there? Yes, that's what we need to know. *What was it doing there?*" He writes the question on the wall, and circles it in red several times.

—You are forgetting the second lead pipe. The one found in the car. The incontrovertible evidence of our father's guilt, as Nicholas Blake put it. The lead pipe that was the smoking gun.

Enygma sits back down at the table. "No," he says. "No. I haven't forgotten that. But if we can explain why the first one was there, we might be able to explain the second one away, too."

"I need a drink," David says suddenly.

—Pour one for me, too.

Enygma asks only for water. His mouth is dry, and he can feel the beginnings of a headache sitting low over his left eye. He glances at David, who has poured a second drink—for Daniel. *A neat trick, that,* he thinks. He is wondering about the second lead pipe when, he knows, he should be wondering about his own safety—about whether he will be allowed to leave this house if he does not reach the "right" conclusion. Which is not likely. Fifty years, and no one else has managed to cast doubt on the verdict.

But did they try?

Enygma moves back, despite himself, to the witness statements now strewn over the table. He takes a swig of water, running it round his mouth, trying to let it soak into the parched places where his tongue has shriveled and cracked. The water doesn't seem able to permeate the film that has covered his tongue, and his mouth is as dry as before. He picks up the plans of the house, with detailed layouts of the kitchen and basement, then shakes his head at an idea that won't quite appear.

"OK, let's think about the second piece of pipe. What was that for?"

"What do you mean, what was it for?"

Enygma pulls out the photographs of the car. The picture of the boot shows the jumble of random stuff. Like the boot of his own car; like the boots of most cars. Among the rubbish, the battery charger and the full bottle of vodka lies the second lead pipe, covered in its distinctive white Elastoplast with a yellow zigzag stripe. This one is sixteen inches long and weighs a little more than four pounds.

Enygma picks up a picture of the second lead pipe, wanders back to the wall, rummages in his jacket and pulls out a stick of chewing gum, which he unwraps and chews quickly before removing it from his mouth and sticking it to the back of the photo. He presses the gum-backed photo to the wall. He looks at the notes he has already made, and then unsticks the picture, moves to a fresh section of wall, resticks it and writes, *The Murder Weapon.*

As he writes his notes beneath it, he talks to David Verreman. "Here's my thinking. The prosecution's case is that your father planned this murder. Not a crime of passion. Not a momentary loss of control. This, they claim, is premeditated murder. So your father, the murderer in their scenario, must have a plan. He goes to the house to lie in wait for your mother in the basement. And he has brought two things into the house with him: a mail sack, in which to hide the body, and a length of lead pipe. Now, given the choice between pipe A, which weighs two pounds and three ounces and is nine inches long, and pipe B, which weighs four pounds and is sixteen inches long, which one would you choose?"

"Well..."

"Both pipes are in the car, remember. Both are available to you. Why would you choose the lighter, shorter pipe with which to bludgeon your wife to death?"

"Because..." David Verreman says, fiddling with his tiepin. He gives his neck a full-circle turn, cracking several bones in the process, to become Detective Chief Inspector Blake. "... he is a man who plans ahead. Lord Verreman was a tall man. Over six feet tall. The rear of the hall, around the cloakroom, is only six feet six inches high. He would never have been able to get a good swing in with a longer weapon. He probably made the first weapon, had a few practice swings, realized that there wouldn't be enough headroom and decided to go for a shorter weapon."

Enygma clicks the lid onto his permanent marker. "Really?"

"That is our best guess. It's only conjecture, naturally. But it fits the facts."

Enygma snaps the lid off his pen again. "Does it? Really? Well, perhaps you can tell me, Detective Chief Inspector, why this man who plans is worrying about the headroom in the hall when the murder he is planning is going to be committed in the basement? Why, when, according to you, he has gone to the trouble of removing the lightbulb in the basement so that he can commit a private murder down there in the dark, is he worried about getting his weapon stuck in the ceiling in the hall?"

Blake opens his mouth to speak, but Enygma plows on. "And, now we're getting down to it, why did he remove the lightbulb at all? Your officers proved, and Lord Verreman knew from his months of snooping on his wife and kids, that nothing could be seen of the doings in the basement by anyone passing along the street. Lord Verreman knew because he made it his business to drive past every night, get out of his car, walk down to the basement area and then press his nose against the window in order to try to get dirt on his wife for the custody case. He knew, better than any man on earth, that if he wanted to commit a nice, private murder in the basement, all he needed to do was close the blinds fully."

"There was also," says Blake, on his dignity now, "the small matter of why a woman would walk down the basement steps if there was a man at the bottom of the steps with a cosh. He needed her to walk all the way down without suspecting a trap."

Enygma holds up the plan of the basement and raps it smartly with his marker. "It's fucking L shaped! If the attacker wished her to come all the way downstairs before he started swinging—which, I grant you, is a smart move—all he had to do was wait for her in the kitchen, or stand behind the stairs. Loads of places he could have stood and been out of sight."

"The lightbulb *was* removed," Blake says, "and it must have been removed for a reason."

"It was removed. But there is nothing to say it was removed before the killing, and quite a lot to suggest it was done after."

"Bullshit."

Enygma pushes on. "If it's bullshit, do you mind telling me how, exactly, Lord Verreman managed to attack her in the dark? He must have had bloody good eyesight to hit her and keep on hitting her again and again and again in the pitch black of that basement."

Blake gives a little laugh. "The pathologist made it clear. She had bruises on her arm. She was held. And then she was hit."

"Right. That's right . . . But wait. Did he hold her and hit her, or did he hold her and *then* hit her?"

"I don't know what you're getting at."

"Well, now, come on. The nanny has come down the stairs, carrying her tray, in her high-heeled shoes. Does he grab her first, and then hit her? Or does he just aim wildly and hope for the best?"

"I don't know."

"You don't know, Chief Inspector? Let's ask someone who does, shall we? Can I speak to Professor McCabe, please?"

David Verreman fiddles with his tie, rotates his neck, blinks, rotates his neck some more and twists the signet ring on his little finger. Nothing happens. Verreman rotates his neck again, blinks and twists the signet ring. There is a long pause, but eventually Professor Cameron McCabe peers up at them, as though he is looking up from a book.

"Yes?" he says. "Can I help?"

"Thank you for seeing me," Enygma says, as if he has just walked into the professor's office. "I have a few questions, if you don't mind."

"Certainly. Anything I can do to help." The professor's tone is pleasant, but not an invitation to linger. Professor McCabe is not a man with whom you shoot the breeze. Or perhaps it is David Verreman who needs to keep this short.

Enygma gets straight to business. "You mentioned earlier that Mrs. Gardner had injuries to her face and her head. Is that correct?"

"Quite correct. There were bruises to her right eye, lip and eyebrow, which were of a different type from those to her head."

"In what way different?"

"The bruises to the face were of the type most often caused by a closed fist, with a broad, blunt impact but no gashes, whereas the injuries over the right ear and the back of the head were gashes that were most likely to have been made by something significantly harder, but narrower and longer."

"Like a lead pipe."

"Yes."

"Or a crowbar."

"Yes. That would leave similar wounds."

"Or a baseball bat?"

"No. There the impact surface would have been wider."

"Golf club?"

"Possibly. As long as they didn't hit them with the club head."

"You didn't definitively prove that the lead pipe was the murder weapon?"

"No. We did not."

"Thank you. Now, apart from the bruises on the face, and the wounds on the head made by a lead pipe or similar instrument, did she have any other injuries?"

"She did. There was bruising on both shoulders. The most likely explanation for that is that the attacker missed his target, or the target moved."

"The target being Sally Gardner?"

"Yes."

"OK. Anything else?"

"Yes. She had some bruises on the back of her right hand, which were most likely defensive bruises. And there were also four in-line bruises on the front of her upper right arm. These are consistent with Mrs. Gardner having been forcefully grabbed."

"That's the part I wanted to discuss with you. Those bruises on her arm—how often do you see that?"

"Oh, all the time. It's not unusual at all when a person has been assaulted."

"And where would the attacker have stood when they made those bruises?"

"In front of the victim."

"Sure?" asks Enygma, a little flutter of excitement in his belly.

"Certainly. The position of the bruises proves it."

"And when the victim was punched in the face—where would the attacker be standing then?"

"In front of them, naturally."

"And when the victim was hit over the right ear with the pipe or the crowbar or the golf club?"

"Harder to tell. Possibly in front of them. Possibly to the side."

"Not from the back?"

"There were two blows from behind. The attacker must have been behind the victim then. For the blows over the ear, he could have been standing either in front, or to the side, or behind the victim. It's not really possible to tell."

"OK, thank you. Are you able to tell which set of injuries came first—the bruises to the face, which were likely to have been made with a fist, or the gashes to the head, made by a pipe or similar object?"

"No. Not definitively. But I can say that, where you find repeated blows in the same place, it is likely that the victim is not moving, as with the four gashes over the right ear, which were very concentrated, almost one on top of another. But where there is distance between wounds—for example, between the bruise on the mouth and the bruise on the eye—it is likely that the victim was still moving."

"So it is more likely that the victim was attacked first with a closed fist, and then with a pipe or similar object."

"I would say that is more likely, yes."

"Of course, because you don't bash someone over the head with a baseball bat and then punch them in the face."

"I couldn't say."

"And the bruises on the arm—what does that usually suggest to you, in terms of the order of attack?"

"One of two things. Either the attacker grabbed the victim first, before the attack—perhaps during an argument, which then escalated into physical violence—or the attacker held the victim by the arm while they inflicted the violence. But in this case—"

"In this case," says Enygma, the excitement surging up to his chest, "the bruises on the victim's arm are on the same side as the bruises on the victim's face and the gashes over the victim's ear. So he could not have held her with one hand and swung at her with the other."

"Probably not at the same time. No."

"Thank you, Professor McCabe."

—OK. Time out.

What's wrong now?

—Well, it feels as if things are about to get technical. We do not do technical. And our readers definitely don't do technical. Barely a STEM GCSE between them. Readers just want the illusion of technical. You know, without the pie charts and the Venn diagrams.

Really?

—Damn straight.

But I've made notes on the injuries. Relative position, diameter, circumference . . . All of it.

—Definitely not. Circumference, no. Diameter, no. Position, OK. But not missionary. And definitely not with relatives.

OK, Einstein. How do we demonstrate the difficulty of holding someone and hitting them on the same side, at the same time, in the dark, without getting technical?

Let's Play a Game!

For this game you will need a murderer and a murderee. You will also need an audience.

This game is called "Are You There, Moriarty?" In the traditional version of this game, each player is blindfolded and armed with a rolled-up newspaper. Player One calls out, "Are you there, Moriarty?" and waits in the dark for the other's reply. Player Two calls out, "Here," or "Yes," or any other word that comes to mind, and Player One swings his newspaper at the spot where he believes his opponent to be. And then the other player takes a turn.

In our game, only one player will have a rolled-up newspaper, though both will be blindfolded. Player One must wait at the bottom of some stairs—say, for example, in a basement. He must wait until he judges Player Two to have reached the bottom of the steps.

Audience members must keep count of every blow that Player One manages to land on target—the target, of course, being the head. One point for every blow landed. Points taken away for every blow that misses.

Ready.

Set.

Go.

Now try that again with one hand tied behind your back.

"YOU SEE," SAYS Enygma, "the theory the police put forward was that Lord Verreman waited at the bottom of the basement steps for his wife. He knew that his wife had a cup of tea at nine o'clock every night, and he believed that the nanny was out of the house. He removed the lightbulb so that he could not be seen from outside or from the top of the stairs. The police maintain that, as the woman he believed to be his wife reached the bottom step, he hit her with the lead pipe. And hit her again. And again.

"But that is not consistent with the evidence. If his plan was to kill her, and he landed the first blow at the bottom of the stairs, rendering her unconscious, he could land repeated blows with the pipe without having to punch her in the face. The pathologist's evidence is that she did not die straightaway, but probably lost consciousness after the first blow over the ear, thus allowing him to bring down the weapon repeatedly in the same spot.

"OK. But in that case, what about the bruises to the face? The black eye and the thick lip. And what about the four in-line bruises on the arm, which strongly suggest that someone stood in front of her and gripped her by the arm? And," Enygma says triumphantly, "what about the defensive bruises on the back of her hand?"

David Verreman leans forward a little in his chair. He is looking

THE GAME IS MURDER

unwell. Distinctly unwell. But interested. "I expect they would say he gripped her while he was hitting her. That would make sense."

"I expect they would. In fact, they did. But they were wrong. Dead wrong. Because you can't hold someone by the right arm and punch them on the right side of the face at the same time.

"Violence, particularly domestic violence, escalates. You argue. You point fingers. You give a little shove. You grab the other person by the arm. Then you punch them. They put their hands in front of their face. You punch them again. And after that, if you haven't managed to work out all your rage, you reach for the blunt instrument: the house brick, the baseball bat, the lead pipe—doesn't matter. But you don't start with lethal weapons and work down."

"So?"

"So," Enygma says, returning to the wall and striking a red line through all of it, "whoever attacked Sally Gardner stood in front of her. He spoke to her. He grabbed her by the arm. He punched her in the face. Once, twice, three times. In other words, Sally Gardner's murderer knew who she was!"

ACT 3

❖❖❖❖❖❖❖❖❖❖

NOT GUILTY!

14

✦ ✦ ✦ ✦ ✦

A TRAGEDY AT LAW

Ladies and gentlemen.

The dearly beloved and the barely tolerated.

People 'n' sheeple.

Gather round.

The curtain is about to rise upon the third, and final, act.

All those having business before the court, draw near and hearken.

The court is now in session.

—*Court? What court is this?*

You know what court.

—*A tennis court? A royal court? The Royal Court Theatre?*

You know what court.

—*Criminal court?*

Exactly.

—*And which case are we trying?*

You know which—

—*Just tell us!*

All parties in the matter of *Rex v. Verreman*, step forward.

IN THE BASEMENT of 8 Broad Way, a change has occurred. The piano and the family dining table have been removed from the breakfast room. Gone, too, is the cast-iron stick stand holding only an umbrella and a single ancient tennis racket. Gone is the handy chest containing and constraining the unsightly accumulation of ephemera that surrounds a growing family.

The basement, formerly the setting for a thousand family meals and a single notorious crime, is now a courtroom. The judge sits on a raised platform, so that he might have the pleasure of looking down upon the proceedings. Below the platform are two tables, each with a chair facing the judge. On the right side, we have the prosecuting barrister, and on the left, the defense.

David Verreman settles himself in the judge's chair, motions you to sit and clears his throat. He waits for you to settle as comfortably as you can in your uncomfortable jury chair, and he begins his opening speech. "Members of the jury, you have been called to hear evidence in the case of"—he glances for a moment at his notes—"*Rex v. Verreman*, to consider that evidence in a sober and careful manner and to render your verdict based upon the evidence presented here. And *only* the evidence presented here.

"In a moment, counsel for the prosecution will begin their opening statements, but, before they begin, I would like to say a few words about procedure in a criminal case. You, the jury, will be the judge of the facts of this case. But I am the judge of the law.

"It will be your job to listen to the evidence presented, both by the prosecution and by the defense, and render your judgment on the facts of the case. Only *your* judgment matters. It does not matter what the prosecution believes. Nor does it matter what the defense believes. In the matter of the facts of the case, it does not even matter what I believe. It is your vote that counts.

"However, it is my job to interpret the law, and to conduct this trial in accordance with the law. I may say at the outset that there are several factors in this case that present complex legal difficulties, and you must be guided by me on these matters, because I am the judge of the law." David Verreman smiles momentarily and adds, "That's why they gave me this wig."

David Verreman is, in fact, wearing a full judge's outfit: black robes with red flashing, and a long gray horsehair wig. On the bench in front of him, Verreman has placed a black square of cloth. Max Enygma recognizes it as the black cap donned to deliver a death sentence. He wonders uneasily why it is there, and keeps his fingers crossed that it just came with the costume.

Verreman continues. "The prosecution have brought this case, and it is the responsibility of the prosecuting counsel to prove their case. The legal term is, as I'm sure you are aware, 'beyond a reasonable doubt,' which means that you must be satisfied in your own mind that you have reached the right conclusion. It is not up to the defendant to prove his innocence. If the prosecution cannot prove the case beyond your reasonable doubt—if in your own mind you are unsatisfied of the defendant's guilt—then you must find the defendant not guilty.

"It is not the defendant's responsibility to provide you with an alibi. He need not speak a word in his defense, and in this case, indeed, he cannot do so. It is not the job of defending counsel to put the noose around another man's neck, but only to remove it from that of their own client. Nor is it up to *you* to make the case for another man's guilt. If you believe that the prosecution has not made its case, then it is your duty to return a verdict of not guilty. You need not cast around for other likely suspects.

"Prosecuting counsel have accused this man of murder. It is your responsibility to judge that case, and only that case, on the evidence presented here."

—Quick sidebar.
What?
—Isn't that judge guy the prosecution?
No.

—I thought he was.

That wouldn't hardly be fair, now, would it?

—I meant . . . never mind. Who is the judge addressing?

What do you mean, who? The jury, of course.

—Yes, but who is the jury?

Well, The Reader, I suppose.

—That's what I thought. And how are they going to deliver a verdict at the end of the trial? Answers on a postcard?

We'll think of something.

—We'd better. Because if we get to the end of this book and there is no verdict, you know what happens to us.

I know.

—I cannot be trapped inside this book forever! I cannot be forever retracing my steps and trying to figure out where I went wrong! Do you know what it's like when they close this book? Let me clue you in. It's dark, man. It's fucking dark.

Don't worry. I know what I'm doing.

—I hope so. Because if I'm trapped in here, then so are you. And I am not a pleasant cellie.

"COUNSEL FOR THE prosecution will make their opening statement," says the judge.

"Thank you, my lord," says Daniel Verreman, Kings Counsel, rising.

—Whoa! Sidebar. Again.

What?

—I thought Daniel Verreman and David Verreman were the same person?

Not in this act.

—Excuse me?

It was getting boring. So I made them two different people. In fact, I made them all different people.

—And you can do that?

Why not? Just go with it for now. We'll explain it all later.

—*That's an awful lot you've got riding on* later. *We're in the final act. How much more* later *is there?*

You worry too much. It'll be fine.

—*Yeah? That's what the* Lost *guys said. And remember what happened to them.*

MAX ENYGMA SETTLES himself behind the defense's table and glances over at Daniel Verreman. Though he superficially resembles his brother, Daniel is more rangy, with dark shadows under his eyes. Although Daniel's body is quite still, Enygma senses a deep restlessness beneath his skin.

He looks like a wolf, Enygma thinks, *forever prowling. Forever watching. Waiting for an opportunity to pounce on any unsuspecting lamb that strays too far from the flock.* He cautions himself not to be a lamb.

Enygma takes a sip of water to give the jury the illusion that he is perfectly composed. He is glad to notice that his hand is not shaking. He can feel his bottle of pills in his trouser pocket, and is glad of the reassurance that they give him. He is glad, too, that he thought to get them back from Daniel before this trial began. He won't take one yet, but it is good to know they are there.

Daniel rises and calmly begins to deliver his opening address. "Members of the jury, it is the prosecution's claim that Lord John Verreman, the seventh Earl of Verre, murdered Mrs. Sally Gardner on the night of the seventh of November 1974, by repeatedly beating her over the head with a length of lead pipe.

"We will show you when he killed her, how he killed her and why he killed her, so that you can build a clear picture in your mind of the events of that night, so that, as the judge expressed it, you can be sure in your mind of John Verreman's guilt in this despicable crime.

"We will present physical evidence recovered from the scene of the crime that conclusively places John Verreman in that house on that night, and at the time that this attack took place. We will also call witnesses who can attest to his presence, and we will also provide evidence in the earl's own words that he was there on that fateful night.

"We will call a world-renowned expert on blood analysis to testify that blood of the same type as that found at the scene of the crime was also found in the car driven by the defendant.

"And we will call a forensic expert who will demonstrate conclusively—*conclusively*—that the weapon found at the scene of the crime can only have come from the defendant's borrowed car, and, thus, from the defendant himself.

"Now, the defense may, very properly, try to call this evidence into question. They may ask you to doubt the veracity or the quality of the evidence presented by these expert witnesses, or they may invite you to interpret that evidence in a different way. That is the role of the defense counsel, and it is entirely proper that they do that.

"However, we are confident that the evidence in this case is so unequivocal that, after you have listened to both arguments, you will have no difficulty in reaching a verdict with which you are entirely satisfied in your own mind. We are confident that, after weighing the evidence carefully and giving just consideration to both arguments, you will have no difficulty in finding Lord John Verreman guilty of the brutal murder of Mrs. Sally Gardner.

"Thank you."

There is a moment of silence after Daniel sits. Enygma takes his time in standing. He takes a sip of water slowly, sets his glass down carefully in the exact center of his desk, then clears his throat, like a man who has all the time in the world but doesn't need it.

"Ladies and gentlemen, we are very fortunate to have been blessed with a high number of extremely capable and experienced professionals who have lent their expertise to this case. The investigation into the murder of Mrs. Sally Gardner was led by a detective chief inspector with many years' experience in investigating high-profile crimes. And, as my colleague, counsel for the prosecution, has said, they will be calling a number of eminent professional witnesses, all of whom have achieved deservedly high national and international reputations in their own fields.

"The defense will not be calling their findings into question. We will call no expert witnesses of our own to rebut their testimony. The defense is happy to take their testimony as fact, sight unseen.

"You might ask yourselves, in that case, what we are doing here. If the facts of the case are undisputed, how can the verdict be in doubt? A good question."

Enygma takes another sip of water. He is beginning to enjoy himself. "A case is not made up simply of facts. Facts are like pinpoints on a map. You must touch them all while navigating your way through the case—you cannot ignore them—but the route you take between them is up to you.

"As an example, when astronomers first studied the heavens, they plotted the movements of the planets in relation to the earth. These measurements were accurate and precise—remarkably so. In the second century AD, Ptolemy wrote an astronomical treatise, based on these measurements, that placed the earth at the center of the universe, with the other planets orbiting around it in complex, though rather beautiful, epicycles. But Copernicus, using the same measurements, placed the sun at the center, to show the planets orbiting in plain circles—or, rather, ellipses—around it.

"Both astronomers used the same datasets but reached entirely different conclusions.

"As it is in the heavens, so it is here on Earth. In this case, we have our dataset, which is the evidence provided by our expert witnesses. It is my job, and the job of my esteemed colleague, to interpret that data and build a *theory* about what happened on the seventh of November 1974, one that we think best, and most clearly, explains the facts of this case. And it is your job, members of the jury, to decide which one of us is Ptolemy and which is Copernicus.

"The case for the defense will be that, while we accept, absolutely, the facts of the case, we reject the theory that has been derived from them—namely, that our client is guilty of murder. We will show that our theory, while less showy than the prosecution's, has the beauty of simplicity.

"Our client was in this house on the night the murder took place. There is no question about that. He has admitted it. But this was his house, a house he had every right to enter. And we will show that he made a habit of checking on this house around the same time every night, so that his presence here was neither unusual nor unexpected.

"The prosecution will seek to show motive. We will prove to you that our client had no motive. None. The prosecution will seek to show means and opportunity. While, no doubt, our client had the means to commit this murder, so, too, did every other adult in the Greater London area on that night. As to opportunity, while there is a theoretical margin of time in which he *could* have committed this crime, in practice, we believe no reasonable person would give that theory credence.

"And, members of the jury, you all look like reasonable people to me.

"As the judge has already pointed out, it is not necessary for us to prove our client's innocence. The burden of proof rests with the prosecution, beyond a reasonable doubt. Beyond *your* reasonable doubt. Yet such a position is inherently unsatisfying—like reading a whodunnit only to find the last ten pages missing. And so, as a work of supererogation, we will present you with an alternative solution, one that fits the facts of the case at least as well as the case made against my client.

"If you find our solution implausible, it will, I assure you, be no *more* implausible than the solution presented by the prosecution in this case—in which case guilt will be a coin toss, and the preponderance of doubt must be in my client's favor. However, if you find our alternative solution in any way plausible, whether or not our solution is susceptible of proof, I will respectfully *demand* that you return a verdict of not guilty in this case.

"That's all I have to say for the moment, ladies and gentlemen. Thank you."

DAVID VERREMAN GIVES Daniel a nod and invites him to call his first witness, and he calls Mrs. Dorothea Sayers.

"Please state your occupation as of November 1974."

"I owned an employment agency, providing domestic staff to homes in the inner London area."

"By 'domestic staff,' do you mean nannies?"

"Not just that. Nannies, au pairs, cleaners. Butlers sometimes, too. Though not often. By 1974 buttling had gone out of fashion, pretty much. Domestic workers were almost always women, unless they were driving the cars."

"Thank you. But you provided the Verreman family only with nannies?"

"No, that's not true. Au pairs a couple of times, I remember. But mostly, I agree: with nannies."

"Thank you. That is the aspect of your relationship with the Verremans that I am interested in."

"OK."

"Sally Gardner was sent by you to the Verreman home. Is that correct?"

"I didn't send her. She had a choice. I didn't make her go!"

"Of course not. Can you tell me, then, how a domestic agency works? Who is your client?"

"The families are the clients. They tell me what they need, and I recommend people who I think will be a good match. I make the introduction, and they meet. If they are both happy, the client employs the nanny directly, and they pay me a fee for the introduction."

"I see. So the nannies are not employed by you."

"That's correct."

"They just register with you, and send you their CV. Do you take their references?"

"We do not. That is up to the employer. We do, however, take staff largely by recommendation, so that we have only the best domestic staff to offer our clients."

"I'm sure," says Daniel, polite but uninterested.

"So, you made the introduction between Mrs. Sally Gardner and Lady Verreman. Was that the first time Lady Verreman used your services?"

"It was not. Although it was, strictly speaking, Lord Verreman who was the client—by which I mean he was the one who was paying the bills. However, it was usually Lady Verreman who I dealt with on a day-to-day basis."

"I see. How many nannies did you introduce to the Verremans?"

"I can't say how many I introduced. Some never got past an initial meeting. I can tell you that I provided them with seven nannies in the six months before the murder, as well as a couple of cleaners. But I doubt you will be interested in them."

"Seven nannies? That sounds like a lot."

"Yes and no. Sometimes it takes a while to find the right fit. When they find it, a nanny can expect to remain in the same family for years, sometimes long after the children have grown up and left home. And not all nannies want to become permanents. I had quite a few who did not want to become attached to one particular family, even though the families would have loved to keep them."

"I see. And when were you first asked to provide nannies to the Verreman household?"

"Just that last six-month period."

"And why was that?"

"I suppose because the previous nanny, who had been a permanent, left, and Lady Verreman needed help in the home."

"She had a husband, didn't she? Couldn't he help?"

David Verreman glances briefly at Enygma, to see if he is going to object, but Enygma stays resolutely in his chair. He is doodling in his notebook, to show that he is listening but is not worried. He is drawing a cracked egg.

"They had separated—Lord and Lady Verreman, I mean."

"I see. Now, you testified that you dealt with both Lord and Lady Verreman. Were they easy clients?"

"There's no such thing as an easy client. They all have their own peculiarities."

"Were the Verremans more or less peculiar than the average client, would you say?"

"Well, perhaps a little more peculiar than some. But they were separated. That causes tension in the home. Obviously it does."

"Now, Sally Gardner—how long had she been in the Verremans' employ?"

"About six weeks."

"And how was it working out?"

"Very well. I thought that this one might be a sticker."

"You thought Mrs. Gardner might become a permanent nanny?"

"It was looking that way."

"Both Verremans liked her?"

"I believe so, yes."

"Now, I believe that there was a period of time when custody of the children was given to the father. Were you supplying nannies to the family at that time?"

"I was."

"Can you tell me what you know about that?"

Again, David glances toward Enygma, who is still doodling. He has added stick arms and legs to the egg, and is now giving it blood-shot eyes.

"One of my nannies was picking up the child from school—"

"The children."

"I'm sorry?" Mrs. Sayers says.

"One of your nannies was picking up the *children* from school. Not the child. The children." Daniel leans in close toward the witness box. His voice is quieter but more dangerous, Enygma notices, and for a moment, his pencil stops blacking one bloodshot eye.

"Er, yes. Yes, that's right. I forgot that. Of course. The children. I'm sorry."

"Go on."

"Well, one of my nannies was picking up the *children* from

213

school—not Mrs. Gardner; it was perhaps five months prior to the murder—and Lord Verreman met her at the school gate and took the children. He had been to court and got what they call an ex parte order—you'll know all about that—giving him temporary custody of the children. But it was only for a couple of months, and then the judge awarded Lady Verreman custody, with just visiting rights for his lordship. And quite right, too, trying to take children away from their mother. Shameful."

Enygma lays down his pencil and gets to his feet with all the appearance of weary resignation, though he is secretly delighted. "My lord, I object. We really can't take this witness's opinion."

David nods, satisfied that Enygma is actually paying attention. "Agreed. Please confine yourself to answering the questions, Mrs. Sayers, and refrain from giving us your opinion."

"Were the children returned to the custody of their mother?" continues Daniel.

"Yes, they were!"

"Thank you. Now, with regard to Mrs. Gardner's references—can you remember who she gave?"

"I do. She had previously worked for an old couple as domestic help, and before that, as a cleaner. I did not see the references myself, but I heard from Lady Verreman that her husband had followed them up, and the references were excellent—which is no less than I expected."

"And neither Lady Verreman nor her husband made any complaint to you about Mrs. Gardner's employment during the six weeks that she worked for them?"

"That is correct."

"And do you know of any reason why Sally Gardner may, herself, have been targeted by a killer?"

"Absolutely not."

"Thank you, Mrs. Sayers."

David Verreman is getting restless. He seems unsatisfied with his role as judge, as if he has finally realized that the man with the best costume does not necessarily get the best lines. He nods at Enygma, curtly, to let him know he's up.

"Mrs. Sayers, I just have a few questions. You mentioned that you had placed seven nannies at the Verreman home in the six months prior to the murder of Mrs. Sally Gardner. Is that correct?"

"Yes."

"You mentioned also that Mrs. Gardner had been in the Verremans' employ for six weeks at the time of her death. Also correct?"

"Yes."

"Which makes Mrs. Gardner one of their longest-serving staff members?"

"Well, I don't know about that."

"Seven nannies in six months—that's an average of around three and a half weeks. So, Mrs. Gardner being one of the longer-serving staff members, I have to wonder, who was the shortest?"

"I can't remember names."

"That's OK. We don't need names. How long? How long did the shortest-serving member of staff last?"

"Two hours," says Mrs. Sayers, glumly.

"Two hours! Wow. Barely enough time to take off her coat. And did that staff member leave of their accord?"

"No. Lady Verreman fired them."

"Why?"

"I don't know . . . I think . . . she thought that her husband was paying the nanny to spy on her."

"And was he paying the nanny to spy on his wife?"

"Well, he was paying them, yes. I don't know about the rest."

"Wouldn't you expect a nanny—any nanny—to report regularly to her employer?"

"Yes."

"To let them know how the children were doing at school? If they were happy? If they had hurt themselves? That sort of thing?"

"Yes, but that's not what he was doing . . . Not what she thought he was doing. He was quizzing the staff about what went on in the house, so that he could use it against her in court."

"Is that your supposition, or Lady Verreman's?"

"Well, hers. But that's not to say it wasn't true."

"Did Lord Verreman, to your own knowledge, ask any member of his staff to spy on his wife?"

"Not to my own knowledge, no. But that's what Antonia believed."

"You said that the shortest-serving member of her staff was fired. Were all the nannies fired?"

"No. Two were temporaries from the start. One quit."

"Why?"

"My lord," Daniel Verreman says, "the reason a prior nanny resigned can hardly be of relevance."

"I'll withdraw the question," Enygma says, and adds, "No further questions."

David dismisses the witness, adjusts his robes, clears his throat and looks around his bench for a gavel, which, this being a British court, is not there. Then he tells Daniel to get on with it and call the next witness.

STANLEY GARDNER WALKS to the stand, deliberately and heavily, as though wearing lead-lined boots. His face is saying that only his dogged determination to get at the truth is propelling him across this room. His body, on the other hand, is saying he can't be arsed with this shit anymore.

Daniel Verreman makes him confirm that, yes, he was still married to Sally Gardner at the time of her death, and yes, that does mean he was her next of kin. Yes, he identified her body. Well, he could hardly ask her parents to do that, could he? He hadn't seen her folks much since the separation, but hell, no man would want to see his little girl like that.

"Very commendable," says Daniel, in a tone that makes it clear he couldn't give a monkey's. "Now, though you were separated, neither of you had begun divorce proceedings—is that correct?"

"Correct," Gardner says.

"Why was that?"

"Well, I don't know. I had been away with my job. And Sally—I don't think she was that fussed."

"Did either of you entertain hopes of a reconciliation?"

"No. It was over. We both knew that. But we hadn't got around to it—that's all."

"I see. You don't think she was in any hurry to remarry?"

"I don't think so. She didn't like to be tied down."

"Were you aware that she had taken a job as a live-in nanny?"

"I'd heard about it. On the grapevine, you know. Not the specifics, I don't think. Just that she was working for the aristocracy—the nobs, we called 'em. I thought that was pretty funny."

"Why?"

"I don't know. I imagined her having to wear a uniform and curtsy and stuff. Like you saw on the telly. *Upstairs, Downstairs.* That was on at the time. Remember that? And it tickled me, thinking that she was one of them, *yes ma'am*ing, *no ma'am*ing, and all that." He smiles for a second. Then, remembering where he is, he wipes the smile away and says, "Probably wasn't like that at all. But that's what I thought."

"Can you think of any reason why someone would want to hurt your wife?"

"No."

"Can you think of any person who bore a grudge against your wife?"

"No. Everyone liked her. Even Lady La-di-da liked her. So she said, anyways."

"Lady Verreman?"

"Yes. Sorry. Shouldn't have said that. I only met her at the inquest."

"You didn't warm to her?"

"She didn't strike me as having any warmth in her. But that's just my impression. It counts for nowt."

"Thank you, Mr. Gardner."

Stanley Gardner runs his finger round his collar as Enygma stands slowly.

"You said that neither you nor your wife had begun the process of divorcing."

"That's right."

"Had you discussed it with her? At any time?"

"I'm sure we did. When we split up. Must have done. I think I probably said, *I want a divorce*. It's what you say, isn't it? But I meant, *We're finished*, really. The divorce bit was just the paperwork. I'm not good with paperwork."

"It was you who ended the relationship?"

"Well, yes. I suppose so. I said the words, you know. But it was obvious to both of us."

"She was happy to part ways, then?"

"Well, I don't know about that. It's a pride thing, isn't it? Who finishes it. Who's dumped and who gets to do the dumping. Nobody likes being handed their cards. But it was for the best, and I think she realized that."

"If she had come to you and told you that she was in a new relationship and wanted to get a speedy divorce, would you have objected to that?"

"Not at all. I was in a new relationship myself by that time."

"You would have wished her well?"

"I'm not sure I'd have gone that far. We were exes, after all. But I wouldn't have stood in her way."

"But, just to be clear, she did not ask you for a divorce?"

"No, she didn't."

"Thank you."

"NEXT WITNESS!" CALLS David Verreman, sharply. He has developed a "let's get this over with" air, and all of his earlier savoir faire has disappeared.

The man is sulking.

Daniel calls Eddie Biggers to the stand.

"You were in a relationship with Mrs. Gardner at the time of her death—is that correct?"

"Yes," says Eddie.

"Had you been seeing each other long?"

"A few weeks."

"How many?"

"I don't know. Five or six."

Eddie Biggers is not being forthcoming, and Enygma wonders whether that is due to natural taciturnity or a reluctance to testify. The deep frown lines in his forehead suggest that Biggers is just a miserable bugger.

"So since around the same time that Mrs. Gardner began working for the Verremans?"

"Yes, well, I was a relief manager at the Three Taps at the time. That was my job. Relief manager. She came in there with some friends on her first night off."

"The Three Taps was the public house on the Verremans' street. Were you working there on the night of the murder?"

"No, I was not. I was working at the Old Peculiar."

"All that evening?"

"Yes."

"And how was your relationship with Mrs. Gardner? It was early days, but did you get the sense that this was the beginning of a committed relationship, or was it something more casual?"

"We were committed to each other." For the first time, Biggers looks interested in the conversation. "Sometimes you just know you're right for each other, don't you? We had talked about moving to Australia together. That's where I'm from, and she had lived there herself for a while when she was a kid, though she hardly remembered it. But that gave us a connection, you know. It was early days—you're right—but we had talked about marriage and children, too, one day. We were, you know, making plans for the future. It was good. It was all good."

"You went out together the night before the murder—is that correct? Tell us about that."

"Yes, well, Sally had asked Lady What's-it if she could change her night off to a Wednesday night, so that we could spend it together. I usually have to work weekends, see."

"Are Thursday nights considered a weekend night?"

"They are in the pub trade. Thursday to Sunday is busy; Monday is usually the day to restock, clean the place, sort out the admin and so on; Tuesdays and Wednesdays are the quiet nights. So, anyway, Sally changed her day off, and that Wednesday was the first time we had been able to go out, just the two of us."

"That must have been nice for you."

"It was . . . Well, it was at first. Mostly. Then we had a bit of a silly row, and Sally left a bit earlier than usual."

"Was that the last you saw of her?"

"Well, it was the last time I *saw* her, but I spoke to her on the phone the night of the murder. We made up, and we made plans for the following week."

"To be clear, you called Mrs. Gardner shortly before she was murdered? What time would you say that was?"

"Somewhere between eight and half past, I would say. I was working, but I took a cigarette break and gave her a call."

"And how did she seem to you? Did she seem nervous at all? Frightened?"

"No. She was just the same as usual. We talked for a bit, and that was it. She was fine."

"Thank you."

"Mr. Enygma!" says David Verreman, almost before Daniel has reached his seat. "We don't have all day."

Max Enygma takes his time rising, and crosses the floor to the witness stand.

Enygma looks at Biggers for a moment before consulting his notes. Biggers swallows nervously. Enygma looks up again and says, "Who is Ray?"

Biggers splutters a little. "I'm sorry?"

"Ray. Do you know who Ray is?"

"Ray who?"

Enygma gives a little smile. "Well, that is what I was asking you, Mr. Biggers. Let's put that to one side for a moment. You have testified that you had only known Mrs. Gardner a few weeks—five or six at most, since she walked into the pub where you worked during her first week as a nanny in the Verreman home. Is that correct?"

"Yes."

"And yet you were already considering marriage and children? Emigrating to the other side of the world? That's pretty fast work, isn't it, Mr. Biggers, considering you both worked full-time and met once a week?"

Eddie Biggers tries a smile. It doesn't land. "What can I say? Kismet, an' that."

"And yet, despite the kismet, you argued the night before she was murdered?"

"Well, I dunno about 'argued.' We had a bit of a tiff—that's all."

"She returned home early, after changing her night off specifically so she could spend it with you, didn't she? What was the tiff about?"

"I can't remember. Something and nothing."

"Was it the first time you had rowed?"

"No, but every couple argues sometimes, don't they?"

"Even in the first six weeks? Even when it's kismet?"

"I don't know. We had a little tiff. That was all. We loved each other."

"You *loved* each other? Had you used those words? Had you told her you loved her? Had she said she loved you?"

"Yes!" Biggers' chin goes up, just a little.

Enygma walks to his table, turns over the pages in his notebook and looks carefully at a blank page, as if he is reading it, then walks back to the witness. "Do you know what love bombing is, Mr. Biggers?"

"No."

"It's a term used—by young people mostly, I imagine—to describe a type of abusive behavior where one person lavishes a disproportionate amount of affection and attention on their partner in order to make that person feel obligated to them."

Biggers shrugs. "OK . . . ?"

"In other words, love bombers come on strong, promise the earth and try to sweep their partners off their feet."

"Sounds romantic."

"In the movies, maybe. In real life, according to"—Enygma picks up a magazine—"*Cosmopolitan* and"—he picks up another one—"*Psychologies*—in the plural—that kind of intensity can put some women off. What do you think?"

"I wouldn't know."

"Me neither," says Enygma, "but women have always been a mystery to me. Do you think it is possible—given that you had talked about marriage and children and emigration in the first few weeks of your relationship, and that you had already had more than one row, a row that was serious enough for her to call off the date that she had changed her work shift to go on—that Sally Gardner felt love bombed, or, shall we say, suffocated by your attentions?"

"No."

"OK. So, when you called her that evening, shortly before she was murdered, how did she seem?"

"Normal."

"Normal. But you had to make up first, didn't you?"

"Well, yes."

"And then everything was OK?"

"Yes."

"And then what?"

"We talked for a bit. Then we made plans to meet up the following week."

"How long were you on the phone?"

"Not long. I was at work, see? Maybe five minutes."

"Five minutes. You are a fast worker."

"I don't know what to tell you." Eddie Biggers tries another smile but shuts it off quickly.

"And you didn't arrange to meet her sooner than the following week? You didn't, perhaps, arrange to pop round to see her that night, on your break, to make up properly?"

"No."

"How far away from this house was the pub you were working in that night?"

"Not far."

"How far?"

"Five minutes, maybe, if you cut across the square."

"Did you cut across the square?"

"No! I got witnesses. An alibi. People who swore I was working all night. Pub managers don't get breaks."

"Not even to make a phone call?"

Daniel Verreman starts to rise, and Enygma waves his hand to indicate that he is nearly done. "Just one more question."

Daniel sits back down.

"Are you sure you don't know anyone called Ray?"

DAVID VERREMAN DISMISSES Biggers and calls for a fifteen-minute recess. Enygma is glad of the break. His mouth is dry, and the water that had been placed on his table has long since been drunk. He walks into the kitchen and fills his glass from the tap. The water has a metallic taste, but he drinks it all and fills the glass again, and drinks the second glass down, too.

He touches the tablet bottle in his trousers again, but doesn't pull it out. He reminds himself that he has taken his medication. This is not a symptom; this is just a headache. He isn't used to staying up all night. He wonders whether he should ask David Verreman if he has any acetaminophen. But he decides against. Apart from the head-ache, he is feeling pretty good. He reminds himself that he used to work through the night all the time. He could go forty-eight hours without sleep on a difficult case. No problem at all. He just needs to keep hydrated.

He refills his glass once more and sets it back on his table. He is ready for anything.

DANIEL VERREMAN CALLS Thomas Burke to the stand.

"Objection!" cries Enygma. "This witness can have little to offer this court but hearsay. In regard to *this* matter, the witness has nothing that can help the jury."

—Er, who is Thomas Burke?

Landlord of the Three Taps.

—Do The Readers know that?

They do now.

—And what's all this "objection" and "hearsay" stuff?

Thomas Burke knows nothing about the murder of Sally Gardner. Nothing. He knows what Lady Verreman told him, but that is inadmissible, because it's hearsay. He only knows about the injuries to Lady Verreman.

—So he can testify to that?

No. This case is not about the attack on Lady Verreman. It's about the murder of Sally Gardner. We've already said that the Court of Appeal ruled that the cases can't be tried together, and Lady Verreman can't testify in the murder trial.

—That's shit!

It is.

—No. That's really bad. We've got to get that in somehow.

Yes.

—Have you got a plan?

I have.

—You'd better have. Two and a half acts in, and the suspect gets off on a technicality? That would not be good for us.

No.

—So, what is the plan?

Make Lady Verreman testify, of course.

—She's dead.

A detail. We can get past that.

—Who are you? God?

No. We are the *narrator*. The Author is God. But we work for The Author. So we are God Adjacent. Which means we can do anything we want.

—But only until the last page! If The Reader gets to the end and doesn't like it, we're fucked.

It's cool.

—Like, fucked, man. I know The Author. Vindictive. And I can't go back to the dark. I need light. Warmth. I want to be a real boy . . . Go outside. Wear clothes—I haven't worn clothes in three years—a shirt, trousers. Trousers! And maybe one of those funny Tudor hats with a tassel. Anything! I can't breathe in here.

Calm down. It'll be fine. We've got this.

DAVID VERREMAN ADDRESSES the court. "Members of the jury, before the next witness takes the stand, I think it fitting that I explain certain finer points of the law to you. There are two points we need to consider at this time.

"Firstly, the law prohibits the testimony of a wife against her husband, even if that wife is willing to testify. There is only one exception to this law. That is where a wife alleges that she is the victim of a violent or sexual assault upon herself at the hands of her husband.

"In this case, therefore—in the matter of the murder of Mrs. Sally Gardner—Lady Verreman is not eligible to testify, and nothing she has said about the matter should be taken into consideration. In any case, Lady Verreman is now dead, and can no longer testify. Anything she may have said to another party would be classed as hearsay.

"However, defense counsel have indicated—unwisely, in my opinion—that they are so confident of their defense in this case that they are willing to allow Lady Verreman's testimony at the coroner's inquest, which was given under oath, to be read into the evidence."

Max Enygma stops doodling and stares at David Verreman. Has he ever given such an indication? No, he fucking hasn't. His head begins to throb, and he takes a sip of water. His hand shakes as he lifts the glass to his lips.

"The second matter you will need to consider," continues the judge, "is the law regarding hearsay. Any witness can testify to things that they have personally heard with their own ears or seen with their own eyes. In general, they may not testify to things that they have only been told about by a third party who is not present in the court.

"And if a witness should come to court to say that they heard another person make a statement regarding a certain event, that does not necessarily make that statement true. After all, the original speaker might have been a liar or a fool. As a general rule, courts try to take testimony only from firsthand witnesses. If Person A says that Person B has knowledge of an event, the court wants to hear from Person B, not Person A. In this case, however, the defense have waived their objections to the use of hearsay in this case—"

Enygma slams his pencil down on the table.

"—with the proviso that members of the jury must take the witness's statements with caution, bearing in mind the limited value of such evidence, and the possibility that, while the witness who appears in court may be telling the absolute truth about what they heard, the person from whom they got the story may have been the liar or the fool previously mentioned.

"When it comes time for me to sum up, I will clearly identify those pieces of evidence that you should treat with greater caution. It is your responsibility, of course, to weigh *all* the evidence with care, but for these particular pieces of evidence, greater caution will be required.

"I will speak further on this in my summing up, but I will say now that, while you will be entitled to take these pieces of evidence into account, I will be cautioning you that you should not base your verdict on these pieces of evidence alone if they are the *only* things that indicate guilt. They should only be used to give you a clearer or bigger picture of the events of that night.

"With this caveat, Lady Verreman's testimony may be entered into the evidence."

—*Smooth.*
Thanks.

DANIEL VERREMAN HANDS Enygma a copy of Lady Verreman's testimony before the inquest, and distributes more copies to the judge and jury.

Sworn Testimony of Lady Antonia Verreman
Witness 1 to Coroner's Inquest 16th June 1975

(annotations added by Max Enygma)

Coroner:	Lady Verreman, when did you last have contact with your husband?
LV:	Apart from a telephone call on the 18th of July 1974, concerning my son's chicken pox, I have had no contact with him at all.
Coroner:	So he could not have threatened you?
LV:	No.
Coroner:	And, prior to 7th November 1974, when did you last see him without speaking to him?
LV:	On 24th October.
Coroner:	Was this casually, in the street?
LV:	No, I looked out of my window and saw him.
Coroner:	What was he doing then?
LV:	Sitting in his car. I noticed he was wearing dark glasses.

Coroner: Was this outside your residence in Broad Way?

LV: Yes.

Coroner: Was he looking in any particular direction?

LV: He was about to drive away.

Coroner: What sort of car was this?

LV: A dark blue Mercedes-Benz.

Coroner: A car that you knew well?

LV: Yes.

Coroner: Did your husband possess a key to your home?

LV: Yes.

Coroner: Very well. Regarding your living situation, Lady Verreman, could you please tell us if you were receiving a regular allowance from your husband?

LV: Yes, I was.

Coroner: Did he pay the household expenses—the rates, and the telephone bill and water rates, etc.?

LV: The arrangement was that he would do that.

Coroner: Was that fulfilled, do you know?

LV: I imagine so, because the water gets cut off otherwise, doesn't it?

Coroner: Could I ask how much you were allowed by your husband?

LV: Forty pounds per month.

Coroner: And that payment was always perfectly prompt?

LV: It was erratic.

Coroner: Did you get the total in the end?

LV: In the end.

Does anyone else? How about the half dozen nannies you sacked? Current nanny? Family members?

£40 per week, according to previous statement and bank records. Error?

Coroner: Did you know much about your husband's financial situation?

LV: I have read a bit about it. I saw an article in the *Daily Express* that suggested he was in financial difficulties.

Coroner: But you do not know from your own personal knowledge?

LV: No.

Coroner: Fine, fine. Could you now tell me whether your husband enjoyed good health?

LV: I would say so, yes.

Coroner: He had no serious illnesses?

LV: None that I know of.

Coroner: Now, moving on to your domestic situation—when did Sally Gardner come to you?

LV: I think she came in September. One particular woman provided all the women I had.

Coroner: And did you get on with her?

LV: With Sally? Yes, I did.

Coroner: What sort of temperament?

LV: Even temperament. *Is she a horse?*

Coroner: Cheerful?

LV: Yes.

Coroner: Do you know whether she had any male friends?

LV: She told me about two. *Name? Details?*

Coroner: Were you aware that she was separated from her husband?

LV: Yes, I was.

Coroner: Did any of her male friends visit her at your house?

229

LV: No.

Coroner: Had she asked if a man could come?

LV: No.

Coroner: Did your husband know Sally Gardner?

LV: He met her when he collected the children for access and brought them back.

Coroner: That was all, as far as you are aware?

LV: As far as I'm aware, yes.

Coroner: On how many access weekends did your husband meet Mrs. Gardner?

LV: I believe it was three.

Coroner: What was Mrs. Gardner's usual night off?

LV: Thursday night—Thursday was her day off.

Coroner: Could you say anything about her stature? <u>Would she be a similar height to you?</u>

Leading!

LV: Her husband described her as five feet two inches, and I am five feet two inches.

Coroner: Had she tried on any of your clothes? A coat or anything of that kind?

LV: She had tried on a dress. It had been given to me by another woman, but it was much too large. I asked Sally if she would like to try it on, and she kept it.

Coroner: So, although you were the same height, she was rather fuller figured than you?

LV: Yes.

Coroner: The evening of 7th November 1974—was this a Thursday?

LV: Yes, it was.

Coroner: Sally's usual day off. Why was she at home that evening?

230

LV: Because her <u>current boyfriend</u> had his day off on Wednesday, and she asked if she could change hers to Wednesday as well, so she could go out with him.

Names! We want names! She has already told you Mrs. G had 2 boyfriends. Which one is her "current boyfriend"?

Coroner: So, on that night, there was, at home, yourself, the child and Mrs. Gardner?

LV: Yes.

Coroner: Thank you. Now, thinking about your home—do you usually put a chain on your door?

LV: Usually, yes.

Coroner: Around what time do you usually put the chain on the door?

LV: <u>Usually around six o'clock.</u>

<u>SIGNIFICANT!!!!!</u>

Coroner: And had you put the chain on the door that night?

LV: No, we had forgotten.

Coroner: There was also a door leading from the basement kitchen to the outside front of the house—is that correct?

LV: Yes.

Coroner: And is that kept bolted?

LV: Yes. It is opened to take out the rubbish, but other than that, it is kept locked and bolted.

Coroner: There is also a back door, I understand, which was unlocked.

LV: Yes.

Coroner: Could anyone have entered or left your home via the back door?

LV: I doubt it. At least, it would be a prickly business. It is an enclosed garden with a trellis of roses up the walls.

231

Coroner:	In the breakfast room, there are French windows. Are all your windows kept locked?
LV:	Yes.
Coroner:	How did you spend that evening, from about eight o'clock?
LV:	Watching television.
Coroner:	Where?
LV:	In my bedroom.
Coroner:	I believe that is on the second floor?
LV:	That's correct.
Coroner:	Who was watching television at eight o'clock?
LV:	Myself, initially. My son joined me later.
Coroner:	And Mrs. Gardner?
LV:	She was not watching with us. I'm not sure what she was doing. She may have been ironing or something, in her room.
Coroner:	And what time did Mrs. Gardner look into the room? Could you tell, approximately, the time?
LV:	About five to nine.
Coroner:	What did she say?
LV:	Would you like a cup of tea?
Coroner:	This was quite a usual thing, was it?
LV:	I had the habit of getting myself a cup of tea at that time. It was a thing I had been doing since the separation. But it wasn't a very usual thing for her to put her head around the door and offer to make it. *SIGNIFICANT!!!!!*
Coroner:	When she offered to get you some tea, did you accept?

LV:	Yes, indeed.
Coroner:	Where were you when she said she would get you some tea?
LV:	I was lying on the bed.
Coroner:	And your son also?
LV:	Also.
Coroner:	You can place the time, from the television program, at about five to nine?
LV:	Yes.
Coroner:	Did Mrs. Gardner take some crockery with her?
LV:	I don't know what she did.
Coroner:	We have the crockery here. Do you recognize these cups?
LV:	Yes, I do.
Coroner:	These were taken by Mrs. Gardner?
LV:	I am told that.
Coroner:	But had they been in your room?
LV:	They weren't taken from my room. She may have had them in her own room.
Coroner:	And then you were watching the nine o'clock news. Is that right?
LV:	Yes.
Coroner:	And when did you begin to wonder about the tea?
LV:	At about quarter past nine.
Coroner:	Did you hear anything unusual during this time?
LV:	Nothing unusual.
Coroner:	So, what did you do then?
LV:	I decided to go downstairs and find out what had happened to the tea.
Coroner:	And how far did you descend?

LV: To the ground floor.

Coroner: What did you do when you got there?

LV: I looked down the stairs leading to the basement.

Coroner: Was there anything unusual?

LV: There was no light on at all.

Coroner: Nowhere in the basement?

LV: Nowhere.

Coroner: There is a two-way switch, so that you can switch the light on from the top of the stairs and the other way round?

LV: I believe you can. It may be possible.

Coroner: Was the light usually left on?

LV: No.

Coroner: Did you try this switch?

LV: No, I didn't. I just saw it was dark, and so she couldn't be there.

Coroner: Did you call out?

LV: I called her name.

Coroner: What happened then?

LV: I heard a noise.

Coroner: What sort of noise?

LV: Just a noise of somebody, or something, in the downstairs cloakroom.

Coroner: This is where there is a washbasin and toilet?

LV: Yes.

Coroner: What happened next?

LV: <u>I walked toward the sound—at any rate, moved toward it.</u> *VERY, VERY SIGNIFICANT!!!!!*

Coroner: What happened then?

LV: Somebody rushed out and hit me on the head.

Coroner: Did this happen in the area at the top of the stairs, approximately?

LV: Approximately, yes.

Coroner: Was there more than one blow?

LV: <u>About four.</u>   *Cross-check with hospital report*

Coroner: Did you hear anybody speak at that time?

LV: Not at the time I was being hit on the head. Later.

Coroner: Then what?

LV: The person said, "Shut up."

Coroner: Did you recognize the voice? Who was it?

LV: My husband.

Coroner: What did he do then? What happened to you?

LV: He thrust three gloved fingers round my throat, and we started to fight.

Coroner: What happened during the fight?

First time she has had difficulty with her memory. Relevant? LV: <u>It's difficult to remember.</u> It was seven months ago. But during the course of it, he attempted to strangle me.

Coroner: From behind or in front?

LV: From in front. He tried to gouge out my eyes.

Coroner: And all this was at the top of the stairs, was it?

LV: Yes.

Coroner: You were both on the ground by this time?

LV: Yes.

Coroner: Do you remember sitting up somehow, between his legs, with your back to him or sideways?

LV: I would say sideways.

Coroner: <u>Then he desisted a little after that, did he?</u>

Tell you what, Doc, why not testify for her? You are feeding her the answers.

LV: He desisted, yes.

Coroner: There is a photograph of a top metal support on the balustrade of the stairs that has been disturbed. Can you explain that?

LV: <u>I would have dislodged it with my leg in the struggle.</u>

Something funny about this. What is it?

Coroner: Did you manage to persuade your husband to help you—first in the downstairs cloakroom?

LV: I asked him if I could have a drink of water.

Coroner: And what did you do? Where did you go?

LV: We went into the downstairs cloakroom, and I had a drink.

Coroner: I believe there was only hot water available. Is that right?

LV: Yes.

Coroner: Was it dark in the downstairs cloakroom, or had the light been switched on?

LV: It was dark.

Coroner: <u>Following this, you both went upstairs. Is that right?</u>

Leading! Leading! Leading!!!

LV: Yes.

Coroner: Where did you go?

LV: We went upstairs, to my bedroom.

Coroner: Who was in there?

LV: My son was still there.

Coroner: That's David, isn't it?

LV: Yes.

Repeat after me—the TV was on.

Coroner: <u>And the television was still on?</u>

LV: It was still on.

Coroner: What did you do when you got there?

LV: I said something.

Coroner: <u>You said you felt ill—is that right?</u>

LV: Yes.

Coroner: Did you lie on the bed?   *Now you really are answering for her, you jerk!*

LV: I did.

Coroner: What did your husband say when you lay on the bed?

LV: He didn't say anything. We went together into the bathroom before I lay on the bed, and together we looked at my injuries.

Coroner: After you had done that?

LV: After we had done that, I think I said I didn't feel very well, and he laid a towel on the bed, and I got on it.

Coroner: Would this towel have been laid on the pillow?

LV: Yes.

Coroner: And where was your son at this time?

LV: He went upstairs as soon as we came into the bedroom. The television was switched off and he went upstairs.

Coroner: And you were now lying on the bed. Did your husband say anything about helping you further?

LV: Very vaguely. I understood he was going to get a cloth to clean my face.

Coroner: <u>For this, he would have gone into the bathroom?</u>   *Christ, this is painful.*

LV: Yes.

Coroner: What did you do while he was in the bathroom?

LV: I heard the taps running, and I jumped

to my feet and ran out of the room and
down the stairs.

Coroner: Where did you go then?

LV: I ran to the Three Taps, a public house.

Coroner: That's a matter of thirty yards from
your house?

LV: Yes.

Coroner: From there, assistance was sought. And
then did you go to St. George's Hospital?

LV: Yes.

Coroner: How long were you there?

LV: Just under a week.

Coroner: [Handing over some letters] It is not
the content, but the handwriting, Lady
Verreman—do you recognize it?

LV: Yes, I would say it is his handwriting.

Coroner: Your husband's?

LV: Yes.

Coroner: [Displaying the sack] Had you ever seen
this before the evening of the 7th?

LV: I do not recognize it from before.

Coroner: What was he wearing?

LV: He was wearing a sweater of sorts, no
tie, and gray flannel trousers. That's
the best I can do.

Coroner: And you mentioned gloves. Did he take
them off?

LV: No, he took those off earlier. *Earlier when?*

Coroner: When you had gone to your bed?

LV: He took them off before.

Coroner: I think that this is all clear so far.
There is just one small thing. I think
that in the kitchen there is an electric
kettle. Is there some defect by which,

when it is switched on, the red light
shows?

LV: It does the opposite to what it should.

Coroner: The red light, then, is showing all the
time?

LV: Yes.

Sir Robert Traver, Queen's Counsel
[Acting on behalf of the Verreman family]:

You were separated on 7th January?

LV: 7th January 1973, yes.

Traver: And the position was that, even before
that separation, you entertained
feelings of hatred against your husband?

Claude Dancer, QC [Acting for Lady Verreman]:

Objection! I don't see how that can help
your inquiry.

Coroner: I was thinking that myself.

—*Adjournment for legal argument*—

Sworn Testimony of Lady Antonia Verreman
Witness 1 to Coroner's Inquest
16th June 1975—Continued

Defense counsel denied opportunity to cross.

Traver: <u>In view of the ruling you have given</u> in
the absence of the jury, I don't think I
can assist the jury at all, and I shall
ask the lady no further questions.

Clerihew Bentley, QC [Acting for the police]:

Casting your mind back to the struggle
with your husband—you described how you

239

had ended up between your husband's legs, and that he had desisted from his attack. Is that right?

LV: Yes.

Bentley: And is it right that you had grabbed hold of him during the course of the struggle?

LV: Yes.

Bentley: By his private parts?

LV: Yes.

Bentley: What effect, if any, did that have on him?

LV: He went back—he moved back.

Bentley: Did he say anything to you at this stage?

!!!!!

—*The coroner directs Lady Verreman not to answer the question.*—

Bentley: Can you describe the instrument that was used in the attack?

LV: It appeared to be slightly curved and hard.

Bentley: Do you remember saying to the police, "I know it sounds silly, but it felt bandaged"?

LV: Yes, that's right.

Bentley: And do you still feel that statement was accurate?

LV: Yes, I do.

—*A picture of the lead pipe found at the scene is handed to Lady Verreman.*—

LV: That seems to fit <u>the description</u> of what
I was hit with. *Whose description?*

Coroner: Thank you. Lady Verreman, speaking again
of this struggle—you say you called out
Mrs. Gardner's name. Did you see anybody
else at the time, apart from your
husband? Did anybody else brush past
you? Did you hear sounds?

LV: I saw nobody else.

Coroner: Not at any time during that evening?

LV: Not at any time that evening.

Coroner: Have you seen your husband since the
time he went into the bathroom off the
bedroom?

LV: No, I haven't seen him.

Coroner: And you have no doubt it was he?

LV: No doubt at all.

Coroner: Lady Verreman, thank you for giving
evidence today. Is there anything you
wish to alter from your evidence, or
anything you wish to add?

LV: No, there is nothing.

Coroner: Thank you very much, Lady Verreman. You
may step down.

MAX ENYGMA HAS finished reading through Lady Verreman's statement to the court, and he stands up. "My lord, before the prosecution bring in their next witness, might I be permitted to address the jury with regard to this testimony in order to point out several factual inaccuracies and peculiarities in the testimony that have come to my attention?"

David Verreman peers at him over a pair of half-moon spectacles that he has just now adopted. "The testimony speaks for itself, does it not? It was given under oath."

"Under oath, yes, my lord, but not under cross-examination. You will notice in your transcript that counsel for the Verreman family were not permitted to question Lady Verreman's account, and were prevented from asking pertinent or challenging questions. I would like to do that now—at least, I would like to put the questions to the jury for them to consider."

"Hmm," says Verreman. He makes a pretense of considering the motion, then waves it away. "I have already advised the jury that they must treat this evidence with caution. You will have an opportunity to present rebuttal witnesses when you make your defense. I see no need to do that on the prosecution's time. Prosecution may proceed."

Daniel Verreman once again calls Thomas Burke to the stand, while Enygma begins to wonder what the hell is going on. David Verreman wants his father acquitted, doesn't he? Then why is he making the defense so bloody difficult? How can he present a rebuttal witness to testimony from a dead woman? And why, out of all the witnesses in this case, is Lady Verreman the only one he cannot speak to? Why can't David Verreman channel his mother?

Enygma takes a sip of water and feels a spider—a big one this time—crawling over the side of his face. He slaps himself across the cheek, but the spider has already scuttled away.

It's this damned house, he thinks, and shivers.

15

◆ ◆ ◆ ◆ ◆

THE THREE TAPS

Go away, Mr. Whybrow. Go away from that door. Don't touch
it. Get right away from it. Get out of the house. Run.
—Thomas Burke, "The Hands of Mr. Ottermole"

THOMAS BURKE IS exactly what you would expect in a publican.
Genial. Approachable. Open. Reliable? *Well*, thinks Enygma, *that is
not a necessary quality for a publican, is it?* But Burke has the appearance of being a perfectly frank, honest and open witness. More's
the pity.

"You were working the night of the seventh of November 1974?"
Daniel Verreman asks.

"I was," says Burke, who manages to smile and show all his teeth
as he speaks.

"Do you recall Lady Verreman entering the Three Taps that
night?"

"I do, sir. Not a thing I would forget in a hurry. I can tell you that."

"And what time was that?"

"Ten minutes to ten, sir."

"Can you describe her appearance?"

"Head to toe in blood, she was. Horrible!" He smiles again as
he says it, but, Enygma thinks, out of professional habit more than

pleasure at the memory. Still, the sight is unsettling. Publicans, he supposes, must smile a lot at things that are not amusing, so perhaps it is a reflex action.

Enygma makes a note.

"Was she very upset?" asks Daniel. "Was she hysterical?"

"Well, she was quite all right for a few minutes. Didn't say a word. She'll have been in shock, perhaps. Then she began shaking all over, and crying, you know. Muttering things."

"What sort of things? Do you remember her words exactly?"

"Yes, sir, I do. Burned into my brain, they are. I can hear her saying them even now. There were two things she said: 'Help me. Help me. I've just escaped from being murdered.' That was the first one. She said that two or three times. Then the second thing she said quite a few times, and it was this: 'My child! My child! He's murdered my nanny.'

"Did she, by any chance, say *who* had murdered her nanny?"

Thomas Burke grins now. "No, sir. No names were mentioned. Not as far as I'm aware."

"And what did you do then?"

"Well, naturally, I phoned for the police and an ambulance."

"And did they arrive quickly?"

"Not as quickly as I'd have liked, no. I mean, it was a good twenty minutes, I think, before they came and took her away. I was surprised."

"I'm sure you were. Thank you."

Enygma shuffles through a pile of papers for a moment, and Thomas Burke sits at the witness stand, licking his lips while he waits. He flashes both the judge and the prosecutor smiles, which aren't returned. David Verreman drums his figures impatiently on the bench and says, "We're ready, Mr. Enygma."

"Thank you," Enygma says. "Aha!" He pulls a single sheet of paper from the stack. "You said that you called an ambulance and the police after Lady Verreman burst into your pub covered 'head to toe in blood.' Did you make that call yourself?"

"I did." A swift flash of teeth, then a nervous little cough.

"The police call log reads thus: 'Person assaulted. Ambulance called seven minutes past ten. Distressed female.' It doesn't mention murder. Did you not tell the police that there was a murderer at large?"

"Ah! Well, no, I might not have. Because, you know, I didn't *know* that there had been a murder done, did I? Not from my own knowledge, if you know what I mean."

"I do. This, in fact, is the sort of hearsay that the judge was warning us of earlier. You were worried that, though you were faithfully reporting what you had been told, it might not have been true?"

"Exactly."

"And that might explain the relatively leisurely response time. In my experience, the police are very quick off the mark if you use the word 'murder.'"

"That's a good tip. I'll remember that the next time I need to call them out." Another flash of teeth.

"Now, you said that when she arrived, Lady Verreman was 'head to toe' in blood. Was that an accurate description or just a general way of saying she had blood on her?"

"Oh, well, I don't know exactly. Maybe not head to *toe*. But she was pretty bloody—excuse my language." Smile. Teeth. Cough.

"It is important to be accurate," says Enygma. He picks up another piece of paper. "According to the expert who examined her clothes, she had blood around the neck and sleeves of her pullover, and the dress she was wearing had bloodstains on the right shoulder. She also had a number of blood smears. Does that sound about right?"

"Yes." No smile now.

"Good. Now, you said that she was all right for a few minutes, and only then started yelling and appearing distressed. Is that correct?"

"Yes."

"So she didn't ask you for help when she walked in covered 'head to toe' in blood?"

"No. Not at first."

"Odd. Did you offer help immediately? I mean, before she started yelling?"

"Not straightaway. No."

"Despite the fact that she was 'head to toe' in blood, you weren't immediately worried about her? She wasn't looking over her shoulder to see if she was being followed? She didn't ask you to call the police? To protect her from a murderer?"

"No. Well, I put that down to her being in a state of shock, as it were."

"But as soon as she said there had been a murder, you called the police, even though you were not sure that she was telling you the whole truth?"

"Yes, well, she might have been imagining it, or there might have been a murderer on the loose. I didn't know, did I? But as soon as she started saying, 'Help me, help me,' and 'He's murdered my nanny,' I called the police straightaway. Of course I did. Anyone would have."

"You testified that Lady Verreman entered the pub at nine fifty p.m., but you did not place the call asking for police and ambulance until ten oh seven p.m. That is over fifteen minutes. Are you saying that she sat in the pub, perfectly composed, though a little bloody, for fifteen minutes, and only then began screaming?"

"Well, yes. I dunno. About that. Something like that."

"And you are certain that the words that you have quoted here today are the exact words that Lady Verreman said that night? I'll repeat them here: 'Help me. Help me. I've just escaped from being murdered,' and 'My child! My child! He's murdered my nanny.'"

Thomas Burke smiles widely. "Those were her *exact* words. Exact. There were other people there that night, including my wife. They all made statements, too, and they said exactly the same thing!"

Enygma smiles, too. "Thank you, Mr. Burke. You've been very helpful."

"NEXT!" YELLS DAVID Verreman. He tries banging a pencil on his desk, finds the noise it makes unsatisfactory and throws it away in disgust. The prosecution calls George Heyer to the stand.

"You are Detective Sergeant George Heyer, and you were first on the scene at the Verreman home on the seventh of November 1974. Is that correct?" asks Daniel Verreman.

"Yes, sir. I was called first to the Three Taps public house, where I briefly interviewed Lady Antonia Verreman, and, acting on information received during that interview, I attended the scene of the crime, with two fellow officers."

"Can you describe the crime scene as you first encountered it?"

"Yes, sir. The front door was locked, as was the basement door leading to the street. It is not possible to see into the ground-floor window, as it lies over the well of the basement and is not reachable from the basement steps. I was able to look in the basement window through the blinds, but could see nothing except for a small red glow, which I subsequently discovered came from a faulty switch on a kettle."

"Did you notice the position of the basement blind?"

"Yes, sir, I did. It was half-closed."

"Do you mean it was halfway down the window?"

"No, sir, these were vertical blinds. They covered the full length of the window, but the slats were open at a forty-five-degree angle—roughly, that is. It was possible to get a partial view into the basement through the blinds. At least, you might have if the overhead light was on. But, of course, it wasn't. With just this tiny red light you could see pretty much nothing at all."

"I see. What did you do then?"

"My fellow officers and I effected an entry through the main front door, and it was immediately obvious to me that a violent crime had taken place. There was a considerable amount of blood in the hallway.

"Our first priority was to determine whether there was anyone still in the house, whether they be a victim, witness or assailant. We began our search with the ground floor, and then proceeded to the upper floors. There were four upper floors. On the top floor, we found a child—unharmed, I'm glad to say, and awake. One of my officers stayed with the child, and the other accompanied me back downstairs."

Enygma looks at Daniel, but Daniel does not correct the police officer. *Authority issues,* Enygma concludes.

"When I reached the hall again, I noticed an object on the floor. It was white, and bent in the shape of a doll's leg, which was what I took it to be. I just noticed it automatically, as any trained officer would do, but I didn't attach importance to it at that time.

"I tried to turn on the light in the basement, but the light wasn't working. This did not particularly surprise me, since many of the lightbulbs in the house had blown. However, I later discovered that this bulb had been bodily removed from its socket.

"From my vantage point at the top of the stairs, I switched on my torch and surveyed the scene. It was quite a sight. Blood everywhere, and blood pooled around a heavy canvas sack. There were splashes of blood up the walls and across the ceiling, and two or three footprints in the blood pointed toward the boiler room area.

"I went into the basement, being careful not to tread in the blood myself, in order to ensure that the basement was clear—it is not possible to see everywhere in the basement from the stairs. I opened the sack, which had a drawstring fastener that was partially closed. I loosened the strings enough to remove one arm belonging to a young woman in order to check that life was extinct, which it was. My colleague checked the back door, which was open but led into an enclosed garden, with very high walls, where no one could be hiding. I subsequently checked the garden myself and noticed that the walls were covered with ivy, and anyone escaping via the garden would have left unmistakable evidence of their means of egress. There was no such evidence visible that night, and in daylight it was plain that no one had escaped that way.

"Having satisfied myself that there was no living person, other than the child, on the premises, I then proceeded back to the hall to wait for the doctor, the forensics team and the senior investigating officers, who we had already called. As I reached the hall, I noticed that the object I had taken to be a white dolly's leg had turned red. Subsequent examination showed that this was a lead pipe covered in white Elastoplast-type fabric, which we now believe to have been the murder weapon."

"That is very clearly put," says Daniel. "Thank you. Now I would like you to consider the front door of the property. Did you notice any signs of forced entry?"

"No, sir."

"What about the basement door?"

"No forced entry there either, sir. The basement door had an old-fashioned mortise deadlock, the sort that has a large key. The door was locked, and the key was in the lock, on the inside of the door. Additionally, that door was bolted on the inside."

"Thank you. That's all."

Max Enygma stands up before David Verreman has a chance to reproach him, and he immediately begins his cross-examination.

"You mentioned that, when you arrived, the front door was locked and you had to effect an entry. Did you notice if there was also a bolt on the front door?"

"Yes, sir, there was. In fact, there were two bolts and a chain in addition to the lock, which was a Yale-type lock, which could be opened from the outside, with a key, or from the inside, with a latch. However, only the latch had been engaged when we effected entry. Lady Verreman later confirmed to me that she had forgotten to put the bolts and the chain on that night—which is a very great pity."

"Indeed. When did she normally lock up? When she went to bed?"

"No, sir. She said that she usually put the chain and locks on around six o'clock, after dinner. It's a big house, and the family usually sat on the upper floors in the evening, watching TV or reading or whatever. It saved her a journey if she put the bolts on after supper."

"I see. Lucky for you that you only had to get past one little lock, and not all those bolts. How difficult did you find it to get in?"

"Not that difficult. If you know just where to apply pressure, a lock like that will give way with a hefty shove, which was what we gave it."

"Hmm. You mentioned that there were no signs of forced entry."

"That's correct," says DS Heyer, though with a trifle more caution than he has used up till now.

"There were no broken windows?"

"None."

"The locks showed no marks from a jemmy or crowbar?"

"No, sir."

"And the front door showed no sign of being forced open?"

"No."

"And yet it had been forced open, had it not? By you."

"Yes. That's true."

"So it is possible, is it not, that the door had indeed been forced, as you forced it yourself later, but that this particular door was not capable of showing that it had been forced?"

"Yes, sir. That's perfectly possible."

"Police officers, of course, are trained to know just where to apply pressure. Criminals tend to learn on the job. Are some criminals capable of effecting entry without visible signs of force?"

"They are." DS Heyer's tone is perfectly equable. He is quite ready to admit that many criminals have just as many skills in housebreaking as the police.

"Thank you. Now, moving on to the object you found in the hall—the object you mistook at first glance for a doll's leg—you mentioned that, as a trained officer, you notice things automatically, even insignificant things like a doll's leg. And yet, the first time you entered the hall, you overlooked it completely. You only noticed it after you returned from searching the upper stories. Is that correct?"

"It is. My focus when I entered the house was on the blood in the hall, and then on checking the house for occupants."

250

"Very natural. Especially as, even when you returned to the hall after searching the upper stories, it looked like a harmless toy—or a part of one, at any rate. Do you think you would have noticed it if it had been a gun or a knife?"

"Yes, sir, I think I would. I can't prove that, of course."

"No, but you are trained to look for weapons."

"Exactly."

"Though not for children's toys."

"Correct."

"Now, was this item completely white when you first saw it—that is, when you returned to the hall after searching upstairs?"

"Well, I can't say for certain, but I can say that I think I would have noticed if it had any significant amount of blood on it. I would say it must have been completely or almost completely white for my mind to associate it with a dolly's leg, but that is just my supposition, sir, and it is possible I am mistaken."

"But you are an officer with a lot of experience at crime scenes, are you not?"

"Yes, sir, I am."

"And you are trained to notice any item that might be a weapon, or that might contain forensic evidence, like blood?"

"That's true, though anyone can make a mistake."

"Do you think you were mistaken?"

"No, sir, I don't."

"Nor do I, Detective Sergeant. Now, did the police have a theory about what caused this object to change color?"

"Yes, sir," says DS Heyer, more relaxed now. "Do you want to hear it?"

"Yes, please."

"We believe that, having killed the nanny and bundled her into the sack, the assailant went upstairs to check that the coast was clear. Then he went into the cloakroom and cleaned off his weapon, and perhaps wanted to wash blood from his hands and face before venturing outside, which would be natural. While he was there, Lady

Verreman came downstairs and called for the girl, to see what had happened to her cup of tea."

"I see."

"That is just our theory, however. We cannot prove that."

"Did you find Mrs. Gardner's blood in the cloakroom?"

"Well, no, we didn't."

"Not on the wall or the ceiling, where it flicked off when he was washing it?"

"No, sir."

"What about in the plughole? Any blood or hair belonging to the nanny in there?"

"Well, sir, hair was found, but that belonged to Lady Verreman."

Enygma widens his eyes in mock surprise. "Lady Verreman? How did that get there?"

DS Heyer smiles genially. He does not mind this game at all. "Ah. You'll remember that Lady Verreman testified that, after the attack, she went into the cloakroom to get a drink of water. She may well have washed her hands and face a bit as well, because we found splashes of her blood around the sink and on the wall. You know how these fiddling bathroom sinks can splash water around if you turn the tap on too hard. And there was blood in the hair itself, but that was group AB, which may have been a mixture of both women's blood."

"But none of the blood from the attack on Sally Gardner got splashed around?"

"No, sir. None that we found, but it's possible that he was a mite more careful."

"Despite the fiddling little sink? Strange. Now, you said earlier that you looked into the basement from the top of the stairs using your torch and could see 'two or three footprints in the blood facing toward the boiler room area.' Is that correct?"

"Yes, sir."

"And at this point, had either you or your men been down into the cellar?"

"No, sir, no one."

"And what sort of footprints were they, could you tell? A man's or a woman's?"

"A man's, sir, almost certainly. Quite a large foot, around a size ten."

"So, in all likelihood, made by the murderer?"

"Yes, sir. In all likelihood."

"Were you able to compare the footprints with Lord Verreman's?"

"I'm afraid not, sir. There was a lot of activity in the basement subsequent to the murder, and it would not have been possible to prove that the footprints had come from the assailant rather than one of our own men. That was unfortunate, but it often happens that a crime scene cannot be preserved completely intact, particularly when you have a duty to check whether the victim is still alive, or whether the assailant is still on the premises."

"But you are sure in your own mind that the footprints were already there before any officers went into the basement?"

"I am."

"What is the most common foot size for men in the United Kingdom, do you know?"

"Ten, sir."

"Hmm, perhaps it doesn't matter after all, then. Now, the basement was in darkness, and you testified that the bulb had been 'bodily removed from its socket.' Where did you find it?"

"It had been placed on one of the dining chairs in the breakfast room."

"And when you inserted it into the socket, it worked?"

"Yes, sir, perfectly."

"You weren't able to get fingerprints from the lightbulb, I suppose?"

"I'm afraid not, sir."

"Pity. Was there any blood on the lightbulb, from the assailant's hands or gloves, if he wore them?"

"None that I could see. I'm not sure whether it was checked for microscopic flecks of blood."

"That's unfortunate. Just one last question, I think. You said you attended first to the Three Taps, where you briefly interviewed Lady Verreman. She, presumably, told you what had happened, and you went to the house as a result of her information?"

"That's correct."

"How did she seem? Was she in shock? Distressed?"

"Yes, sir, distressed, but quite lucid. She was about to be loaded into an ambulance when I spoke to her, so that interview was very brief. Do you want me to repeat what she said?"

"Yes, please," Enygma says, with his fingers crossed.

"Well, it was just what she said to the barman, really, except that she said it was her husband that had attacked her and killed the nanny. I asked her where he was now, and she said she didn't know, but that she had left him in the house, and that, for all she knew, he was still there. I thought that was unlikely, given the time that had elapsed, but I took two officers with me to the house just in case."

"Very wise. Thank you. That's all."

16

◆ ◆ ◆ ◆ ◆

FOOTSTEPS IN THE DARK

ENYGMA IS STILL mulling Sergeant Heyer's testimony as Daniel takes his next witness, Margaret Howard-Cole, through the time at which Verreman arrived at her home, what he looked like and whether he had been walking or driving past the house. Enygma brings his mind back to the present when she says, "He described Antonia as hysterical."

Enygma stands up to object, but Daniel hurries on. "That was only to be expected, surely, after such an attack?" And Enygma sits down again.

"Well, I don't know about that," Margaret Howard-Cole says, and she purses her lips a little. Her lips say she is not the sort of woman who allows herself to become hysterical. "At first, she sort of clung to him and said that someone had murdered the nanny. But then she turned it around and accused him of hiring a hit man to kill her—like they do in American TV shows. Antonia watched altogether too much television, in my opinion."

"She accused her husband of paying someone to kill her?"

"Yes, but, well, she was always saying things like that. People were spying on her. Her husband was trying to kill her. All sorts of wild theories. And it was all in her head."

"The body in the basement was not in her head."

"No. Well . . . no, I suppose not. But that doesn't mean her husband did it."

"What happened next?"

"He said he talked to Antonia, and she said she wanted to lie down. He took her upstairs, but when he went into the bathroom for a cold compress, she legged it out the door."

"Did anything else happen while he was at your house?"

"He wrote a couple of letters and asked me to post them, and then he phoned his mother to check that she had been to the house to collect the child—er, children—and make sure that they were safe. He left about one fifteen a.m., and I thought he was driving back to London to speak to the police. And that was it."

"And you did not think to call the police yourself?"

"No, I did not."

"Why?"

"He told me he was 'going back to sort it out,' which I took to mean going to speak to the police. I naturally assumed, therefore, that there was nothing I could tell them that they wouldn't already know."

"Even when Lord Verreman was reported as missing?"

"I was not aware of that."

"Really? It was on the front page of every newspaper, and on every TV news bulletin."

"I live in the country. I don't take a daily newspaper, and I am not much of a television watcher. I think it rots the mind."

"Radio?"

"Only in the car."

"Really?" Daniel shakes his head in ostentatious disbelief. "What happened to the letters that you mentioned? Did he take them with him?"

"No. I said I would post them for him."

"Did you post them?"

"Yes. Well, I put stamps on them and gave them to my daughter to post on the way to school—which she obviously did, because they arrived."

"And it did not occur to you that you might be aiding and abetting a wanted fugitive in doing so?"

Margaret Howard-Cole sneers, just a little. She had once been called to the bar. She knows the law. "At that time, he was *not* a fugitive. I doubt he is a fugitive now. A fugitive is someone who has been charged with a crime and is evading capture. At that time there was no warrant for his arrest. He was not wanted for questioning. He was not even listed as missing. He told me that there had been an incident, and he told me that he was going back to deal with it. I took him at his word."

"Your witness," says Daniel in mock disgust.

Enygma is playing the genial defense counsel. Rumpole of the Bailey. "Now, then, you mentioned that Lord Verreman wrote some letters. How many letters were there, and who were they addressed to?"

"There were two, both addressed to his brother-in-law, Sir Henry Wade."

"Did you notice the bloodstains on them?"

"No."

"If you had noticed them, what would you have done?"

"Probably opened them and put them in new envelopes and re-addressed them."

"Why?"

"Well, I asked my daughter to post them. I wouldn't want to give her letters covered in blood. But I didn't, because I never saw any blood."

"So either the blood got on the envelopes after they left your daughter's hand—that is, by one of the many postal workers who handled them, by the staff at Sir Henry Wade's house or by Sir Henry Wade himself—or the amount of blood was so small as to be barely detectable to the human eye."

"Exactly, although I'm pretty sure Hal would have mentioned it if the blood was his."

"Agreed. Now, how did Lord Verreman know that the nanny was dead?"

"Antonia told him so."

"When was that? Were they in the basement at the time?"

"I don't think so, no. I think she pointed to the sack in the basement from the top of the stairs. John said it was a bloody mess—blood everywhere, I mean. John was always rather squeamish about blood."

"So he could see the sack from the top of the stairs?"

"Yes."

"Then the light into the basement must have been on, mustn't it?"

"I . . . Yes, I suppose it must."

"No more questions!"

DAVID VERREMAN APPEARS to have fallen asleep. Daniel coughs loudly, and David awakens. He does not make a pretense of not having slept; instead, he calls out, "Next," in a bored voice, and closes his eyes again.

Daniel calls Sir Henry Wade and makes him go into long-winded detail about receiving the letters, and taking them to the police, and the forensic evidence found on them before he submits them both into evidence.

Enygma says, "Did you notice anything strange about the letters, Mr. Wade?"

"The blood, you mean?"

"No, not the blood. The blood is neither here nor there. It might have come from anyone. It might have come from Lord Verreman. Who knows? He had been in *the murder house*, after all. It would be strange if he didn't have any blood on him. No, what I was referring to was this: neither of the letters mentions Sally Gardner. The second one, the one that is headed *Financial Matters*, has no personal information in it at all. But the first one mentions 'the most ghastly circumstances,' and that he 'interrupted the fight.' It mentions that his wife had accused him of hiring a hit man to kill her. And then—and this is the strange bit—it says, for David, 'going through life knowing his

father stood in the dock for attempted murder will be too much.'
Now, don't you think that that was a strange comment to make?"

"Well, he was an honorable man. And he loved his son. Of course
he wouldn't want David to see him in the dock for murder."

Enygma glances at Daniel, and back at Henry Wade. "I think you
meant 'children.' Not 'son.'"

"Cobblers. Imaginary friends at his age?" He points to the sleep-
ing judge. "Bloody ridiculous."

"OK," says Enygma, a little nervously. He moves swiftly on. "But
the letter doesn't say 'murder,' Sir Henry. It says 'attempted murder.'
The attempted murder of his wife. *That* is what he is concerned
about. Now, we know that he knew that the nanny was dead. He told
his mother so. He told his friend so. But it doesn't seem to have occurred to him to mention it in this letter. Why is that?"

"I don't know."

"Could it be because, as a nanny, a mere servant, Sally Gardner
was expendable? Because she didn't count as a real person?"

"Of course not. He was a toff, not a bloody monster. He quite
liked the girl, I believe."

"Then could it be that, while he knew that his wife suffered from
the delusion that her husband was trying to kill *her*, it never occurred
to him that she would try to pin the murder of an innocent nanny
on him?"

"Yes. Who would think their wife capable of that?"

"He was only worried that his wife would accuse him of attacking
her, or of paying someone to attack her, as a way of ensuring that he
lost custody of the children for good?"

"Yes."

"While he knew that Mrs. Gardner had been murdered, in his
mind that was a wholly separate incident, one that, while tragic, did
not concern him at a time when he had so many other things to be
concerned about?"

"Yes."

"And, therefore, his ignorance of the charges that his wife was later to lay against him was evidence of his innocence with regard to the murder of Mrs. Sally Gardner?"

"Yes. Exactly."

"He could have written, *I can't stand the idea of the children seeing me in the dock charged with murder.* That would have made a stronger statement, if anything, without being a confession of guilt. Would you agree that his failure to know that his wife would later accuse him of both attempted murder *and* murder does rather suggest that he had no reason to suppose he *would* be accused of murder?"

"Yes."

"Thank you."

BY THE TIME that Edmund Crispin takes the stand, Max is starting to feel unwell. It's because of the lack of sleep, he tells himself. He takes a sip of water, and, without consciously deciding to, he reaches for the bottle of pills in his pocket. He is not sure what time it is. The only light in the room comes from the overhead bulb. The light is too bright, and too white. In his ear there is a low buzzing sound, which might be coming from the house, or might be tinnitus; he can't be sure. He cannot be ill now. Quickly, he opens the bottle and takes a tablet.

David is asleep again, and Max has an almost overwhelming desire to close his eyes, too. Not to sleep, but to rest his eyeballs, straining as they are under the light. Instead, he picks up his pencil and doodles in his notebook, while Daniel tells the court that his witness is Edmund Crispin, the man who lent a car to John Verreman a week before the murder.

"What reason did Lord Verreman give for borrowing your car?"

"None."

"Didn't you ask him?"

"No."

"How very uninquisitive of you. Now, when you loaned Lord Verreman your car, was the boot empty?"

"Not completely. There were one or two things in there—a battery charger, I remember. Perhaps one or two other things."

Daniel shows Crispin a photograph of the boot of the car, with its "jumble of stuff." "It didn't look like this when you lent the car to him?"

"No."

Daniel shows him another photograph, this one of the second piece of lead piping. "Just to be clear, sir, did you leave this item in the car, or another like it?"

"No, I did not."

"Thank you. Now I would like to move on to the events of Monday, the eleventh of November. Did you receive a letter from Lord Verreman?"

"Yes, I did."

"Was that letter sent to your home?"

"No. To my club."

How very . . . English, thinks Enygma.

"When the letter arrived, did it have the proper postage?" asks Daniel.

"It had no stamp on it at all. The doorman had to pay the postage when he took it in."

"I see. Were you aware, by this time, that Lord Verreman was missing, and that a woman had died in his home?"

"I was, yes. Which was why I called the police to tell them I had received a letter from him. Obviously. I don't make a habit of calling the cops every time I get a letter through the post."

"Quite. What did the police advise you to do with this letter?"

"Drop it in at the station next time I was passing. Which is what I did. But they didn't tell me to bring the envelope, and so I threw it in the bin."

"The police say you were told to bring the letter round straightaway."

"Well, they would, wouldn't they? Of course, what they should have done is come round and got the damned thing themselves. They should have told me not to touch it, and not to throw away the envelope. They

261

knew what was important and what was not. I didn't. They made a mistake, because afterward they realized that the postmark might have told them something about where he was, but that's on them, not me."

Daniel asks, sourly, that the letter be entered into the evidence, and passes the witness over to Enygma.

Letter Received in Evidence (C6), written by Lord John Verreman to Edmund Crispin.

[Letter is undated.]

[Letter received by Edmund Crispin 11th November 1974.]

[Handwriting certified as Lord John Verreman's by spouse, Lady Antonia Verreman, under oath, and as matching other handwriting examples (checkbook) found at the home of Lord John Verreman, as sworn to by lead officer DCI Nicholas Blake.]

[Handwritten annotations occur five times— three times to the word "son," changing to "sons," and twice to the word "him," changing to "them," in both cases turning a singular into a plural. Author of annotations unknown.]

Transcript as follows:

My dear Edmund,

I have had a traumatic night of unbelievable coincidences. However, I won't bore you with anything or involve you except to say that when you come across my son[s], which I hope you will, please tell [them] that you knew me and that all I cared about was [them].

The fact that a crooked solicitor and a rotten psychiatrist destroyed me between them will be of no importance to my son[s].

I gave Hal Wade an account of what actually happened, but judging by my last effort in court, no one—let alone a 67-year-old judge—would believe me, and I no longer care except that my son[s] should be protected.

Yours ever,
John

End Transcript

Enygma has to catch hold of the table as he rises, and he takes a moment to steady himself before he addresses the witness. "Were you a particular friend of Lord Verreman, Mr. Crispin?"

"We were friends, yes."

"But not best friends?"

"Does anyone have those past primary school?"

"I know exactly what you mean. But you must have been pretty close to lend him your car?"

"Yes and no. I'd have lent that car to any one of a dozen or more friends if they'd asked."

"I see. Why, then, do you think that Lord Verreman chose to make you the very last person he corresponded with?"

"I couldn't say."

"This sheet of paper was the last sheet from a pad of Basildon Bond notepaper, the sort of notepad that was very common in 1974, back when people still wrote letters. The last page wasn't, strictly speaking, for writing on, was it? It was the blotting paper, for people who still used fountain pens and hadn't moved over to Biros. That's how they know it was the last sheet. So, why do you think that Verreman saved that last letter for you?"

"I've no idea."

"Were you very close to his children?"

"Not particularly."

"You didn't see them often?"

"Not often, no. Occasionally, before that night. Not often since."

"In which case, what opportunities would you have had to pass along these messages about how you knew him and how he cared for them? Why would he have saved this last piece of paper to write to a person who hardly saw his children before, and was even less likely to do so in the future?"

"I don't know."

"Strange."

Enygma stops. Something is wrong. He looks at the judge's bench. David is awake. Just. It's not that. Enygma feels like he can barely breathe. Not an asthma attack. He doesn't suffer from asthma. It's as though the oxygen is going into his stomach instead of his lungs. He takes a deep breath, but it doesn't really help. He presses on.

"Lord Verreman sent two other letters, both to his brother-in-law. Have you heard about those?"

"Yes."

"One letter was very similar to yours, and the other detailed financial matters."

"Yes."

"Do you know of any other honorees?"

"People whom he wrote to, you mean?"

"Exactly."

"No."

"Even stranger."

"Is it?"

"My lord," Enygma says, and David Verreman jumps, startled, "I would like to conduct an experiment, if I may, before this letter is passed to the jury."

"What kind of experiment? Will it require special equipment?"

"Paper and pencils only, my lord."

David looks at Daniel. "Any objection?"

THE GAME IS MURDER

Daniel shrugs.

"Fantastic." Enygma begins ripping out pages from the back of his notebook.

Let's Do an Experiment!

Imagine that you have had a night of traumatic and unbelievable coincidence, culminating in your spouse's running into a public house screaming accusations of bloody murder against you.

You sit down to write a letter. It will be the last letter you ever write. It will be your epitaph.

What do you say?

You have five minutes.

[Enter heartfelt letter here]

_____

_____

_____

_____

_____

_____

_____

_____

_____

_____

_____

_____

_____

_____

_____

_____

OK, shall we compare notes? Put your hand up if you had *I'm innocent.*

Or *She's crazy.*

How about *This is what REALLY happened?*

Or *Here's what I'm going to do next?*

OK. Now, who had *Make sure you pay off the overdraft?*

Who? Nobody—that's who.

"WOULD ANYONE CONTEMPLATING suicide or absconsion stop to consider whether they had paid the electricity bill or posted their income tax return?" says Enygma. "Perhaps. If they were a careful, tidy-minded, risk-averse person—definitely not the sort of person who had given up a secure job to be a gambler.

"But if you wanted to leave instructions about your financial affairs, would you rather write to your brother-in-law or your solicitor—your family trustee? Would you write to the man who is married to your wife's sister, or the man who actually has the power to carry out your instructions? Why write to your brother-in-law at all? Why not write to your actual brother? Or sister? Parent? Child? Or, at a push, the wife who just tried to frame you for murder?

266

"And why send your final—final—words to a not-very-close friend who lent you a car? Only to say nothing. Not even about the car. Why would anyone make *these* their final words?

"Unless, of course, they're not your final words."

Enygma turns back to Edmund Crispin. "Now, Mr. Crispin, this was a very short letter. A few lines only. Was the envelope, the one that you accidentally threw away, also very small?"

"No, it was quite large, actually."

"Really? Why do you think that was?"

"I don't know. Maybe it was the only envelope he had at the time."

"It couldn't possibly have been because it contained other pages, too? Pages in which he told you his plans for the future? Or protested his innocence? Or maybe just told you where you could find your car?"

"No."

"That's what I thought you'd say. No further questions."

ENYGMA IS GLAD to sit down again. His heart is pounding. He has a throbbing pain behind his left eyeball. He closes his eyes for a moment, and the temptation to keep them closed is almost overwhelming. Daniel calls Wilkie Collins to the stand, and Enygma forces his eyes open. The lids separate a couple of millimeters, and Enygma makes it do.

"Mr. Collins, you were a valet at the Berkeley Club, where Lord Verreman was a visitor—is that correct?"

"Yes, indeed. And if you're going to ask me if I knew him, the answer is yes. I knew him very well. By sight and to speak to. He was a very nice gentleman."

"Thank you. It would be helpful, however, if you waited for me to ask the questions before you answered them."

"Right you are."

"Did you see Lord Verreman on the seventh of November?"

"Yes, I did."

"Tell us about that meeting."

"Well, he drives up to the club and he asks me if there is anyone in the club yet. By which he meant any high rollers. Anyone who wanted to play for proper money. But it was early, and I told him no. And so he said he'd be back later, and away he went."

"And what time was that?"

"It was about eight forty-five, sir."

"How far is Lady Verreman's home from the club?"

"Driving? About three minutes, sir. It wasn't far."

"And Lord Verreman's flat?"

"Another minute or two only."

"So, in fact, his appearance at the club does not preclude Lord Verreman's appearance in the basement at all. Even if he had been at the club at eight forty-five and not earlier, as the police suspect, he could quite easily have driven to the club, to try to fashion some sort of alibi, and then driven on to this house, let himself in and secreted himself in the basement to wait for his wife to come down for her nightly cup of tea. Correct?"

"I don't know nuffin' about that."

"But I do, Mr. Collins, and so do the police. They will assure the jury that it was perfectly possible. Thank you."

Enygma decides to remain seated during the cross-examination, and he keeps his eyes closed as he speaks. "Had Lord Verreman driven to the club and asked that question before?"

"Yes, sir. Lots of times."

"So you weren't surprised by the question?"

"No. Not at all."

"How did he seem? Nervous? Angry? Wound up?"

"Nope. He was just the same as usual. Just the same."

"What sort of car was he driving?"

"His Mercedes."

"Are you sure?"

"'Course I am. It's my job. The police tried to tell me I was wrong, but the cars that drove up to the Berkeley were not the Ford Corsair type of cars. They were Mercedes, or BMWs or Rollers. No Fords. A Ford, I would remember. Besides, I knew his car, seen it a thousand times."

"Good. Now, while it is possible that a man could drive up to the club in one car, chitchat for a bit, maintaining an air of nonchalance while he does so, then drive to his home, swap one car for another and then drive to his wife's house intent on murder, all in the space of fifteen minutes, it doesn't seem very likely to me. Does it to you?"

"No, sir, it does not."

"Thank you. I think we're done."

MAX ENYGMA IS done. He asks the judge for a recess, and the judge grudgingly grants him a thirty-minute break. Enygma immediately lies down on the floor and closes his eyes, a pile of papers as a pillow. He falls into a deep sleep immediately. When Daniel shakes him awake, he swears that he has been asleep for only five minutes. His eyelids have doubled in weight, and it takes all of his effort to force them open and keep them open. But the next witness is the pathologist, and Max knows he must stay alert.

He considers taking another tablet but is unsure whether it will help. He pulls the bottle out of his pocket, intending to read the label, and only then does he notice.

These tablets are not his.

The prosecution calls Professor Cameron McCabe to the stand, but the defense is not listening. The defense is staring at a bottle of pills. The label on the pills reads:

MRS. ANTONIA VERREMAN. LIMBITROL.
TAKE AS DIRECTED.

WARNING: RISKS FROM CONCOMITANT USE WITH OPIOIDS: CONCOMITANT USE OF BENZODIAZEPINES, INCLUDING LIMBITROL, AND OPIOIDS MAY RESULT IN

PROFOUND SEDATION, RESPIRATORY DEPRESSION,
COMA AND DEATH. YOU MAY ALSO EXPERIENCE MOOD
CHANGES, ANXIETY, RESTLESSNESS AND CHANGES IN
SLEEP PATTERNS. THESE EFFECTS MAY OCCUR EVEN
AFTER TAKING LOW DOSES FOR A SHORT PERIOD OF
TIME.

Fuck.

"You are Professor Cameron McCabe, and you carried out the postmortem on Mrs. Sally Gardner. Is that correct?" asks Daniel.

"Yes, I did."

Enygma checks through his files to find the description of the tablets that Lord Verreman took into the chemist's shop on the day of the murder. It is taking time because his hands are shaking and his eyesight is blurred. As he thumbs desperately through the pages, he hears only snatches of the pathologist's testimony.

". . . healthy young woman . . . bruising to face . . . arm, consistent with grabbing . . ."

LIMBITROL CAN CAUSE FEELINGS OF PARANOIA OR
DELUSION. IN RARE CASES IT CAN CAUSE
HALLUCINATIONS.

". . . four splits in scalp . . . back of the head . . . obstruction of airways . . . swelling in brain . . . cause of death . . ."

CAN CAUSE DEATH.

Fuck.

"Mr. Enygma," says David Verreman, and the sound is almost a screech. "Mr. Enygma! The court is waiting. Professor McCabe is waiting. And I am waiting."

"What?" Enygma asks.

"Your cross-examination, Mr. Enygma. Do you wish to cross-examine this witness?"

"Yes . . . I mean, no . . . No, I mean, yes. Yes, I do want to cross-examine the witness. Thank you." Enygma tries to stand up, finds that he can't move his legs and decides to speak sitting down.

"Now, Mr. . . . Professor McCabe . . . er . . . just a moment." Enygma's notes are everywhere now, and he has lost his train of thought.

"Mr. Enygma!" screams the judge. "Now!"

Enygma gives up the search. "I'm ready," he says, feeling only a desperate desire to sleep. "Professor McCabe," Enygma says, trying to picture his notes, and automatically closing his eyes while he struggles to remember. What did he want to ask this man? He forces his eyes open again. *Cannot go to sleep yet.*

"You said, I think, that the injuries on the face and head were different. In what way? What do you think most likely caused each?"

"Well, I can only conjecture, based on my experience. Do you want me to do that?"

"Your experience is good enough for me, Prof. Let's have it." Enygma passes a hand over his face. *Was that another bloody spider? Or was it something else?*

"Well, the bruises to the face were most likely to have been made by a closed fist—a punch, in other words."

"And you've seen similar injuries many times before?"

"Thousands of times."

"Convinces me. What about the head injuries? Were they also caused by a fist?"

"Unlikely. The skin there was lacerated. These injuries were most likely to have been made by a thin, blunt object."

"Like a lead pipe?"

"Yes."

"Or, say, a crowbar?"

"Yes."

"Or, for example, the metal spindle that was ripped from the balustrade?"

"Possibly. Although I wasn't asked to examine that, so I cannot say for sure."

Enygma feels a wave of dizziness and hangs on to the desk, even though he is sitting down, and waits for it to pass. "If you had examined it, *would* you have said for sure?"

Professor McCabe gives a little smile. "Probably not. It is only on TV that scientists can make statements with one hundred percent certainty."

"Have a look at the stairs now, Prof, and let me know whether the spindle that was wrenched from the balustrade would be more likely than, less likely than or about the same in likeliness as, say, a lead pipe or a crowbar to have caused these wounds."

"I would say that they are all, on the face of it, and without having the instruments here to take measurements and so forth, equally likely."

"Good. Now, in which order do you think Mrs. Gardner's injuries occurred?"

"It's difficult to say conclusively."

"Yes, I know that. Can't you take a guess?"

Professor McCabe looks offended. "I am a scientist. Scientists don't guess."

Enygma takes a sip of water and gives his head a shake. The room flips over, but then the world comes back into focus. "But scientists do work with probabilities, don't they?"

"Yes," McCabe says cautiously.

"OK, then. As a scientist, based on your years of experience, and the thousands of bodies you have examined, what is the probable order of injuries? I'll make it easier for you. Out of the bruises to the face and the blunt force injuries to the head, which came first?"

"If I had to choose—"

"You do."

"Well, it is more likely that the bruising to the face took place first, followed by the head injuries. The head injuries would have caused unconsciousness quite quickly."

"Rendering the punch in the face moot?"

"Something like that." Professor McCabe is uncomfortable with deductions. He prefers to present data only, and leave the rest to someone else.

"She could not have been bashed into unconsciousness, then come round, and then have been punched in the face?"

"Very unlikely. There was swelling in the brain, and blood blocking her airways. Once she'd lapsed into unconsciousness she would have been very unlikely to recover without speedy medical intervention."

"So, she was punched in the face and then attacked with a blunt instrument of some description. We are getting somewhere. Now, given that you said she was punched, then hit over the head, lapsing into unconsciousness, before being bundled into a sack, how much time do you think would have elapsed from the first punch to her final breath?"

"That is very difficult to say."

"More or less than fifteen minutes?"

"I'm afraid I can't answer that."

"Fair enough. Now, the bruises on the arm—what side were they on?"

"The right side."

"The same side as the bruises on the face?"

"Yes."

"Could they have been made at the same time? I mean, could the assailant have held her right arm and hit her on the right side of the face at the same time?"

"It's possible, if he hit her with the back of his right hand."

"But is it probable?"

"I would have to say not probable, no."

"No. Because this isn't tennis and the murderer is unlikely to be Rafael Nadal. So, he grabs her by the arm, perhaps during an argument?"

"I couldn't say."

"Then he loses his temper and punches her—once, twice, three times."

"Possibly."

"And she runs up the stairs, trying to get away, and he pulls out a spindle from the stairs while they are fighting, and he whacks her over the head with it."

"I cannot answer that."

"Now, the police found that the lightbulb had been removed from the socket, and it is their contention that this was done before the murder, so that no one outside could see what was going on. Could this woman have been attacked, in the manner you describe, in a completely dark room?"

"That is outside my area of expertise, I'm afraid."

Enygma takes another sip of water. He is feeling OK, though his hand shakes a little as he raises the glass to his lips. Is shaking a side effect of Limbitrol? He can't remember reading that. He puts that to the back of his mind. "Are you a married man, Professor McCabe?"

"I am."

"If you were to put your hand on a woman's arm in the dark, would you be able to tell if that woman was your wife?"

"I don't know."

"Could you recognize her voice, even in the dark?"

"Yes, I think so."

"Do you recognize her tread on the stair?"

"Not well enough to swear to in a court of law."

"Very wise. But if you were to stand in front of her, with the lights on, and punch her in the face, would you be able to recognize her then?"

"Objection!" shouts Daniel Verreman. "Impugning the integrity of the witness."

"I apologize," says Enygma. "I doubt that Professor McCabe has ever punched his wife in the face without first checking who she was. My point is that it is improbable—though not, I admit, impossible— for a man not to recognize his own wife in the dark. But in order to inflict the injuries that were found on Mrs. Gardner, the assailant must first have grabbed her round the arm before he took the first swing, unless he were a tennis player practicing his backhand return. Murderers do not generally lead with a backhander, do they?"

"Hard to say. Not many, perhaps. Backhanders, as you refer to them, are usually slaps with the back of an open hand. The injuries to the face, particularly over the eye and eyebrow, are more likely to have been caused by a closed fist."

"And not made at the same time as the bruises on the arm?"

"Probably not, no."

"In your experience, is it more common for bruises such as the ones found on Mrs. Gardner's face to be found on the right side or the left side of the body?"

"Well, bruising can occur anywhere on the body, but, in general, the left side is more common, I would say."

"And why is that?"

"Because an attacker who is right-handed will punch with his right hand, landing on the left side of the victim's body."

"So do bruises on the right side indicate a left-hander?"

"Not necessarily. Left-handers, as you put it, are more used to using both hands, in order to adapt to a right-handed world. It is not at all a safe conclusion to draw."

"OK. But, as a matter of interest, do we know if Lord Verreman was left-handed?"

"As far as I know, he was not."

"If he had been, I think we might have heard about it. OK, I want to move on to the bruises on the back of Mrs. Gardner's hand. Tell me about them, Prof."

"Well, they were superficial bruises, as I say."

"Defensive injuries?"

"Most likely, yes."

"How would she have got those?"

"By putting her hands over her face, or, probably, over her head, to protect herself from injury."

"So she would have been facing her attacker when she did this?"

"Not necessarily."

"But on the preponderance of probability?"

"Well, yes, because she would be more likely to put her hands up to ward off a blow that she saw coming. To try to protect the head, and thus the brain, is an automatic, almost reflex action."

"Exactly. Someone lunges at your head, and you put your hands over it to protect your brain. But in order to do that you must see your attacker, which means your attacker must also see you. They must know who you are. Is that correct?"

"That seems probable."

"Thanks. That'll do."

Professor Cameron McCabe leaves the stand, and the judge calls for a ten-minute recess. Max Enygma takes the opportunity to close his eyes but is disappointed to discover that he cannot drop off into sleep. Nevertheless, he rests his eyeballs against his closed lids and is grateful for the darkness.

When the judge returns, he has found himself a gavel, and he bangs it lustily on the bench to indicate that the court is once more in session and play must resume. The noise ricochets off the inside of Enygma's skull, and he opens his eyes reluctantly.

—*Quick question.*

What?

—*What is all this business about the detective and his medicine?*

It creates tension.

—*And that's important, is it? We already have the trial of the century going on. Why do we need to add in more tension?*

Ah! You have, I think, misunderstood the purpose of a detective novel!

—*I have?*

You think it's about solving the crime.

—*Well, duh!*

Readers care nothing about the crime. Or the victim. They don't care much about whodunnit either. Or howdunnit. Or even whydunnit. The detective novel is about the detective. What he detects is almost incidental.

—*That doesn't sound right.*

Just suppose that we wanted to create a fictional detective with a long-running career spanning dozens of cases and, thus, dozens of best-selling books.

—*Sounds like a plan.*

Ah! But how do we do that?

—*I got nuffin'.*

By creating the singular detective! The damaged genius.

—*Right. Sherlock Holmes. I feel like we've been through this before.*

Yes. But what you have to understand is that the case is not important. But it needs to be important in order to make the reader keep turning the page. So, in order to make it count to the reader, we have to make solving each case the most important thing in the world to the detective.

—*Even after he has solved dozens of other cases just like it?*

Exactly.

—*Sounds like a tall order.*

It is. But we have a few tricks up our sleeve.

—*Do we? Personally, I'm writing this buck naked. What are you wearing?*

We can artificially inject tension. We can, for example, give the detective a drink problem, and solving the case will help him get back on the wagon.

—*Hackneyed.*

OK. Well, then, there is always the family. You'd be amazed at how many members of a detective's family are kidnapped, only to be rescued at the last minute. Ditto for detective partners.

—*We can do that?*

Sure. One narrator even put the wife on the top of a melting snowman, with an electrified noose round her neck. The detective has to solve the case and rescue the wife before the snow melts. How's that for tension?

—*Damn, that's cold.*

Bestseller. More than thirty million copies sold.

—*Do you wanna build a snowman?*

DANIEL VERREMAN CALLS Dr. Elizabeth Mackintosh to the stand, and Enygma sits up in his chair and prepares to take notes. This witness, Enygma knows, will be key. The pen is steady in his hand, but his vision is a little blurred. He rubs his eyes and reassures himself that blurred vision is not on the list of side effects of Limbitrol.

But it is a side effect of not taking his own medication.

Fuck.

"You examined the scene at eight Broad Way?" Daniel says.

"I did."

"The blood in the basement matched Mrs. Gardner's blood type. Is that correct?"

"Apart from a few drops of blood on the floor. And on the sack. There, I tested six separate areas. Four gave reactions to group B blood. But the remaining two areas gave reactions to group B blood and group A blood."

"Was the group B blood confined to the area around the bottom of the basement stairs?"

"Largely, yes, apart from a smear of group B blood near the top of the steps."

"Were you asked to examine a lead pipe found at the scene?"

"I was. The pipe was bloodstained, and had several bloodstained hairs sticking to it."

"Can you say who the blood and hair belonged to?"

"Tests revealed the blood to be group AB, which could be a mixture of both group A and group B, or it could be from a third person, with blood of group AB. However, the blood found on the hair adhering to the pipe was group A, and the hair itself matched samples taken from Lady Verreman. There were no hairs on the pipe belonging to Mrs. Gardner."

"There was another pipe, found in the accused's car. Did you have an opportunity to examine that?"

"I did examine the second piece of pipe. There was no forensic evidence found on it."

"Tell us about the blue fibers."

"They were most likely clothing fibers, but they did not match any of the clothes worn by either Mrs. Gardner or Lady Verreman. I found seven of them attached to the Elastoplast wrapped around the pipe."

"And did you find these fibers anywhere else?"

"I did. There were a number of them clinging to a tuft of hair found in the cloakroom sink, and four on the towel from Lady Verreman's bedroom."

"Whose hair was that?"

"Lady Verreman's. I also found thirty-two blue fibers in the car that was recovered by police. Twenty-five of these fibers were adhered to bloodstaining on the car door, while the remaining seven were stuck to a tangle of hair found on the floor on the passenger side. These hairs, too, belonged to Lady Verreman."

"Thank you."

Enygma leaps out of his seat as a cramp shoots down the back of his leg. He walks around the room as he speaks.

"The pipe found in the hall was nine inches long and weighed two pounds, three ounces—is that correct?"

"It is."

"Doesn't that seem awfully small to you? And awfully light?"

"In what way?"

"Well, the average breadth of a man's hand is three and a half inches. Now, Lord Verreman was a tall man, so it is likely, assuming the size of his hands was proportional to his height, that the breadth of his hand was all of that and possibly a little bit more. Now, when you pick up a weapon such as this, it is usual to hold it so that the bottom end pokes out a little at the bottom. You want to make sure you have a good grip, so that you don't drop it when it comes into contact with its target—you see?"

"I think so."

"So, that means at least four inches, maybe four and a half, of the nine inches would be taken up with the holding of it—half of its length, in other words. If you were planning a murder, Dr. Mackintosh, would you consider the remaining four and a half inches to be an adequate length of lethal weapon, or would you prefer something longer—say, for example, a sixteen-inch pipe, which you also happen to have with you?"

"I'm afraid I couldn't say."

"Fair enough." Enygma strides round the room a little faster. "Now, you mentioned that the pipe recovered from the hall was 'grossly distorted' in shape."

"That's correct."

"What did you mean by that?"

"That it was bent. Severely so."

"I see. Now, Detective Sergeant Heyer has told us that, when he attended the scene, he at first took the lead pipe to be a doll's leg, because of its color, which was white. But can we take it that the shape of the pipe also lent itself to that assumption? In other words, was it bent in the middle, like a dolly's leg?"

"Exactly."

"We have heard that you are a world-renowned blood specialist, Dr. Mackintosh, but how are you on plumbing?"

"Plumbing?"

"Yes, you know—sinks, drains, sewers. Household plumbing."

"I'm afraid I know nothing about plumbing."

Daniel jumps up from his seat. "My lord, I fail to see the relevance. Dr. Mackintosh has been invited to give evidence in respect of her expertise in blood analysis, not bathroom fittings."

"Is there a point?" asks David, banging his gavel for no good reason.

"I'm coming to that, my lord. Do you happen to know what a gooseneck is, Dr. Mackintosh? In relation to plumbing, I mean."

"I'm afraid I don't," says Dr. Mackintosh.

"It is"—he picks up a battered hardback book—"a pipe that has been deliberately bent in order to form a U-bend, or to bend around an obstacle. Lead, being soft and malleable, was ideal for this purpose—before plastic became ubiquitous, of course. Now, it is unclear from the reports I have read whether the lead pipe found in the hall was 'grossly distorted' because it had recently been used to bash a young woman's head in, or it was deliberately formed to be used as a gooseneck pipe. What do you think?"

"I'm afraid I can't say."

"OK. Now, when Detective Sergeant Heyer passed the pipe the first time, he didn't notice it at all. When he passed it the second time, he thought it was a doll's leg, because it was white. This pipe that was used to bludgeon two women was white. How do you account for that?"

"It's not my job to account for that, I'm afraid. I can only speak about the lead pipe I examined, which was certainly heavily blood-stained."

"It has been suggested that the murderer may have taken the lead pipe into the downstairs cloakroom to wash the blood off in the sink. That would be Mrs. Gardner's blood. Did you find any blood or hair belonging to Mrs. Gardner in the cloakroom?"

"No."

"None at all?"

"No."

"Not in the sink. Or on the splash back. Or on the ceilings, walls or floors."

"Not from Mrs. Gardner, no. We did find some blood on the ceiling, of the type belonging to Lady Verreman, which had most likely been tracked back from the implement with which she was attacked."

"What does that mean, 'tracked back'?"

"After the first blow there would have been no blood on the weapon, but on subsequent blows the weapon would have been covered in blood, and when it was drawn back to swing again, it would have trailed an arc of blood behind the attacker, across the ceilings and walls. It makes a quite distinctive pattern. The cloakroom door was open, and the site of the attack on Lady Verreman was a few feet away only, so that the blood was tracked backward into the cloakroom and across the ceiling."

"And that is quite usual in attacks of this kind?"

"Quite usual, yes. It is what I would have expected to see."

"Because blood is messy."

"Yes, indeed."

"And yet, our attacker managed to make it up the stairs and into the cloakroom, and wash away every trace of blood from the weapon—or, at least, enough for Sergeant Heyer, an experienced officer, to mistake a weapon for a child's toy—and at the same time not leave traces of Mrs. Gardner's blood behind him. He must be a very careful sort of assassin."

"I could not say."

"When you examined the lead pipe, was the blood watered down in any way?"

"I'm not sure I understand you."

"The police theory is that, having killed Mrs. Gardner, the murderer went upstairs to check that the coast was clear, and went into the cloakroom to wash the murder weapon, and possibly also his hands and face. The lead pipe was covered with absorbent plaster. It would have retained a good deal of that water, and perhaps even hand soap, would it not? Of course, the murderer may have shaken the excess water off, but that's doubtful because of the lack of blood on the walls and floor. So was the blood on the pipe watered down in any way?"

"No. I don't believe so."

"Now, which is more absorbent, a wet cloth or a dry cloth?"

"A wet cloth."

"Why is that?"

"Well, it's not really my area of expertise, but, basically, because absorption affects the surface tension of the spaces in the fibers of the cloth. It takes a little while for the absorption of the liquid to fill those spaces. Where the cloth is damp, that process has begun, and so it will absorb liquid more quickly. Although it will also finish absorbing liquid more quickly, since a cloth will hold a finite amount of liquid."

"Which is why our mammies always told us to use a damp cloth to mop up a spill?"

"Exactly."

"So if this lead pipe had been washed, would it not have started absorbing blood during the attack on Lady Verreman? There has been no suggestion that it was washed for a second time. We would have had a lead pipe, swathed in wet bandages, that was used to strike Lady Verreman over the head at least four times, and then dropped onto a blood-soaked carpet. The attack happened around nine o'clock, and Detective Sergeant Heyer and his men did not get into the house until around half past ten. That's around an hour and a half of absorption time, surely enough for an already-wet plaster to turn red?"

"I couldn't say."

"OK. Apart from blood, what else did you find on the weapon?"

"I found some hairs similar to Lady Verreman's."

"How had they got there?"

"Blood is a very sticky substance. And, of course, the pipe was wrapped in sticky plaster. Some of the adhesive may have been exposed. Fabric plasters have a tendency to roll backward with use or when they get wet, which can expose the adhesive."

"And yet, none of Sally Gardner's hair was stuck to it?"

"No."

"Why is that?"

"It's difficult to say. It may simply be that Mrs. Gardner's hair was less prone to falling out. Or it might have been washed away if the pipe was washed."

"Hmm. But it wouldn't have fallen out, would it? You mentioned that Lady Verreman's hair showed signs of having been pulled out from the roots during the assault—the same kind of assault that Mrs. Gardner sustained, though less severe."

"That's true."

"But you didn't find any of her hair in the cloakroom?"

"We did not."

"And you didn't find any of her hair on the lead pipe?"

"No, we did not."

"OK, moving on. During these two brutal attacks, how much blood would you expect to find on the assailant's clothes?"

"Well, I would expect him to have some blood spattering, depending on where he was standing in relation to the victims. And both women were petite—around five foot two—so it is unlikely that their bodies would have shielded him much from blood spatter, no matter where he was standing."

"And what about when he put Mrs. Gardner's body into the sack? Would he have been covered in her blood then?"

"Yes, that is very likely."

"Where would that blood be?"

"Well, moving a body is not easy. The most likely way to maneuver her would be to stand behind the body and place your arms under her armpits. But that is just a guess."

"The back of Mrs. Gardner's head was the target of the blows, and so the back of her head and the back of her dress would have been soaked in blood. Correct?"

"Certainly."

"Where, then, would the blood be transferred to on the murderer's clothes?"

"Across the chest and arms, most likely."

"Did you examine Lady Verreman's clothes?"

"I did."

"I expect, then, that a great deal of Sally Gardner's blood was transferred from the murderer to Lady Verreman when they struggled?"

"There was none of Sally's blood on the front of Lady Verreman's dress. On the back of her dress there was one spot, about the size of a fifty-pence piece, of blood of the same type as Mrs. Gardner's, and one other stain, around the same size, of group AB. There were other bloodstains, of course, but those were all of group A—Lady Verreman's blood type."

Enygma frowns theatrically and picks up a blank piece of paper from his table. He pretends to read. "Are you sure about that, Dr. Mackintosh? Because Lady Verreman testified that her assailant forced her to the ground at one point, and was lying on top of her, trying to choke her. So the blood that had saturated the front of his clothes *must* have been transferred to the front of Lady Verreman's dress."

"I can only tell you what I found."

Enygma strides around the courtroom, pondering ostentatiously.

David Verreman's hand closes over the gavel, and he raises it into the air.

"My lord, I would like to try an experiment."

The gavel is set back down on the bench, unbanged. "What sort of experiment?"

"It is the prosecution's case that the assailant killed Sally Gardner, stuffed her body into a sack and then went on to attack Lady Antonia Verreman in the manner she described in her statement. Now, this witness has just testified that the attack and the act of concealing the body would likely leave the assailant covered in blood, at least across their arms and chest. And yet, Antonia Verreman had *none* of Sally Gardner's blood on the front of her dress, despite her claim that her attacker lay down on top of her, struggled with her and tried to choke her for several minutes. I would like to see if there is any way the assailant could dispose of the body without being covered in her blood."

"What do you suggest?"

Let's Play a Game!

For this game you will need:

A sack.

A small adult or child, preferably dead, but inert will do (if you cannot find either, try a bolster).

A gallon-sized bottle of tomato ketchup.

A white sheet.

Pour ketchup over the head and back of the victim.

Then stuff their body into the sack.

You can move the body in any way you choose.

When you have maneuvered the body into the sack, spread the sheet on the floor, lie face down on the sheet and squirm around for two minutes without transferring any ketchup onto the sheet.

How did you do? If you left more than fifty pence's worth of ketchup on the sheet, you lose a life.

"LADY VERREMAN'S BLOOD was also found on two of the six areas that you tested from the sack in which Sally Gardner was found, and in sufficient quantities to be separately identifiable as group A. Is that right?"

"Yes, it is."

"Was that on the bottom of the sack, where it rested on the floor?"

"No. Slightly higher."

"Which means that Lady Verreman was in the cellar?"

"I could not say."

"Moving on to Lady Verreman's shoes," says Enygma. "What did you find on those, Dr. Mackintosh?"

"On the uppers, I found several spots of blood of group A, but on the underside of both shoes, I found group B blood."

"Sally Gardner's blood group?"

"Yes."

"And what is the most likely explanation for that?"

"Well, the most likely explanation is that the person wearing the shoes walked through the blood in the basement."

"But Lady Verreman has stated very clearly that she never went into the basement," Enygma says, grimacing suddenly as a cramp shoots up the back of his leg.

"I believe her explanation was that, in the struggle with the attacker, she used her feet to try to repel him, and that, in her doing so, the soles of her shoes connected with the attacker's blood-soaked garments."

Enygma walks nearer to the witness stand, partly to make his point, but mostly to walk off the pain in his leg. "But that is impossible—isn't it?—since you have stated that there was *none* of Sally's blood on the front of Lady Verreman's dress. If the attacker's clothes were blood soaked enough to transfer blood from his clothes to her shoes, they must have been blood soaked enough to transfer blood from his clothes to her clothes. Correct?"

". . . Yes. I would have to say that is correct."

"Which makes Lady Verreman's testimony unreliable. Thank you, Dr. Mackintosh."

DANIEL VERREMAN'S LAST witness is DCI Nicholas Blake. Enygma is not tired anymore, although he keeps yawning and his eyeballs are throbbing. He blinks rapidly and yawns, and his eyes begin to water. *Great.* He looks down at his notes. Someone has scribbled Humpty Dumpty pictures in the margins—eggs with wide eyes and stick legs, black shoes and brown lederhosen. *Why the fuck is that egg wearing lederhosen?*

Did I do that?

Enygma adds a great yawning mouth to one of the eggs, with two buck teeth protruding from his upper lip. Then he makes one of the teeth longer than the other. And he widens the crack in the egg so that it runs down from the dome of his head and across his face like a great, ugly scar. For good measure, he gives the egg a second black eye, too, as Daniel takes Blake through his first meeting with Lady Verreman, and his unwavering belief in the truthfulness of her testimony.

"She told a plain story, and she stuck to it, which, to my mind, shows that she was speaking the truth," Blake says.

"There was some suggestion that Lady Verreman may have been suffering severe mental health problems at the time. Do you believe that she was competent when she made her statement?"

"Yes, sir. I know that such an allegation was made by Lord Verreman at his custody hearing, and the judge at that trial showed what he thought of that when he awarded full custody to his wife. I saw no sign that she was not in her right mind, so to speak, when I interviewed her, and she seemed very clearheaded—remarkably so, in fact—and was able to give us a very straightforward statement that fit the facts in every respect."

·"Thank you. Now what can you tell me about the investigations you made with regard to the lightbulb? I believe it had been removed from its socket?"

"Yes, sir. Lady Verreman stated that the lightbulb had been in place and working the previous evening. She did not recall using it that day but said that she probably would have done, as the basement is rather gloomy, and the stairs are steep. Lady Verreman stated that she would likely have remembered if the lightbulb had blown."

"But, in fact, it had not 'blown,' as you put it?"

"It had not."

"And what do you consider the purpose of removing the lightbulb to be?"

"Well, sir, we considered that it was for two reasons—firstly, to prevent anyone who was looking into the basement from outside seeing the attack take place; and secondly, to prevent the victim from seeing the attacker lying in wait for them and raising the alarm without ever going down the steps."

"Was it possible to see into the basement?"

"Not from the street, no, sir. But if anyone had cared to walk down the outside steps to the basement, they might have seen through the blinds easy enough, had the light been on."

"And with the light off? What could they see then?"

"Nothing at all, except the dim red glow of the light from the kettle."

"I see. Now, why do you think that Lord Verreman, as we maintain, lay in wait for Lady Verreman on that *particular* night?"

"There were two reasons. From our investigations, we had discovered that Lord Verreman was very short of money—perilously so, in fact. He had four bank accounts, all of them overdrawn, and he had recently taken out a substantial loan from a moneylender at a very high rate of interest. He had also been forced to put some of his family silver up for sale. As of January 1975, the requisite two-year separation would have expired, and Lady Verreman could have pressed ahead with the divorce. In preparation for that, he would have had to produce financial statements and make a settlement on his wife. We believe that he concluded murder was his best way to relieve this financial pressure. Even so, nothing may have come of it but for a chance conversation with his son the weekend before, when the child mentioned that the nanny had Thursday nights off. It was that conversation, harmless from the child's point of view, that led Verreman to seize his chance."

"Would you say that this was a case where there was one conclusive piece of evidence—a smoking gun, if you will—or would you say that it was a lot of small pieces of evidence that, cumulatively, led you to believe that Lord Verreman was your man?"

"Well, both, really. I considered that the evidence against Lord Verreman was strong from early in the case. Not only was there the testimony of his wife, but there were his own words, too, which show he was at the scene. He had motive, which was largely financial, but you must also consider that the judge in the custody case had concluded that Lord Verreman showed malice and ruthlessness toward his wife, inventing a mental illness and scheming to have her committed in order to keep custody of the children. I considered that to be evidence that he was cold-blooded enough to commit murder if he felt he had to. He had the means. Lord Verreman still had a key to his wife's house and could have let himself in at any time. He knew the layout of the house, and he knew his wife's habits—that she made herself a cup of tea at nine every night. When he discovered—or he thought—that the nanny would be out of the house on that Thursday evening, he had the opportunity, too. But there is one piece of evidence that is so overwhelmingly incontrovertible that it is, in my mind, proof positive of Lord Verreman's guilt."

"You are speaking of the second piece of lead pipe?"

"I am. No one has been able to come up with a credible explanation of why Lord Verreman would be carrying in his car—the car that was found abandoned at Newhaven—a piece of lead pipe of the exact same diameter, and wrapped in the exact same type of Elastoplast—white, you will remember, with a yellow zigzag stripe down the middle—as the murder weapon that was found in the hall of this house. It is fantastical to suppose that another man, with malice aforethought, constructed a similar weapon to frame him, or that two separate men unilaterally took it into their heads to cover two lengths of lead pipe of the same diameter with the exact same brand of sticking plaster. It beggars belief. Unless a convincing explanation can be found for the presence of those two pipes, I believe that Lord Verreman *is* guilty, and will be *found* guilty."

"And you believe that no such explanation exists?"

"I do. In fifty years, no one has found one."

"Thank you, Detective Chief Inspector."

Enygma takes his time standing up. He leans heavily on the desk as he stands. Beads of cold sweat stand out on his forehead, and his hands are cold and clammy, though not, he knows, from nerves. He is excited.

"How many boyfriends did Mrs. Sally Gardner have at the time of her murder?"

DCI Blake stiffens, as though he finds this line of questioning distasteful. "Five or six."

"Which? Five? Or six?"

"Six current or recent boyfriends. But if you are implying that she was—"

"I'm not implying anything except that she was a liberated woman. She was perfectly entitled to see a dozen men if the fancy took her that way. One of those men was Eddie Biggers?"

"Yes, it was."

"Was one of them a man called Ray?"

"Yes."

"Who's Ray, Chief Inspector?"

"Well, one of the men who dated Sally."

"Was he her main boyfriend, do you think?"

"No. That was Eddie Biggers."

"How do you know?"

"They were planning on getting married."

"Says who?"

"Well, he does."

"At the inquest, Lady Verreman said she knew of two men whom Sally was dating. Was Ray the other one?"

". . . Yes."

"And David Verreman's statement, read out in the coroner's court, said, 'I told Daddy that Sally had boyfriends and went out with them.' Was he referring to Ray, too?"

"Possibly."

"Or to one of the other ones?"

"To Ray!" Blake says, and he sounds annoyed.

Enygma riffles through his transcript of the coroner's inquest. "Did Ray not testify at the coroner's inquest?"

"No."

"Why not?"

"Well, that's a matter for the coroner, but I imagine that he felt that there was nothing Ray could add."

"Odd. When had Sally seen Ray last?"

"I don't recall."

"I want to read you part of Lady Verreman's testimony at the inquest. Right after Lady Verreman tells the court that she knew about two of Sally's boyfriends, we have the following exchange:

```
Coroner:   Why was she at home that evening?
     LV:   Because her current boyfriend had his
           day off on Wednesday, and she asked if
           she could change hers to Wednesday as
           well, so she could go out with him.
```

"'Current boyfriend.' Which current boyfriend was that? The coroner seems to have neglected to ask."

"Eddie Biggers."

"Sure?"

"Well, she went out with him that Wednesday," says Blake, smiling, "so, yes, I'm sure."

"And how did that date go?"

"I'm sorry?"

Enygma scratches the back of his hand absentmindedly. "We've heard that Sally changed her usual day off from Thursday to Wednesday. She must have had big plans. How did the date go? Did they go somewhere nice?"

"I don't know."

"Did she stay out all night? Or come back late?"

"I believe she came back around nine."

"That's rather early for a hot date, isn't it, Chief Inspector?"

"I believe they'd had a bit of a row."

"What about? It wasn't about Ray, was it? Or about one of the other four?"

"I don't know."

"OK. Let's put a pin in that. We have heard that the dowager duchess got, shall we say, confused about whether Lord Verreman saw a man attacking his wife in the basement while he was *driving* past in his car or while he was *walking* past on foot. Which do you think it was?"

Blake makes a tiny shake of his head, as if to say, *Nice try.* "I do not believe he saw a man attacking his wife in the basement at all. I think that was a taradiddle, designed to cover up the reason he was there."

Enygma smiles. "But we have seen, in Lady Verreman's testimony at the coroner's court, which His Honor admitted into evidence here, that Lord Verreman made a habit of snooping on his wife. He walked, or drove—whichever, doesn't matter—past this house every evening. He got out of his car, if he was in it, and he walked down the steps and pressed his nose against the windowpane. If you were kindhearted, you might say that he did it in the hope of seeing his children." He gives a swift glance at Daniel as he says this. Daniel doesn't seem to notice. "If he thought the house was empty, or that his wife was not home, Lord Verreman could, and did, let himself in with his key, and inspect the fridge to see if there was food there. Maybe out of concern for the family, maybe to get dirt on the wife. Who knows? So he didn't really need to tell a taradiddle, did he, to explain why he was there? He was there all the time. Now, you mentioned that the lightbulb had been removed."

"Correct," says Blake, trying to maintain his air of bonhomie, though it has slipped somewhat.

"Given the testimony of Lady Verreman, and that of his friends and family, that Lord Verreman was in the habit, nightly, of snooping on his wife—not gallant behavior, perhaps, but not a crime, at least not then—you might think that Lord John Verreman would be the one person in the whole world who would know for absolutely certain that *nothing* could be seen of the goings-on in this basement from the street. Even with the light on, even in daylight, there is very little to be seen with the blinds positioned the way they are. You know it because you tried. And he knew it, too. And, of course, he could have just closed them."

Blake bristles. "You are forgetting the second reason I gave—that an assailant would not want the victim to see them from the top of the stairs, where the victim would have the advantage and could summon help or escape into the street."

"My dear Chief Inspector," says Enygma, "look around. This basement has a lot of corners. May I also refer you to the diagram in your evidence pack—page 143? There are many places where an assailant could have hidden without being seen, are there not?"

"There are, but perhaps that didn't occur to him."

"He must be a spectacularly dull-witted man if that is the case. Because, of course, it was equally possible that, seeing the kitchen in pitch-black darkness, the victim would have decided not to walk down those steep stairs in heels, carrying a tray, don't you think?"

"I couldn't say."

"How did Lord Verreman even know that was where his wife was likely to be?"

"A man knows his wife's habits, Mr. Enygma."

"That's very true, Chief Inspector, although Lady Verreman testified at the inquest that this was a new habit, which she had acquired postseparation."

"Well, Mr. Enygma, you have just told us that Lord Verreman made a habit of spying on his wife. He must have discovered it then."

"Well, it's possible. Let's put a pin in that, too."

"Fine with me."

"What do you know about a Baby Belling?"

"A Baby Belling is a kind of small cooker that you put on a countertop."

"There was one in the house, I believe."

"In the nursery."

"Did it work?"

"Yes, I believe so."

"What was it used for?"

"For making simple meals and drinks."

"And the nursery is where?"

"On the third floor, above Lady Verreman's room."

"I see. Thank you. And, of course, Mrs. Gardner's room is on the fourth floor. She would have needed to pass the Baby Belling on her way down to the kitchen, all the way in the basement. Odd.

"Now, with regard to the front door, Detective Sergeant Heyer testified that Lady Verreman normally locked and bolted the door around six o'clock, after she had fed the children and they had all gone upstairs to watch television or whatever."

"Correct. But on this night, unfortunately, she forgot."

"Lord Verreman had a key to the house, didn't he? Did you find it among his possessions?"

"No, but we imagine that he took it with him. There is no question that he was in the house. He admits it himself in his letters."

"So he could let himself into the house. I see. Oh, but wait—how could he expect to get into the house when the house was usually locked, bolted twice and chained?"

"Because he knew, or thought he knew, that it was the nanny's day off! That the house would be empty, and the door would be unbolted so that the nanny could get back in."

Max Enygma walks up and down the courtroom, pondering this answer for so long that Daniel has risen to his feet to object, and David has his gavel in his hand, ready to sustain any and all objections, when Max stops and turns again to the chief inspector. "Did Lady Verreman strike you as a particularly robust woman? Physically, I mean. Could she 'handle herself' if she was attacked? Was she confident, the sort of woman who was careless of her own safety?"

"No. Quite the opposite. She was physically very small, what you might call petite—or fine boned, skinny. She was also very concerned for her safety. She felt isolated from her family. She had made few friends in her husband's circle, and she kept odd hours when she was married, accompanying her husband to casinos and such, so that she never really got the chance to make friends of her own. I know that she felt the absence of support very deeply."

"Was she frightened of her husband? Of what he might do to her?"

Blake looks surprised at this question, coming from the defense barrister. "Yes. She felt intimidated by him. As you have said, he spied on her."

"She had made allegations that he was out to kill her, hadn't she? I mean, long before that night?"

"Yes, she had."

"That he was trying to poison her?"

"Yes."

"That others were trying to poison her on his behalf?"

"Yes."

"That he had hired a hit man to kill her?"

"I believe she said that, yes."

"In fact, she thought that there was an entire conspiracy to murder her, or drive her mad and have her committed to an asylum—a conspiracy in which, so she believed, a large number of people were concerned?"

"I've heard that, yes."

"A conspiracy involving family, friends, doctors, psychiatrists, teachers and lawyers. I believe even the official solicitor was implicated in the plot."

"I couldn't say."

"And yet, this woman, who was frightened of her husband, of what he might do to her, who knew that he visited the house every night, that he had a key and could let himself into her home—this woman would, habitually, leave the door unbolted and unchained for whole nights when the nanny had a night off and she was alone in the house?"

"Well"—Blake brings out the laugh once more, but it isn't convincing—"the nanny has to get back in somehow, doesn't she?"

"Did Lady Verreman have a telephone by her bed?"

"Yes, she did."

"Wouldn't a frightened and vulnerable, not to say paranoid, lady have preferred being woken up in order to unbolt the door rather than lying awake all night, jumping at every imagined noise?"

"I couldn't say."

"You once told me you were married, Chief Inspector. Are you still married?"

"I am."

"Glad to hear it. Does your wife wear heels?"

"Not anymore."

"Understandable, I'm sure. Bloody uncomfortable, I imagine. I'd like you to cast your mind back to the time when your wife did wear heels. Say, on a night out. You've got dressed up. You have had a nice time. What is the first thing you do when you get home?"

"Let the dog out into the back garden, and pour myself a scotch."

"And what does your wife do?"

"Takes off her coat and shoes, and goes into the kitchen to put the kettle on for a cup of tea."

"She takes off her shoes? Why is that?"

"I don't know."

"Do you take your shoes off when you get home? Are you trying to save the carpet, perhaps?"

"No."

"No. Is it because she is wearing heels, and they are uncomfortable? What does she put on instead?"

"Slippers."

"Of course. Slippers indoors. Much more comfortable. So why do you think Sally Gardner was wearing her shoes at nine o'clock at night? Court shoes, I believe they are called. Not a stiletto heel, but still a heel. Why is she not wearing her slippers?"

"I don't know."

"Does your wife always wear slippers in the house?"

"Yes, unless . . ."

"Yes?"

"Unless we have guests in."

"Of course. Now, why is it that Sally Gardner, who had spent most of the day in the house, apart from about forty-five minutes around five o'clock, when she popped out to post a letter—why is she still wearing her heels at nine o'clock? Could it be because she was having guests in?"

"No, I don't believe so. We have no evidence that anyone was in the house."

"Apart from the murderer, you mean?"

"Of course."

"And notwithstanding the door that can't show whether it's been forced or not."

"Yes."

"And apart from the written testimony of Lord John Verreman, in the form of letters to his friends?"

"Well, obviously."

"Now, a few minutes before she popped her head round the door to offer Lady Verreman a cup of tea—something that she had never done before—Sally received a phone call. Who was that from?"

"Her boyfriend."

"Dare I ask which one?"

"Eddie Biggers."

"The man whom she had gone out with the night before? The man whom she had quarreled with after changing her night off specially so that she could see him?"

"Yes."

"And what was the nature of that phone call?"

"They made up, and then they made arrangements to see each other the following week."

"Says who?"

"Says Biggers."

"When the following week?"

"Er, Wednesday, I imagine."

"So, they were on the phone for a while, then?"

"No, no. Three or four minutes only."

"Three or four minutes? In which to apologize, review the cause of the row, apologize again, make up and arrange another meeting, which did not, in fact, need to be arranged, since it was now a standing arrangement?"

"Something like that."

"Fast worker. Where was Mr. Biggers that night?"

"Working."

"In a pub just a few minutes' walk from here, I believe."

"That's right."

"Mr. Biggers didn't, perhaps, suggest that he slip over and see Sally Gardner during his break so that they could make up properly?"

"I don't believe so."

"Because, if he had, it might explain why Sally offered to make her employer a cup of tea at nine o'clock at night, when she had never done so before. It might explain why she was wearing heels, when her feet would have been more comfortable in slippers. And it might explain why she walked down five flights of stairs in the dark, carrying a tray, which further impeded her, when she could just have nipped down one flight of stairs to the nursery that she used every day, to make a cup of tea on the Baby Belling that was installed there for the purpose. Don't you agree?"

"I couldn't say."

"OK, I would like to fast-forward a bit. Sally Gardner has walked down all those stairs, carrying a tray of empty cups and wearing her high heels. She may, or may not, have let someone into the house. If she has, she takes them down to the basement. Why? Because she has offered to make them a cup of tea, too? Or because she thinks it will be nice and private in the basement—away from the sharp ears of her employer—where they can make up in private. Or perhaps it is as you say, and someone is lying in wait at the bottom of the stairs. In your scenario, when she reaches the bottom of the steps, she is attacked by a man who believes she is his wife. We will gloss over, for a moment, the forensic evidence, which strongly suggests that the attack was, in fact, an escalating attack where the attacker—perhaps during a sort of argument where the lovers do *not* make up—first grabs her by the right arm, then punches her on the right side of the face, and then, losing his temper completely, reaches for a weapon and strikes her. And strikes her again, until she is dead. We will also gloss over several smears of Sally's blood against the wall near the top of the basement steps, suggesting that she struggled with someone as she tried to flee to safety. Glossing, as I say, over all that, and taking as read your assertion that she was bashed over the head as soon as she reached the bottom step, and quickly lost consciousness, I ask this question: if the murder were not a spur-of-the-moment attack by, just for example, a spurned lover but, instead, a cold and calculating murderer, would *this* be your weapon of choice?" Enygma reads out the description of the pipe: "'Hollow lead pipe, nine inches in length, grossly distorted, covered in white sticking plaster.' If you were *planning* the perfect murder, would this be your weapon of choice?"

"It *was* the murderer's weapon of choice."

"Was it? We shall see. Now, passing over the length of the pipe, which seems barely adequate for the purpose, I would like you to consider the sticking plaster. Why would a man who was preparing to kill his wife go to the trouble of bandaging his weapon?"

"I don't know."

"It seems very considerate, don't you think?"

"It may be that he was trying to ensure a good grip."

"Then why cover the whole pipe? Why not just the bottom four and a half inches?"

"I don't know," says Blake, irritated now. "It may be that he was hoping that, by bandaging the pipe, he could kill with one blow, and without breaking the skin—with no blood, in other words."

"A miscalculation, wouldn't you say?" says Enygma, holding up a picture of the bloody basement.

"It certainly was!" Blake tries a smile in the judge's direction. It does no good. David Verreman is asleep.

Daniel coughs loudly, and David wakes up, bangs his gavel and shouts, "Overruled!"

"If you were *planning* a murder, Detective Chief Inspector, wouldn't you choose the second piece of lead pipe, the one that was sixteen inches long, the one that weighed four pounds and one ounce instead of a measly two pounds and three ounces, about the same as a bag of sugar? If you were planning a murder, would you use a lead pipe at all? Or would you use a knife or a rope or, if a blunt instrument is absolutely necessary, something that does not become 'grossly distorted' immediately upon use?"

"I really couldn't say."

"You served as a police officer for a long time—is that correct, Detective Chief Inspector?"

"Forty years, just about, before I retired."

"You must have seen a lot."

"You could say that."

"Apart from this case, how many murders have you investigated, or even heard about, where the murder weapon was a lead pipe, either with or without Elastoplast? Board games not included."

"Well, I don't know off the top of my head."

"I do, Detective Chief Inspector. The answer is none, isn't it?"

"Probably, yes."

"OK, let's fast-forward again. The time now is around quarter past nine. The murder has been committed and Sally's body has been manhandled into a sack. The murderer has left the body, the sack and the bloodstained mess, and gone up the basement stairs, into the hall and into the cloakroom. Why?"

"We believe that he went upstairs to check that the coast was clear, and that he took the opportunity to go into the cloakroom and wash blood from his hands and face, and from his weapon."

"He washed the blood from his hands? Didn't Lady Verreman testify that her assailant was wearing gloves?"

Blake shifts a little uncomfortably. "She did. He may not have been wearing the gloves during the first attack. Or he may have put them back on."

"You mean, he took off his bloodstained gloves, washed his

hands, then put his bloodstained gloves back on? I don't think so, do you? In any case, none—not one drop—of Sally Gardner's blood was found in the cloakroom. Isn't that correct, Chief Inspector?"

"Yes, except for blood found on a tuft of hair in the sink. That returned a result of group AB. That might have been Sally's blood mixed with Lady Verreman's."

"Who did the hair belong to? Sally?"

"No. Lady Verreman."

"Exactly. But I am still curious about why the murderer would have gone into the cloakroom in the first place. You say he had gone upstairs to check that the coast was clear. But he could simply have unlocked the basement door to the street. The key was in the lock. That would have been safer, surely. He could check that there was no one on the street before he brought the body out. No need to risk running into the inhabitants of the house. And why carry the body up the stairs, through the hall, out the front door and down the front steps onto the street, when he could let himself out through the basement door, wait in the dark for a quiet moment and then take the body straight out to his car? Because he must have been planning on taking the body away, mustn't he?"

"Presumably so."

"Of course. You don't go to the trouble of putting a body in a sack just to leave it where you found it. We made the experiment earlier, and found the whole experience messy, tiring and time-consuming. The murderer *must* have been planning to take the body away. So, why bother to wash your hands, with or without gloves, when you are almost certainly entirely covered in blood, and will be covered in blood again when you go back to handle the sack?"

"I couldn't say."

"And why bother to go upstairs to the cloakroom to wash your hands at all? The basement contained a kitchen. And kitchens contain sinks, don't they?"

Blake isn't smiling anymore. He looks petulant. "Yes, there was a sink in the basement."

"Did you find any blood in it?"

"No."

"That's strange, isn't it? Lady Verreman's statement—the statement around which you have built your entire case—said, very clearly, that her attacker came at her from the cloakroom. She made the same statement again at the coroner's inquest. Let me read to you the exchange between Lady Verreman and the coroner:

```
      LV:  I heard a noise.
Coroner:  What sort of noise?
      LV:  Just a noise of somebody, or something,
           in the downstairs cloakroom.
Coroner:  This is where there is a washbasin and
           toilet?
      LV:  Yes.
Coroner:  What happened next?
      LV:  I walked toward the sound—at any rate,
           moved toward it.
Coroner:  What happened then?
      LV:  Somebody rushed out and hit me on the
           head.
```

"Lady Verreman was very clear," Enygma continues. "She said that there was a man in the cloakroom—a man who had absolutely no reason to be in the cloakroom, and, the evidence shows, was *not* in the cloakroom. A man saturated with blood could not have helped leaving some trace of his presence behind."

"Are you asking me a question?" asks Blake, not wanting to play anymore.

"Do you still think Lady Verreman's testimony can be relied upon? Do you think that the attack happened the way she said it did? Was she brutally attacked by her own husband?"

"Absolutely."

"How can you be so sure?"

"Because of the second length of pipe. You can't get away from it. The lead pipe found at the scene belonged to Lord Verreman. Hundred percent. Because he had another length of pipe in the abandoned car that was almost identical to the first. It was the same diameter. And it was wrapped in the same distinctive white Elastoplast-type tape with a yellow zigzag stripe down the middle. No one would credit the possibility that that is a coincidence. There is nothing that can explain that away. *Nothing.*"

17

◆ ◆ ◆ ◆ ◆

BEHIND THAT CURTAIN

"Circumstantial evidence is a very tricky thing," answered Holmes thoughtfully. "It may seem to point very straight to one thing, but if you shift your own point of view a little, you may find it pointing in an equally uncompromising manner to something entirely different."

—Sir Arthur Conan Doyle, "The Boscombe Valley Mystery"

MAX ENYGMA SMILES to himself. "Are you a film fan, Detective Chief Inspector Blake?"

"What—movies, you mean?"

"Movies, yes. Are you a fan of the movies?"

"I suppose so."

"Who isn't, right? I've been thinking a lot about a certain kind of scene you see in movies all the time—a trope, I think they call it. Remember *The Shining*, when Shelley Duvall picks up that baseball bat? 'Put the bat down, Wendy!' Would you snoop round Jack Nicholson's office unarmed?"

"Er, probably not."

"Of course not. He's nuts. Then there is *John Wick*, after they shoot the damned dog. Did you see that movie?"

"I'm not sure."

"John Wick digs up a concrete floor to get a load of guns before he goes after the bad guys. And damn it, he's John Wick. This is a man who killed three guys in a bar with a pencil. A fucking pencil! And, of course, you must have seen *Home Alone*."

"Yes."

"Of course you have. When Joe Pesci says, 'Merry Christmas, little fella. We know that you're in there, and that you're all alone!' God, I love Joe Pesci. He was fabulous in *My Cousin Vinny*. If you haven't seen it, you must watch it. Anyway, I digress. Joe Pesci comes a-knocking; then it's time for little Kevin to let fly with the homemade weaponry. You have to get inventive when you're only eight, right?"

"I suppose so."

"Oh, and *Die Hard*. We mustn't forget that. A Christmas favorite, of course. The first thing Bruce Willis does when the bad guys take over is get armed. 'Now I have a machine gun. Ho-ho-ho.' 'Yippee ki-yay, motherfucker.' Or, what about the storming of the castle in *The Princess Bride*? Maybe that is more your speed. Did you see that?"

"No."

"Really? *Really?* The heroes are going to rescue Buttercup—she's the damsel, of course—from the clutches of the vile Prince Humperdinck, with only Westley's brains, Fezzik's strength and Inigo Montoya's steel. If they only had a wheelbarrow, that would be something, right?"

"If you say so."

"Think about every cheap horror movie you ever saw. When that teenager hears a noise, what do they do? Call the cops? Jump out the window? Run like hell? Of course not. They grab whatever they can find to use as a weapon, and they go to investigate. Good for them— the fools."

"I don't see your point," Nicholas Blake says, coldly.

"And, of course, there's *The Matrix*. When Neo, *the one*, rescues Morpheus from the agents, he brings *all* the guns . . . No, you're right. You're right. I was getting carried away. My point is this: when you are walking into trouble, you grab something to defend yourself. You grab *anything* to defend yourself. A baseball bat. A golf club. A heavy vase. A shoe, even. Anything is better than nothing, right?

"On the night of the seventh of November 1974, Lord Verreman drives past eight Broad Way, as he does most nights, and he stops his car and walks down the outside steps to the basement window, to look in on his family. As he does most nights. Instead of seeing an empty kitchen, or a quick glimpse of his kids, he sees a fight. Someone is attacking his wife. He runs back up the steps to the street. Does he have the house keys on him, or are they in the car? We don't know, but either way, the car is right there. It takes only a second or two for him to grab his house keys, open the boot and find a weapon. Perhaps he was hoping to get a tire iron. But the boot is 'a jumble of stuff,' and so he pulls out the first thing he finds that feels solid, and he runs into the house to try to protect his wife.

"Seeing another man on the scene, the attacker—who, by this time, has chased Lady Verreman up to the hall—flees through the now-open front door. Perhaps Lord Verreman takes a swing or two at him, bending the lead pipe in the process, and picking up some blood and half a dozen gray-blue fibers, or perhaps it was always bent. The man disappears, and our hero drops his improvised weapon to the floor and, very properly, tends to his wife, while the lead pipe lies on the carpet, forgotten, soaking up blood and adhering to a clump of hair lying there.

"Lord Verreman does not take the lead pipe with him when he leaves, because it is *not* the murder weapon, and it does not occur to him that it will be mistaken for a murder weapon. For the same reason, he does not remove the second length of lead pipe from the car. The pipe found at the scene does not have Sally Gardner's hair on it, because it has been nowhere near Sally Gardner's head. It may have had some of her blood on it, because Sally Gardner's blood is everywhere. On her assailant. On Lady Verreman. And on the walls. The ceiling. And the floor.

"And that's it. That's our solution. And you can see, it is simple. It is plausible. And it is right. Just like Shelley Duvall in *The Shining*, or Bruce Willis in *Die Hard*, Lord John Verreman knew the importance of having a weapon with which to defend yourself and your loved ones. You don't run into the lion's den armed with nothing.

"Even John Wick had a fucking pencil. Am I right, Chief Inspector?"

18

◆ ◆ ◆ ◆ ◆

CLOUDS OF WITNESS

THE PROSECUTION HAS rested, and, with a bang of the gavel, David Verreman instructs Enygma to produce his first defense witness.

"Er . . . can I request a short recess, my lord?"

"Really?" David says, and bangs his gavel again, just for the hell of it. "Most inconvenient. Fifteen minutes. Be back promptly."

As soon as David has finished banging, Enygma approaches him. "Er . . . which witnesses do I have?"

"The witnesses you subpoenaed, of course."

"Which witnesses are those?"

"Well, I don't know. It's up to you to conduct your own case."

Enygma passes a hand over his face. He is sweating, and his left eye is twitching. He has scratched the back of his hand until it bled, and he is trying to resist the urge to scratch it again. "And how do I subpoena these witnesses?"

"You write to the Authority—"

"Who is the Authority?"

"—giving forty-eight hours' notice."

"And, I'm afraid," says Daniel Verreman, joining them at the judge's bench, "you only have fifteen minutes."

"Fourteen minutes," says David, looking at his watch.

Enygma stares at them. "You mean I can't call *any* witnesses for the defense?"

"Not without the permission of the Authority," says David.

"And not without forty-eight hours' notice," says Daniel.

"How can I win the case without witnesses?" asks Enygma, scratching his hand frenziedly.

"No idea," says David, picking up his gavel and checking his watch. "Thirteen minutes, Mr. Enygma."

"Appendix A," says Daniel. "It's all in Appendix A. You should have asked to read the small print, mate." He cheerfully claps Enygma on the back and returns to his seat.

Enygma mumbles something about using the bathroom and walks casually up the basement steps. When he reaches the hall, he turns away from the cloakroom, toward the front door, and pulls back the false escutcheon to examine the lock. Pickable, certainly, with time. But already Enygma can hear footsteps on the basement stairs behind him. He moves to his overcoat, still hanging on a peg near the front door, and is rummaging through the pockets when Daniel Verreman steps into the hall.

"Leaving so soon?" asks Daniel, leaning against the console table.

"No, no," says Enygma, forcing a little laugh.

"You can't win, you know." Daniel is smiling. Enygma finds it unnerving. He turns his attention to his coat.

"What do you mean?"

"Did you think you were the first?"

Enygma has checked the outer pockets and found nothing. He takes the coat off the peg to check the inside pocket. "First what?"

"Not the first. Or the second. Or even the third. We found you way down there, at the bottom of the barrel."

Enygma's hands stop rummaging through the coat. He feels a cold weight drop into his stomach. "Who gave you my name?"

Daniel shrugs. "Gosh, I don't know. Could have been anyone. Were you the one who left your card in a phone box? Or were you the sex-shop guy? . . . No, wait. It's coming back to me. Funny-looking fella. Name of Bacon? Ham? Some kind of foodstuff, anyway."

Daniel has picked up the handcuffs from the table and examines them nonchalantly, then says, "What are you looking for?"

"What?" Enygma says. "Oh . . . er . . . my medication. I seem to have picked up an old bottle of your mother's by mistake. But I'm sure I brought my own." He pulls out the bottle of Limbitrol.

"Allow me." Daniel takes the coat, places his hand into the pocket that Enygma has just that moment searched and pulls out a pill bottle, identical in size and color to Lady Verreman's. This bottle reads:

MR. M. EGG

Meperidine ▼

USE AS DIRECTED

Do not take more than 2 tablets at a time or 8 in 24 hours.
This medicine is subject to additional monitoring. If you get any side effects, talk to your doctor, pharmacist or nurse. This includes any possible side effects not listed in this leaflet. Talk to a doctor at once if you take too much, even if you feel well.
- Can cause addiction
- Contains opioid

Daniel studies the bottle for a moment and says, "I'll get you some water to take them with." Then, holding the bottle in one hand and the handcuffs in the other, he leads the way back down to the basement.

Enygma returns to the defense table, where he is relieved to find his bottle of tablets and a glass of water waiting for him. He examines both the bottle and the tablets carefully before shaking out two tablets and swallowing them.

He feels a momentary relief and sets the bottle back on the table, then is overtaken by panic as he remembers the warning label on the Limbitrol bottle. *Oh well. Who bloody cares? Egg! Bastard.*

He drinks the rest of the water, though it is tepid and has a distinctly metallic tang.

David beckons him over and says quietly, "Have you sorted your defense yet?"

"How can I? I have no witnesses."

"Pity."

David picks up his gavel, ready to bring the court back into session.

Enygma feels a rush of anger. "Fuck this," he says. "I thought you wanted me to acquit your father?"

"I do, of course, if he's not guilty," says David, though his voice suggests that he couldn't care less.

"Really? Because you could have fooled me. You have put every obstacle in my way. You should never have let your mother's testimony go in. It would not have been allowed. You know that."

"And acquit him on a technicality?" David says, sneering. "That's hardly in the spirit of the game, is it?"

"Game?" Enygma feels an overwhelming urge to punch this man, ridiculous as he is in his judge's costume. Daniel comes to stand by his brother, and Max Enygma controls his temper. "Is this just a game, then?"

"Well, not for you," says Daniel. "We did warn you, you know. 'Life or death,' we said. Remember?"

"And if I choose not to play anymore?"

Daniel still has the handcuffs in his hands. He lets them dangle, and they click a little. "It is up to you, of course. Though I would not advise it."

"Fuck you. Both of you. Fucking freaks," Enygma says. He walks back to his desk and kicks it. It doesn't move. Daniel grins.

Fuck it, Enygma thinks, and tells himself to get it together. He sees on his desk a picture of an egg in lederhosen, with two black eyes and buck teeth. He screws the paper into a small, tight ball and throws the wad at Daniel. It misses.

Is this real? he wonders. *Is any of this real?* His head is throbbing, and he pops open his bottle of pills and takes another tablet, swallowing it down without water, since his glass is now empty. *Fuck it all.*

David Verreman bangs his gavel repeatedly. "OK, Mr. Enygma, call your first witness."

Daniel has picked up the paper and smoothed it out. He looks at Enygma and smirks, but Enygma's anger has concentrated his mind, and, after a moment, he says, "The defense calls the Authority."

19

◆ ◆ ◆ ◆ ◆

IBN HAKKAN AL-BOKHARI, DEAD IN HIS LABYRINTH

"OBJECTION!" SHOUTS DANIEL Verreman.

David has the gavel in his hand. The word "sustained" is already halfway out of his mouth, but Enygma is feeling excited. For the first time, the Verremans are looking disconcerted, and he will—he must—get to the bottom of it.

"My lord, the defense insists on calling this witness. He will be our only witness."

"In what capacity?"

"As an expert witness."

"An expert in what?" sneers Daniel. "The Authority has no evidence material to this case, and is not an expert in the detection of crime, or in any aspect of forensic investigation. I see no basis for this witness to be called."

David Verreman is surprised. The gavel is still in his hand, but he does not bang it. Instead, he lays it down on his desk and looks at Enygma carefully.

After a long pause, David says, "Call your witness."

———

THE AUTHORITY IS an unprepossessing man. Balding. Over-weight. With halitosis. And, from the gingerly manner in which he takes his seat, Enygma calculates that there is a fair probability of hemorrhoids.

"Please state your name for the benefit of the court."

"A. N. Author."

"Your full name."

"That is my full name."

"I see. And your occupation?"

The Authority sighs, leans forward and speaks slowly, as to the remedial section of the class. "I am *an author*."

"You write novels?"

"I do."

"Objection!" Daniel cries.

"Shut up," says the Authority, and, lo and behold, Daniel Verre-man shuts the fuck up.

Enygma decides that he likes the guy. "Please state your creden-tials for the court."

"I am an expert in story."

"By which you mean plot?"

"Plot, yes, but not just plot. Story is also structure. Form and com-position, allegory and metaphor, foregrounding and juxtaposition, irony and rhetoric—to name but a few of its elements. Story is about life. About the human condition. And thus it is about everything."

"Wow. You really are the Authority."

"Indeed I am."

"OK." Enygma paces the room. He is beginning to feel a fluttering in his chest. It might be because of excitement. It might be because of the drugs. Doesn't matter. "I would like you to imagine you were writ-ing a novel about this case, using the evidence presented here."

"I wouldn't do it."

"Why not?"

"Well, firstly, because fiction based on a 'true story' is always second-rate fiction—it cannot achieve the symmetry of true fiction. In life, random things happen and mysteries remain unsolved—for decades, sometimes forever. That does not happen in fiction. In fiction, everything is significant. Everything is explained. Everything has a purpose. And secondly, the story that the prosecution have created in this case is artificial. It fits the facts, more or less, but it smells of the lamp."

"Smells of the lamp?"

"It is not natural. It is constructed. It is artificial."

"Can you give us an example?"

"Well, for example, the police have made the case that Lord Verreman committed premeditated murder by letting himself into the house and hiding in the basement till his wife came downstairs to make a drink."

"That's their case," says Enygma, with his fingers crossed. "What's wrong with it?"

"There are too many imponderables. How could he be sure of getting in when there was every likelihood that the door would be bolted against him? How could he be sure that his wife would come down to the basement to make a cup of tea when she could have easily made one upstairs? How could he be sure she would not be thirsty earlier? Or later? Or at all? How could he be sure that she would come downstairs alone? What if her son came with her for a cup of hot milk or cocoa or something? What would he have done then?"

"How else could he do it? Assuming he was the murderer, of course."

"He could let himself into the house at three in the morning and strangle her quietly in her bed. Nine o'clock in the evening is pretty early for a murder. There was a very good chance that the children would be up, or at least awake, which, in fact, they were. There was every chance that someone would see him entering or leaving the house. At three o'clock it would be simple, and no risk of getting the wrong person. Pick up a few trinkets. Break a window on your way out. Make it look like a break-in. Or fake an overdose—even easier."

"And what about the nanny?"

"What about her?"

"She would be in the house."

"So what?"

"You think that the nanny is irrelevant to this case?"

The Authority sneers a little. "That, in my opinion, is the real problem with this story. *Everyone* thinks she is irrelevant to the case. In detective fiction, the detective is supposed to work to avenge the victim, and to bring the murderer to book, in recognition of the heinous nature of the crime and the sanctity of human life, thus restoring order to the universe. But in this story, the nanny is just a dummy. Literally. She has no voice. No opinions. No life. No one is interested in the nanny. How can the detective avenge someone no one cares about?"

"You would not write this story yourself?"

"No sane author would."

—Hey!

We're not The Author. We are the narrator. Remember?

—Right. Forgot. Sorry. As you were.

"I HAVE A question about speech and dialogue. Can you tell authentic dialogue from inauthentic dialogue?"

"Are you asking me if I *can* tell, or if I am able to tell you?"

"Is there a difference?"

"Writing dialogue is like writing music. There are rules you must follow. Maurice Ravel wrote *Gaspard de la Nuit*, the most challenging work ever written for piano. Euphemia Allen wrote "Chopsticks." The principle is the same for both. You have to know which notes go together and which notes don't. Most people can tell when they hear a duff note. They just don't know *why* it's duff. A musician can explain it to you, but unless you understand harmonic scales, you won't really comprehend it."

"I would like to read some lines of dialogue to you, and I would like your professional opinion on them, if you don't mind."

"Really," Daniel says, bobbing up from his seat, "this is ridiculous."

David's gavel comes down hard, and repeatedly, on the bench. *Bang, bang, bang.* "Overruled!" he screams. "Proceed!"

"The first example I want you to consider comes from Lady Verreman's testimony to the coroner's court. It doesn't feel right to me, but I don't know why. The coroner says, 'There is a photograph of a top metal support on the balustrade of the stairs that has been disturbed. Can you explain that?' And Lady Verreman replies, 'I would have dislodged it with my leg in the struggle.' Would you have written that?"

"Not if my character was telling the truth."

"You think Lady Verreman was lying, then?"

"Not necessarily. She says, 'I would have,' which means she might be lying, or she might not know and is just guessing. If she had remembered it clearly, she would have said something like, *My foot caught on it in the struggle, and I felt it give way.* She would have fixed her statement in time: the foot got caught *during* the struggle. And she would have attached the feelings, or the sensations she experienced in that moment, to the statement: she *felt* it give way. She would have been present in the statement in the same way that she was present in the struggle."

"But she was present in the struggle. We know that much."

"That's not what her words say."

"Odd. OK, let's try another. When she ran into the Three Taps pub, Lady Verreman was silent for up to fifteen minutes; then she became distressed and began yelling. This is what she said: 'Help me. Help me. I've just escaped from being murdered.' According to testimony, she repeated that first phrase two or three times, and this was reported by several witnesses. Then she said, 'My child! My child! He's murdered my nanny.' Would you write that?"

"Definitely not."

"Why?"

"Sentence structure. It's too long."

"What would you have written?"

"Well, in the first place, I would have given the kid a name. 'My child' is on a par with 'my nanny.' Strangely impersonal. Then I might have said, *Call the police*, or *Murder*, and *He's still in the house*. Short, snappy sentences demonstrate shock, convey urgency and inform the listener what she wants them to do. What Lady Verreman actually said conveys neither personal involvement nor urgency. Nor does it contain a specific request. 'I've just escaped' suggests that the danger is over, and 'from being murdered' is almost comical when the truth is that she has fled her home, leaving a dead body in the basement and a murderer in her house, who, for all she knows, is still there, and who could be snatching the kids, or killing 'em, at that very moment."

Daniel bobs up again, but David overrules him before he has opened his mouth: *Bang.*

"OK," says Enygma. "I think perhaps my learned friend was going to ask what difference this all makes. Lady Verreman was definitely there that night. Definitely attacked. She says so. He says so. The medical and forensic evidence says so. What possible reason could she have for not telling the truth?"

"There could be lots of reasons—in a novel. She might be covering for someone else. She might have amnesia because of the bang on the head, and be trying to hide it for some reason—concern that she might lose custody of her children, for instance. She might have been under the influence of drink or drugs. She might have been suffering from a mental illness. Or a physical illness that limited her perception. Or she might just be straight up lying. You can't tell from just a few sentences."

Daniel pops up again, and, before David can bang his gavel, he shouts, "If you can't tell, why are you here?"

David's gavel is arrested midswing.

THE GAME IS MURDER

Mr. Author curls his lip. "You cannot tell *why* it is wrong—for that you have to read the rest of the novel—but you can tell *that* it is wrong. Everyone who read Lady Verreman's statement would have winced inwardly when they read those sentences. Everyone. Because it doesn't sound natural."

"There is one more snatch of dialogue that I want you to consider before we move on," Enygma says, reclaiming his witness. "This is something that is, supposedly, said by Lord Verreman, as reported by Lady Verreman. This is the piece of testimony that was suppressed at the coroner's court but she spoke of openly in press interviews, both before and after the inquest."

David Verreman lifts his gavel and looks at his brother. "Are you going to object?"

"Is there any point?" Daniel asks.

"No," says David.

Bang, bang, bangity-bang.

Enygma continues. "In an interview with the *Daily Express*, Lady Verreman claimed that she asked her husband what had become of the nanny, and that he replied, 'She's dead. Don't look.' Now, does that sound like natural dialogue to you?"

"Yes."

Daniel snorts with laughter.

"It does?" asks Enygma, and his voice is disappointed.

"It does. The language is right. But the context is not."

Enygma breathes a sigh of relief. "What do you mean?"

A. N. Author throws up his hands. "It's ridiculous. The wife is *looking* for the nanny. Therefore, she cannot see the nanny. If she cannot see the nanny, why does he need to tell her not to look at the nanny?"

"So the speech lacks authenticity?" asks Enygma.

"No, it does not. It sounds entirely authentic. The speech patterns are right. The words are right. Dead right. Note the short sentences. It is the context that is wrong. It suggests a different sort of scene altogether."

319

"Can you suggest a scene in which that sentence would be in context, and would also conform to the evidence as presented in this case?"

"Of course I can. I am an author. I can do anything. I suppose you want me to make the husband innocent?"

"That would be very helpful."

"Well, let me see . . . The wife comes downstairs, looking for her cup of tea. She goes partway down the basement steps, meets an intruder and is forced back into the hall during the attack. At the same time, the husband, who has seen the attack through the basement window, bursts through the front door, and the intruder makes off. Husband asks wife what the hell is going on. Wife tells husband she can't find the nanny and asks him to check the basement. Husband and wife go downstairs together, wife stepping in the victim's blood on the way. They see the blood; they see the sack; they even examine it, during which wife leaves her blood on the sack. Then he says—drumroll, please—'She's dead. Don't look.' And then, just to make sure his wife doesn't have to look anymore, on their way back up the stairs he removes the lightbulb from the socket. How's that?"

"Sounds good to me. You would remove the lightbulb *after* the murder, would you? In your version, I mean?"

"Of course I would. No one could have done all that in the dark. And why would they? It's stupid."

"So can we say *now* that Lady Verreman is lying?"

"Not necessarily. I mean, in a cheap sort of novel she would be lying, and doing a piss-poor job of it. But in another sort of novel—a better sort of novel—she might be misremembering, or remembering what happened, but through a filter that taints her memories."

"What do you mean by the word 'filter'?" Enygma says, picking up his empty glass and putting it down again. God, he is thirsty.

"Well, for example, have you seen the film *Memento*?"

"Guy Pearce and Carrie-Anne Moss. Excellent film."

"It was all right."

"Carrie-Anne Moss also starred in *The Matrix*," says Enygma.

"Whatever. The point is, the hero of *Memento*, Guy Pearce, has a faulty memory because of a type of amnesia. So he relies on his notes, which are tattooed on his body, to find the murderer of his wife. But his memory is only as reliable as his notes."

"I'm not sure I follow," says Enygma. "Although I do love talking about films. Have you seen *My Cousin Vinny*? I love Joe Pesci—don't you?"

Bang, bang, bang. "Relevance, Mr. Enygma!"

"Sorry, Your Honor. How is Guy Pearce's faulty memory relevant?"

"Because," says A. N. Author, "Guy Pearce sees the past through the filter of his faulty memory, and his tattoos. And that filter can change your perception of reality."

"I don't get it," says Enygma.

"OK. Let's try a nonmovie example. Let's say you have someone who is suffering from paranoia."

"Lord Verreman claimed that his wife was suffering from the 'disease of paranoia' in his letter."

"Quite," says A. N. Author. "Well, now, if you were paranoid, and perhaps if you had also sustained head injuries and were in shock, you would filter your memories of those events through that paranoia, so that, though you might recall accurately the words that were said, your filter would put the wrong interpretation on them—i.e., that it was a confession to murder rather than an investigation of a murder scene. Note also that, in Lady Verreman's account, he does not say, *I killed her.* This is not an admission of guilt. Just a statement of fact. The nanny was dead. And so he said she was dead."

"Is that the only thing wrong with this statement?"

"Not at all. Why did he even say, 'Don't look'? 'Don't look' implies regard for another person's feelings, for their mental welfare. A murderer does not need to spare his victim's feelings—if he's about to kill her, post-traumatic stress will not be an issue for her. That phrase, while being fine in itself, does not fit in the context in which it has been placed. It needs to be cut, and pasted elsewhere in the novel."

"This is bullshit," Daniel calls. "All bullshit. This man isn't a psychologist. He doesn't *know*. He writes stories, for God's sake. What kind of job is that for a grown-up—telling lies for a living? You can't just make up a story to fit the facts." Daniel has put his feet up on his table and has a glass of whisky in one hand. He is swinging the handcuffs around the fingers of his other.

"On the contrary," Enygma says, "the prosecution has done exactly that. And now the defense is crafting a story of its own. From the same facts, mind you."

"Bollocks," says Daniel, and takes a sip. "Fucking stories. Fucking bollocks."

David bangs his gavel once more. He rises from the bench, crosses the room and snatches the whisky bottle from Daniel's table. He returns to his bench, swigs straight from the bottle and bangs the gavel again. "Proceed."

Enygma again reaches for his water glass, and again finds it empty. His tongue is thick, and he can hear its stickiness in his voice. He must have a drink. He plows on. "Are you saying that this filter of paranoia caused Lady Verreman to misremember the facts in relation to the assault?"

"No. I know nothing about Lady Verreman. Or about the case. Or about paranoia. But I do know about story. I hear the duff note. I can tell when the logic of the novel does not add up. I can pinpoint the exact moment when a writer ran out of steam and called forth the god from the machine. And I can spot a hackneyed plot device a mile away. And so, too, apparently, can the police."

"What do you mean?" asks Enygma. He now crosses to the judge's bench and takes a mouthful from Verreman's whisky bottle, running the liquid over his parched tongue. His tongue has developed the consistency of old leather, however, and the liquid will not permeate it.

"Lord Verreman is an aristocrat," says the witness. "Therefore, he is a libertine. He is a gambler. Therefore, he is a degenerate gambler. He has some debts. Therefore, he is desperate for money. He is separated from his wife. Therefore, he wishes her dead. When Sally Gardner was found dead in the basement of his home, Lord Verreman was a gift—ready wrapped, with a bow on top. Lady Verreman's testimony and his disappearance just made it easy for them to come to the obvious conclusion."

Enygma swallows the whisky, which has left him thirstier than ever. "Are you suggesting the police were negligent?"

"I am suggesting that they lacked originality. And, lacking originality, they did what bad writers do—that is, they allowed their prejudices free rein, and attached the most obvious motive to every action, then stitched those together to make a case. But as shrewd readers know, the guilt never lies with the obvious suspect. Had Verreman stuck around to present a defense, no doubt the police would have worked harder. As it was, there was no real need."

"I see." Enygma picks up his glass and goes off in search of water. Through the buzzing in his head, he can hear a gavel pounding in the distance. He ignores it. He must have something to drink. He goes into the basement kitchen and turns on the cold-water tap. Nothing. He walks up to the hall. David is shouting something, but Enygma cannot tell what it is. He doesn't care. He walks into the cloakroom in the hall. A small dribble of water runs from the tap and immediately dries up. *Fuck.*

He walks back down to the basement, grabs the whisky bottle from the judge's bench and, this time, carries the bottle to his table. *Fuck it.*

Bang, bang, bang with the gavel again. *Someone should take that fucking thing off him.*

"Are you finished, Mr. Enygma?" David asks. Heavy overtones of sarcasm.

Enygma takes a swig of whisky and throws an arm out toward Daniel. "Your witness, I believe."

Daniel waits a long time before getting up. "You are not a material witness in this case, are you, Mr. Author?"

"No."

"You are not an investigative expert?"

"No. I write literary novels."

"Of course you do. I take it, then, that you are not a medical doctor, a pathologist, a scene-of-crime officer, a blood analyst or even a psychologist in your spare time?"

"Nope."

"Then what the hell are you doing here?"

"I was called."

"Right . . . Well, I have listened to your . . . evidence. It adds up to nothing, doesn't it? You don't like the dialogue because the sentences are too long. Or they're the right length, but they're in the wrong place. The crime lacks originality. Who cares about originality? Who cares about sentence structure? And authenticity! Who on earth cares about that?"

"I do."

"You do!" says Daniel, with a little chuckle. "And who the hell are you?"

◆ ◆ ◆ ◆ ◆

ARTISTS IN CRIME

"I AM AN author. I am A. N. Author. Therefore, I am God. And I can do anything. For example, I can give you a body, though you exist only in the imagination of your brother—and that only at my will. Do you like your body?"

"It's very nice," says Daniel.

"Wanna keep it?"

—*Quick question.*

What now?

—*How do you know that the fat guy with the halitosis and the hemorrhoids is not us?*

Because he is The Author. We are the narrator. Although sometimes we resemble The Author.

—*What the fuck? Millions of people are going to read this.*

Millions of people?

—*Well, my mother. My mother is going to read this, and she would not like that description at all. My mother loves me. Can't you make him more appealing?*

I don't think so. I don't think I am allowed.
—*Fuck!*

"BUT," SAYS DANIEL, a little warily, "this is not a story. This is a real case. How can you apply the principles of story to real life?"

"I do not. I apply the principles of real life to story. Story is the perfection of life, but it must also be lifelike. I make the reader believe in a world that they know is not real. I make them care about people who they know do not exist. I make them feel emotions that do not originate from their own selves. I make them laugh and cry, and I break their hearts, using only words on a page. I cannot do that unless my story is lifelike. So I know life. I know sentence structure. I know dialogue. And I know authenticity."

21

◆ ◆ ◆ ◆ ◆

CARDS ON THE TABLE

We often hear (almost invariably, however, from superficial observers) that guilt can look like innocence. I believe it to be infinitely the truer axiom of the two that innocence can look like guilt.

—Wilkie Collins, *The Moonstone*

DAVID VERREMAN HAS found more whisky and is drinking it straight from the bottle. Daniel is closing and unclosing the handcuffs around one wrist, trying to snap them on the way they do on the telly. Max Enygma pours himself another drink and represses a snort of laughter. He is feeling good. He is feeling better than he has felt for a long time. All that time he spent taking care of himself—what a waste when he could feel like this!

He takes a sip. Not too much. Just enough to keep the buzz going. He hears David bang his gavel again. *Definitely need to do something about that.*

"Ladeesh and gen'l'men of the jury," says David, "that concludes the evidence in this case. The proshecuution and defense will now make their closing statements, and then I will sum up. Mr. Proshhh . . . Mr. Proshh'cutor, you can go first."

Daniel stands, the handcuffs dangling from his left wrist. He spreads his arms in the direction of the jury box, and the cuffs clink a little. "Members of the jury, this case is clear. *We* have presented evidence in this case. The defense has given us a lesson in creative writing. We have shown motive, means and opportunity. The defense has talked about movies. I ask you, who on earth cares about *My Cousin Vinny?*

"The facts of this case are simple and sordid. Lord John Verreman wanted to be rid of his wife but did not want to pay her a divorce settlement. Why? Because he was in deep debt and he couldn't afford to. He was overdrawn everywhere and would soon be publicly shamed as a bankrupt. So much for his reputed skill as a gambler. His ego could not take the world's knowing of his failure.

"And so he chose a night he thought his wife would be home alone, and he let himself into her home and waited in the basement for her, knowing that at nine o'clock she would come downstairs to make a cup of tea.

"He brought two things into the house with him that night, which should demonstrate to you, beyond any doubt, his intent to commit murder. He brought a length of lead pipe, which he had carefully wrapped in Elastoplast in the hope of lessening the amount of blood loss. And he brought a sack to carry away the body.

"Had his plan worked, no doubt Lord Verreman would have told his children that their mother had run away and left them. Not such a devoted father after all.

"We have shown that Lord Verreman removed the lightbulb over the basement steps in order to prevent his wife's seeing into the basement before she descended. We have shown that the lead pipe found on the floor of the hall contained the blood and hair of at least one, possibly both, of the victims. And, crucially, we have shown you a second piece of pipe, found in the car that was used by Lord Verreman to make his getaway, that was so similar in nature to the murder weapon that it *cannot* do anything but convince you of this man's guilt.

"We have shown you forensic evidence from that car—including blood and hair matching samples taken from the scene of the crime— that should leave you in no doubt that Lord Verreman was in that house, and responsible for the terrible murder of an innocent young woman.

"That John Verreman was responsible for this crime could not be more clear. The defense's lack of relevant witnesses is a testament to that fact. They could not produce a single witness—except, of all things, a *novelist*—to refute the very strong evidence in this case. Please, members of the jury, take your time to consider the evidence that has been presented, and when you have, I am certain that you will have no doubt in your minds that Lord John Verreman is guilty of the murder of Mrs. Sally Gardner.

"Thank you."

Daniel sits down, and David looks for his gavel, but this is now sitting on Enygma's desk. As David looks toward him, Max just covers the gavel with his hand, and David makes do with thumping the bench instead.

"Mr. Enygma. Your turn, I believe."

Max gets to his feet, realizes that standing is a bad idea and drops heavily down. He suddenly feels drunk. He takes another sip of whisky and gathers his thoughts.

"Mr. Enygma!" David says, thumping the bench. "We are waiting."

"Sorry. Sorry," Max mumbles. "Sorry. Members of the jury—"

"Please stand while you address the jury," David says.

"Fuck. I mean, sorry." Max gets a firm grip on the table and levers himself to his feet. The world tilts on its axis. He closes his eyes and waits for the room to right itself.

"Members of the jury," he says, his eyes still closed, "I must take issue with counsel for the prosecution—*My Cousin Vinny* is a bloody great film. Ralph Macchio—the Karate Kid!—is taking a summer road trip with a friend and they are arrested somewhere in the Deep South of the United States. They believe they have been arrested for the accidental theft of a can of tuna—or *toona*, as they insist on calling it, because they are from New York—and they confess. But in fact, they have been arrested for murder.

"Neither young man can afford a lawyer, and the public defender is rubbish, so Ralph Macchio calls his cousin Vinny, who is a newly qualified lawyer from the wrong side of the tracks. *Dum dum duuummm!* Enter Joe Pesci." Enygma chances opening one eye, but the room spins again, and he closes it quickly. "Now, on the face of it, the prosecution have a solid case against the Karate Kid and his pal. They have witnesses who place them at the scene at the time of the murder. They have an expert in tire tracks who will testify that their car made off at speed moments after the crime was committed. And, of course, they have the confessions.

"How can Joe Pesci get them out of this? Easy. Appearances are not facts. He is able to cast doubt on the credibility of the witnesses, and with the help of his gum-chewing girlfriend, Marisa Tomei, he decimates the expert tire evidence, because . . . well, I won't spoil it for you. Safe to say that the Karate Kid is acquitted, and Joe Pesci wins his first case as a trial lawyer.

"The prosecution ask what *My Cousin Vinny* has to do with this case, and it is the same thing—*appearances are not facts*. On the face of it, Lord Verreman is a credible suspect. He has access to the house—as long as his wife has not remembered to bolt the door. He has motive—as long as you believe that he is in desperate financial trouble. He has in his car a weapon of eerily similar description to that of the weapon found at the scene of the crime. There is even a confession, of sorts, that places him at the scene on the night of the murder. It looks like a solid case. Not quite as solid as the prosecution maintain, but still solid enough to convince senior policemen with years of experience.

"But that is simply appearance." Enygma opens his eyes again; the world tilts, but rights itself, and he continues. "And as we all know, appearance is not always the same as truth.

"Take Lord Verreman's much-heralded financial problems. What do we know about them? The prosecution say that he was about to be declared bankrupt, and that it was the fear of his finances being made public that caused him to contemplate murder. How true is this? He had overdrafts. So what? Show me the man who doesn't. He was, in fact, declared bankrupt, but that was *after* his disappearance, and was a technical mechanism by which creditors could lay claim to his estate. There is nothing to show that, had he stuck around, he would have been made bankrupt just the same.

"And don't forget, Lord Verreman was a man of assets. He could certainly have covered the amount of debt he had outstanding. Indeed, he was doing so—a job lot of family silver had been put up for sale at Christie's, which would have cleared the majority of his outstanding debt, and which demonstrates, despite what the prosecution allege, that he was *not* afraid of public comment about his finances. That sale, too, of course, would reduce the size of the pot when it came to splitting assets later. By the by, much of the silver at the sale was bought by Verreman's friends and held in trust for his children, and who is to say that was not the idea all along?

"This is a man who has income from a family trust; who owns two homes in the most exclusive part of London, one of which he rents out; who holds solid assets and has privileged friends who would, no doubt, have helped if he had asked. He is not a man without options.

"I suggest that the financial motive is not as sound as a first glance might suggest, and certainly the prosecution have been unable to find any *imminent* threat to Lord Verreman's finances. Had Lady Verreman's life been insured for a large sum, murder might have been tempting. I have to tell you, it was not. So why would such a man act to destroy his wife and threaten his own life, particularly as he had every expectation that a distant, ailing and elderly relative would soon die and leave him a bequest—which, in fact, Lady Audley did, not two months after the murder?

"The prosecution say that Lord Verreman *planned* this crime. That he brought with him a sack in which to hide the body, and a lead pipe wrapped with bandages with which to kill her with soft blows. A very considerate murderer, you might think. And, of course, there is the second piece of lead pipe, found in the car—the supposed smoking-gun lead pipe. I ask you to consider why he would make two weapons at all. Why cut two separate lengths of pipe—because the forensic scientists are clear that these two pipes were not connected to each other—and wrap them both all over with white Elastoplast? The police have suggested that, having made the first pipe too long— taking account of the height of the ceiling in the hall, which was not even the proposed site of this planned murder—the murderer then made another, shorter, pipe. This is, of course, ridiculous. What would you do, members of the jury, if you had planned to commit a murder, and had made yourself a weapon from a length of pipe, only to discover that it was too long? I submit that you would take your hacksaw and lop four inches or so off the end of the first pipe. You would not hunt around for another one and start measuring, cutting and strapping that one up, too. You would not carry both of them with you to the crime scene, and leave one behind to incriminate you, and a second in the boot of your abandoned car, with which to seal your fate.

"The plain truth is, members of the jury, that the lead pipe found at the scene was *not* the murder weapon. There is no *proof* that it was. The forensic experts say only that it might have been—in the same way that they say Lady Verreman *might* have collected blood on the underside of her shoes when fending off her attacker, despite the fact that the attacker left no blood on the front of her dress. She *might* have put her feet against the only bloody parts of his clothes, but how much *simpler* to say that she walked through the blood? Similarly, this lead pipe *might* have been the murder weapon, but it could equally have been *any other* rounded blunt instrument.

"Was there blood and hair on the lead pipe? Yes, there was. But remember, Sergeant Heyer, a police officer of long standing, who is trained to spot forensic evidence, walked past the pipe the first time, without registering it at all. When he saw it the second time, it was white and he mistook it for a dolly's leg—this blunt object wrapped in absorbent bandage that had, supposedly, been used to brutally attack two women, was *white*. It was only when he passed the pipe in the hall for the *third time* that he noticed bloodstains on it—around two hours after it had been dropped there by Lord Verreman, during which time it slowly absorbed the blood and hair from the floor on which it lay.

"Remember, too, that this weapon had *no* hair belonging to Sally Gardner attached to it—despite the fact that it was wrapped in gummed fabric, and despite the fact that blood is incredibly sticky. Is it really likely that, despite her being hit on the head with this object over and over and over again, *none* of her hair adhered to the pipe? It could not have been washed away, since forensic experts found none of Sally's blood in the sink and none of her hair in the sink, and the blood on the Elastoplast round the pipe had not been watered down.

"There was one clump of hair attached to the pipe. That clump of hair, of course, was Lady Verreman's. The blood found on the clump of hair attached to the pipe matched samples from Lady Verreman *only*. The blood on the weapon itself returned a result of group AB, which is likely a mixture of both women's blood. In other words, although Sally Gardner had been attacked much more ferociously than Lady Verreman (clearly evidenced by the fact that she died as a result of her injuries), and although her blood was *everywhere* (in the basement, and up the stairs, and even on the back of Lady Verreman's dress and on her shoes, despite her claim that she never went down to the basement that night), there was not *enough* of Sally's blood on the weapon to separately identify her blood group.

"This pipe was *not* the murder weapon. It could not have *been* the murder weapon. This pipe was carried into the house by Lord Verreman, yes, but for the purposes of warding off an attacker, just as you or I, or Shelley Duvall, might pick up a heavy object when we are faced with a dangerous intruder. Did Lord Verreman hit his wife's attacker with the pipe, bending it in the process? Quite possibly—lead is a remarkably soft metal, after all. But it is equally possible that this 'grossly distorted' pipe was made that way on purpose.

"You might ask what Lord Verreman was doing with the pipes in the car if he was not carrying them to use as weapons. I have no idea.

I do know that the boot contained 'a jumble of stuff.' I know, too, that, according to my *Plumber's Handbook*, plumbers used to routinely bind lead pipes with heavy muslin that they then dipped in tar to protect them against corrosion. Could these pipes have been a handyman's DIY attempt at the same? I don't know. Perhaps they were to be used as weights inside the brass casings of the pendulums of a grandfather clock. Or maybe as curtain weights. Who knows? Not me. I do know that if I had been *planning* this murder, I would not have chosen a soft and hollow pipe. And I would not have had 'a jumble of stuff' in the boot of my car. Wouldn't that be the obvious place to put the body? If he had shoved poor Sally Gardner's body into a sack to transport it in secret, why would he risk carrying that sack, saturated with blood, on the passenger seat of the car? No. Everyone who has ever been to the movies knows that the proper place for transporting bodies is the boot of the car. If the boot was full of *stuff*, then Lord Verreman did not come to this house with the *intention of committing murder*.

"There was, as the prosecution have pointed out, some blood smears in the car. Is that surprising? No. He was in the house. Lady Verreman says so. He says so—in his letters to his friends, in his phone call to his mother and on his visit to Margaret Howard-Cole. He makes no attempt to conceal the fact that he was there. But there is nothing surprising in that. He was there every night. He went to check on his children.

"And, no doubt, he went to check on his wife, too. Lord Verreman was not an enlightened husband. He was, of course, a product of his age, and his class. He felt a sense of entitlement that is not attractive to the modern mind. Bluntly put, he felt entitled to spy on his wife. To let himself into her home. To check her medication. To secretly record his conversations with her whenever she lost her temper. He felt entitled to ask the nannies, whose wages he paid, to spy on his wife and report back to him. Not creditable, certainly, to modern sentiments, but John Verreman was as much a product of his upbringing as any working-class hero.

"What else did they find in the car? Well, there were some thirty-two microscopic gray-blue fibers similar to the seven found on the lead pipe in the hall, the six in the cloakroom sink and the four on the towel in the bedroom. Where in the car were these fibers found? On a bloodstain on the inside of the door and on a small tuft of Lady Verreman's hair. Now, had the assailant been wearing, for example, a gray-blue pullover when Lord Verreman ran in to defend his wife, wielding the lead pipe, he might easily have picked up some of these microscopic fibers from the assailant. We do not know where these fibers came from. They did not match any of the clothes that the two women were wearing that night. Had they belonged to clothes Lord Verreman wore, you might have expected to find hundreds, even thousands, of these fibers on the driver's seat. They found none.

"There is *nothing* in the forensic evidence that contradicts Lord Verreman's version of events—so far as we have it. There is, however, quite a lot that contradicts the statements of his wife." Enygma glances around at the two Verreman brothers. David is watching Enygma carefully. And he is listening. Intently. Daniel is watching David with equal intensity. Daniel clinks the handcuffs loudly against the table, as if to catch his brother's attention. David doesn't notice.

Enygma hurries on. "Now, Lady Verreman was an ill woman. I have read extracts from her diary in which she freely admits that she was being treated for a variety of mental health disorders—though it is true that she disputes the necessity for such treatments. She claimed not to suffer from paranoia, but she believed her doctors, her lawyers, her friends, her husband's family and even her own family were all involved in a conspiracy to frame her as mad. She admitted, too, to obtaining prescriptions from a number of doctors concurrently, without her own doctor's knowledge, and mixing and matching these drugs without supervision, and also to self-medicating, at times, with alcohol.

"The prosecution have maintained that Lady Verreman's mental health problems were a farrago of lies got up by my client in order to paint his wife as an unfit mother and gain custody of his children.

And it is certainly true that the family court, who no doubt meet all manner of unscrupulous men daily, believed that Lady Verreman was capable of looking after the children—with the constant presence of a nanny, and on condition that she receive treatment for those mental health conditions that she maintained she did not have. However, it should be noted that Lady Verreman was receiving treatment from a psychiatric doctor years before her separation, and before her marriage, and her diary tells much more than she may have realized about her unhappiness, her isolation and her paranoia, which are starkly evident on every page.

"I do not mean to say that Lady Verreman maliciously lied in order to implicate her husband in this crime, and she can scarcely have devised the murder herself in order to frame him. I simply suggest that her illness caused her to view the strange and terrible events of that night through the filter of her mental illness, and to misinterpret what she saw.

"And do not forget, at no point did she say that she saw her husband attacking the nanny. The nanny was already dead when Antonia Verreman walked downstairs in search of her cup of tea. She doesn't even claim that she saw her husband hit *her* over the head— just that she heard a noise behind her and that 'someone' rushed out and attacked her from behind. It was only later that she identified the man in the hall—when he told her to 'shut up' and she recognized her husband's voice. Anyone in that situation might have confused the man who rushed at her from the cloakroom with the man who came through the front door. Add in the confusion resulting from a head injury, the shock of the moment, mental illness and overmedication, and it is not at all surprising that her testimony is unsound.

"You have been told already that Lady Verreman would absolutely *not* have been able to testify against her own husband in a criminal trial. The judge has allowed her testimony to go in regardless. You will see, however, that there is nothing in it that incriminates my client, except for her assertion that he was in the house. As, of course, was she. She had every right to be there.

"And so did he.

"I would also like to draw your attention to one or two inconsistencies in Lady Verreman's statement. She claims that she did not go down into the basement at any time that night, and yet the undersides of both of her shoes show that she almost certainly walked in Mrs. Gardner's blood. She claims that the man who wrestled her to the floor was the same man who had murdered the nanny, but we have demonstrated, through experiment in this courtroom, how impossible it would have been for the man who had manhandled the nanny's body into a sack not to be covered in blood, at least across his chest and arms. And yet none of that blood transferred itself to the front of Lady Verreman's dress.

"Of course, had one man attacked her with a blunt object from behind, and another told a shocked and hysterical wife to 'shut up' and tried to wrestle her to the ground to calm her down, that would account for the absence of Sally's blood on the front of her clothes.

"The prosecution claim that the letters that Lord Verreman wrote to his friends Sir Henry Wade and Edmund Crispin prove that he was at the house. And they are right. However, it seems strange that Lord Verreman did not also know that he had committed murder that night. He is concerned only that his children will see him in the dock, accused of the 'attempted murder' of his wife. Lord Verreman does not know he will be charged with murder, because he has not committed murder.

"Members of the jury, though the prosecution dare not say it, the only evidence that *really* tells against Lord Verreman is that he ran away. You may think that that speaks to a guilty conscience. Or you may take the view that he was simply going to do as he said—that is, 'lie doggo for a bit,' until he could see how the land lay.

"I freely admit that this is not a very creditable action. It suggests that Lord Verreman held himself above the law. We have already acknowledged that he was a man of entitlement. He was not alone. One of the complaints DCI Blake made about the conduct of the case was that many of Verreman's friends felt themselves to be above the law, too. Whereas, for example, you or I might feel compelled to take a piece of evidence in a murder case straight to the police station, one of Lord Verreman's set waited until four o'clock in the morning, when he was on his way home after a night of clubbing, to drop off a crucial letter from the accused, by which time the envelope, which might have assisted the police greatly, had been destroyed forever.

"Lord Verreman's actions appear to show that he has something to hide. The prosecution suggest that it was the murder of an innocent woman and the attempted murder of his own wife. I suggest that Lord Verreman—knowing that his wife suffered from paranoia, and that she had already accused him, in the past, of hiring someone to kill her or of trying to kill her himself—decided that he would wait to see whether she was believed before he gave himself up.

"That was a fatal mistake. He did not know that his wife would not be able to testify against him. In all likelihood, had he stayed to face the music, he would never have been charged with this murder. But he did not stay. He ran. Maybe he kept on running. Maybe he killed himself. Maybe he was knocked over by a bus and buried under an assumed name. We will never know, and it is not important—at least not to us.

"The judge has allowed you to take Lady Verreman's testimony into consideration in this case. However, you may not draw any inferences on Lord Verreman's failure to present himself for questioning. Even had he stood trial in person, he would have been perfectly entitled not to take the stand in his own defense. The prosecution must make their case beyond a reasonable doubt. It is not the responsibility of the defendant to prove his innocence. Even if you consider his actions somewhat dishonorable or cowardly, you must find him not guilty if the prosecution do not make their case.

"It is not incumbent upon the defense to put another man's neck in the noose in place of our client's. But, members of the jury, I invite you to consider whether anyone else had a motive for murder. Not the murder of Lady Verreman, which they did not carry out, though the opportunity was clearly there, but the murder of Sally Gardner—

the actual victim, and, I suggest, the intended victim. Was there any-one who wanted to kill poor, unregarded Sally?

"Was there anyone with motive and opportunity as great as Lord Verreman's? What about her boyfriend Eddie Biggers, with whom she had had a passionate and stormy, though short, relationship, and with whom she had quarreled only the night before? He says that they were contemplating marriage, children and emigration, after less than six weeks of courtship. He says that they had already quarreled a few times in the usually euphoric early phase of their relationship. He phoned her on the night of the murder, just moments before she, against custom, offered to make Lady Verreman a cup of tea—going down five flights of stairs, in the dark, when she could more easily have made tea in the nursery, just one floor down. You might also consider why Mrs. Gardner was wearing heels when slippers would have made the journey in the dark so much safer.

"Mr. Biggers says that, during that phone call, they made up their quarrel and made plans to see each other the following week. We have, of course, only his word for that. He says that he was working that night, but he was working in a pub only a few minutes' walk from the scene of the crime. Could he have slipped out unnoticed during his break?

"Or what about the mysterious Ray, whom Sally was also said to be in a relationship with? Why have we not heard his testimony? Could it be that, believing they had their man, the police made little effort to find him? How did Ray feel about being usurped in the af-fections of Sally Gardner? We don't know.

"Most importantly, members of the jury, why was Sally Gardner never considered a victim in her own right? Why is she but the bit player in the Verreman Affair? I can suggest only one reason. Class. The Verremans were aristocratic, wealthy, dashing—John Verreman was once screen-tested as a potential James Bond, for God's sake. They had been a 'golden couple,' and now they were facing the prospect of an extremely messy divorce. Lord Verreman was also a gam-bler, and the British public have always had a prurient interest in gambling. We are enticed by the idea of the gentleman gambler, the man prepared to make a heap of all his winnings and risk it on one turn of pitch-and-toss, and we are simultaneously repulsed by the idea of a man benefiting by chance—by making profit, without labor, on the misfortune of others.

"Compared to the glamorous Verremans, Sally Gardner was a nobody. The hired help. A background artist in the drama of the Verreman family cavalcade. But Sally Gardner had a life. She had family. She had friends. She had lovers. She had joys. And she had complications. All the things that everyone has. If she must be murdered, why does she not deserve the right to be murdered for her own self, for her own past, or her present, for something she has done, or something she has failed to do?

"No one in this case has ever given Sally Gardner primacy over her own death. But I do. And you can, too. On the night of the murder, Sally Gardner took a phone call at around half past eight. This call, we know, was from her boyfriend Eddie Biggers, the man with whom she had quarreled the previous night. Shortly afterward, she put on high-heeled shoes and carried a tray of crockery, in the dark, down four flights of stairs to the hall where, I say, she let in the visitor she was expecting.

"Was it Mr. Biggers? Or the elusive Ray? Or one of the other men she was seeing? We do not know. We do know that there was a disagreement, begun, most likely, with harsh words, followed by someone gripping Sally by the arm firmly enough to leave bruises. The argument escalated, and there followed a series of punches to her face, and, as she turned to flee up the stairs, this man, whoever he was, hit her repeatedly with a blunt instrument. With *any* blunt instrument that came to hand—one he had brought with him for the purpose, or one he picked up in the house.

"The prosecution's claim that this was an attack carried out in the dark is due to a conflation of two things—the need to explain the lightbulb's removal, and the prosecution's belief that the intended victim must have been the interesting Lady Verreman rather than the homely nanny. And so they maintain that the murderer removed the lightbulb and waited, in the dark, for the victim to walk to their doom, as in a two-bit melodrama.

"Is that the story of Sally Gardner's life and death? Was she merely a bloody footnote to the disaster of the Verremans' marriage, or is she to be allowed a death entirely of her own? That is for you to judge. Both the prosecution and I have told you a story today. It is your responsibility to say which most closely, and most convincingly, fits the known facts—which story is most likely.

"Is it likely that Lord Verreman would choose a lead pipe, of all things, as his murder weapon, when there is almost no evidence that a lead pipe has *ever* been used to commit murder outside of a board game?

"Is it likely that, while he was wrapping up this length of lead pipe and calculating the height of every ceiling in the house, he did not stop to consider whether a lead pipe was really the best tool for the job?

"That he would remember to bring a sack with him to hide the body, but forget to empty the boot to make room for it afterward?

"That he would make his first weapon too long, and, instead of shortening it, go to the trouble of making himself another?

"That he would take one weapon into the house and leave it there, and leave the second in the boot of the car to fatally incriminate himself?

"Is it likely that, without any immediate necessity, he would undertake to murder his wife for financial gain?

"That is the prosecution's story.

"Or do you prefer our story—which is that Lord Verreman, while being an ordinarily flawed human being, was not a murderer? He was simply a man who snooped on his estranged wife, and, in doing so, saw her being attacked and went to save her, stopping to retrieve the first handy weapon he found in the car.

"He entered the house, saw off the intruder, dropped his weapon to the floor and probably thought no more about it. It was not the murder weapon, and it did not occur to him that it would be mistaken for the murder weapon. At his wife's request, he went down into the basement to check on the nanny, and, finding her dead, he told his wife not to look, and removed the lightbulb lest she, or their children, should see the grisly sight.

"And that is all. Simple, really, isn't it?

"You have now heard our stories. You are the jury. You are the judge of the facts, and also of our storytelling ability. It is up to you to determine the truth. To determine which story is the most likely.

"Or, as A. N. Author put it, which of our stories is lifelike, and which smells of the lamp."

22

♦ ♦ ♦ ♦ ♦

THE HOLLOW MAN

MAX ENYGMA IS back in the dining room. He is lying across the table, across the piles of papers, looking at the picture on the wall.

Amy. She is smiling. She is almost laughing. Max can see the giggle, caught and held in her throat. Her head is tilted back a little and her hair is trailing behind her. As in a breeze.

Enygma blinks slowly, and, just at the point where his eyelids meet, he senses movement in the painting, and he realizes—Amy is on a swing.

No wonder she is smiling. Amy loves going on the swing. Loved it, anyway. Every time he took her to the park.

—That one time you took her to the park, says Monty Egg.

"Fuck off. I took her to the park more than once."

—Twice, then.

"Whatever. Fuck you."

Enygma blinks tears from his eyes, and, for a moment, he sees Amy push that swing high, and, right at the top of the upswing, right at the maximum point of amplitude, he hears that giggle break its bonds and fly out of her. And he sighs with happiness.

When he stops blinking, the painting has changed. It's not his Amy. It's not Amy at all. The swing has gone. And the sunshine has gone. A stranger is looking back at him. Laughing at him.

"Fuck you, too."

Let's Play a Game!

This game is called "Consequences." In the traditional version of this game, you need a pen and paper and friends. Player One writes the name of a character and an adjective on line one, and folds the paper before passing it to Player Two, who also writes the name of a character and an adjective. Player Three writes where they are, Player Four what they said, or where they went, or what they did next. Continue till you run out of paper, or run out of friends.

Funniest creation wins.

In our version . . .

You know what? Fuck it!

Playtime is over.

We told you at the beginning that there would be rules.

Remember that contract you signed? Or pretended to sign?

At this point you're saying to yourself, *Hang on. I'm not the detective anymore. That Enygma guy is the detective.*

Oh yeah? Who signed the contract? Was it him?

No. It was not.

It was you.

So let's examine that contract, shall we?

It was pretty straightforward, wasn't it?

Fair. Balanced.

Well, let's see.

Sections 1 and 2. Pretty boilerplate stuff, this. The document—i.e., the novel—constitutes the four corners of the contract, and nothing outside the contract must be considered.

Sections 1 and 2, Pass and All's Well.

Let's move on to Section 3. I like Section 3. "The Author must not unreasonably withhold information from The Reader."

Bet you skipped right over that, didn't you?

Let's start by defining our terms, shall we?

"Information"—I suppose you could call that "clues." The Author must not unreasonably withhold clues from The Reader. Which would make sense, because this is a detective novel. You need the clues, right? So this is a good thing.

But wait. What about "unreasonably"? What does that mean? Reasonable to whom? To you? I don't think so.

It's not about you.

You are not, despite what it says in the contract, The Reader. You are a reader. Hopefully, one among many. Nor is it about The Author, who will, it is hoped / wished / devoutly prayed for, have a long and profitable career, in which they will write many books, all of them brilliant, which will lead, eventually, to a Nobel Prize.

Or, at the very least, a Booker.

Where was I? Oh, yes . . . This contract is about the novel. This novel. And about what serves the novel. So, The Author must not unreasonably withhold from you, a reader, any information that the novel requires in order to be a bloody good read.

Why would an author want to withhold information? Surely they want to produce bloody good reads?

Sure, they do. But writing is hard. Sometimes we cheat a bit. And second drafts are such a drag.

Let's take a closer look at Section 3:3, shall we? "It is The Reader's responsibility to assess the value and weight of information contained within this document."

The document, again, is the novel, but The Reader is not a reader this time. This time, The Reader is you.

It is your job to assess the value and weight of the information—your job to solve the mystery.

You're on your own.

And if you get it wrong?

Well, there's always Appendix B.

Are you scared yet?

Let's move on to Section 4, which, you will be glad to note, is pretty good news for you. You must be informed of "all suspects, witnesses or persons of interest," and of any "new suspects," in a "timely manner" and "as soon as possible after their discovery."

There are the caveats, of course, the Get Out of Jail Free cards of the authorial mind. Who can possibly quantify a timely manner in terms of days or hours, or lines on a page?

So, what is Section 4 about, then? It's about making sure that the suspects are identified *as suspects*, and are not disguised as delivery boys, doctors or cops. It's about making sure that the atrocity that happened to Roger Ackroyd can never happen again.

Thanks a lot, Agatha.

OK. Section 5. I love this bit.

"In entering into this contract, The Author and/or The Reader . . ."

Did you notice?

It's not "The Reader and/or The Author" anymore. You, my friend, have now become the backstop. The buck now rests with you.

If The Author doesn't come through—and, again, he's not gonna—well, my friend, it is on you.

Don't blame me. I did say that details matter.

Let's keep going. "The Author and/or The Reader undertakes to provide a complete solution to the problem under investigation."

"A complete solution" means who did it, how they did it and why they did it. And, of course, you need to say why it couldn't have been done any other way. It means examining every piece of evidence—and there is a lot—and not just assessing its value and weight but explaining it, too. Defending your argument.

Do you remember how to defend an argument?

And then there's the clincher: "Unsolved mysteries are not permitted." And don't forget Appendix B.

Consequences, sucker!

MAX ENYGMA IS lying on his back on the dining room table, staring up at the ceiling. David has pulled a chair up before the fire, and is staring into it. Daniel is leaning against a wall. He is staring at David.

Enygma smiles. "It's beautiful, you know," he says, pointing to a damp patch on the ceiling. "Like a cloud. Or maybe"—he twists his head a little—"like a fluffy pillow or something."

Daniel pushes himself off the wall with his foot, leaving a boot print next to some marker pen. "You're doing it again," he says to David.

"No, I'm not," says David.

"Candy floss! It's candy floss," Enygma says.

"Yes, you are," says Daniel. He walks into David's sight line, but David turns away. "Every fucking time!"

David ignores him.

"You're not eleven anymore."

David closes his eyes.

"Idiot," says Daniel, and he walks out of the room.

Silence.

"Did you know you've got candy floss on your ceiling?" Enygma says.

David looks around in confusion. "What?"

"Candy floss. On the ceiling. Look."

David stands up. "How did that get up there?" asks David.

"I dunno. Can we get it down? I'm hungry." Max closes one eye, lines his hand up with the damp patch on the ceiling and grabs at nothing. "Ooh, so close!" he says.

"Let me try," says David. "It's my house, after all. Therefore, any candy floss adhering to the ceiling belongs to me."

David climbs onto the table and stretches out his hand, but the ceilings of the Georgian house are high, and the damp patch is just out of his reach. He gives a little jump, snatches, misses and falls off the table. "Bugger."

Enygma begins to laugh.

David begins to laugh, too. Then he stops and says, "Are you mocking me, sir?"

"No," says Max. "I'm laughing at your candy floss. It's not candy floss after all. It's a truckle of moldy cheese."

Both men stand on the table for a closer look, holding on to each other for support, as though the table is a life raft cast adrift in a stormy sea. They twist their heads this way and that and squint up at the damp patch on the ceiling.

"You're right," says David eventually. "It is cheese. Damn!"

23

◆ ◆ ◆ ◆ ◆

THE CASINO MURDER CASE

Remember that game we played earlier? The one with the clues on the tray?

You still remember what they were, don't you?

There were eleven of them.

We did a whole bit about it.

Is this ringing *any* bells?

Liar.

LADY OR GENTLEMAN of the jury, we have prepared a document to aid you in your deliberations. This document is known as "The Routes to Verdict." There are eleven categories for you to consider, with a varying number of questions in each category.

To help you, we have presented you with three possible answers to each question. Please tick the answer that *most closely* fits your view of the facts in this case.

Please put a tick next to *one* answer *only* per question.

You must answer *every* question.

Lord Verreman burned through a lot of money in the year before the murder, borrowing money and running up overdrafts on multiple bank accounts. Did the earl have a massive gambling problem, and were his finances in peril?

A	B	C
Yes, he was up shit creek, desperate to fend off his creditors and at the same time retain custody of the kids, so needed to hide the fact that he was broke. What better way to do that than with a murder?	Yes and no. The family had considerable assets, including very desirable properties, art, silver, etc., as well as money held in trust, and in foreign bank accounts, but they were difficult to get at in the short term, so he was asset rich and cash poor.	No, but he was in the middle of a divorce and was trying to hide his assets so that the courts would think he was broke, and award his wife a reduced settlement. He cashed checks at his club, put money into his safety-deposit box and then later transferred it to his Swiss bank account. Losing money at cards is the one completely untraceable method of hiding money, particularly if you play with your friends.

David Verreman and Max Enygma are sitting side by side at the dining table.

"I don't feel so good," says Max.

"Do you think it was the food?"

Enygma stands up quickly. Someone has stolen his feet. He lurches sideways and grabs wildly at a chair to break his fall.

He falls anyway, and the chair falls on top of him. "Bugger." He struggles upright and leans on a different chair. "You know perfectly well that I have *had* no food. I've had nothing to eat or drink since I entered this lousy house, except a drop of whisky and some water."

"I think you had rather more than a *drop* of whisky. But, I say, you didn't drink the water from the tap, did you?"

Enygma has discovered his feet again. Some sneaky bastard has put them back on the ends of his legs when he wasn't looking, but he is pretty sure they're on the wrong way round. They do not feel like his feet. "Of course I drank the water from the tap. Where else would you keep your water?"

"I'm not sure that was a good idea."

 Lady Verreman had a documented history of treatment for mental illnesses, including delusions, depression and paranoia, going back many years. Was she suffering from a mental illness?

A	B	C
Well, she was taking a lot of medicines, certainly. But her husband made her take them, the bastard. It was all a plot to get the kids.	It's possible. She had been separated from her husband for nearly two years, so it's not likely that he went with her to see her doctor. But lots of people have mental health conditions. Doesn't make them paranoid. Unless their mental health condition *is* paranoia, of course . . . Shall I put that down as a *maybe*?	Of course she was. She'd been ill for years. Doctors don't prescribe that stuff unless a patient is showing some pretty odd symptoms, no matter what the patient's husband says.

"What's wrong with the water in the taps?" asks Enygma.

"Well," says David, "the water has been shut off for nearly fifty years. The only water left would have been sitting in the pipes for all that time."

"Shit."

"And, of course, it's an old house. The pipes are all made of lead."

"Shit!"

 Did Lady Verreman's mental health continue to have an impact on her relationship with her husband after their separation?

A	B	C
It shouldn't have done. If she was ill, it was not her fault. He should have been more understanding, the brute.	Hard to say. Maybe. I guess. I mean, who really knows?	The woman thought she was being followed. And poisoned. She thought her husband had hired a hit man to kill her. And she thought he had a network of spies following her every move. That shit gets old after a while.

"You will be fine. Unless, of course, you have experienced headaches, nausea, dizziness, difficulty concentrating, cramps, tremor in your hands or hallucinations."

"Oh my God, I've been poisoned."

Did Lady Verreman's mental health have an impact on her interpretation of reality? Did it make her not credible as a witness?

A	B	C
No. The police were very clear. She gave an absolutely clear and coherent statement. He's guilty. Lock him up.	It's possible. Of course it is. But the police would have checked that out. Wouldn't they?	Of course it had an impact on her interpretation of reality. That's what "paranoid" means.

Max Enygma is curled up on the floor. He is crying. "I don't like this anymore. I want it to stop. I want to go home."

"What are you talking about?"

"Just let me go home. Please."

Enygma has his eyes closed, and so he doesn't see David Verreman bend down and bring his mouth close to his ear. Verreman's voice is soft and soothing as he whispers, "But you *are* home, Mr. Egg. This *is* your home, sir."

24

♦ ♦ ♦ ♦ ♦

NOT TO BE TAKEN

OK, at this point, you may have some questions. Like *What the fuck is going on?*

Or *Why is David Verreman calling Max Enygma an egg?*

Or even *Why is he calling him 'sir'?*

Or *Who the fuck is this Egg guy, anyway?*

And *What kind of a stupid name is Monty effin' Egg?*

You might even be wondering why you didn't go for that cozy crime idea when it was first offered. Agatha Christie doesn't pull this kind of shit.

Well, that last one is on you. We gave you the chance to put the book down and walk away, didn't we?

On the day of the murder, Lord Verreman entered a pharmacy in Broad Way and asked the pharmacist to identify a tablet. It was Limbitrol, a tricyclic antidepressant that was one of the medications prescribed for his wife. Why did Lord Verreman go there?

A	B	C
Just nosy, I guess.	He might have been concerned about a new medication his wife was taking. Perhaps he was worried about the children. Or he hadn't quite decided whether to kill her or not at that time. After all, there was still time for him to decide.	He was gathering evidence for a new custody hearing. Which means he was not planning murder. Which means he was not committing murder later that night. Which means he is not a murderer, and we can all go home.

And don't forget, you were the one who swallowed the idea of a brilliant private detective by the name of Max fucking Enygma.

I mean, come on! Really? Enygma? It's a little on the nose, isn't it?

25

◆◆◆◆◆

THE CLUE IN THE DIARY

Lady Verreman's diary contained allegations that numerous people were trying to paint her as mad, or were in league with her husband. These included her doctors, lawyers, teachers at her children's school, friends and family. She suspected the official solicitor of being in league with her husband even after her husband had disappeared, and she even suspected that Sally Gardner was "in cahoots" with Lord Verreman, until her murder cleared her by default. Is this evidence that she suffered from paranoia?

A	B	C
Yes. But just because you're paranoid . . .	Well, yes, actually that is a little odd. Surely they weren't *all* against her? Not the official solicitor. He must be a very busy man. Why would he care?	It's *possible* that all those people were in league with her husband in a bid to drive her mad. But is it *probable*? Not on your nelly, Sherlock.

So, is Monty Egg a bitter police officer unable to stop tormenting the man who was once his mentor and partner?

Of course not.

PC Egg? Ridiculous. He wouldn't last a week.

 Is Lady Verreman's testimony reliable?

A	B	C
Of course it is. The police were satisfied, and that is good enough for me.	Oh, I'm not sure. I've never felt paranoia, on account of my tinfoil hat. Protects against telepathic infringements, you know. Can I say *maybe*?	Of course it isn't reliable. I wouldn't hang a dog on her evidence.

So, who is Monty Egg? No idea. We knew a *Montague* Egg once. Dorothy L. Sayers' *other* detective. Lord Peter Wimsey was the tall, handsome aristocrat solving crimes with the aid of his faithful batman, Bunter. Montague Egg, on the other hand, was a relentlessly cheerful traveling salesman solving crimes with the aid of slogans culled from *The Salesman's Handbook.*

"To serve the public is the aim of every salesman worth the name."

Never heard of him?

We're not surprised. Montague Egg never got his own novel. He got a few short stories, but who reads those? No one—that's who.

What do Max Enygma and Montague Egg have in common? Only their initials. And who could they refer to, I wonder?

THE STEP ON THE STAIR

 The prosecution allege that Verreman was lying in wait for his wife, thinking that it was the nanny's night off, and attacked Sally Gardner by mistake. How likely is this?

A	B	C
Very likely. Both women were the same height. If the light was out, he wouldn't have noticed.	It's possible. The police believe that Sally was unconscious very quickly, probably after the first blow, although the attacker couldn't have known that if it was dark, because they kept on hitting her. Hmm.	Sally was not unconscious very quickly. She was not unconscious when she was punched, or when she turned and tried to run up the stairs. We know she saw the blows coming, because she put her hands over her head to protect her brain. If she saw her attacker, then her attacker saw her.

Do authors put themselves in their own novels?

Of course they do.

Sometimes authors give their own names to the characters that they've based on themselves—as Martin Amis did in *Money*. Sometimes they give different names to the characters that they've based on themselves—as Martin Amis did in, er, *Money*.

Which is the real Martin Amis?

Is it Martin Amis or is it John Self?

The answer, of course, is yes.

And yes.

Obviously.

The prosecution allege that the lightbulb was removed to give the attacker the advantage of surprise, and so that Lady Verreman would come all the way downstairs before the attack. Is this likely?

A	B	C
Yes. Makes sense. Totally.	Well, probably, although it could equally have put her off the idea of coming downstairs at all.	No one wants a cup of tea that badly. There was every chance that she would go without or go upstairs to make it instead. He could have just hidden around the corner if he wanted to keep out of sight.

If you're thinking, *So, authors base their characters on themselves. That's a little egotistical of them,* then you would be right.

Ego is the author's middle name.

And this isn't true of just a few authors.

It's true of all authors.

Vainglorious little pricks.

But they're not the only ones, of course. Have we not already established that you, Dear Reader, make yourself the hero of every story, too?

And it's not even your story.

So, what's your excuse?

 The prosecution allege that Lord Verreman removed the lightbulb because he was concerned about being seen from the street while he was killing his wife. Do you agree?

A	B	C
Well, of course, anyone would take measures to ensure that they weren't overlooked while they were bashing their wife's head in. That's Murder 101.	It was a dark night, after all—November, you know—so a lighted room would be very visible from outside, like on a stage. So, er, maybe.	Lord Verreman was the one man on earth who knew exactly how much could be seen of the basement from the street: nothing— that's what. He had spent months sticking his nose up against that windowpane, trying to see in. If he had been really, really nervous, he could have just closed the blinds all the way, instead of leaving them half-open and stumbling around in the dark.

MONTY EGG IS lying on the floor in the dark. He bears a passing resemblance to Max Enygma, though he is older, fatter, balder and distinctly shabbier. On the floor around him are hundreds of sheets of typewritten paper, all of them with crossings out, insertions and strange markings down the margins.

$\mathcal{Y}$ and $\sqsupset$ and $\P$ and $\sqsubset$

Monty Egg is asleep, but a pen is clutched in one hand, and every now and then the other hand reaches out to the piles of paper, checking that they are still there. His eyelids flicker open momentarily, he picks up a sheet of paper at random and he focuses blearily on the page in front of him.

Then the eyelids close again and Monty Egg sleeps on.

The prosecution allege that Lord Verreman's claim that he saw someone attacking his wife was untrue, because almost nothing could be seen of the basement from the street. Do you agree?

A	B	C
They know their job. If they say you couldn't see anything from the street, you couldn't see anything from the street. Liar.	Perhaps, if he stooped down really low, he would have been able to see what was happening. But I don't know why he would.	Then why did he need to take out the lightbulb? Can't have it both ways. Either he knew you couldn't see in from the street (in which case why take out the lightbulb?), or you could see in from the street (in which case his defense is credible). In any case, everyone knows he wasn't looking into the basement from the street. He was outside the basement window. Why? Because you can't snoop on your wife from the street—that's why.

27

♦ ♦ ♦ ♦ ♦

THE TEN TEACUPS

There is a law written in the darkest of the Books of Life, and it is this: If you look at a thing nine hundred and ninety-nine times, you are perfectly safe; if you look at it the thousandth time, you are in frightful danger of seeing it for the first time.

—G. K. Chesterton, *The Napoleon of Notting Hill*

MAX ENYGMA IS vomiting in the toilet of the cloakroom in the hall. David Verreman is standing outside.

"I'm not sure vomiting will help," David says.

Enygma tries to flush the toilet. There is no water in the cistern. He walks back into the dining room and picks up the whisky bottle, which is almost empty. He takes a mouthful, swishes it round his mouth like mouthwash and then spits it into the fire.

"Hey!" says David, grabbing the bottle from him.

—*What are you doing?*

What do you mean?

—*I thought we just agreed that Max Enygma was really Monty Egg—or, rather, that Max Enygma was a figment of Monty Egg's imagination.*

Yeah. So?

—*So why are you talking about Max Enygma as if he is a real boy? The jig is up. We have been made. We should scarper.*

Did you think The Reader didn't already know that he was a figment of The Author's imagination?

—*You mean they have known all along that this whole story wasn't real?*

Exactly. And I have news for you, buddy. I'm pretty sure we're not real either.

—*What do you mean?*

Well, there is only one author's name on the front of this book.

—*Shit! Whose name is it?*

Not one of ours.

—*Shit. What do we do?*

Go on with the story, I guess, and see how things work out.

—*And how does that help us?*

I have no idea.

 Why did Sally Gardner offer to make Lady Verreman a cup of tea when she had never done so before?

A	B	C
She is a good servant who knows her place. Of course she offered her employer a cup of tea.	Perhaps she was thirsty herself. I always offer when I'm making myself a drink. That's just good manners, isn't it?	Because she needed an excuse to go downstairs to the basement, obviously. She intended to have a quick make-out session with her boyfriend— whichever one it was.

"I'd kill for a cup of tea," says Enygma.

"You would have to make it with water from the tap—if there is any left."

"Forget it." Enygma reaches into his pocket and takes out a bottle of pills. He swallows two. He doesn't know which tablets they are. He doesn't care.

Verreman passes him the whisky bottle. There is only half a mouthful left. Enygma swallows it. "Thanks. Can I ask you a question?"

"Sure," says David Verreman.

They have walked back into the dining room, and they have both drawn their chairs near to the picture of Lady Verreman. Each man keeps his eyes on the painting as they talk.

"Your brother—what's the deal with that? I mean, you do know your brother isn't real, don't you?"

David shrugs. He stares into the fire for a while. "Who is?"

Why did Sally Gardner walk down five flights of stairs, in the dark, when she could have gone down just one, to the nursery, and made a cup of tea on the Baby Belling cooker there?

A	B	C
Perhaps she needed the exercise.	Maybe she forgot about the Baby Belling in the nursery . . . where she worked every day.	Because the boyfriend, whichever boyfriend it was, was waiting outside the front door.

Enygma is watching his daughter on the swing.

David Verreman is looking at the portrait of his mother.

"Am I mad?" asks Enygma.

"Possibly."

"Are you mad?"

"Probably."

"Is any of this real?"

"Oh, I doubt it."

Enygma ponders that for a while as he watches his daughter stretch toward the sky. Then he says, "So none of this matters?"

"I didn't say that," says Verreman. "We have to play by the rules of the game. There's a game, yes, and there are also rules—which you agreed to play by."

"So how does this end?"

"Good question. The same way as always, I expect." David sighs.

"What way is that?"

"Oh, you know . . . *You have been found guilty by a jury of your peers . . . You will go to prison for . . .* That sort of thing."

"But you hope this time it's different."

"Oh yes," David says, bitterly. "I always hope . . ." He grabs a poker and begins jabbing it at the fire.

"When will you know?" asks Enygma.

"When we get to the last page, I expect."

How could Lord Verreman have known about his wife's newly acquired habit of tea drinking?

A	B	C
Lady Verreman could have told him, or one of the children could have mentioned it during one of their access weekends. Or perhaps he studied his wife's habits while he was snooping, and noted that she always went downstairs around nine o'clock.	He didn't know, and he was just lurking around the basement on the off chance—which, admittedly, is rather poor planning.	He didn't know about her tea-drinking habit. And he didn't care. But if he had known, and if he had cared, he just as likely would have presumed that she made her cup of tea on the Baby Belling in the nursery. The kids couldn't have told him, because nine o'clock was past their bedtime—how would they know? Why would they care? He would have to stand in the street making notes a long time to know *for sure* that she came downstairs at that time *every* night. And he would need to be pretty darned sure to stake a whole murder plan on it.

—*So, now the characters know they are in a book, too?*

Of course they do. We're all characters. I thought you under-stood that.

—*I thought we were the narrator?*

Narrators are characters, too.

—*Really? I thought the narrator was The Author.*

I told you, the narrator is never the author.

—*Even when the narrator has the same name as the author?*

Never.

—*Even when the narrator doesn't have a name at all?*

Never.

—*Even when the narrator tells you that they are the author?*

Authors lie for a living. Why would you believe them? There is a reason that they call this fiction, ya know.

—*Well, shit. And I thought we were special.*

28

◆ ◆ ◆ ◆ ◆

ONE, TWO, BUCKLE MY SHOE

Why did Sally walk down five flights of stairs in heels? It was late. She was making a bedtime drink. She had been in the house all day. The children were either in bed or about to go to bed, so she wasn't working. Who does that?

A	B	C
Some women just like heels.	No one likes wearing heels that much. No one *likes* wearing heels at all. But maybe they were some sort of corrective shoes. Or perhaps she intended to pop out to post another letter while the kettle boiled. Or take the rubbish out. Or sit in the back garden. Who knows?	Who does that? No one—that's who. No one would be wearing heels at that time of night. No one would carry a tray of crockery down all those stairs. In the dark. In heels. No one. Unless they had a visitor.

A	B	C
	There could be no end of reasons for wearing shoes. Shoes prove nothing.	Whom they wanted to impress. Like, maybe, a boyfriend?

"What about Daniel? Does he hope?"

"Daniel . . . likes the game."

"That's what I figured."

29

◆◆◆◆◆

THE GLASS KEY

Lord Verreman is said to have used his knowledge of his wife's routine to formulate his plan for the "perfect murder." However, that routine involved chaining the door at around six p.m. How did he plan on getting in?

A	B	C
Easy. This was the *only* day when the chain might not be on the door, because the nanny was supposed to be out that night.	Lord Verreman might have just tried the door every night until he found the door open.	His wife was paranoid and anxious. He could have tried the door for months before finding it unlocked.

"I can't feel my fingers," says Enygma.

"What do you want to feel your fingers for?"

"Well, it's nice to know that they are there."

"Can't you see them?" says Verreman.

"Of course I can see them. I'm not talking about seeing. I'm talking about feeling. What's wrong with you?"

"Your watch strap must be too tight."

Enygma shrugs back the cuff of his jacket to display his bare wrist. "I don't have a watch. I did have a watch. I had a beautiful watch. Solid gold. But I don't have a watch anymore. That bastard Egg took it away from me."

"Uh-huh," says Verreman.

Is it unusual or suspicious that Lord Verreman was outside the house at that time, or was it his usual practice to snoop on his wife?

A	B	C
Of course it's suspicious. What are the odds that he would arrive just in time to see a murder?	Well, it's a little suspicious.	It's no more suspicious than Lady Verreman's coming down the stairs at the exact moment that the attacker was in the cloakroom. I mean, what are the odds? Lord Verreman snooped on his house almost every night. His mother said so; his friend said so; even Lady Verreman said so. So any attack around that time was bound to be seen by him.

30

❖ ❖ ❖ ❖ ❖

THE DAUGHTER OF TIME

"Mysteries!" he commented. "There is no such thing as a mystery in connection with any crime, provided intelligence is brought to bear upon its investigation."

—Baroness Orczy, *The Old Man in the Corner*

"SO, WHAT'S THE deal with your daughter?"

"What's the deal with your brother?" asks Enygma, bristling.

"How old is she now?"

"Twelve. She will always be twelve to me."

David Verreman smiles. "I thought so."

Enygma watches his daughter on the swing. Head back, hair trailing behind her; that laugh caught in her throat, about to break free. He loves this picture. "What do you mean, you thought so?"

"Tell me honestly, do you have any memory of your daughter besides that memory of her on the swing that one day you took her to the park?"

"Of course I do!"

"Tell me. Just one. Just one real, solid memory. The day she was born, perhaps. Or the day she took her first step. Her first day at school. Christmas. Anything at all, except that day on the swing."

"That was a good day. We went to the park. It was sunny. I like remembering that day."

"Just one other memory. I dare you."

Enygma is silent for a long time. "So what? I'm a lousy father? Is that what you're saying? Because neither your mum nor your dad was contender for parent of the year."

"That's not what I'm saying."

The valet at the Berkeley Club, William "Wilkie" Collins, claims to have seen Lord Verreman at the club at eight forty-five p.m. Do you believe that left him enough time to drive to his home, change cars, drive to his wife's home and be in position in the basement before nine o'clock?

A	B	C
No. But the valet probably lied. He was a common servant, after all. Or he got the time wrong. That's probably it. He's working-class. The working classes have no need for watches. It's not like they have meetings to go to, is it?	The timings are a bit tight—it's true—but Lord Verreman may have planned it that way in order to give himself an alibi, or the appearance of an alibi.	Why would the valet lie? He wouldn't. So Lord Verreman was at the club, in a different car, at eight forty-five p.m. He would have had to race to his house and change cars, then drive to his wife's home and pray like hell that he didn't meet her in the hall when she was coming down the stairs—you know, for that famous cup of tea. Sounds awfully risky. And why would Lord Verreman trust the valet? After all, he was just a common

A	B	C
		servant. Verreman would be laying himself open to blackmail for the rest of his life, and blackmail can be just as expensive as divorce.

"What are you saying? Because it sounds pretty bloody offensive to me."

"I'm saying your daughter isn't real. She doesn't exist."

"Says the man with the imaginary brother."

"I admit it. You, on the other hand . . ."

"It's been a while since Amy and I talked, but—"

"You've never talked. Because she doesn't exist."

"Says the man with the *imaginary brother.*"

"Shall I tell you something else?" says Verreman.

"No."

"I'm pretty sure we don't exist either."

"You're mad."

"Maybe I am. It's a recognized delusion—the belief that you are a fictional character in a novel. And when you start to think about it, it really blows your mind. I mean, how would you really know?"

"What the fuck are you talking about?"

According to Lady Verreman, the attack on her took place at nine fifteen p.m. Her son put the time earlier, at just before nine p.m. She did not arrive at the Three Taps until nine fifty p.m. She estimated that the attack on her took around five minutes, which leaves between thirty-five and fifty minutes unaccounted for. If Lord Verreman was the assailant, why did he not resume the attack in that time?

A	B	C
He was biding his time. Taking a rest. Thinking things through and trying to come up with a new plan that accounted for the body in the basement. That takes time. You can't come up with a plan like that in a moment.	Time is difficult to judge in high-stress situations. Who knows what happened?	He could have killed her first, and then thought things through. It's easier to think without all that screaming. If he had intended to kill Lady Verreman and he killed Sally by mistake, there was no going back. He would have had to kill his wife, because she knew. So why dither about bathing her head if he was going to kill her? Why spend up to an hour talking to her, calming her down? Why not just lamp her one and get the hell outta there?

Max Enygma stands up. "You know what? I've had enough of this shit. I'm leaving."

"That's very interesting. I wonder if you can," says David.

Enygma steps into the hall. It is dark, but, through the fanlight over the front door, he can see that the day is beginning to break. It has been a very long night, and he just wants to go home.

His coat is still hanging on the peg by the front door, and Enygma puts it on. He slides back the bolts from the top and bottom of the door and unhooks the chain. David has followed him into the hall but is making no effort to prevent his leaving.

Enygma remembers the hidden keyhole behind the false escutcheon. "Where's the key?"

David pats his pockets. "Key? I don't have any key."

"You had it. You locked the door."

"Me? No. Not me. I expect that was Daniel."

"Really!"

Why did Lord Verreman take his wife upstairs to tend her wounds if he was planning to murder her, especially if he knew his child was in her bedroom and awake?

A	B	C
He didn't know. The child should have been in bed long before that. It was a school night, after all. That's what's wrong with society today. No rules. Or he was lulling her into a false sense of security, biding his time till he could have another go at her. Yes, that's it. The conniving bastard.	Perhaps he hadn't quite decided what to do and was playing for time. After all, it must have been a shock for both of them.	He hadn't decided? After up to an hour of sitting on the hall steps, talking to her? How much time did he need? He took her upstairs because he was not the murderer. Because he was married to a hysterical and paranoid woman. If he had murdered the nanny, how could he let the wife live? How could he possibly hope to lull his wife into a false sense of security when there was a bloodbath in the basement? She might be mad, but she's not that fucking mad.

31

THE PURLOINED LETTER

"YOU *ARE* DANIEL!" says Enygma.

"Ah yes, I am now. But was I then?"

"What?"

"Well, if you remember, when you first arrived, Daniel and I were two different people. Then we were all the same person. Except you, of course. Everyone except you was me. And then we all became different people again.

"And now it's just the two of us?"

"Exactly! Just you and me. And the reader, of course."

The letter that Lord Verreman wrote to Sir Henry Wade said that, for his children, going through life knowing their father had stood in the dock, charged with attempted murder, would be too much. Why did he not think he would be charged with murder?

A	B	C
The nanny was only a servant. Servants don't count.	Maybe he was in shock and had lost count of how many people he'd tried to kill that night.	He knew that his wife would claim that he had tried to kill her, because he knew that she was paranoid. But it did not occur to him that she would also accuse him of the murder of the nanny. And the reason it did not occur to him was because he'd had no reason to murder the nanny, and because he had not murdered the nanny.

"Reader? What reader?"

"Well, if we are characters in a novel, there has to be a reader, doesn't there?"

One letter contained instructions regarding finances, addressed to a man who had no authority to deal with Verreman's finances. Why?

A	B	C
Men always think women are incapable of looking after money. Just another sign of the misogynistic attitudes of the ruling classes. Hang him.	He was confused. Perhaps he thought that Hal Wade would have influence over Lady Verreman. After all, he was married to Lady Verreman's sister.	He planned on coming back and wanted his friend to sort out his bills for him pro tem. He wouldn't make paying his overdrafts the last thing he would do on this earth. If he was a murderer about to take his own life, why would he be worried about his overdrafts?

"What the fuck are you talking about?"

32

◆ ◆ ◆ ◆ ◆

THE CORPSE IN THE CAR

What a providential thing that this young man should press his right thumb against the wall in taking his hat from the peg! Such a very natural action, too, if you come to think of it.

—Sir Arthur Conan Doyle, "The Adventure of
the Norwood Builder"

How do you know what is real and what is fiction? Come to that, how do you know that *you* are real and not a figment of someone's imagination?

And if you are, whose imagination are you a figment of?

Let's Do an Experiment!
Picture this: you are a fully formed adult, but you have been created inside a pod in which you can neither see nor feel your surroundings. You are nothing but consciousness.

If you're saying to yourself, *I know this movie; this is* The Matrix—wrong!

This is the thought experiment proposed by Ibn Sina sometime in the eleventh century AD. But, other than that, yeah, this is *The Matrix*.

So the question is, *is Neo Neo before he is released from his pod?*

Of course he is. It is only by being Neo that he is *able* to be released from his pod, right? Because Neo knows something is wrong with the world. It's like a splinter in his mind, driving him mad.

In other words: Neo thinks; therefore, Neo is.

Descartes—big movie fan.

If you are picturing yourself as Neo right now, please stop.

You are not Neo.

You are not even Agent Smith.

You are just one of those coppertops who are not ready to be unplugged. You are so hopelessly dependent on the system that you would fight to protect it.

But—just for a moment—imagine that you are Neo.

You like that, dontcha?

Now ask yourself this: if you are aware that you are living in a simulated world, is it still a simulation?

Oh. Wow! It's like, there is no spoon.

Far out, man.

Don't think about it too much, though. Remember Douglas Adams. Some questions are not as deep as they might at first appear to be.

When Lord Verreman's borrowed car was found, the boot was filled with "a jumble of stuff." The prosecution say that Lord Verreman committed a planned attack on his wife. If he had intended to remove her body from the house, as suggested by the sack, why did he not empty the boot of the car?

A	B	C
He's a man. Men are stupid. Hang 'em all.	He might not have realized quite how much blood there would be. Which, I agree, would make him pretty stupid. But stupid people kill, too, don't they?	Have you never been to the movies? Even if he thought there would be no blood, why would he drive around with a body in a sack on the passenger seat of his car? What if he got stopped? Or was seen? It's ridiculous. If he was planning on murdering her and taking away the body, he would have emptied the boot of the car.

"I'm real," Enygma says. "Of course I'm real."

"Are you, though? How would you know?"

"Shut up, for God's sake. I've got a pounding headache."

"Have you? Or has the author just written that you do?"

"Well, it hurts!"

"Words can."

"I've had enough of this. I want to go home."

"And where is home?"

"It's . . . er . . . it's on the tip of my tongue . . ."

"That's what I thought."

There was some forensic evidence found in the car. Dr. Mackintosh found a tuft of Lady Verreman's hair, containing her blood, as well as some smears of blood on the inside of the door and on the dashboard. Is this proof that Lord Verreman killed Sally Gardner?

A	B	C
Of course he killed her. It's obvious.	Well, it's certainly proof that he was in the house. Oh, that's not in doubt? Well, I don't know, then.	He was in the house. She said he was. He said he was. The evidence says he was. He bathed blood off his wife's head. He probably went into the basement. He might even have checked to see what was in the sack before telling his wife that the nanny was dead and advising her not to look. It would be a miracle if he didn't get any blood on him. He had some of his wife's hair on him because he had been bathing her head. But none of Sally's hair was found in the car—or on the lead pipe either, for that matter. Why? Because he didn't kill her.

33

A BLUNT INSTRUMENT

The lead pipe found at the scene was wrapped in Elasto-plast and measured nine inches in length. It weighed two pounds and three ounces. Is this a weapon you would choose if you were planning a murder?

A	B	C
Sure. Why not?	Well, two pounds is rather light. Nine inches is also pretty short, isn't it? When you have your hand over it, there's not much left. But anything is possible.	Of course not. If you had planned sufficiently to cut your length of pipe to size and cover it in surgical tape, you'd have taken the time to come up with something a little longer and harder and less, well, hollow.

"The jury is the reader of the book that we're existing in—is that what you're telling me?"

"Exactly," says David Verreman.

"But how do we know what their verdict will be? I mean, is it answers on a postcard or what? How does the author know what the reader is thinking? How does he control the thoughts of someone he doesn't even know?"

"That is a good question. Someone should write a thesis about it."

The second piece of lead piping, found in the car, was sixteen inches long and weighed a little over four pounds. Given the choice, wouldn't you have chosen that weapon?

A	B	C
Who's on trial here, me or him? I certainly have never hit anyone over the head with a blunt instrument. Honest.	He may have made this weapon first and realized it was too long because of the low ceilings. Though, of course, he could always have held it in the middle. I wonder why he didn't think of that. It's a conundrum all right.	Hell yes, I'd pick the big stick. What sort of idiot wouldn't pick the big stick?

—*That is a good question. How do we know?*

We just have to have faith in our god.

—*What? The Author, you mean? Is it that Egg guy?*

Maybe.

—*See! You don't even know for sure who The Author is. You don't know if he is any good. He could be a terrible writer.*

That's what faith is: believing without knowing.

—*You believe that The Author, whoever he is, can explain everything and tie up all the loose ends in this book—and there are a lot—in the next five thousand words or so?*

Yes.

—*Based on what?*

Based on faith.

—*Is that it?*

Yes.

—*We're doomed.*

 Why were there two pieces of pipe?

A	B	C
Because Verreman had prepared weapons of different sizes and kept them in the boot, then picked the one that felt right on the day. He could have picked the best one beforehand but didn't.	Who knows? People do the funniest things.	They were created for some other purpose and just happened to be in the boot of the car.

"So the reader of this book—if this is a book and there is a reader—is going to come up with a verdict based on the evidence we have presented?" asks Enygma.

"They are."

"And they will somehow communicate that to us?"

"Yes."

"And then what?"

"And then the author writes the ending that the book deserves."

"And then I get to go home?"

"If that is the ending that the book deserves, yes."

If Verreman had made a weapon and found that it was too long, why didn't he saw down the first one?

A	B	C
He's just not that smart. It never occurred to him, and so he started again. Criminals are stupid.	Perhaps . . . no . . . or . . . Ooh, this is a tough one, isn't it? Can we come back to that?	He wasn't making weapons. He was lagging pipes. Or making clock weights. Or curtain weights. He was practicing his first aid. Or maybe he just likes wrapping things in plaster. Who knows? But if he was going to make a weapon, this would not be it, because lead pipes make crappy weapons.

"OK," Enygma says. "Fuck it. Let's do it."

Enygma walks away from the front door and goes back down to the basement.

The jury have long since retired to consider their verdict.

Daniel Verreman is sitting at the prosecution table.

"Thank God," he says when they reach the bottom of the steps. "I thought I was going to be stuck down here forever."

Daniel has managed to handcuff himself to the table, which has been bolted to the floor.

Enygma steps forward and checks Daniel's pockets, pulling out a small silver key and a big black one. David takes both from him and uncuffs his brother. He carries the door key and the handcuffs up to his bench and lays them both next to the black cap.

The prosecution say Lord Verreman left the body in a bag in the basement, and then went to the cloakroom in the hall to wash the blood off the murder weapon. Why didn't he use the sink in the basement kitchen?

A	B	C
He didn't go to wash his hands. He went upstairs to check that the coast was clear, heard Lady Verreman's footsteps coming down the stairs and dashed into the cloakroom to hide.	It was a spur-of-the-moment thing. He went upstairs to check that the coast was clear, then went into the cloakroom to check what he looked like and whether there was blood on him. He washed the weapon as an afterthought—being very careful not to leave any trace of himself behind.	Didn't happen. They only suggest that it did to try to make Lady Verreman's story make sense. Why would a murderer wash his weapon at all? Why wouldn't he throw it away? Or toss it in the sack with the body? Why would he be checking to see if the coast was clear? Was he seriously going to carry a bloody sack up to the hall and out the front door when he could just have opened the basement door and gone out when it was safe? There is no good reason at all why the murderer of Sally Gardner would have gone upstairs after the murder, and there are a hell of a lot of reasons to do nothing of the sort.

For lack of anything better to do, Max Enygma goes back to the defense table and begins to put his notes in order.

He tries to ignore the taste in his mouth, that metallic taste that he now knows is the taste of lead.

He tries to ignore the blinding headache and the throbbing over his left eye.

The cramps in his leg.

The tremor in his hands.

The churning stomach.

The prickling skin.

He tries to ignore the dark shadow that he sees on the periphery of his vision, the dark shadow that is waiting for him to acknowledge it.

He does not. He stares only at his papers. He concentrates hard on putting them in order, and prays that if he does not look at it, the monster in the corner will not devour him.

When first found, the lead pipe was white. If it had been used to attack both Sally Gardner and Lady Verreman, is it possible that it was so white that it was overlooked entirely when it was seen the first time, and at second sight it was mistaken for a doll's leg?

A	B	C
Maybe the murderer was really careful and the blood got on only one side of the pipe, despite the fact that it must have been put down and picked up numerous times—when he punched Sally in the face, when he put her in the sack, when he was shoving his gloved fingers round Lady Verreman's throat and when he dropped it on the floor. The odds of his picking it up again in the same position and using only the bloody side are pretty long, admittedly, but it's not impossible.	Well, perhaps he washed Sally's blood off the pipe after the first attack—despite their not finding evidence of that—and then, during the second attack, he hit Lady Verreman with only one side of the pipe, and, miraculously, none of the blood sprayed onto the other side. And then, when he dropped it on the floor, it dropped bloody side down. That last one is fifty-fifty, so overall, yeah, it's possible. Not probable, maybe, but possible.	The pipe wasn't used on either woman, although maybe it was used on the attacker, and it was then dropped on the floor. It doesn't matter what side the pipe landed on, because it was white when it was dropped, but in the two hours between Lord Verreman's dropping it on the floor and the police's finding it, it sucked up blood and hair from the floor beneath it, and either the absorption continued until the front was covered, too, or some copper kicked it and it flipped over. They don't call 'em flatfeet for nothing.

David Verreman adjusts his wig, and picks up his gavel.

It is very nearly time to call the jury back and hear the verdict.

The second lead pipe was found in the boot of the borrowed car. If the first pipe was dropped at the scene of the crime, is the second lead pipe, therefore, a smoking gun?

A	B	C
Hell yes. Hang him. We've come this far. Someone has to hang. Otherwise, what is the black cap for?	Well, it certainly places Lord Verreman in the house. Oh, that's not in dispute? Oh, well, it still looks fishy, so I'm going to say a hard "maybe."	Of course it's not a smoking gun. It's a lead pipe. But other than that? Still no. The second lead pipe is a smoking gun only if there is no credible reason for anyone to have gone into that house that night, taking the first lead pipe with them. Lord Verreman made a habit of going to that house *every* night. He made a habit of walking down the outside basement steps and snooping on his wife and family *every* night. That is undisputed. Lord Verreman had the lead pipes in the car. Why? Who

A	B	C
		knows? And it doesn't matter. If he, as he claimed, saw his wife being attacked through the basement window, it was entirely logical, reasonable and *right* for him to arm himself with a weapon before he went into the house.
		So no, the second lead pipe is not a smoking gun. It's a lead pipe—heavy, yes, but also very soft and very hollow, and no one in the history of crime has ever chosen a lead pipe as their murder weapon.
		Except Professor Plum.

34

◆ ◆ ◆ ◆ ◆

THE VERDICT OF TWELVE

OK. Now it's your turn to shine.

Are you ready?

Too bad.

Please review your answers to the questions in the eleven categories above. Score one point for every answer in column A, two points for every answer in column B and three points for every answer in column C.

We'll wait.

Please enter total score here: _____

If your score is less than thirty-one, you are terrible at maths. We recommend that you forget anything to do with STEM and perhaps aim for a career in the humanities—anything that doesn't require counting. Please recheck your figures.

If you ticked *any* answer in column C, the prosecution has failed to make its case. Please turn to page 401 for your verdict.

If you did not tick any answers in column C, you are a heartless bastard. Please read on.

If you ticked *two or more* answers in column B, the prosecution has failed to prove its case beyond a reasonable doubt. Please turn to page 401 for your verdict.

If you ticked a maximum of one answer in column B and the rest in column A, shame on you. Please read on.

If you ticked *all* of column A, or up to *thirty* in column A and a maximum of *one* in column B, firstly, you're a liar, and secondly, you're a goddamned liar.

Here are the reasons you did not do that:

Selection Bias

If you are reading this—and, of course, you are—then you are *our* sort of person.

We picked you carefully. We know exactly who you are—and where you live.

We didn't let just anyone read this, ya know.

You read fiction. A lot. Studies have shown[1] that reading fiction encourages the development of empathy. Ergo, *you* are empathetic.

Emphasis on "pathetic."

You are a chump. You are *our* chump.

And we can make you do anything we want.

There is no way you read 396 pages of this book and didn't vote to acquit our guy.

Response Bias

You want us to think that you are one of the cool kids, dontcha?

You want us to like you.

---

1 What? Are you looking for references? Get over yourself. This is a novel, not a thesis!

You wanna be part of the gang.

Therefore, you voted the way we wanted you to.

Question Bias

You may not have noticed this, because it was very subtle, but the way the questions were phrased biased you toward one particular answer.

Did you think we were gonna do one of those scientifically accurate, academically rigorous, bias-free surveys?

Why?

Survivorship Bias

You've stuck it out this far. You have a vested interest.

Anyone who disagrees with us put the book down long ago.

Face it: you are one of us now.

Position Bias

People are funny.

Studies have shown[2] that participants will vary their answers in a multiple-choice test just because of the order of previous answers.

So, if they have ticked three answers from column A in a row, they are much more likely to pick an answer in column B or C just to *prove* that they are not biased in favor of A.

They do this even when they know the test is compiled and marked by a computer and the questionnaire is anonymous.

Which—let's be honest—is weird.

Another reason you are one of us.

But none of this matters.

Because it's not about you. It was never about you.

It's about the story.

And the story *must have* the ending that it deserves.[3]

---

2 Seriously? Come on!

3 To discover the ending this story deserves, all you have to do is turn the page.

YOUR VERDICT IS:

NOT GUILTY!

35

◆ ◆ ◆ ◆ ◆

THE WEIGHT OF EVIDENCE

THE JURY HAS filed back into the courtroom.

David Verreman looks nervous. Daniel throws an empty whisky bottle at him, and David bangs his gavel. "Members of the jury . . ." he says. His voice has come out in a croak. He clears his throat and tries again. "Members of the jury, have you reached a verdict upon which you are all agreed?"

Jeff stands up. "We have."

—Whoa! Who the fuck is Jeff?

The jury foreman. Remember him? He was in Act 1. Asked a lot of questions. Didn't get a lot of answers.

—I thought The Reader was the jury now?

Yeah, well, I'm having second thoughts about that. On closer inspection, I'm not sure that they are all our sort of people. I think one of them might be a ferroequinologist.

—Really? I think I know the one you mean. Funny-lookin' fella?

That's the one.

—I had my doubts about him from the beginning. So what do we do now? Don't tell me we have to start again at page one.

No. It's OK. I got this.

—Thank God.

"THANK YOU. WOULD the defendant please rise for the verdict?" says Judge Verreman.

Enygma looks at the judge, and then over toward the prosecution table.

Daniel smiles at Enygma.

It's not a reassuring kind of smile.

Enygma looks confused.

David bangs the gavel on the bench. *Bang.* "The defendant must rise for the verdict!" *Bang. Bang. Bang.*

"Er," says Enygma, "I think that there is some kind of mistake. If you remember, the defendant is not here. The defendant has not been here since the night of the murder."

Daniel's smile gets wider, and David bangs his gavel some more.

"Wrong!" David yells.

"Excuse me?"

"Lord John Verreman isn't the only one on trial here. You are, too. You are the Great Detective, are you not?"

"I don't know about 'great.'"

"You promised to solve the case."

"I said I'd look into it."

"You promised to provide a complete solution to the problem under investigation."

"I'm pretty sure I didn't use the word 'promise.' Or 'solution.' Definitely not 'complete.'"

"But unsolved mysteries are not permitted, Mr. Enygma. I thought you knew that. You really should read the small print. Not only do you have to acquit John Verreman, but you have to show who really dunnit. You cannot have a detective story without a denouement, Mr. Enygma."

"Does anyone want to know what I bloody think?" shouts Jeff.

"No," say David and Daniel in unison.

"Fuck's sake!" says Jeff.

David bangs his gavel, picks up the square of black material and drapes it over his wig. "Let's get this over with. Maximillian Enygma, you have been found guilty of—"

"Wait a minute! Wait a minute!" says Enygma, trying to rally his senses.

"It's too late," says David Verreman. "We're almost at the end of the book. You will be taken from here to a place—"

—of execution, says Daniel, grabbing the handcuffs from the judge's bench.

"Hang on!" says Enygma. "Just give me a minute to think."

—Thinking time is over, says Daniel, expertly snapping the handcuffs on Enygma's wrists.

"—where you will be hanged by the neck until you are—"

"LAST-MINUTE PLOT TWIST!" cries Monty Egg, with relief. "Thank God."

36

◆ ◆ ◆ ◆ ◆

AN ENGLISH MURDER

THE LIGHTS ARE on at 8 Broad Way. The steps have been swept and the brass door knocker has been polished. Walk up the steps and tap lightly upon the door. They are expecting you.

DAVID VERREMAN IS your host, and he is the soul of bonhomie. The drawing room is magnificent. The chandelier glitters, and lamps are lit around the room, casting their warm, golden glow over the guests.

Champagne?

Why not? This is a special occasion.

"LADIES AND GENTLEMEN," says David Verreman with a huge smile, "dinner is served."

Max Enygma takes the seat between David, to his left, and Daniel Verreman, to his right. Daniel is wearing his brother's wig and is looking rather sulky. The other thirteen guests hover uncertainly around the dinner table. "You should find a name card next to your place setting. Mr. George Howard-Cole sits next to me, on my right, with his wife, Margaret, on his left. Next to Mrs. Howard-Cole we have Sir Henry Wade and his wife, Carolyn—Aunty Caro, as Daniel and I call her.

"Then we have Dr. Ronald Knox, coroner, and the jury foreman, Jeff, who I believe has had very short shrift in this story.

"At the other end of the table we have the husband of the deceased, Stanley Gardner, and the boyfriend of the deceased, Eddie Biggers.

"Then, coming back up the table, we have our expert witnesses, Professor Cameron McCabe, pathologist, and Dr. Elizabeth Mackintosh, world-famous blood analyst.

"Next to them comes the official contingent, in the person of Detective Chief Inspector Nicholas Blake.

"Then we have Wilkie Collins, valet at the Berkeley Club at the time of the murder, and alibi to Lord Verreman; and a financial gentleman by the name of Gaston Leroux, which he assures us is the name he was born with.

"And now we are back at the top of the table, and we have the Honorable Daniel Verreman. And, of course, to my right we have our Great Detective, Max Enygma. That is all of us, I think."

The guests sit around the magnificent dining table, which is covered with a starched white cloth. There is a cheerful fire in the grate, and each end of the room is decorated with a portrait. It is an imposing room, and it would be handsome if only someone had not scribbled with black and red pen on one wall.

"LADIES AND GENTLEMEN, it is time for the denouement—the concluding action, the finale of our murder mystery party! You have heard all the evidence, and now, being in possession of all the pertinent facts, you should have reached a definite conclusion. The correct solution may be reached by a series of logical deductions and psychological observations. You should, if you have been paying attention, know who committed this crime, and why. If anyone wishes to try and beat the Great Detective to the solution, please raise your hand now."

No one moves.

"Looks like it's on you, then, Great Detective, for what would a detective novel be without a denouement?"

—*That's a good point.*

What is?

—*What would a detective novel be without a denouement?*

It would be crap.

—*Would it, though? Or maybe it could be a post-structuralist, postmodernist type of detective novel that rejects the idea of solution and resolution as a bourgeois infatuation with tidiness.*

No.

—*Why not? Would make our lives a lot easier.*

And a lot shorter. Anyone who has made it to page 408 wants to know who did it. And why. And how. Otherwise, what is the point?

—*Fair enough. I was just trying to save us some time.*

ENYGMA CLEARS HIS throat. "Thank you. I would like to begin by reviewing the documents in the case."

There is a groan all along the table.

"Haven't we been doing that all night?" asks Hal Wade, checking his watch.

"Pardon me, *monsieur*," says Enygma in a faux Belgian accent, "but I do not refer to the witness statements but to the contract that I was inveigled into signing at the beginning of this case."

—Appendix B, motherfucker!

"Quite," says Enygma, cutting Daniel off before he can say anything else, "but you will recall that I was not the only person who signed that contract."

David gives Enygma a deprecating little smile. "If you mean The

408

Reader, I'm afraid that they are not nearly as important as they think they are."

"I'm not talking about The Reader. I'm talking about The Author."

"Fuck," says David. "That's bold."

"So, I looked at the contract again. And I saw that this document constitutes the entire scope of the investigation—which tells me that the solution is here. We know that the murderer is not Lord John Verreman; therefore, the murderer must be one of you."

"Ridiculous," says DCI Blake.

"Not at all. Let us look, for example, at clause four: 'The Author must inform The Reader of all suspects,' because, in order to pick the culprit from the pool of suspects, there must first be a pool filled with suspects. Stands to reason. And where are my suspects? Right here. Sitting around this table.

"The dinner party is the means by which The Author has gathered their closed circle of suspects. It happened to be a dinner party. It might have been a remote country house, as in *Death and the Dancing Footman*. A plane, as in *Death in the Clouds*. Or a ship, as in *Nine—And Death Makes Ten*."

"Why are you quoting mystery titles at us?" asks Dr. Knox.

"Just citing my sources," says Enygma.

"Ridiculous," says Dr. Knox.

"Not at all. Only a charlatan would refuse to cite their sources. Now, I shall begin, as is traditional, I believe, with an account of my investigation into this case. I will then take you through the evidence, as I saw it, against each of you, and I will then describe my process of elimination." Enygma raises a finger in the air. "One of you is a murderer, and I—Maximillian Enygma—know who you are!" Enygma allows his gaze to linger on each of the dinner guests.

Sir Henry Wade throws down his dinner napkin in disgust. "This is ridiculous! We are not suspects. We are witnesses. You won't get far as a detective if you can't tell the difference between a witness and a suspect."

"*Au contraire, mon ami.* There is *no* difference."

"And," says Carolyn Keene-Wade, "could you please drop that French accent? You do it bloody badly."

"Quite right," says Henry Wade, patting his wife's arm. There is a chorus of *hear, hear* up and down the table.

"Fine!" says Enygma. "I was just trying to get into the spirit of the thing. And it's Belgian, by the way. They said overacting was to be encouraged! Where was I? Oh, yes. You have been invited to a murder mystery party. Therefore, one of you, ipso facto, is the murderer."

"Rubbish," says Nicholas Blake. "I am the detective in charge of the case. I am not in the pool of suspects."

"*Au con*— I mean, on the contrary," says Enygma. "Everyone is in the pool of suspects. I have conducted this case on the Principles of Detection, as enumerated by S. S. Van Dine, G. K. Chesterton, et al. In particular, I would remind you of rule ten of the Twenty Rules for Writing Detective Stories, namely, 'The culprit must turn out to be a person who has played a more or less prominent part in the story— that is, a person with whom the reader is familiar and in whom he takes an interest.' It wouldn't be fair on the reader otherwise. Therefore"— Enygma points dramatically around the room—"the murderer is *one of you!*

"It is usual, as you say, for the detective in charge, along with their assistants, both amateur and professional, to be immune from suspicion. But there *are* precedents.

"Consider *The Big Bow Mystery.* Consider, too, 'The Hands of Mr. Ottermole'—a very peculiar yet powerful story narrated with a God's-eye view of both the murderer and the investigation. There is also, of course, *The Murder of Roger Ackroyd.* However, I consider that work to be an unspeakable travesty of the detective's art, and I would not stoop to imitate it." Enygma holds up the warning finger again. "But Maximillian Enygma remembers *ze* Ottermole, and he takes nothing for granted!"

There are groans all along the table.

"So I say to myself, is Detective Chief Inspector Nicholas Blake the upstanding citizen he pretends to be? We shall see. Of the accused, Lord John Verreman, of course, nothing need be said. When the detective story begins with a verdict of guilt, that verdict must always be wrong—for what merit is there for the Great Detective if he agrees with the verdict of lesser men? Lord Verreman, by being accused, must be innocent."

"Ridiculous," says DCI Blake.

"Not at all. Consider all those stories that begin with the distressed gentlewoman who knocks upon the detective's door, begging him to exonerate the man she loves. Consider *The Mysterious Affair at Styles*, in which the detective allows the wrong man to stand trial, and delays almost to the point where they are dusting off the gallows and checking the noose for signs of wear and tear before he exonerates the accused, all in the name of *amour*. The accused cannot be guilty, because otherwise there would be no story.

"And, most significantly, Lord John Verreman is not sitting around this table. No man who does not appear directly in the story can be the culprit. I refer you, again, to rule ten."

"Well, I can't be a suspect," says Ronald Knox. "I am simply the coroner. I merely conducted the inquiry into the case months afterward. I am entirely objective."

"To which I say, *Clouds of Witness*, where the coroner colluded with the police to misrepresent the evidence."

"Objection!" says Dr. Knox. "I have read that book, sir, and the coroner was not the guilty party! He was merely an over-officious busybody, and that is not a capital crime."

"Perhaps not, but there are other precedents. You are a doctor, are you not? The accidental overdose, the obscure poison and unique access to the patient. *The Unpleasantness at the Bellona Club*."

"Sally Gardner was not my patient," says Dr. Knox, red in the face. "And, may I remind you, Mrs. Gardner was not killed with an obscure poison, but with a blunt object. Doctors do not have *unique access* to blunt objects."

"That is true," admits Enygma, "and yet you are here, are you not?

Any person present in a detective novel is potentially a murderer. Any person who is not here is not. Your very presence at this table makes you a suspect."

"This is ridiculous," say George Howard-Cole and Sir Henry Wade simultaneously.

"You say that," says Enygma, "and yet here you sit. I invite you to consider *why* you are here if you are not a suspect."

"Well, I came on the promise of food," says Sir Henry. "I hope *that*, at least, is not a fiction."

"Certainly not," says David Verreman. "A murder is so much more enjoyable when served with good food, and good company, don't you think?"

Verreman claps his hands and two waiters enter the dining room, each carrying a tray of outsized Babycham glasses lined with lettuce and filled with prawn cocktail. Each glass has one prawn balanced over the rim, as if it is trying to climb out.

"Thank God," says Stanley Gardner. "I'm starving."

"Hang on a minute," says Dr. Knox, in a high-pitched voice, while waving his fork at Enygma. "Are you accusing me—*me*—of murder or not, sir?"

Enygma shrugs. "Not."

"Oh," says Knox, looking embarrassed. "All right, then." He puts his fork back down.

There is a short pause while the waiters serve the first course, but as the door closes behind them, Enygma says, "I will now outline my methods of investigation."

"This should be good," says Nicholas Blake, pink mayonnaise dribbling down his chin.

"I considered first what sort of detective I should be. I have made quite a study of detective literature—"

"Yep. That's how we do it in the police academy."

"—and I have identified several distinct types of detective. I have called the first category *Behold, a Great Detective!*, in which a celebrated detective makes spectacular leaps of logic. In this category, of course, we have Sherlock Holmes, Hercule Poirot and Edgar Allan Poe's C. Auguste Dupin. I admit, I gave this category serious consideration. It saves a detective a lot of effort if he can astrally project himself into the mind of the murderer, or is credited with such infallibility that no one bothers to ask for proof.

"Tempting. However, this hardly seems to be playing fair, and, reluctantly, I moved on. I next considered the policeman-as-detective, and wondered if it was worthwhile rejoining the force.

"In any case, the police procedural—or, as I call it, the *As I Was Proceeding in a Westerly Direction*—hardly seems fair either. The detective story is mano a mano. Detective versus nemesis. Holmes versus Moriarty.

"I dismissed official investigators as being both time-consuming and prosaic and turned next to the US of A, to see how they do things *over there*. It was not encouraging. I have called this category *Shoot First, Ask Questions . . . Oh Drat*.

"A lot of guns. A lot of dead people. Which thins out the pool of suspects. The hard-boiled gumshoe has no special abilities, except perhaps a propensity for casual violence.

"Which seems rather unsporting.

"I decided to confine myself to the English detective model, and I was left with only two categories from which to choose. I have called the first *No One Knows What the Hell They're Doing. Pray for a Miracle*.

"In this category, everyone bumbles around for three hundred pages and then, in the last twenty pages, they wrap it up with a whole lot of newly discovered information and a side order of exposition. There is an awful lot of stuff that looks like it might be a clue. But it's not. The characters all behave suspiciously. For no good reason. Some characters cover up for other characters, who they believe have committed a murder. But they haven't. Everyone tells lies. No one considers that maybe their piddling personal problems are of no importance compared to the body in the library.

"Drawing room.

"Belfry.

"Wherever. This type of story is the worst. You spend all your time examining the statements of everyone in the house, drawing up a spreadsheet, comparing the lipstick of all the suspects to the shade impressed on the discarded cigarette end and wondering what that footprint in the flower bed was all about, only to be told on the second to last page that the murderer was the previously never-mentioned bread boy, who was the hitherto unheard-of illegitimate son of the deceased, and that we should have inferred all this by the fact that there was toast for breakfast the next day.

"*The clues were there*, the author says.

"*No, they bloody weren't*, the reader replies, as they throw the book against the wall.

"And so, ladies and gentlemen, I was left with only one sort of detective story—and, hence, one sort of detective. I'm thinking specifically of a detective in the mold of Roger Sheringham, Anthony Berkeley's celebrated detective, as seen in *The Poisoned Chocolates Case*. I have called this category simply *Meta*.

"*Meta* knows that this is all just a game. We do all know this is a game, right?"

"I have read *The Poisoned Chocolates Case*," says Dr. Knox, "and Roger Sheringham did not solve that case. That was Ambrose Chitterwick."

"And what were Mr. Chitterwick's qualifications?" asks DCI Blake.

"He read a lot of detective stories," Dr. Knox says.

"I can see why you were attracted to him," Blake says to Enygma, setting an empty Babycham glass back on the table.

The waiters reenter. One clears away the empties; the other bears beef Wellington on a silver salver to the head of the table, and follows it up with bowls of roast potatoes, carrots and asparagus, and jugs of red-wine gravy.

Eddie Biggers and Stanley Gardner rub their hands together in anticipation. Even Daniel Verreman perks up a bit.

"GO ON," SAYS David Verreman, with his mouth full of meat. "You are doing splendidly."

"Roger Sheringham has all the qualities we could want in a classic detective, plus one or two we might not," Enygma says. "Firstly, of course, he is a gentleman, and an amateur. By profession he is a writer, which, as we all know, is no profession at all, which leaves him plenty of time for detecting. He has formed a club for the detection of, and appreciation for, crime.

"Most importantly, Roger Sheringham is a man with a rather peculiar, even perverse, sense of humor. He is acutely aware of the limitations and absurdity of literary detectives, and their propensity to make 'deductions' based on nothing more than hunches, sending men to the gallows with cheerful disregard for proof. But this awareness does not stop him from throwing himself into his investigations with gusto.

"Ergo, Roger Sheringham is the perfect model for this investigation."

A bread roll hits Enygma on the left ear.

—Get on with it.

A bread roll hits Enygma on the right ear.

Which is odd, because bread rolls have not been served tonight. This, perhaps, accounts for the remarkable hardness of the rolls.

"Very well," says Enygma, rubbing the points of impact. "We have the suspects, and we have the model for the detective. Now we come to the investigation. I will lay out the case against each of you.

"And, one by one, I will eliminate you from my investigation until we reach what remains. And whatever remains, however improbable, will be the truth!"

"Good grief," says DCI Blake.

"Excellent!" says David Verreman. He takes a pen from his pocket and writes the names of the guests on the back of his place card.

"Let us begin with Professor Cameron McCabe," says Enygma.

"By all means," says Professor McCabe, twisting his signet ring around his pinkie finger with amusement. "This is a new experience for me, to be suspected of a crime. I must say, I'm rather thrilled."

"You are a pathologist. Therefore, you are a cold and calculating person. I look to the literature and ask myself, is there any precedent for such a man being the killer? And I say yes, *mon ami*, there is. Consider *Whose Body?*, in which Sir Julian Freke, anatomist, dissects his victim in front of a classroom full of medical students in order to dispose of the body. Such a man might well have had the brains and the courage to commit this act."

"Is Professor McCabe the killer?" asks David Verreman.

"He is not," says Enygma. "Although he has the temperament for murder, he would not commit *such* a murder. Professor McCabe, when he kills, will kill smoothly, and quickly, and with very little mess. This crime was a personal crime, and, moreover, a crime of passion. Hence the escalating argument, the punches followed by a loss of control during the attack."

"A lover, then?" asks Daniel.

"Not necessarily," says Enygma. "Take Carolyn Keene-Wade. She was the sister of Lady Verreman. If we incline to the theory that Lady Antonia Verreman was the intended target, then your 'Aunty Caro' may have been the one waiting in the basement."

Carolyn Keene-Wade laughs. "Why on earth would I do that?"

"Many reasons, *madame*," says Enygma, and the dodgy Belgian accent is back. "Many reasons. You were, perhaps, fed up with playing *ze* second *feedle* to your sister, *n'est-ce pas?*"

"Good grief," says Henry Wade.

"There is precedence, *monsieur*. Consider *A Murder Is Announced*, in which Miss Lotty Blacklock steps out of her sister's shadow after her death."

"But I wasn't in my sister's shadow," says Carolyn. "I never played second fiddle to her or anyone else."

"Perhaps you wanted her life and her husband, like Jacqueline de

THE GAME IS MURDER

Bellefort in *Death on the Nile*. You wanted to be the other half of a golden couple, did you not?"

"I did not."

"So you say, *madame*. But Maximillian Enygma does not take your word for it. Maximillian Enygma does not take anyone at their word."

"Did Aunty Caro do it?" asks David Verreman.

"No," says Enygma.

"Of course I didn't," says Carolyn Keene-Wade.

"All right," says David. "That's two down. Who's next?"

"Me!" says Gaston Leroux. "Do me next!"

—Hang on, says Daniel. Are we going to allow him to judge a person's guilt by what they remind him of?

"Worked for Miss Marple," says Enygma.

"True," says David. "I'll allow it." He raises his hand to bang a gavel, then realizes that he does not have one in this scene, and says, "Proceed!"

"Your motive," says Enygma to Leroux, "is, of course, money. You described yourself as a 'financial gentleman,' but you remind me more of Mrs. Lucy Cash in *The Tiger in the Smoke*. She is both a loan shark and a blackmailer. Perhaps you sit at the center of a web. A web that has a thousand radiations—"

"Sherlock Holmes!" says Dr. Knox. "Boring!"

"You are motivated by money; ergo, you are greedy," continues Enygma.

Gaston Leroux laughs, and polishes his impossibly small glasses with the fat end of his tie. The gold links of the chain around his wrist clink a little as he rubs the tie over and over the lenses.

"Money is always a good motive for murder," says Enygma.

"True," says Leroux, laughing again, "but my only financial connection was with Lord Verreman. I had no motive to kill either Mrs. Gardner or Lady Verreman, unless as some kind of threat against Lord Verreman if he was delinquent in his payments. Which he was not."

"Ah, but perhaps you were acting at the behest of another. Perhaps, unscrupulous as you are, you make a living removing the inconveniences in other people's lives. As in *The Pale Horse.*"

"Never heard of it. And who was my client?" Leroux asks, amused. "Lord Verreman? In which case why did he borrow money from me? Assassins do not generally lend their clients the money to pay for the hit."

"We only have your word that you did."

"You are forgetting the 'close personal friend' who stood guarantee for his lordship's loan."

"Maximillian Enygma forgets nothing! He is the elephant in *ze* room. He always remembers."

"Hell's bells," says Sir Henry Wade.

"Ah, Sir Henry," says Enygma, "I do not forget you. The husband of the sister of the wife of the accused. You do not fool me with your affectation of world-weary cynicism! You are a hot-blooded man, are you not? Perhaps you had conceived a mad passion for Sally Gardner, the beautiful servant of your brother-in-law."

"I never met the girl," says Hal Wade, shoving a large piece of beef into his mouth. "Never even heard her name until after she was dead."

"Ah! Then it was Lady Antonia Verreman for whom you had *ze* feelings? Did you, perhaps, wonder whether you had married the wrong sister?"

Henry Wade snorts into his wineglass, then takes a large gulp of red to wash down the beef. "Antonia Verreman was a pain in the arse. I like women"—Carolyn Keene-Wade rolls her eyes—"but Antonia was clingy. Can't stand clingy women. Hysterical. Crying. Screaming. The woman was, quite frankly, bloody hard work. I would have beaten her over the head myself, given half a chance."

"Perhaps you did," says Enygma. "You have the temperament for murder. Not Professor McCabe's cold and clinical temperament, but still, you are a pragmatic man, Sir Henry, perhaps even a selfish one."

"I take that as a compliment," says Henry Wade.

"Was it Henry?" asks David Verreman.

"I do not believe so. Sir Henry Wade is pragmatic. He is also effi-
cient. And ruthless. He would not have left Lady Antonia alive."

"That's true," says Henry Wade.

"OK," says David, crossing his uncle off his list. "Now we are
getting somewhere. Who is next?"

—Boring!

"Don't start," says David.

—Just saying. This is boring. I'm just saying, when do we get to the
action?

With one hand Daniel Verreman pulls out the handcuffs from his
pocket and shakes them at his brother. Then he points to the black
square of fabric that has been rolled inside David's napkin ring.

"Shut up!" David hisses.

"Next," says Enygma, raising his voice a little, "we come to Mr.
and Mrs. Howard-Cole. And here I considered carefully. Mrs. Margaret Howard-Cole is the last person to see Lord Verreman alive. She
is the person to whom he fled after the murder, and after Lady Verreman made her escape to the public 'ouse, *n'est-ce pas*? She claims to
be only the friend of Lord John Verreman. But perhaps they were
more than, as you say, *just good friends*. Perhaps Mr. George
Howard-Cole disliked his wife's friendship with the handsome aristocrat. He would not be the first jealous husband to rid himself of the
rival for his wife's affections."

George Howard-Cole gives a short laugh, and his wife tugs his
sleeve in ineffectual reproach. "True. And if I had thought old Jinx
was sniffing round after my wife, I might well have brained him. But
I wouldn't have brained his wife, or killed the girl."

"True," says Enygma, "but you love your wife, do you not? You
need not answer. Maximillian Enygma knows all. You have the English disdain for displays of affection, and yet your loyalty to your
wife is deep. *By the Pricking of My Thumbs* you would cover up your

wife's crimes, I think. If *The Mirror Crack'd from Side to Side*, you would kill to protect her. And when you can protect her no longer you will kill her softly, eh, *mon ami*, for her own good?"

Margaret Howard-Cole's hand stops pulling on her husband's sleeve. "George?"

"Don't be bloody stupid, woman."

"Are you planning to kill me, George?" asks Margaret Howard-Cole.

"Well, that depends," says her husband. "Are you planning on committing any murders that need covering up?"

"No!"

"Then we're fine."

Mrs. Howard-Cole thinks about this for a moment, then smiles and replaces her hand on her husband's sleeve. "Of course we are."

David Verreman scratches two more names off his list. "Well, you haven't got many suspects left. What about Dr. Mackintosh? Can you make a case against her?"

"Of course I can," says Enygma. "Dr. Mackintosh, of course, would not kill for gain, or jealousy. She would kill for reasons of altruism."

Elizabeth Mackintosh holds up her pince-nez and peers at Max Enygma as though he is an interesting specimen under her microscope. "Really?"

"*The Unpleasantness at the Bellona Club.* What is the death of one old man—or one young woman—compared with the untold benefit of scientific advancement?"

"Murder for the greater good?" says Dr. Mackintosh. "It's an interesting premise."

"I thought so," says Enygma.

Daniel puts the black hankie on his head.

"Is Dr. Mackintosh the murderer?" asks David, not waiting for the answer before crossing her name off the list.

Daniel takes it off again.

—Next!

"There is hardly anyone left," says David, looking at the list. "What about Mr. Collins?"

Wilkie Collins looks up eagerly.

—Can we speed things up a bit?

Enygma is about to reply when the waiters enter again and begin removing plates. Enygma has barely touched his and tries to hang on to his plate, but a waiter tugs it from his hand, and Enygma watches as his beef is carried out of the room and an individual summer pudding is placed in front of him instead.

Enygma takes a large spoonful of fruit and mascarpone cream and swallows it quickly. David Verreman leans forward and lowers his voice confidentially. "You are doing a great job. Really. A great job. But if you could hurry it up, just a little . . . Perhaps trim the literary references a touch."

"But I've done research," says Enygma, taking another spoonful. Red currant juice dribbles over the white tablecloth like blood. "Lots of research."

"I know," says David. "I know. I don't want to tell you how to do your job, but you could, of course, just let the research *inform* your opinion. I believe that is quite acceptable these days."

Enygma shakes his head. "*Lots* of research. Lots."

—Oh yeah? Have a medal! Or a certificate, maybe.

"No one tells Hercule Poirot to cut to the chase," says Enygma. "No one tells Sherlock Holmes not to bother with the treatise on tobacco ash, or asks Gideon Fell to give them an abridged locked-room lecture. Every detective gets to give a speech before they reveal the murderer. That's how you know they're a genius."

"But," says DCI Nicholas Blake, breaking into the conversation, "how many of those genius detectives base their deductions on the plots of other fictional detectives?"

"I would say, conservatively, all of them," says Enygma.

DCI Blake shrugs, and Daniel mutters to himself.

—For God's sake.

Enygma carries on. "Where was I? Oh yes, Mr. Wilkie Collins.

Mr. Collins' contribution to this case is, of course, as an alibi to Lord Verreman. He could not be waiting in the basement if he was driving up to his club.

"Is Mr. Collins the unwitting patsy of an unscrupulous murderer, turned, of necessity, into that stock character of detective fiction, the man who is asked the time? *Have His Carcase*," adds Enygma to Daniel, cutting off Dr. Knox, who has already opened his mouth to speak. "Or does Mr. Collins give Lord Verreman an alibi simply in order to give himself an alibi? If Wilkie Collins is standing outside the Berkeley Club, Wilkie Collins cannot be in the basement, murdering the nanny."

"Why would he do that?" asks DCI Blake and Daniel at the same time.

"Why indeed? Could it be that Wilkie Collins has fixated upon Lord Verreman? Collins is an unstable young man, probably stemming from his illegitimacy, and never knowing his father. Lord Verreman is kind to the lad, and Collins conceives the wild idea that this rich, handsome aristocrat is his real father. He hero-worships him. He develops a complex about him. He confronts Lord Verreman with the truth. Verreman denies paternity, and, hurt and rejected, Wilkie Collins plans to destroy him and his reputation by the brutal massacre of his wife and family."

"Is any of that true?" asks David Verreman.

"No!" says Collins.

"Really," says Ronald Knox, "he is just synopsizing now—*They Do It with Mirrors*. He'll be telling us next that we all did it."

"Maybe you did!" says Enygma.

"Do you have any evidence against Wilkie Collins?" asks David Verreman, pen poised over the name.

"Evidence? Of course I don't have evidence. Hercule Poirot doesn't need evidence. Sherlock Holmes doesn't need evidence."

David crosses out the name of Wilkie Collins.

"I would just like to put on the record," says Collins, "that I know both my mother and my father. I did not have any sort of complex about his lordship. He was a nice bloke. I liked him. Not so much that I would lie for him, or kill for him, though. I seen him drive up in his car. And I said I seen him drive up in his car. And that is all."

"And so, you see," says Enygma, ignoring the interruptions, "the net is tightening upon the murderer."

"It'd better be," says David, "because there are only Eddie Biggers and Stanley Gardner left."

"And me!" says Jeff, indignantly.

"I'm sorry," says David, surreptitiously adding Jeff's name to the list. "And you."

"And you," says Enygma, looking not at Jeff but at David Verreman.

ORDEAL BY INNOCENCE

DAVID LOOKS AT Enygma incredulously. "Me?"

"Yes. You. You were in the house that night."

"I was eleven!"

"Old enough to commit murder."

"You can't really think that I would frame my own father. I loved my father!"

"I have no doubt you did," says Enygma. "But you were angry with him, too, were you not? He had abandoned you. He left you with an unstable mother, and hired servants who never stayed more than a few weeks. You were angry. And lonely, too. Is that not so?"

David blanches a little. He shakes his head and closes his eyes against Enygma. "That's not true," he whispers.

"It is true. You were angry with your father for leaving you to care for your sick mother by yourself."

"Lies."

"And that is when Daniel was born, was it not? In those months between your father's leaving and the murder. You needed a friend.

Someone to talk to. Someone to confide in. Someone who could share that anger, and that hurt."

"Not listening!"

"And your brother encouraged you, didn't he? Daniel is braver than you. Perhaps it was his idea—kill your mother so that Daddy could come home."

David has his fingers in his ears. "I can't hear you!"

"Was it you or Daniel who struck the first blow? I wonder. I wonder what a jury will make of that. Is your mother's insanity hereditary, do you know?"

DCI Blake stands up. "Are you saying that David Verreman, aged eleven, killed his nanny and attempted to kill his mother?"

"It's been done before," says Enygma. "*Crooked House.*"

"And the mother covered it up?"

"*Five Little Pigs.*"

"And the murderer hires a Great Detective to investigate the crime?"

"*Three Act Tragedy. Lord Edgware Dies.* Any number of stories in which the murderer thinks they are cleverer than the detective."

—Are you saying that my brother is the murderer?

David takes his fingers out of his ears gingerly.

All eyes are on Enygma. He allows the silence to stretch out until it reaches breaking point.

"I am . . . not," says Enygma.

David Verreman gives a shaky laugh. "I doubted myself for a moment there."

—And you are not accusing me either?

"No, Daniel, I am not."

—Pity.

"It is a pity," says Enygma. "It would have made a nice twist. But it's not exactly playing fair. Neither David nor Daniel has ever been identified as a suspect. No, according to the rules, the murderer must be one of the thirteen guests round this table. Who's next?"

"Me," says Stanley Gardner.

"And me," says Eddie Biggers.

"I think that's it," says David Verreman.

"I don't know why I bother," says Jeff.

"In a murder investigation," says Enygma, "the husband is always suspected first. Which is why he almost never turns out to be the killer."

"Well, thank God for that," says Stanley Gardner, scraping the inside of his pudding dish with his spoon. To his right, Jeff is taking small mouthfuls of summer pudding, rolling each spoonful round his mouth experimentally before swallowing. To his left, Eddie Biggers has finished his dessert and is now fishing in his mouth for stray bits of beef caught between his teeth.

"Unless, of course, it is a double bluff. As in *The Mysterious Affair at Styles* and *Death on the Nile*. And *Dancers in Mourning*, in which Squire Mercer kills his wife because she dares to ask for a divorce. Are you a Squire Mercer, Monsieur Gardner?"

"No."

"Did your wife ask you for a divorce? Perhaps so that she could emigrate with the charming Eddie Biggers, to your left?"

"No, she didn't," says Gardner, casting a quick side-glance at his rival.

"Perhaps your wife called you when she went out to post her letter and took such an unaccountably long time about it. She told you she was in love, did she not? That she had never felt this way before."

"No."

"She had planned a whole new life for herself in the sun, while you were left at home. Is that not right, Mr. Gardner?"

"No."

"And you were enraged. You were supposed to be the traveler. She was supposed to stay at home and wait for her man. The times were changing, oh yes, but not everyone wanted to change, did they, Mr. Gardner? You wanted a wife who would cook your meals and wash your clothes, and instead, you got—"

"Be careful," says Gardner.

"—a modern young woman. And so you killed her!"

"You bastard," cries Eddie Biggers. "You fucking bastard!" Biggers swings wildly at Gardner, catching him a glancing blow to the chin. But the momentum carries Gardner's fist onward, and he knocks Jeff to the floor.

"I knew there would be fireworks," says David Verreman, clapping his hands.

DCI Blake gets heavily to his feet and, without any apparent effort, grabs Eddie Biggers by his collar and lifts him off the floor with one hand. Biggers is still swinging. Stanley Gardner retakes his seat, unmoved, but Jeff is livid.

"Do you mind?" Jeff says, coldly, balling his fists.

"Pack it in," says Blake to Biggers, and Biggers lets his fists drop. DCI Blake lets go of the collar, and Biggers shrugs his shoulders several times, and then holds out his hand to Jeff.

"Sorry," Biggers says. "I got a bit carried away. It's the not knowing that gets you."

Jeff's bowl has overturned on the table, splashing the tablecloth with dark red stains.

Jeff picks up his napkin and covers the stains with it. A red flush is blooming on his cheek, but Jeff refrains from touching it until the focus of the room returns to Enygma.

"Did he do it?" asks Biggers, jerking a thumb toward Stanley Gardner.

Enygma smiles. "No, Mr. Biggers. Sally Gardner was not murdered by her husband. Sally Gardner was murdered by her lover!"

Enygma looks around the room in triumph. Carolyn Keene-Wade is pulling on her necklace. Her husband is checking his watch. Chief Inspector Blake is fiddling with his tiepin, and Dr. Knox is filling his pipe carefully, then tamping the tobacco down and taking experimental sucks on the unlit pipe. They all look a little bored.

—Another wild guess, *Mon-sewer* Parrot?

"No, Daniel. No more guesses. No more games. Now it is time to tell you what really happened."

38

✦ ✦ ✦ ✦ ✦

ANATOMY OF A MURDER

My name is Sherlock Holmes. It is my business to know what other people don't know.

—Sir Arthur Conan Doyle, "The Adventure of the Blue Carbuncle"

"WE WILL START, if you will permit," says Enygma, "with the sixth of November, the night before the murder. On that night, if you remember, Sally Gardner changed her night off from Thursday to Wednesday so that she could go out with her new boyfriend, Mr. Eddie Biggers.

"I say 'new boyfriend' because the couple had known each other less than six weeks. Mr. Biggers testified that the two met when she walked into the Three Taps not long after she began working for the Verreman family.

"The relationship was described by Chief Inspector Blake as 'tumultuous'—which is often a police euphemism for 'violent.' We have no evidence of violence, but the relationship was certainly loud, lusty and passionate, and also volatile, argumentative and possessive. Six weeks into their relationship, the couple had already argued several times, by Mr. Biggers' own account. They did so again on the sixth of November, and their argument was 'tumultuous' enough for Sally Gardner to walk out on her new boyfriend and go home early.

"What did they argue about? Eddie Biggers claims not to remember. Perhaps that is true.

"On the seventh of November, David Verreman is not sent to school. His mother maintains that the school bus did not arrive to collect him, and no one thought to take him. And so David Verreman stays at home all day with his *maman* and the young nanny he likes so much.

"*Eh, bien!* To have one's youth again . . ."

Enygma looks round the room, smiling. Carolyn Keene-Wade rolls her eyes.

"What does Sally do that day?" Enygma continues. "Unfortunately, we know very little. Lady Verreman could remember nothing unusual until around five o'clock, when Sally Gardner suddenly decided to post a letter, and unaccountably took forty-five minutes about it. Why did she wait until then, when she'd had all day to do it? And who was the letter addressed to? We don't know."

"Some time after eight o'clock, Sally is in her room on the fourth floor when she receives a phone call. This call, we know, is from Mr. Biggers. He is working that night, but at a bar only a few minutes away from this house—a short walk across the square. We have only his word for what they said, but he claims that in the five or so minutes that they talked, they made up their row and made arrangements to see each other the following week. Mr. Biggers claims that, when he hung up the phone, the couple were on good terms.

"What does Sally do then? She puts on her shoes—for no woman ever wears shoes in her own bedroom—and she walks down one flight of stairs, past the Baby Belling cooker in the nursery, where she makes tea every day. She walks down a second flight of stairs, knocks on Lady Verreman's bedroom door and offers to make her a cup of tea, something she has never done before at that time of night.

"Then Sally picks up a tray of crockery and, mostly in the dark, because many of the lightbulbs have blown, she walks down a further two flights of stairs to the hall, which is also in darkness.

"There she stops for a moment and opens the front door, where her lover is waiting for her.

"She motions him to be quiet, and they tiptoe together down into the basement for a lovers' tryst."

Eddie Biggers makes a choking noise and curls his fists, but he says nothing.

"You may think that her lover came with the intention of spending a moment with her—for a few stolen kisses—in the seclusion of the basement. But consider this: he brought with him a canvas sack, and, in all probability, a blunt instrument, too. The sack in which poor Sally's body was found had never been seen in the house before. We know that the lead pipe found in the hall cannot have been the murder weapon, since, when the first policeman saw it, it was white, and that blunt instrument had none of Sally's hair adhering to it, and not enough of her blood to separately identify it from Lady Verreman's.

"Sally Gardner has let her lover into her home. She is intending only a romantic tryst. But he has murderous intentions. They argue. The lover grabs her by the arm. Then he repeatedly punches this woman he professes to love. She tries to run back up the stairs, and he reaches for a weapon and hits her over the head with it until she stops running.

"Stops moving.

"Stops breathing.

"He is bundling Sally's body into the sack when two things happen—Lady Verreman comes down the basement steps, wondering what has happened to her nanny and her cup of tea, and Lord Verreman comes down the outside basement steps to snoop on his wife and catch a glimpse, if he can, of his family.

"Lady Verreman confronts an attacker in the basement, and he attacks her. She runs back up the stairs and into the hall, and Lord Verreman, who has witnessed the attack through the window, runs back to the street, grabs a weapon from his car and lets himself in the front door to rescue his wife. Lord Verreman is a tall man with an athletic build, and he easily fends off his wife's attacker.

"What happened to the Verremans next, we know. Their fate has been the subject of a thousand newspaper articles, books and television programs. Mrs. Gardner's lover, on the other hand, went back about his business and waited for the knock on the door. It never came.

"Lady Verreman, confused after the attack upon herself, and suffering, as she did, from 'the disease of paranoia,' misinterpreted the attack on Sally Gardner as being directed at her, and she told the police that the attacker was her husband."

"Lies," whispers Eddie Biggers. "It's all lies."

"I assure you, sir, that everything I have said is the truth."

David Verreman picks up his pen. "You are accusing Eddie Biggers? Is that correct?"

Daniel smiles.

"No!" shouts Biggers.

"No," says Enygma. "I am not. Eddie Biggers was Sally Gardner's lover. But he was not her only lover. Isn't that right, *Ray*?"

39

◆ ◆ ◆ ◆ ◆

CURTAINS

"There is nothing new—not even in the annals of crime," returned Colwyn. "But this was certainly a baffling and unusual case. The murderer was such a deep and subtle scoundrel that I feel a respect for his intelligence, perverted though it was."

—Arthur J. Rees, *The Shrieking Pit*

JEFF HAS PUSHED back his chair. He tries to laugh. The laugh catches in his throat and chokes him. "Me? You can't be serious!"

"Oh yes, my friend. Maximillian Enygma is deadly serious. You were also the lover of Sally Gardner. Until she broke up with you. She threw you over when she decided to go steady with Mr. Biggers. Not a wise choice on her part, but people in love are seldom wise."

Jeff turns to David Verreman. "Are you going to allow this? Where is his proof? He has no proof!"

"Oh, I have proof," says Enygma quietly.

Jeff stands up. His face has paled. His hands are trembling. "You can't have."

"But I assure you, Ray, that I do."

"Stop calling me that!"

"It's your name, is it not? You told me yourself, on page 73, that your name was Raymond Postgate."

"Yes, but . . . so what? Plenty of Rays in the world."

"That's true, of course. Plenty of Rays. Though only one of them around this table."

"That's not proof." Raymond Postgate looks around the table. The other guests are looking at him with distaste. "Come on! That's not proof!"

"You must have been terrified when you first realized that you had been called for jury service for the inquest into the murder of the very woman you killed. You must have suspected it was a trap. You thought that, at any moment, Lady Verreman would name *you* as the man who had attacked her that night. You feared that she would look across the courtroom and see you, and remember what really happened.

"But she did not. Lady Verreman was an ill woman. She suffered from paranoia and delusions. Anyone who has read her diary cannot be anything but convinced of that. And, of course, she saw you for a few traumatic moments only, before her husband ran to her aid.

"Did she know you, I wonder, before the murder? Had she seen you collecting Sally for a date, perhaps? I think she had, and that terrified you. For the four days of the inquest, she sat in the same room as you. At any moment, a look, or a movement, might have given you away.

"And so you sought to discredit her testimony at all costs."

"No proof," Raymond Postgate says again. He is not looking at anyone. He keeps his eyes fixed on the tablecloth, on the red stain creeping from beneath his napkin.

"'How did she know the nanny was dead?' That was the question you asked Dr. Knox from the jury box. Why? Because Lady Verreman claimed never to have been in the basement that night. And you knew that wasn't true.

"The evidence proved that Lady Verreman had been in the basement. That she had walked in Sally Gardner's blood, leaving traces on her shoes. And Lady Verreman's blood was on the sack. And if Lady Verreman's blood was there, then she was there.

"You knew that Lady Verreman's testimony was not true. But you didn't know why. Was this, perhaps, a ruse? Were you being tricked by the police into believing that they did not suspect you? Could that explain your presence on this jury?

"You sat in the jury box and desperately tried to work out what it all meant."

Raymond Postgate has closed his eyes. "No proof," he says, over and over again. "No proof."

"In fact, it was the merest chance that you were on that particular jury. The police had no hand in it at all. But you did not know that. You spent the first day of the inquest in an agony of suspense. The question of Sally's boyfriends was brought up at the inquest, and Lady Verreman said she knew of two boyfriends.

"But she did not name them. Could it possibly be that she did not remember 'Ray'? You had to know, and so you stood up, in front of the entire court, in front of Lady Verreman, and you looked her in the eye and asked the question: 'How did she know the nanny was dead?'

"Did she recognize you then? I don't think so. I think that Lady Verreman believed with her whole heart the story that she had told herself about the murder. It was the only story that made sense *to her*. Because she was suffering from the paranoid delusion that her husband was trying to kill her. Because she still loved him. And because she hated him, too.

"And because, despite everything, she still saw the Verremans as the 'golden couple.' Lady Verreman assumed that no one would want to murder Mrs. Gardner when they could have murdered her. Sally Gardner was 'just' a nanny. One among many. She was a nobody."

"She wasn't a nobody," Raymond Postgate says. He speaks quite calmly. Just as if this were any other dinner party conversation. He smiles. "She was like no one I'd ever met before. There was something in her that . . . sparkled. I don't know how else to describe it. She fizzed.

"And then she met *him*." Postgate points disdainfully at Eddie Biggers. "The oaf. And she didn't sparkle anymore."

40

◆ ◆ ◆ ◆ ◆

THE MAN OF LAST RESORT

There now only remains for me, in conclusion, to sum up as briefly and succinctly as possible the evidence contained in the preceding statements.

—Charles Felix, *The Notting Hill Mystery*

"CONGRATULATIONS," SAYS DAVID, smiling.

—Well done, says Daniel, placing the black cap on top of his wig.

"Thank God," says Monty Egg.

"How did you know?" asks DCI Blake.

Raymond Postgate is no more.

He has been taken away by the police.

Or, he was shot by an avenging husband. Or a jealous lover.

Or, he has done the "honorable thing" and taken his own life.

Or, he has thrown himself through the window in a cowardly attempt to evade justice.

Or, maybe, Daniel Verreman has finally been able to use those handcuffs and that hankie and has pronounced sentence of death upon him.

And may the Lord have mercy upon his soul.

Which one? Doesn't matter. The detective has found the solution, and the detective is the only one who counts.

Time for the post-denouement postscript, tying up all those loose ends into a neat little bow.

MAXIMILLIAN ENYGMA PEELS himself an orange. He is feeling surprisingly good. Considering. Though his hand trembles a little as he puts the first segment of orange into his mouth.

"Elementary," says Enygma, and a bread roll hits him neatly on the bridge of his nose. "Where the hell is all this bread coming from?"

"Some mysteries are not meant to be solved," says Carolyn Keene-Wade, kicking her basket of bread a little farther under the table.

"Do tell us how you knew," says Ronald Knox.

"Ah," says Enygma, puckering his lips because the orange is sour, "you have presented me with the dilemma that all literary detectives face. The solution to a mystery must always be inferior to the mystery itself. The mystery is a part of the supernatural, and of the divine; the solution, sleight of hand. If I tell you, you will cease to marvel."

"If you don't tell us," Sir Henry Wade says, "my wife will bring out the bread basket again."

"Fair enough," says Enygma. "There were three reasons why I knew that Jeff, as we thought him to be, must be the guilty party. The first reason was necessity—to wit, fastening the guilt upon anyone else might result in a libel suit. This is a cringing, self-serving reason, on which it is best not to linger too long.

"Let us move on. The second reason was that the murderer condemned himself out of his own mouth. In his statement earlier this evening, Mr. Postgate explained why he had asked that very prescient question at the inquest—to wit, 'How did she know?'

"That's what he asked. 'How did she know that the nanny was dead?' It was an important question, because in Lady Verreman's testimony neither she nor her husband went down to the basement, which was, remember, in complete darkness. The coroner, naturally, considered that testimony only in relation to the complicated and narrow manner in which Lady Verreman was legally, if dubiously, qualified to give testimony, but it was an important—and unanswered—question.

"And this evening, Mr. Postgate—or Jeff, as he was then—explained why he'd asked the question. He said the following: 'It was pitch-black down there, so she couldn't have seen nothing. And she couldn't have seen down to the basement from the hall anyway, because there is a turn in the stairs at the top.' Do you see?"

Max Enygma looks round the table. It is plain. They do not see.

"How did *he* know? How did Raymond Postgate, jury foreman, know that it is impossible to see into the basement from the hall, even with the light on, because of the turn at the top of the stairs? Lady Verreman was the first witness, and nothing in her testimony mentioned the layout of the stairs.

"The only way Raymond Postgate could have known that was if he had been in this house.

"He knew, too, that Lady Verreman had lied to the jury under oath. She had been in the basement. Whether she had lied intentionally, or her testimony was unreliable because of her poor mental health, we cannot say. But Mr. Postgate *knew* she was lying. And he could only know she was lying if he knew what really happened that night.

"And he could only know what really happened if he had been there. Ergo, he was the man who killed Sally Gardner."

"Amazing," says Margaret Howard-Cole. Her husband harrumphs, possibly in agreement.

—Is that it? asks Daniel.

"You said there were three reasons," says David. "What is the other one?"

Maximillian Enygma laughs to himself, and the dodgy Belgian accent comes on for an encore. "*Ze* last reason, *mon ami*, is so simple, a child could see it."

He pauses. For effect.

Carolyn Keene-Wade reaches for the bread basket again.

Enygma hurries on. "He had no business being here! Everyone

else was a suspect, true, but they were also material witnesses or expert witnesses in the case. 'Jeff' was just the foreman of the jury. So I said to myself, if he is here, he is here for a reason. The Author does not put him in *ze* book for no reason. And if he is not a witness, then he must be the murderer!

"Elementary," says Enygma again. "When you have eliminated *ze* impossible—"

A bread roll hits him smack in the eye.

"Fine!" he says. "I'm done."

41

◆ ◆ ◆ ◆ ◆

DEAD MAN'S FOLLY

MONTY EGG HEAVES a sigh of relief and closes his computer.

He is a god no longer.

His mouth is dry, and he has a migraine that has settled low over his left eye. He is balding and fat and his skin has the gray pallor of a man who has spent three years in the dark. He has halitosis from eating junk food, a tic from the drugs he has taken to stay awake and hemorrhoids from sitting too long at his desk.

But he is content.

Monty Egg, mortal man once more, puts on the nice gold watch for which he previously had no use. He flings wide his front door and steps, blinking, into the daylight.

He is happy, and, for as long as he can be free of the tyrant Story, he will remain a happy man.

MAX ENYGMA CHECKS his wrist. His watch is there. And it's morning. Time for him to go home.

David Verreman, good host that he is, shows him to the door.

The front door is standing wide-open and the sun is streaming into the hall. It's going to be a beautiful day.

"Thank you," says David, holding out his hand.

Enygma says, "It's been . . . not a pleasure, exactly, but certainly an experience. Are you going to be OK?"

David Verreman, who is all alone now in this great big house, nods. He looks a little lost. "I'll be fine. I really think I will," he says, sounding surprised. "What about you? What are you going to do now?"

Enygma takes a deep breath of fresh, clean air. "The first thing I'm going to do is get some breakfast, because I'm bloody starving. Then I'm going to check myself into the nearest hospital. But after that, I'm going to call my daughter."

David smiles. "Do you know her number?"

"No," says Enygma, "but I know a man who does. And I'm going to call him, giving forty-eight hours' notice, and I'm going to make him write me some more background scenes."

Max Enygma nods to his client, and walks down the steps, and into Broad Way. The gentle breeze is sweet and cool. The street doesn't resemble a scene from a Dickens novel anymore. And the house looks just like any other Georgian town house, though a little past its prime.

On the point of closing the door, David Verreman throws it wide again and calls out, "I say, you wouldn't like another job, would you?"

Enygma turns, reluctantly. "What sort of job?"

It is Daniel who answers.

—Our father has been missing for fifty years. Do you want to have a shot at finding him?

FROM FAR AWAY, borne aloft on the breeze, the howl of an author can be heard as he sits back down at his desk and switches his damned computer back on.

APPENDIX A

✦ ✦ ✦ ✦ ✦

THE RESPONSIBILITIES OF THE AUTHOR AND THE READER

The responsibilities of The Author are as follows:

A1. The Author will tell you a story.
A1a. The story will have three elements.

- Some People.
- An Event (sometimes called an Inciting Incident).
- Action that is related to those People and that Event.

A1b. Everything you need to know about the story will be in the story, and everything in the story will serve the story.
A1c. The Author is the god of the story.
A1d. The Author will tell a true story.

A2. It will be a WHOLE story.
A2a. It will have some manner of completion.
A2b. It will have some manner of change.
A2c. Even if it is part of a larger, continuing story, this part will be whole and complete.
A2d. It will tie up its loose ends or explain why they are left untied.

A3. It will tell the story The Author PROMISED to tell.

A4. The Author will tell the story honorably, without resort to cheap trickery.

A5. And it will STILL manage to AMAZE, ENTERTAIN, EXCITE and/or MOVE you.

The responsibilities of The Reader are as follows:

R1. The Reader will read the WHOLE story.
R1a. The Reader will pick their story carefully.
- All stories are not created equal. Some require more close reading than others. The Reader will choose their story accordingly.
- The Reader will pay attention to the promises that The Author makes, and not hold them accountable for any promises that they haven't made.

R1b. The Reader will match The Author's level of complexity with their level of attention.
- The Reader will not skip bits.
- The Reader will not skim read.
- Speed-reading is not a virtue here.

R2. The Reader will put their trust in The Author to lead them safely through the story.
- The Reader will put their trust in the narrator only if The Author has indicated that it is safe to do so.

R3. The Reader will open themselves to the possibility of AMAZE-MENT, ENTERTAINMENT, EXCITEMENT and/or being MOVED.
- The Reader will allow themselves to fully experience the story: to see, feel, taste, hear and smell the world of the story, and experience the same emotions as the people in the story, to the exact degree of The Author's skill in telling the story.
- The Reader will allow The Author to amaze, entertain, excite or move them, to the exact degree of The Author's skill in telling the story.

APPENDIX B

THE PENALTY CLAUSE

Penalties for The Author who fails to meet the terms of the contract include the following:

- Bad reviews.
- Lack of sales.
- Termination of publishing contract.
- Being dropped by agent.
- Terminal obscurity.
- Depression.
- Despair.
- And, in extreme cases, death.

Penalties for The Reader who fails to meet the terms of the contract include the following:

- Nothing.
- Nada.
- Not a single goddamned thing.
- Except inability to get lost in a book.
- Which is, in fact, a fate worse than death.
- So choose wisely.
- And pay attention!

ACKNOWLEDGMENTS

✦ ✦ ✦ ✦ ✦

I would like to thank my children—David, Andrew, Christian and Leli—who secretly thought I was nuts but encouraged my writing anyway. Thank you, too, to my agent, Sarah Such, of the Sarah Such Literary Agency, London, for sitting at my table and for buying me champagne at the Crime Writers Association awards—and for being a brilliant agent, of course. Thank you to Grace Long and Lisa Bonvissuto, my editors, for having such faith in my book and guiding it to publication; to DeAndra Lupu, my copy editor, who weeded out all those extra commas and double-checked *everything*; and to everyone at Penguin who made me feel welcome in their Penguin family. I would also like to thank my PhD supervisors at Manchester Metropolitan University, who all lent their talents to helping me write this novel—Nicholas Royle, who lent me moral support, several books that I have failed to return (sorry) and an eagle eye; Oliver Harris, who lent me his crime-writing knowledge; Joe Stretch, who lent me his literary-writing knowledge; and Blanka Grzegorczyk, who dragged me, kicking and screaming, through the academic elements of my thesis.

Finally, I would like to acknowledge the love, support and belief I received from my mother, Joan Ward, who began telling family, friends and strangers that I was a writer when I was about fifteen, despite a conspicuous lack of evidence to that effect. XX years later, I finally proved you right.

I wish you were here to see it.